Stan Barstow has published seven
novels and three volumes of short
stories. His dramatisation of his Vic
Brown trilogy (*A Kind of Loving, The
Watchers on the Shore* and *The Right
True End*) was seen on the ITV
Network in 1982. The Royal Television
Society gave him its Writer's Award in
1975 for his dramatisations of his own
A Raging Calm, Joby and Winifred
Holtby's *South Riding.* Stan Barstow is
an Honorary Master of Arts of The
Open University. His books have been
translated into ten languages. He is
married, has two grown children, and
lives in his native Yorkshire.

A Kind of Loving

Stan Barstow

But little do we perceive what solitude is, and how far it
extendeth. For a crowd is not company, and faces are but a
gallery of pictures, and talk a tingling cymbal, where there is
no love.

BACON: *Essays*

BLACK SWAN

A KIND OF LOVING
A BLACK SWAN BOOK 0 552 99186 4

Originally published in Great Britain by
Michael Joseph Ltd.

PRINTING HISTORY
Michael Joseph edition published 1960
Corgi edition published 1973
Corgi edition reprinted 1974
Corgi edition reissued 1977
Corgi edition reissued 1982
Corgi edition reprinted 1982
Black Swan edition published 1986
Black Swan edition reprinted 1987

This book is set in 11/12 pt Mallard

Black Swan Books are published by
Transworld Publishers Ltd., 61-63 Uxbridge Road,
Ealing, London W5 5SA, in Australia by Transworld
Publishers (Australia) Pty. Ltd., 15-23 Helles
Avenue, Moorebank, NSW 2170, and in New Zealand
by Transworld Publishers (N.Z.) Ltd., Cnr. Moselle
and Waipareira Avenues, Henderson, Auckland.

Made and printed in Great Britain by
The Guernsey Press Co. Ltd., Guernsey, Channel Islands.

For Neil

Part One

1

I

It really begins with the wedding – the Boxing Day Chris got married – because that was the day I decided to *do* something about Ingrid Rothwell besides gawp at her like a love-sick cow or something whenever she came in sight. I'd been doing this for about a month before Christmas, I remember. I don't know what started it. Does anybody know what starts these things, why a bint can be one among dozens about the place one day and somebody special the next? Or it seems that way. Well anyway, it was that way with me and I'd been at it for a month, or maybe six weeks, and I'd got to the stage where I knew I'd have to do something about it.

The wedding was about the only thing anybody had been talking about at home for the last six months – ever since Chris and David came right out into the open and bought the ring – and I really thought that after all the talk and planning it would have to be something out of the ordinary for it not to fall flat. But then I was a novice at this kind of thing. I'd never been involved in a wedding before and I have to admit it's what you might call an experience.

There's about five hundred people staying overnight before the day, to begin with, and on the morning they're getting ready in lumps all over the place. The house is like a lot of backstage dressing-rooms like you sometimes see in musical pictures and you wouldn't be surprised to see some young lad marching round knocking on all the doors and shouting, 'Five minutes, please,' like they do. I think I've never seen so many strange faces and the surprising thing is they're mostly relatives of mine. Or they're supposed to be. I wonder where on earth the Old Lady's dug them all up from and I don't think even she knows them all for sure. I know for a fact she realizes she's overdone it with the offers of accommodation. And as for the Old Man, he said last night that if he'd known he wouldn't be able to get up to bed for people kipping down on the stairs he'd have put a bell-tent up on the lawn.

He's lucky he could go to bed. I've spent the night on the front-room sofa and the last four or five hours hanging about trying to get into the bathroom. By the time I do manage to get in there I'm feeling a bit sour at having all these people barging about the place, and thinking about a couple of thousand more that live in the town and have to be transported to the church. Being in a bit of a flap I forget to shoot the bolt behind me and it doesn't improve my temper when the door flies open and young Dorothy and Angela catch me without pants. This amuses them no end and I wonder if I can't arrange to fall downstairs and break a leg and give them a real laugh. A couple of proper horrors, Dorothy and Angela, twins, belonging to Auntie Agnes, one of my mother's sisters. I know the Old Lady can't abide them and she only had Chris ask them to be bridesmaids because she didn't want to get across with Auntie Agnes who's one of them sensitive types who go through life looking for any offence left lying about for the taking. I've only had one glimpse of Chris as she nipped across the landing and from the tight little smile she gives me when I make a crack that's supposed to be cheerful I guess she won't be sorry when it's all over and she's with David on the 3.45 to the Great Metropolis. It's even affected the Old Man. I'm just about to go downstairs to get started when he calls me into the bedroom and I find him standing in his undervest and trousers in front of the wardrobe mirror.

'Here, Vic,' he says; 'come an' tell me what you think to these new trousers.'

I sit down on the edge of the bed and look him over. 'Very nice, Dad. They seem to hang all right. Can't really tell, o' course, without your jacket on.'

'I'll just pop it on.'

He does this and then takes another look in the glass. He begins to work his shoulders about as though the tailor's left a few pins in. 'Seems a bit on the slack side to me,' he says.

'Well that's the style now, Dad,' I tell him. 'You'll feel better when you've got your shirt and waistcoat on. And I can't wait while you do that,' I say, as he begins looking round for them.

He's a tall, spare sort of feller, the Old Man is, and really a suit hangs well on him when he lets it. This one's a dark blue, nearly navy, with a faint double stripe in grey. 'I think he's made a right good job of it.' I lean forward and finger the material. 'A nice bit o' cloth an' all.'

'Oh, aye,' the Old Man says in that self-satisfied way he has sometimes; 'you can't diddle me when it comes to pickin' cloth. I know a good length o' cloth when I see one . . .' His voice tails off. He's not at all happy this morning. 'It's t'makin' up 'at worries me,' he says. 'I just don't feel right in it, somehow.'

'But he's one of the best tailors in Cressley, Dad. I wouldn't have recommended him otherwise.' I get up off the bed. 'Look, there's nowt wrong with my suit, is there?'

He eyes me over through the glass and says nothing. 'He charges t'best prices, any road,' he says. 'He fair made me sweat when he told me how much. I've never paid more na ten or eleven pound for a suit afore.'

'That'll be a suit when you've forgotten how much you paid for it,' I tell him. 'And that's looking a long time ahead.' I'm a bit fed-up with this conversation because we've had most of it out before.

'Happen so.' The Old Feller takes his jacket off again. 'All t'same, I wish I'd gone to Liversidge's like I allus have afore.'

'Aagh! Mass production. They cut suits with a bacon slicer there.' It's no use trying to do anything for the Old Man; you might just as well let him to his own sweet way. He still thinks in terms of wages at three pound ten a week and suits fifty bob apiece off the peg.

'Anyway,' I say, 'I'll have to be off.' And then just as I'm turning round to go out I catch sight of these brown shoes under a chair.

'You're not thinkin' o' wearing them today, are you?'

'Eh?' he says. 'What?'

'Your brown shoes.'

'Why not? They're me best.'

'Look,' I say, mustering my patience, 'you don't wear brown shoes with a blue suit. You've heard Stanley Holloway, haven't you?'

'That war a funeral,' he says.

'Well it applies to weddings an' all. You'll have our Chris curling up with shame. Remember there'll be a lot of eyes on you while you're up at the front.'

'They'll never notice me for our Christine.'

'Some of these folk here today make a point of noticing everything,' I tell him. 'Not that three parts of 'em know any better anyway.'

'Oh, damnation,' he says, getting his rag out at last, 'Is'll be glad when it's all over. I don't seem to be able to get owt right some road.'

'You won't be told.'

'Well I can't wear old shoes wi' a new suit,' he says, getting stubborn now.

'An' you can't wear them brown 'uns. I'll ask me mother what she thinks when I go down.'

This is the ace. The Old Man lifts his hand up. 'Ho'd on a minute. There's no need to bring your mother into this: I'm havin' enough trouble as it is.'

Just then I hear the Old Lady shouting from the bottom of the stairs. 'Victor! Are y'there, Victor? The taxi's waiting. Hurry yourself up or you'll have us all late.'

'She'll be bringing herself into it if I don't get a move on.' I start to go out again. 'Now just remember – no

12

brown shoes.' And I go out and leave the Old Man standing there staring into the glass with a baffled look on his face.

'Come on, Victor, come on,' the Old Lady says. She's standing at the bottom of the stairs like a battleship at anchor, big and solid, with her hair, greying fast it is now, newly trimmed and set. 'You know we've no time to spare.'

I know we haven't because I've planned the calls. 'I was just fixing me dad up.'

'Oh, your dad,' she says, rolling her eyes. 'A fat lot o' use he is on a day like this.' I stop in front of the hallstand to run my comb through my hair. 'You'll do, you'll do,' the Old Lady says. 'It's not you 'at's gettin' married.'

'Catch me.'

'One of 'em will one o' these fine days.'

'She'll have to be up early.'

'There's plenty willin' to do that to get a presentable young chap with a steady job an' no bad habits.'

I cock a wary eye at her. Is she after marrying me off next? The wedding bug must have bitten deeper than I thought. I chuck her under the chin. 'What do you know about my bad habits?'

'Oh, go on with you,' she says. 'Get off an' get your job done.'

I pull my jacket down and straighten my tie. 'Well I'm ready. Where's our Jim?'

'He's in the front room. He's been ready a good half-hour.'

A good mark for the scholar! I go through into the front room to find him. It's bedlam in there. Somebody's switched the wireless on and it's playing a record request programme at full blast. Standing in the doorway I feel like shouting, 'Would anybody like the wireless turning up a bit?' There they are, milling about, pulling at their clothes and messing about with make-up as they jockey for position in front of the glass. Somebody's knocked an ashtray on to the floor and the last of the three plaster geese flying across the wallpaper is

13

doing a nose-dive into the carpet. Over in one corner, curled up as peaceful as if he's by himself in the middle of a field, there's young Jim, with his nose in a book, as per.

I reach past somebody and touch his knee. 'C'mon, Einstein.'

He gets up, thin, fifteen years old and too tall for his age, and marks the place in his book and follows me out. He's ushering at the church. You wouldn't think he's noticed anything unusual going on and when we get out on the front step and look at this big Rolls with white ribbons and white seat covers, he says, 'Just like a wedding, isn't it?' and I have to laugh.

Well I'm glad to be out of that lot and I take a butcher's at my list. 'Auntie Miriam first.' I give the driver the address and Jim and I get into the taxi. Jim opens his book and retires again; but I can't afford to; I've got a lot to do before eleven and I hope Geoff Lister, my cousin, who's looking after the other taxi, keeps his end going as well. I check the list for the umpteenth time, wondering if we can get them all there on time. It's a tight list and I'm proud of that because I'm saving David's money by having one less car than they thought. But it makes no alllowance for lost time, so I'm hoping everybody's ready and waiting.

The taxi turns round in the street and moves off. The wedding's under way.

II

It's snowed twice heavy in the fortnight before Christmas and it's still lying about in like little grimy mountain ranges on either side of the road where it curves down the hill. It looks as if there's more to come as well because the sky's like a thick grey blanket hanging behind the chimneys and rooftops with a reddish flush over the bottom half where the sun's doing its best to break through. Cressley Town Silver Band's pitched in

14

the forecourt of the Prince of Wales on the corner and I get the sound of 'Hark! the Herald Angels Sing', as we slow down for the turn coming louder as I wind the window down and give them a shout.

'Oi! Call at number thirty-seven. There's ten bob in it today.'

The conductor lifts his hand to show he's heard me and the band carry on playing in the cold. I know the Old Man'll be glad to have them call this morning because he'd be out with them but for the wedding and he says it's the first Boxing Day play-out he's missed in more than twenty years.

I begin to think about things – the wedding and all that – as the taxi bats down through town and young Jim goes on reading in his corner. I reckon you can take all of us – me, my mother and father, Chris, young Jim, and probably David as well – and the only one enjoying it is the Old Lady. *She's* having the time of her life; you can tell this by the way she's fussing about snapping everybody's heads off. She's been waiting years for this day. Chris is twenty-seven now and I think there have been times when the Old Lady was scared she was being left on the shelf, just another schoolmarm with nothing to look forward to but retiring on pension and maybe living with somebody else in the same fix. But I never saw any reason for worrying; I knew all along Chris would get married. I didn't see how she could miss, what with her looks and personality; because even if she is my own sister and I do say it myself, she's one of the grandest girls any bloke could hope to meet. As I saw it, it was only a matter of time before the right chap came along and snapped her up. But the Old Lady isn't a big believer in right chaps; all she thinks of is position and income and character; and the duller and plainer they come the more character she seems to think they bring with them. Good-looking blokes are all very well on the pictures or television, but you keep your eye on them in real life because you can't expect them to be any better than they should be with all the temptations that must come their way.

That's the way the Old Lady thinks – or thought – and it's probably why she didn't fall over herself to welcome David at first, because he's good-looking and talks with a cut-glass accent and comes from the south. And she knew nothing about him except he was Senior English master at the Grammar School. That was a point in his favour, though, because the Old Lady thinks that schoolteachers were first in the queue when brains and general strength of character were handed out. She should have seen some of them from where I was sitting not so long ago and she might have modified her ideas a bit. Anyway, it bothered her because she couldn't chew the fat about David's background. (His mother was a so-and-so – y'know, they kept that draper's shop in Whiteley Street – and his father was a somebody else. He had a sister that ran away with a feller from Wigan and left three kids for the husband to bring up.) All that kind of stuff; it's the breath of life to the Old Lady, and she had to pacify herself by worming as much as she could out of Chris. Such things as David was taken prisoner in North Africa when he was only eighteen, his mother and dad were killed in the London blitz, and his girl friend got tired of waiting and writing letters and went and married somebody else. She'd never have got a hard-luck story like that out of David himself but she got it out of Chris bit by bit; and then she went and turned right round and couldn't do enough for him. She mothered him till I'm surprised he's lasted till the wedding. But that's the Old Lady all over: hard as nails on top and soft as a brush underneath.

Anyway, we make the first call and pick up Auntie Miriam and Uncle Horace, who aren't very important and won't have to mind being first and having to hang about at the church half the morning. I drop Jim off with them and give him his orders.

'Now get your nose out of that book and watch what you're doing. You show the bride's guests to the left and the groom's to the right. Okay?'

'It's all so complicated,' Jim says. 'You should have put somebody more intelligent on the job.'

'You're all we could spare, so watch what you're doing or it's a clip on the ear.'

'Bribery will get you nowhere,' Jim says, and I have to laugh because he's a real wag at times.

'All right, have it your own way.' I whip the book out of his hand 'But I'll take this and then mebbe you'll keep your mind on the job.'

'Here, what am I supposed to do between times?' he says.

'Look at the gravestones. See'f there's anybody you know stopping there.'

I look at the title of the book as I get in with the driver – *Philosophy from Plato to the Present Day* – and pop it in the compartment under the dashboard. There's times when young Jim unnerves me, he's got so many brains. I wonder how I come to have a brother like him, or a sister like Chris, for that matter. And looking at it that way, it's me who's the odd man out.

At a quarter to eleven prompt, like I planned, we leave the church for the last trip – home for Chris and the Old Man. All without a hitch, I'm thinking, pleased with myself. Everybody there for time and all going nicely, thanks. On the way we pass the Old Lady doing her impersonation of Lady Docker, with the two brats, Dotty and Mangy, making hideous faces through the back window.

And just after this it happens. We swing round a corner and there's this dirty great piece of broken milk bottle lying jagged edge up in the road. There's a crack like a gun going off and bumping as the front offside tyre goes flat. The taxi swerves off the road across the pavement and stops with its front end up the bank. The driver lets it roll back on to the road and then we both get out and look at the damage. He pushes his cap back, bending down with his hands on his knees, and whistles.

'Now what?' I say. And everything's rushing into my mind at once: Chris and the Old Man waiting at home, the church full and no bride, and the Old Lady getting more ratty every second that goes by.

'It's bad,' the driver says.

'I've noticed that,' I tell him. 'It's ten to eleven. What do we do?'

'Change t'wheel,' he says. 'There's nowt else for it.'

He takes his white coat off and then starts to peel off about fifteen layers of pullovers and waistcoats that he has on underneath; all nice and steady like, as though it's Sunday and he's at home in his backyard and out to make a morning of it. I hop round to the boot and rummage about for a jack. I slam it into position and begin to crank, praying we shan't be bothered by some copper with time on his hands and a lot of silly questions to ask. I can't imagine this driver ever changed a wheel before; somebody must always have done it for him while he was stripping for action. As it is, he's hardly reached the working minimum when I've got the spare wheel in position and I'm tightening nuts like mad. It's just after eleven when we get the car moving again, and nearly ten past by the time we pull up at our gate.

The Old Man's on the front step with his hand over his eyes like a sailor up in a crow's nest looking for land. 'Where the hummer have you been?' he says with panic in his voice. 'We're late.'

I'm tempted for a second to give him a cheeky answer, like we've called for a drink or something, but I see he's worried out of his wits so I just show him my dirty hands and tell him we've had a puncture. Chris comes out meantime and though she's got a coat on over her frock it doesn't hide that she looks a real picture, just like somebody in one of them glossy women's mags.

'You'll knock'em sideways,' I tell her. 'You'll knock'em for six.'

Well, once they begin it doesn't seem to matter that Chris was late. After all it'll give her and David something to laugh about later on. I slip her coat off for her and stay at the back where I can get out first when it's all over. The organ switches from this soft background music it's been playing and starts on the wedding march, booming out and filling the church. There's a shuffle as all the guests stand up and Chris and the Old Man, with Dotty and Mangy behind, start down the aisle to where the vicar and David and his best man are waiting for them. A real picture Chris looks, all in white, and her hair shining under this little cap of net and flowers, Chris's hair is a sort of reddy brown like the Old Lady's was when she was young, but Jim and I are both dark like the Old Man. I look down at the Old Feller's feet and see he's remembered what I told him. There's a bit of a lopsided look about the congregation because our family's out in force and course David has no family, just the few friends he's made since he came to Cressley.

The organ stops and there's dead quiet for a minute. Then the vicar chimes up. 'Dearly beloved, we are gathered together to join this man and this woman in holy matrimony . . .'

I'm real happy for them; I really am; because David's a good bloke and he's getting a real gem in Chris. I've always thought there was something special about Chris and I suppose that's a bit funny because a lot of lads I know can't abide their sisters. But I know I'll be lucky if I find a girl as nice as Chris to marry. I'm always kind of half-looking for this girl I'm going to find one day. She'll be everything you could want in a girl: talking, laughing, sharing, making love, and everything. I never say anything about this to anybody and as far as my mates are concerned I'm interested in bints for just one thing. This is the way you have to be because if you told them all you think they'd laugh and say you were sloppy and soft in the head.

And now I begin to think about Ingrid. I'm always thinking about her these days and wondering what she thinks of me – if anything. I wonder if I'll be lucky enough to see her tonight and what I'll say to her if I do. Because I'm going to say something if it kills me. I've hung about and gawped for long enough.

Outside the church, when it's over, the photographers get busy, both the amateurs and the bod paid for the job.

We get them to make it snappy because it's too cold to hang about. Then I slip the coat round Chris's shoulders and let my cousin Geoff take her and David to the reception and I follow on behind with the Old Lady and the Old Feller. We drive away leaving confetti in the snow and the deep puddles in the gutters.

The Old Man seems restless in the back seat, as though he's lost something, and the Old Lady says to him, 'What you seekin'?'

I'm lookin' for me speech,' the Old Feller says, rummaging through his pockets. 'I had it when I –'

'Your speech?' the Old Lady says, and this is the first I've heard of it as well.

'Aye. I've jotted a few points down on a bit o' paper but I can't find it . . . Ho'd on, here it is.'

'I hope you're not goin' to show us all up,' the Old Lady says. 'All you need do is tell them we're pleased to see 'em and thank 'em for comin'. That's all. No need to get on ramblin' all round the houses.'

'It wa' your idea to have t'reception in t'best hotel in Cressley,' the Old Man says, 'so wes'll have to come up to scratch. Who ever heard of a posh weddin' wi'out speeches? If you'd had t'bandroom like I wanted you to I might not ha' got on me feet at all.'

'T'bandroom,' the Old Lady snorts. 'Allus on t'cheap. D'you mean to tell me you begrudge your own daughter – your only daughter – a decent send-off to her married life?'

'There's a difference between a decent send-off an' a Society do,' the Old Feller says. 'I'm nobbut a collier, y'know, not a mill-owner.'

'An' you don't let anybody forget it . . . Anyway, we've had all this out before.' I think the Old Lady's just cottoned on that the glass partition's open and the driver's taking all in and having a quiet smile about it.

'Aye, we have,' the Old Man says.

'An' we decided that the Craven Arms was the best place.'

'Aye, we did,' the Old Man says.

I know the driver's not the only one laughing but the Old Lady can't see this, not being one of the quickest to see a joke.

'An' if it bothers you just remember 'at you've no more daughters an' t'next wedding in the family somebody else'll pay for.'

'Ah!' the Old Man says.

III

When Chris and David go off to catch their train a lot of the guests go home, because the wedding's officially over like. But some of them, the closest family and friends, come back to our house. We live in Meadow Lane, in a big old stone-fronted house that my mother talked the Old Man into buying before the war when houses were dirt cheap compared with what they're asking for them now. You get a nice view from the bedroom windows with the town on one side and the park on the other with the infirmary sitting on top of the hill where it looks at night a bit errie, all old and lit up, like Castle Dracula on a party night. There's a lot of these people come back with us and we have to borrow some chairs from the neighbours for them to sit on; but this doesn't help much because then out of common politeness we have to invite the neighbours in as well, them that haven't already been to the wedding, that is. The Old Lady says she's never seen the house as full since her father's funeral. But this is no funeral. They haven't had a get-together like this in years and they're out to make the best of it and bury all the family differences.

The Old Man's speech has done as much as anything towards this. Nobody expected much when he stood up with his bit of paper on the table behind the mince pies, and they expected even less when he started humming and hawing and feeling in his pockets like he'd done in the taxi. I knew straight away he'd lost his glasses and he can't read anything much smaller than a newspaper

21

headline without them. Anyway, he coughed and mumbled a bit and then all at once he opened up. It was just as if something had got into him, kind of inspired him, seeing all the family sitting there like that, all them familiar faces looking at him, wondering what old Arthur was up to like. Well he starts with Chris and David and then goes on to the family in general, telling them all how silly they are to fall out about silly things and nurse grudges and spites, and wasn't this a good time to start thinking about the family again and forgetting all these little things that poison family life. He got 'em. He cut some of them right to the quick and one or two of the women were in tears. The Old Lady was flabbergasted and I could see her timing the Old Feller as he went on like he did this every day of his life. Chris was all full up as well and when it came to her turn all she could say was thank you everybody and then she turns to the Old Man and hugs him till he goes red in the face he's so embarrassed.

Uncle William, the Old Man's eldest brother, comes up to him after and says, 'By gow, Arthur, I didn't know you had it in you, lad.'

'Neither did I, William,' the Old Feller says, and he lowers his voice. 'You don't think I made a fool o' meself, do you? Is'll catch it from Lucy if I have.'

'A fool of yerself! It's finest thing 'at's happened in t'family for years.'

And so everybody else seems to think. Except Auntie Agnes, who's taken everything the Old Man said as being directed personally at her and gone home in a huff. Good riddance to bad rubbish, I say.

So we have a party on the strength of it and when we've eaten what's left over from the reception and practically everything else in the house besides we decide to play some games. Uncle George takes charge now. Guaranteed to keep any party going, Uncle George is. He specializes in the kind of game where you're blindfolded and made to make a fool of yourself in front of everybody else. A laugh every ten seconds with Uncle

George and no hard feelings at a pin stuck in your behind or a lemon-cheese tart smeared across your face, because it's all good clean family fun. When everybody gets tired of this and they're all worn out from laughing till they cry, Uncle George shows what a versatile lad he is by getting on the piano and playing for carol singing. They have the Old Man getting his trombone out now and he plays 'Just a Song at Twilight' and his favourite – 'Bless this House'. Just as he hits the high note near the end of this the light bulb bursts all over the place. I've heard of a singer smashing a wine glass but never a trombone player breaking a light bulb. There's a good bit of larking about and squawking in the dark while I strike a match and get a spare out of the cupboard.

Round about half past eight, though, the party begins to break up because some of them have a way to travel and there's a lot of looking for coats and hats and hand-shaking and kissing and wishing compliments of the season; and then by nine there's only us and Uncle William and Auntie Edna, who're staying the night, left among the wreckage. In a minute or two young Jim beetles off to bed.

'Looks as though we've had a football match,' the Old Lady says, looking round. The chairs are all out of place and there's still a few about that don't belong to us. There's cushions on the floor and empty glasses and full ashtrays on everything. The fire's nearly out because we've kept ourselves warm the last couple of hours, and the air's thick with tobacco smoke. I bend down to pick a glass up before somebody kicks it over and find a ciga-rette burn in the corner of the carpet. I keep quiet about it, though, thinking tomorrow's early enough for the Old Lady to know about it.

'Somebody's gone without her gloves,' the Old Lady says. 'I wonder whose they are.

'I think they're Millie's,' Aunt Edna says. 'Let me look . . . Yes, they are. I remember admiring them outside the church.'

'I'll drop her a line about 'em after the holidays.' The

23

Old Lady wanders about the room picking cushions up and punching them into shape. 'Just look at these cushion covers: clean on today and there's lemon-cheese an' all sorts on 'em.' She laughs. 'Eeh, but he's a card, isn't he, George? A real tyke. One of the best of husbands, though. Elsie's never had a minute's bother with him all the twenty year they've been married. He never had a steady job before he knew her, y'know. He took bets for a bookie in town at one time. Allus his name in the paper, being fined. Me father nearly kicked him off the step the first time he came to call for her. 'Get yoursen a decent job afore you come courtin' a daughter o' mine,' he said. An' George did. He went to Fletcher's mill an' got set on. He's never been out o'work since. A foreman he is now, at some engineering shop Keighley way . . .

'Could you do with a cup o' tea?' she says.

'Not just now,' Auntie Edna says. 'You sit yourself down and have a minute. You've been at it all day.'

The Old Lady sits down and folds her hands in her lap. 'It's been like a real tonic to have 'em all here together, laughin' an havin' fun, just like old times. When you have a party like that you wonder how anybody can fall out with anybody.'

'It's the way of the world,' Uncle William says. 'It's allus been like that an' it allus will be. As long as you can get together now an' again an' forget it all.'

'Only Agnes had to spoil it by going off like that . . .'

'I think I offended her,' the Old Man says. 'She thought I wa' gettin' at her.'

'An' so you were, Arther,' Uncle William says. 'Who else but daft silly women like her?'

'I've given over bothering about Agnes,' the Old Lady says. 'You can't do right for doing wrong with her. I've sucked up to her for years, telling meself it wa' just her way an' she was all right underneath. Well now I've done. She allus has to spoil everything.'

'How does it feel then to have one less?' Auntie Edna asks in a minute.

'Oh, you have mixed feelings when it comes to the

time, y'know. I shall miss her, no doubt about that. She's a good lass, our Christine. Allus was . . . But it's high time she settled down an' started a family. Many a lass at twenty-seven's got 'em growin' up an' at school.'

'Seems a nice young feller she's married,' Uncle William says.

'Oh, David's one of the best. A right grand lad. She'll be all right with him; I haven't a minute's worry on that score.'

'Such a nicely spoken young man,' Auntie Edna says. 'Lovely manners, too.'

'He's educated, David is,' the Old Man says, as though this accounts for everything. 'Educated.'

'And not a bit o'side with it, neither,' the Old Lady says. 'Oh, we couldn't have wished for a better match for her.'

Auntie Edna cocks a look at me where I'm slumped down in the easy-chair taking all in and saying nothing. 'I suppose it'll be Victor next,' she says. I like Auntie Edna but I do think she's a bit of a busybody at times.

'No, we shan't be going to Victor's wedding yet awhile,' the Old Lady says, talking about me as if I'm not there. 'Give him time; he's not twenty-one yet. And I don't even think he's courtin'. Course, I suppose I'll be the last to get to know when he is. I'm not bothered about him, though. If they were all as steady an' content as him we'd do well enough. It's young Jim 'at worries me sometimes. Allus studyin', y'know. Never seems to give his mind a rest. He fancies bein' a doctor an' I suppose he'll have to work hard if he's going to pass for college; but I sometimes think he overdoes it a bit. I found him one night, Edna – and this is without a word of a lie – I found him sitting up in bed in the middle of the night, fast asleep, with his books open all round him. Fast asleep, he was. Y'see he can't even leave it alone when he's supposed to be resting. His mind never rests; it's allus on the work. I don't like it. He's growin' fast and he never did have Victor's constitution. Like a young horse from the day he was born, Victor was. Never a minute's worry over illness with him – except the usual kid's ailments, o' course, an' that time he fell on the railings an' cut his head open.'

Auntie Edna looks round at me and gives me a sort of fond smile. I wink at her and she twinkles at me.

'Jim's certainly shot up since we saw him last,' she says.

'Aye, too fast for his strength. He's taking all his strength into his brain instead of his body. I've been thinking I'll have a walk over to the doctor's with him after the holidays and get his advice.'

'If he's happy it'll help a lot,' Uncle William says. 'He's a very intelligent lad, you can see that; and lads like that have to have plenty to occupy their minds or they get restless and run down. I shouldn't worry too much about him, Lucy. See what the doctor says, by all means, but don't fret.'

'Aye, that's all very well, William, but when you have 'em you fret about 'em. It's nature.'

I don't really think the Old Lady should have said this because Uncle William and Auntie Edna haven't any kids and I think they miss not having them sometimes.

'Well we want him to make the most of his chance,' the Old Man says. 'I only hope we'll be able to keep him till he can earn for hisself. It wasn't so bad with our Christine – she had scholarships; but they tell me scholarships are nobbut a drop in the ocean when a lad's studyin' medicine.' He fishes for his pipe and bacca, then remembers the big box of cigars he has in the cupboard. 'Here, William,' he says, 'try one o' these. David bought me 'em. Very good of him, wasn't it?'

'Very good indeed, Arthur.' Uncle William takes a cigar and sniffs at it. 'I thought you'd been treating yourself.'

'You thought wrong,' the Old Man says. 'I'm not in t'cigar class.'

'Not far off, surely, Arthur?' Uncle William says, and I see a gleam in his eyes as he lights up. 'The new aristocracy, living off the fat o' the land, sending your lad to college to study medicine. And you should have some brass if anybody has. You're not the one to go out swilling it every night.'

'Ey up! Ey up!' the Old Feller says, rising to it. 'Just because we're gettin' a decent livin' wage after all this time everybody's on to us.'

'I wish I war earning twenty pound a week,' Uncle William says, 'and they could all be on to me as liked.'

'Earn it,' the Old Man says. 'I'm glad you said earn it. I tell you what I tell everybody else, William. If You think you can addle twenty pound a week in t'pit, you can come an' have a try. It can be done, an' there's fellers takin' that kind o' money out reg'lar. But they work like blacks for it. Aagh! all these fellers proppin' bars up and openin' their mouths. The hardest work they ever do is lift a pint glass. They wouldn't last a shift down t'pit. I've done some coal-gettin' an' I know. I'm glad I haven't to do it now. I'm a deputy an' there's many a man under me earnin' more than I do; but I don't begrudge 'em it because I've addled money t'same way an' I know what it takes to do it. And there's another thing –'

'Now then, Arthur, that's enough,' the Old Lady says. 'There's no need to get arguin'. William's entitled to his opinion.'

'No man's entitled to an opinion till he knows the facts. I'm just straightenin' him out . . .'

The Old Lady and Auntie Edna look at one another and I decide it's time I was on my way. I get up.

'Are you goin' to bed, Victor?'

No, I'm going out. There's a special dance on in town. I thought I'd go over for an hour.'

'What, at this time?'

'They'll only just have got warmed up.'

'Well, better take a key. And don't be too late; you've been on the go all day, y'know.'

'Have a good time, Victor,' Auntie Edna says.

IV

The first thing I do when I get upstairs is take a look at myself in the dressing-table mirror. It's one of those with three glasses in and if you get the knack of adjusting them you can see what you look like from the side as well as straight on. It seems to me I'm spending altogether too much time these days either looking in mirrors at home or catching sight of myself in mirrors outside. I never knew there were so many mirrors; the world's full of them, or shop windows with the blinds down, which amount to the same thing as far as what I'm talking about's concerned. When I'm washing my hands at the office I can see another pair of hands just like mine doing the same. If I go to the pictures ten to one I'll climb the stairs and come face to face with my twin brother coming up from the other side. (Only he's not strictly my twin because he's the opposite hand to me.) And I've only to look out of a bus at night to see this same opposite-handed me looking in from outside. It's not that I'm conceited – at least, not most of the time – and when I see myself in a window or something I don't think what a swell-looking geezer, but try to look at myself as though I'm somebody else and wonder what I think of me. And it's actually that I'm not a swell-looking geezer. At least, not most of the time. I never used to be like this. I can remember when I didn't give a monkey's what I looked like or what anybody thought of me. But now it's different; because now, you see, I'm conscious of women. Very conscious of them in fact.

When I'm looking in my mirror at home like I am now, I don't think I'm so bad. Whichever way you look, and whoever's doing the looking, you couldn't call me ugly. Not *handsome*, maybe, but not ugly. My face is sort of square and what an author might call open, and it's a good colour. (Thank God I'm not one of these blokes who's plagued to death with boils and spots and blains and whatnot). The scar over my left eye where I argued with the railing doesn't help, though I wonder sometimes if it doesn't make me look a bit tougher. I don't know. And there's always my hair. No two ways about that, I've got a head of hair any man would be proud of, thick and dark with a natural wave that needs only a touch of the fingers after it's combed and glossy without a lot of cream. No doubt about my hair. And I have it cut every fortnight and never miss. Or only now and again. I could do with a couple more inches on my height. I've always had a yen for just two more inches. But still I'm not a little runt because I've got a good build . . . a nice deep chest that I'm not scared of showing off in swimming trunks, and square broad shoulders. And then my clothes. Now there's no denying I know how to dress. I don't pay the earth for my suits but I know where they give you the right cut and I always keep my pants pressed and my shoes clean. And if my shirt's just the least bit grubby at the collar, into the wash it goes. Ask the Old Lady. She says it's like washing for an army keeping up to me alone.

So there I am – Victor Arthur Brown, twenty years old, one of the lads, and not very sure of himself under the cocky talk and dirty jokes and wisecracks. Take me or leave me, I'm all I've got. And what does it matter what you look like anyway? Every day you see the niftiest bints with the gloomiest-looking blokes; blokes you wouldn't think any self-respecting bird would look twice at. And what do clothes matter? At least, decent clothes, because it seems you get on best if you look a freak these days and you're always seeing wenches clinging like mad to bods in suits I wouldn't wear as far as the front gate.

So what the hell!

I'm as presentable as the next bloke and I don't see why Ingrid shouldn't think the same way. Only, that's what I think here in my own room; and the second I lay eyes on her I feel about as fetching as something dreamed up for a science-fiction picture.

I pull myself out of the glass and go and have a wash in the bathroom. Then I decide to go and borrow Jim's new tie, the blue knitted one with the horizontal stripes. There's a light showing under his door and I find him sitting up in bed with an exercise book on his knee and a pencil in his hand.

I pick the tie up off the drawers. 'Lend me this?'

He mumbles something. I don't suppose he could care less. I start to put the tie on in the glass. Another glass.

'I've never seen anybody make so much fuss over tying a tie,' he says in a minute.

'What fuss?'

'All that twisting and turning and threading through. Why don't you tie a knot an' have done with it?'

'That's a Windsor knot,' I tell him. I pull it into place and smooth my collar down. 'When you tie a tie like that it makes a neat knot and it stays put.'

'It'll be all creased up now when I want it.'

'What do you care?'

'Hmm,' he says, and goes back to his books.

'It's a nice tie.'

He says nothing.

'Like to flog it?'

'Eh?'

'The tie. Would you like to sell it?'

'I didn't buy it. Me mother bought it.'

I look in the glass. It really is a smart tie; too good for Jim who doesn't care about clothes anyway. 'I'll give you half a crown for it.'

'It cost a lot more than that.'

'You didn't buy it.'

'No, and how can I sell it when I didn't buy it?'

'You'd like the half-crown better, though, wouldn't you?' I say, looking at him through the glass. He's always broke, Jim is, because he's always buying something or saving up to buy something, like guinea pigs or rabbits to keep in the shed, or stamps for his collection, or something.

He's watching me, turning something over in his mind. 'I'll tell you what,' he says, 'I'll let you wear it whenever you like at threepence a time. And you owe me threepence now for tonight.'

30

'Why did I open my big mouth?' I fish in my pocket. 'I haven't any change, only a bob.'

'That'll do. You'll have three more times to your credit.'

I chuck him the bob. 'You don't want to waste your time with medicine, laddie; you want to go into business. You'll be a millionaire by the time you're thirty.' I go over to him and stick my chin out. 'Do I need a shave, d'you think?'

'Save it till the Easter holidays,' he says.

'How d'you mean? I'm shavin' every day now.'

'If you want to go to all that trouble . . . Are you going somewhere?'

'To a dance.'

'At this time?'

I look at my watch. 'Quart' to ten. The night's but young, me boy.'

'Going out at this time to shuffle round a floor with a lot of smelly people to a so-called band,' he says.

'You wind your head in an' get on with your Latin.'

'How do you know it's Latin?'

'I'll bet it's not *Lady don't turn over*.'

'What's that?'

'Never mind.'

'As a matter of fact,' he says, 'it's maths. And while you're here, there's a bit I don't quite follow.'

'No use asking me. It's all Greek to me.' I realize I've made a corny joke. 'How's that, eh? Maths – all Greek to me.'

'Ha, ha,' Jim says, very sarcy. 'And you can knock it off, Vic. Old Cartwright was on to me the other day. He said he expected better maths marks from Vic Brown's brother.'

This is enough to bring me out of the mirror again. 'He said that? Old Carthorse? I don't believe it.'

' 'Strue,' Jim says. 'I daren't let on who I am in the French class but old Cartwright seems to think you were pretty good.'

Ah, well . . . who cares about lousy old French anyway?

I go back to the bed and pick Jim's exercise book up.

'What's the trouble, laddie?' I say, imitating old Carthorse's rumble.

'Here.' Jim points it out in his text-book. 'I can't get this one out. I've been struggling with if for half an hour. I think the book must be wrong.'

'I've never met one yet.' I go through his working out step by step and spot it as soon as I come to it. I drop the book in his lap. 'Try putting that last equation the other way up.'

He looks. 'Gosh . . . Well fancy me not seeing that.'

'It's not seeing things like that 'at makes you fail exams.'

'All right, bighead.'

I rub my hand over my chin and fancy I hear the bristles rasp. 'Well, I haven't time for a shave anyway. I'm late enough.'

'Won't she wait?' Jim says.

'Who?'

'Who?' he says, grinning. 'Brigitte Bardot, of course; who else?'

For a second I wonder if he's found out. Then I realize he can't have because nobody knows but me. Even she doesn't know yet. But she soon will now. She jolly soon will.

Outside it's sharp and clear, real clean winter weather. From the look of the sky this morning we were in for some more snow but now it's full of stars and the frost nips your cheeks. I think about if for a minute and then start walking instead of waiting for a bus because it's too cold to hang about. In a minute I hear a bus topping the hill behind me and I break into a trot and beat it to the next stop. I get a threepenny into town. There's nobody else upstairs and I get in the back seat and have another butcher's at this book of pin-ups and nudes Willy Lomas lent me before the holidays. *Chérie* it's called and it's French, with a bint on the cover in a suspender belt and black nylons and nothing much else but a you-know-what look. 'Lush,' Willy said, and he was dead right. These Frenchies certainly know how to put a book like this together. Your guts melt when you look at some of these bints in there. There's some birds in their underwear or nylon nighties, just covered up enough to set your imagination working and some others where you don't need any imagination at all. There's some writing as well that makes me wish I'd taken more notice in the French class at school because if it's anything to do with the pictures it must be pretty hot stuff. When I'm looking at these tarts I wonder for the three-thousandth time what It must be like, and I reckon I'd never manage to find out with these birds because it would be all up with me if one of them so much as came near me in the flesh.

The funniest thing though is I don't think about Ingrid this way at all. Not that she isn't attractive, because she is; just about the most attractive girl I know. Only the way I think about her is sort of clean and pure and soft, as though just to touch her cheek would be better than anything these other bints could give me.

Once I get thinking about Ingrid I forget about everything else and I overshoot my stop and have to walk back.

Walking down Illingworth Street I begin to feel pretty good about everything. I've got a good suit on and I'm clean and spruced up and my heels ringing on the pavement seem to give me more confidence, somehow. I know it'll be the interval at the dance so I call in at the Ram's Head, this pub up the street, for an odd one to put me right on top and a looksee if any of the lads are about. I go into the lounge. It's jam-packed with the interval trade from the Gala Rooms and I can see across the bar into the smoke room where the band boys are having a quick one in them nifty fawn jackets they wear with maroon bow ties. I scramble for a glass of bitter and when I look round who should I see but Willy Lomas waving to me from a corner table. I go over an' this lad he's with – Harry Something-or-other, his name is – shoves up and makes room for me to sit down. They haven't got their coats on and I ask them if they've been in the dance.

They both nod, and Willy says, 'Packed out. Everybody dancin' on your feet.' He's looking about as cheerful as he always does. I think it's his face that does it. It's long and white, like a clown's, and his hair's jet black and slicked back without a parting, smooth and shiny as your shoe toecap. He lifts his leg up and shows me a torn turn-up.

'Put me leg out in a quickstep,' he says. 'Next thing I know some tart has her heel in me trouser bottom. Nearly went arse over tip.'

'Any interestin' talent?' I say.

'Usual crowd,' Harry says, which tells me nothing that I want to know. Anyway, I don't think they know Ingrid.

'I rather fancy that singin' bit they've got,' Willy says.

'A bit out o' your class in't she, Willy?' Harry says. 'It'd cost you a fortune to keep her in stockings.'

'Well I can fancy it free, can't I?' Willy says.

'Anyway, she's married,' I say.

'How d'ye know?' Willy says.

'Because she wears a wedding ring, clot, that's how.'

'I sometimes think the married 'uns are the best in the long run,' Harry says. 'Least, they know what you're after and you don't have to break 'em in.'

'I don't want any fifteen-stone husband breathing down my neck,' Willy says. 'Give me the single 'uns every time. What I like is a nice willin' little virgin who's grateful to you for showing her how nice it is.'

He's bragging now and I grin at Harry as he gives me a sly wink.

'Trouble is', Willy says when he's had a pull at his pint, 'every bird I take a fancy to's either wed or courtin'. You know, I picked one up at the Trocadero the other week. Smashin' bit she was and she had that look about – y'know, no limit for the price of a bag of fish an' chips. She let me walk her to Greenford – two mile – an' then when I tried to steer her into a shop doorway to do a spot o' neckin' and fix up for another time, what d'you think she said? 'Me fiancy wouldn't like it,' she said. Her fiancy! Four mile I walked that night, for damn all!'

I laugh. I have a theory about Willy. I think he'll end up married to a tart six-foot tall and as plain as the side of a warehouse and be bossed about for the rest of his life.

'Aye, women are murder,' Harry says, so it looks like he's got troubles too. 'I wa' goin' steady with a bint some time back. Twelve month I'd been courtin' her an' we were even thinking about getting engaged. She was allus on about it. "When're we goin' to get engaged, 'Arry?" she says. Allus on about it.'

'Oh, I've never thought about that,' Willy says, and I have a quiet grin thinking about this six-foot tart who's about some where waiting for him.

'Well, I didn't mind,' Harry says. 'She wore me down like. I wa' ready to give in for a bit o' peace an' quiet. Then one week-end she goes over to stay with a cousin of hers in Warrington. Next thing I know she's over there every week-end an' I'm ditched for a bloody Yank.'

'Aye, uniforms an' brass,' Willy says. 'You can't compete with 'em.'

'Have to get yourself a bus conductor's job,' I say. I'm thinking I'll be as miserable as them if I stop here much longer. As it is, I'm all a-bubble inside from the thought of seeing Ingrid.

It's quieter in the pub now and when I look round I can't see any sign of the band boys so the interval must be over. I'm wasting good time.

'Oh, by the way, Willy . . .' I fish out *Chérie* and pass it to him, covering the tart on the front with my hand. 'Thanks.'

Willy pockets it like a conjurer. 'Think to it, Vic?'

'Very nice. There's one or two in there I wouldn't mind getting friendly with.'

'I'll say,' Willy says. 'By, but I'll have me a holiday in Paris next year – and to hell with Blackpool. Just see if I don't.'

'You don't think they walk about streets wi' nowt on, do you?' Harry says.

'Course not,' Willy says. He leans over the table and lowers his voice. 'But I'll tell you what, though: there's wenches over there 'at open their coats when they see you comin' an' they've got nowt on underneath.'

I start grinning and Harry says, 'Gerraway!'

'It's right,' Willy says. 'I know a bloke what goes over reg'lar: one of the travellers at our place. He's had it with more different bints than a lodging-house cat. An' besides they've got knocking-shops on every corner, run by the gover'ment. All above board. You walk in, pay your money, an' take your pick. Just think if we had one'r two here in Cressley. We shouldn't need to run after bints in dance halls: we could go an' get what we wanted when we wanted it.'

'I'm all for it,' Harry says; 'but you're a bit late about Paris, Willy. They've shut 'em all up.'

'Eh?' Willy says. 'How d'ye know?'

'I read it in a book a bit back. They closed 'em just after the war.'

'Well anyway,' Willy says, a bit disappointed like, 'you don't have to look far for it.'

'You're a feller 'at's lookin' for summat he won't get rid of so quick,' Harry says.

'Aw, come off it,' Willy says. 'Science, man, science.'

'What does a bint on a street corner know about science?'

Well they look like they're settled here so I get up to leave them to it.

'You're not goin', are you, Vic?' Willy says. 'Have another afore you go.'

I say no. I'm all on edge to get down to the Gala Rooms and look for Ingrid. I'm not much of a drinker, anyway. Willy could keep a brewery in production but an odd one's enough for me.

'Anyway, I'll see you later,' I say, and they both say, 'Yeh, see you later, Vic,' and go back to their argument about the tarts in Paris.

I pop a piece of spearmint chewing gum in my mouth to clean my breath as I go down the street to the Gala

Rooms. I pay my three bob admission at the desk in the entrance and go down to the cloakroom to park my coat. Some bloke with a few too many inside him is singing in one of the cubicles and the attendant keeps looking over that way as though he's wondering if he ought to throw the bod out. I comb my hair and straighten my tie and go upstairs. When I open the big door into the hall I walk slap into a wall of attar of sweat and eau-de-kerniff that you could cut with a knife. It nearly stops me in my tracks. I stick it, though, thinking I'll get used to it in a couple of minutes, and go in, trying not to breathe through my nose.

The place is chock full like Willy said and there's a big crowd just inside the door. I work my way through and edge across the corner of the floor, nearly getting bowled over by a couple prancing about in a kind of private war-dance. The bloke's wearing a bottle-green corduroy jacket, a yellow check shirt without a tie, and black pants with what look like fourteen-inch bottoms. This bint he's doing his stuff with is a real case, all eyebrows and lipstick with a white complexion that makes her look like death warmed up, and two at the front under her black sweater that stick out like chapel hat-pegs, brassièred till it must be agony, and nearly taking this bloke's eye out the way he's half doubled up breathing all over her chest. They don't like jiving and rock 'n' roll and whatnot at the Gala Rooms and they have notices up saying so. Sure enough, while I'm still there, the M.C. comes up and taps the cove on the shoulder and says something to him. They both give him a killing look and switch to a straightforward quickstep, Gala Rooms style.

There's no sign of Ingrid, though I stop there about half an hour listening to the band, which isn't bad for a semi-pro outfit. Then I decide I might spot her if I circulate a bit so I get up to dance and pick a bird who looks okay from a distance and pongs like beef gravy gone off close to. I'm glad when this is over; if there's anything I can't stick it's a bird who smells. Now I go up on the balcony where I can see everything except the crowd up near the door. While I'm up there they play a slow waltz and douse the main lights till there's only this sphere with all the mirrors on it spinning slow high up under the ceiling and sending little flecks of light flitting over everybody. I wish I was down there dancing with Ingrid and holding her close because I can get real romantic dancing a slow waltz with the lights down. But she isn't there; I have to admit it now. And she's not likely to be coming now at this time. I wouldn't have come myself if I hadn't heard she'd be here, and now I feel all empty and let down with disappointment. Maybe she's gone to the Trocadero, I think. Or perhaps she's just at home watching television, or in bed even. I smoke a cig and hang on till the lights go up for a last look round, hating to give it up. I see Willy and Harry down below but I'm not interested in their company tonight so I go down and get my coat and beetle off home. I have to walk because the buses have stopped running by this time.

2

I

The holidays over, it's back to the old routine with the same old crowd on top of the bus. Most of them get buried behind their papers and they're so quiet you'd hardly know one from the rest; but there's one or two you might call characters. There's the country squire type who gets on a couple of stops down the hill. He wears these thick hairy tweeds and a pepper-and-salt hat with the brim turned down all round, and a sporting gun would look more at home under his arm than the *Daily Telegraph* he always carries. Every time I look at this bloke's face it reminds me of a blood orange, all red with broken veins and this great big shiny conk jutting out in the middle like something he presses into place every morning after he's shaved. He's a fresh-air fiend, this bloke, and all the chaps on the top deck shrink up in their seats the second they hear his brogues clatter on the steps. He always takes the same seat down the middle of the bus (unless somebody strange happens to be in it first – and whoever it is gets a dirty look for trespassing) and slams open every window in reach till the wind whistles through the top deck fit to blow your hat off. Wind, rain, sleet, snow, or even fog; it doesn't matter what the weather is, it's all the same to him – he lets it in through the windows. I reckon the saddest day of his life must have been when the open-air buses went out.

Bloodnok, I call this bloke after that feller in the Goon Show and I don't think he's so bad, really. You can stick him provided you're well wrapped up. It's the talkers you have to watch out for, like this little elderly cove that gets on the stop after Bloodnok and always comes and sits with me like we're old pals or something. He has opinions on everything, this chap, and he's such a cheerful type, which is why everybody likes him so much.

'Well,' he says this morning, after he's parked himself at the side of me as usual, 'you wait months for it and then it's off in a couple of days.' He has a voice with a built-in megaphone that carries all over the bus, and all the regulars get a glassy look in their eyes when he opens up.

'Aye, that's right,' I say. Always agree with him, that's the drill. Never encourage him or you're done for.

He broddles about in his pipe a bit then lights it and puts a smoke screen up round us. He grows his own tobacco, he's always telling people, and he'll hold his hand out to show you this dry yellow stuff that looks like horse-shit that's been in the sun all day. Nobody contradicts him on this because nobody can think of a brand of tobacco that stinks so foul. It's when this bloke lights up that we're glad of Bloodnok and his open windows. 'I reckon we shan't be back more than half an hour before it seems as though we've never been away,' he says, sucking at his pipe, which he must have had since he was a young chap because the bowl's all burned down at one side and the stem's tied round with insulating tape where it's been broken. I reckon he must be either very fond of it like, or too skinny to buy a new one. I decide it's because he's too skinny, because blokes who talk like him are usually tight with their money.

'I reckon so,' I say.

'Don't know why we bother with Christmas,' he says at the top of his voice. 'There's no religion left in it; no real feeling. It's just a mockery. Shopkeepers like it. It's all right for them, they can sell all they've got and more besides. All it is for anybody else is guzzling and swilling and sitting round dozy-like watching television ... A mockery.'

He whips his hanky out and blows his nose with a loud noise and wipes his little grey moustache. He looks in the hanky to see what he's brought down before he puts it away again. 'Not that I'm a churchgoer meself,' he says. 'Full of hypocrisy and humbug, that's the churches today. And the parsons . . . all mealymouthed little toads enjoying an easy living where they know they won't get sacked unless they offend somebody by preaching a sermon with a bit of honest to goodness hell-fire in it . . .'

'That's it.'

'And this television. I wouldn't have a set in my house. The wife's allus on about getting one. I've told her, though. 'If you've got enough to buy a television set,' I said, 'you buy one. But the day it comes into this house, I go out . . .' I just don't know what we're coming to. It's got the whole country. It's riddled with it. Riddled, from top to bottom.'

And so on, and on, and on . . .

But I'm all right this morning because I can shut myself off by thinking about Ingrid. I'm going to get talking to her today. I don't know just how, but I am. We've been nodding to one another for a couple of years now, but it was only a month or so before Christmas that it dawned on me what a marvellous bint she really is. And she'd been there under my nose all the time . . . Now I've reached the pitch where I've got to do something about it. I just have to. I've no idea of my chances, that's the trouble. I don't know whether I'm somebody special to her or just another tuppence-ha'penny draughtsman, one of thirty-odd in the firm. What I do know is I'll never find out unless I pull my socks up and *do* something. And the first step is to get talking to her.

I buy my morning paper in the bus station and cross over to wait for the other bus. I'm half-way between two islands when I see her in the queue and for a second all the people round me seem to vanish and I'm out there on my own with all the queue looking at me and me thinking about her and feeling as if everything in my mind is written plain across my face for them all to see. I think

I'm going to colour up and I only just make the queue in time. Of course I only thought *she* was looking. In fact she only glanced my way and then went on talking to Miss Price from the typing pool. Why should she notice me in particular? Who am I? Just another bod from the D.O., and not one of the important ones either. I bet she never gives me two thoughts together. I bet if I left Whittaker's this week she'd hardly notice I'd gone. Oh, it's rotten the way you flog yourself like this: up one minute, down the next, and never knowing which is nearest the mark.

I step a bit out of line and watch her over the top of my *Mirror*. Ah, but she's a smart piece! Always so neat turned out and clean as clean. I hate bints with bitten fingernails and mucky hair who smell like last week's joint gone off and warmed up again. I could nearly throw up when I run into one of them. But Ingrid looks as if she has a bath every morning and her hair's always soft and clean and shining, lighter brown than mine and lighter still when the sun catches it. And these skirts and blouses and jumpers she wears are always washed and ironed and fit well and show her trim little figure off a treat. I reckon her legs are just about the best thing about her; they're a lovely shape and she wears high heels that set them off and nylons with never a ladder or a hole. I've never known a bint like her in all my born days and it isn't a bit of good me mooning over her because I haven't a chance in a million. Not a dog's.

I lift the paper up quick because it's just as though she knows somebody's watching her when she turns her head and looks straight at me.

The bus trundles in and stops. The conductor nips off the platform and round to the front for a lean on the radiator and a quick drag with the driver. By the time I reach the door the top deck's full and people are coming back down to stand inside. The usual second bus pulls in behind and most of the queue stand back to get on this. This is what I'd do usually but today I get on the first bus and stand. This way I'm all the nearer to Ingrid. She's sitting up at the front next to the aisle with a woman I don't know. I edge forward till I'm standing one seat behind her. The floor gives a shudder as the bus starts and I reach up and hold the bar and stand looking at her till the conductor's voice brings me to again. Now this bloke's well known on this run as a bit of a card. They say he's an ex-army sergeant and everybody knows he doesn't give a damn for anybody. You get the feeling that if the Archbishop of Canterbury got on in full rig-out he'd get the same treatment as anybody else, with maybe a bit of extra leg-pulling on the side. He's got more neck than many a comedian at Cressley Alhambra, and that's saying something. He gets up off the platform. 'Nah, then, you workers, getcha fares ready, perlease! An' look cheerful, for cryin' out loud. Think about them 'at started at half past seven while you lot were still in bed . . . Yes, miss? Three-pennorth of the best? Ta! . . . What's your pleasure, madam? A fourpenny one? Just like the geezer give his owd woman, eh? . . . Yessir?'

He makes his way down the bus, giving with this horrible corny patter and I feel for some cash. I find a ha'penny in my overcoat pocket, what's left over from a tanner after riding down into town and buying the paper. I unbutton my coat to get at my trouser pockets, and there's nothing there. And nowhere else, either, except on the dressing-table at home. So I'm without my fare . . . It's a thing that's never happened to me before, though I've heard of other people doing it. If there's nobody you can borrow from you give the conductor your name and address and pay later. But all my mates are upstairs and I can see myself explaining to this bod and him making sport of it. In front of Ingrid as well! It's the sort of thing you think's funny after, but not at the time. And the conductor works his way up towards me I take a quick scan of the faces. Sure enough, they're all upstairs. I'm in foreign territory here.

There's only two ways out of it, then. I can bluff it out with laughing boy or . . . or I can borrow the fare from Ingrid. But I can't ask *her* for money. I hardly know her

43

. . . but then again, isn't this the best chance I'll ever have of getting to know her? Haven't I been wanting a chance, wondering about it all during the holidays?

Before I've time to think it over too much I'm leaning forward and touching her shoulder and catching the scent of her hair as she turns her head. Then she's looking straight into my face at a distance of one foot and my knees are weak and I can't think for a second what I'm supposed to be saying.

'Look, I'm in a bit of a spot. I've left my money at home and I wondered if you . . . I don't know anybody else down here, y'see.' Then she catches on and starts opening her bag, her neck going a bit pink. 'No,' I say, 'you get both fares.' And I straighten up and watch the pink spreading over her neck to her ears and over the one cheek I can see, and I love her madder than ever. I go all weak inside with it.

At our stop I stand back and wait for her to get off. I try to give her a smile but I can feel it doesn't amount to much.

'Thanks for saving me life.'

'Oh, that's all right.'

We start off up the lane to the Works.

'I'll see you get it back as soon as I get some money.'

'Oh, don't worry about it.'

'I never picked it up off the dressing-table. I had sixpence in my overcoat pocket so I never noticed till I was on the other bus, y'see. One of the lads'll help me out.'

'Well I'm not frantic for it,' she says. 'It's only threepence.'

'No, but it's your money and you want it back.'

'You can pay my fare some time.'

'Be glad to.'

Just give me the chance! And that's only the beginning. There's pictures and dances and theatres as well. Not to mention chocolates and nylons and bottles of scent and whatnot. She can have every penny I have. She's only to say the word.

We're both quiet now and I'm thinking, This is it, what I've been waiting for. I'm talking to her. What can I say? 'Dear Ingrid, I've been mad about you for months (well, one month, anyway). How do you feel about me? Will you make me the happiest bloke in Cressley and come to the pictures with me tonight?'

'Not a bad morning, is it?' I say.

'No, not bad at all, to say.'

To say what? That it's winter, I suppose. 'I wonder if we shall have some more snow soon.'

'I shouldn't wonder. It's cold enough for it.'

And who the heck cares? I can love her in snow or sunshine. If only I knew what she thinks of me. She seems friendly enough, but that could be plain ordinary politeness and not mean a thing. I'm pleasant myself every day with people I don't really like at all. What I want to do is give her a hint . . .

'Funny, isn't it?'

'Hmm? What?'

There she was, miles away, thinking about something else altogether. Or may be some*body* else. What then? Suppose she already has a boy friend? Oh, Lord, I've never really asked myself that one. Not straight out, anyway. I've always skated round it. But you never know. It's more than likely, if you think about it . . . how attractive she is an' all . . .

'I was just thinking we've worked at the same place for two or three years and we've never talked to one another before.'

'Yes,' she says, 'it is funny, isn't it?'

So it's funny. We're agreed on it. We fall quiet again and I beat my brains out. Why doesn't *she* say something? I hear somebody tramping up behind and I look round and see Miss Price coming up fast, striding out like a man.

'Good morning, Mr Brown. Are you returning refreshed from your holiday?'

'That's right.' Well, that's it. I've had it now.

Miss Price nods and sticks her big chin out as she falls

in with us. She throws the end of her long muffler back over her shoulder and plants her feet down square in step with mine. Miss Price embarrasses me. She's too good to be true. She should be under contract to J. Arthur Rank by rights because I always think she looks as if she's lost her way from a British comedy picture. *She's* got a voice as well. Some of the staff say it's been known to carry the length of the Works, given the wind in the right quarter of course, and I wonder what it would be like to put her and the cheerful cove together in a railway tunnel.

'Have you had a nice Christmas, Vic?' Ingrid says, and I'm so tickled to hear her say my name that I can't think what to say for a minute. Not Mr Brown, like Miss Price. Not Victor, even; but Vic, just like my mates.

'Oh, so so, y'know,' I say. 'We had quite a time Boxing Day. My sister got married.'

'A charming girl,' Miss Price says, telling everybody for five hundred yards either way as well as Ingrid and me. 'And the groom – a most pleasant and intelligent young man, so my sister tells me.'

I remember now that she has a sister, another Miss Price, who's Domestic Science mistress at the Grammar School. She's come since my time.

'Was it a white wedding, Vic?' Ingrid asks, and I see I've got her interested now, anyway. Funny how birds are interested in weddings, even when it's somebody they don't know. 'What did your sister wear?' she says, wanting to know all the details.

I'm a bit out of my depth here and I flounder about for a minute till Miss Price comes to the rescue.

'My sister and I went to the church.' (Funny, but I never saw them.) 'She was so keen to see young Mr Lester marry, and I love a wedding at any time.'

There – even the ones who're past it!

Anyway, she trots out all the gen Ingrid wants and she says, 'I'd love to see the photos, Vic, when you get them.' We're just inside the door of the office building by now and Miss Price says, 'Cheery-bye,- and stalks off down the long corridor.

46

Ingrid giggles. 'Isn't she a case?'

I say, 'Hmm.' I look after her where she's walking away. I don't know, I always feel a bit sorry somehow for people like that.

The bell rings while we're standing there and Ingrid says she'll have to go.

'Yes, okay. I'll try to get hold of the photos when they're ready.'

'Yes, do. I'd love to see them.'

She walks away after Miss Price and I go up the stairs. Bringing the photos will give me another chance to talk to her if I can't manage it any other way before then. I want to lean over the rail and watch her go, but there's too many people about and Jimmy Slade, my mate at the office, comes up with a muffler on and bike clips and carrying his bike pump that he doesn't leave in the shed for fear somebody pinches it.

'Now then, cock.'

'Now then, Jimmy.'

'Back to it, eh?'

'Aye, back to it.'

We go up the steps together.

II

Whittaker's is about the biggest engineering works round Cressley. All down the side of the erection shop there's the name spelled out in white bricks – DAWSON WHITTAKER & SONS, LTD, ENGINEERS. This is so when you're on the train you'll know what that big mucky place was you passed just before Cressley Junction.

The first thing you think when you go into the offices is that whoever built them meant them to last a while. There's solid oak doors all over the place and a lick of varnish every ten years or so is all that's needed to keep them in trim. The top halves of most of the office walls are glass and when you stand at one end of the ground floor you can see right down through office after office where people are working at their desks or talking to one another with maybe their hands going, but you can't hear a thing, like watching television when the sound's gone. The drawing office is the biggest and it takes nearly all the length of the upstairs floor on one side of the building. There's more glass here than anywhere else. It's half glass on the corridor side and there's big windows out on the lane. Then the roof's half glazed and there's this big window, like a church window but with plain glass, up in the end wall. You've got plenty of light to work with all right but it's like a greenhouse in summer and a refrigerator in winter. The boards are in three lines and there's enough for thirty-five draughtsmen and designers. At the side of every board there's a plan press which gives a flat top for your drawings and filing room for all the old drawing that have been piling up since the firm began back in eighteen-seventy something. You have a drawer for yourself as well where you put your own stuff, such as sandwiches, the *Manchester Guardian*, the *Daily Mirror*, *Snappy Nudes*, *Sporting Pink*, and even reference books and drawing instruments, all depending what sort of bloke you are and what you're interested in. There's three smaller rooms open off the big office, one for the estimators, one for the tracing lasses, and one where the prints are done. The print machine's a carbon arc job and it looks a bit like one of them mechanical pianos where you put a penny in and it plays a tune that was in the Top Ten during the Boer War. The prints are done by a young lad called Laisterdyke and a lass called Phoebe Johnson. Then at the top end of the office there's two glass cubicles, one belonging to the assistant chief, Miller, who everybody likes, and the other to the chief, Hassop, who nobody much cares for.

The real boss is Mr Althorpe, the Chief Designs Engineer, and he has his own office (private – no glass) with his name on the door along the corridor. The work comes from him and Hassop and Miller pass it out to the section leaders. Each section leader has a team and this can vary from two or three to a dozen blokes depending how big the job is they're doing. You'd think in an office this size there'd be bags of chance for experience but each team specializes and once you know a particular job you can find yourself stuck with it year after year. Anyway, that's the D.O. at Whittaker's.

I'm not sorry to be back because I quite like both the office and the work. I don't like either as much as I did the first two or three years I was here but I haven't got to the stage where I can't stand it any more so I don't mind. And besides, I've got another interest at work now.

I don't see her again till dinner-time and then it's in the canteen with three tables and about thirty people between me and her. She's sitting facing me and though she doesn't look at me I can't keep my eyes off her. She has a way of breaking off what she's saying to throw her head back and laugh (she's got rather a carrying laugh actually), and as I watch her I see how her neck curves and I wonder what it would be like to run my hand up over it and under her chin. There's a scar on her neck under her left ear and I want to put my fingers on that as well because I can't bear the thought of the knife cutting into her.

Ken Rawlinson's sitting next to me with enough fountain pens and propelling pencils for half the office in his top pocket. He asks me to pass the water and this takes my mind off Ingrid for a minute. He's wearing that tie clip again. There's a few things about Rawly that get on my wires and this tie clip's one of them. It's one of these glider clips with a bit of fine chain on it. The idea is to slide the clip on to your shirt and let the chain hold your tie; but Rawly always wears it with the clip on both his tie and his shirt and the chain hanging down for fancy like. I've often wanted to put him right but I always think why should I? He's one of these blokes with ten bob each way on himself and so why should I care if he looks a clot?

He fills his glass up and says, 'I saw a very good French film last night.'

'Oh, yes?'

49

'Gervaise,' Rawly says. 'Based on a novel by Zola.' He pokes about on his plate as if he expects to uncover something nasty. 'Do you know his novels at all?'

' 'Fraid not.' Zola? Sounds like a game, like bingo or ludo or canasta.

'An excellent writer. Surprisingly modern to say he wrote sixty or seventy years ago.'

'Oh?'

'Very outspoken for his time. They banned his books in this country. Wouldn't wear them.'

'Sexy, eh?' This is more like it.

'Shall we say 'direct'?' Rawly says and I think he can call it any name he likes as far as I'm concerned. I decide to take the mickey a bit.

'Was this picture hot stuff?'

'Oh, X certificate and all that,' he says. 'Nothing pornographic about it, though. An adult film.'

'Be in French, I suppose?'

'Oh yes. Subtitled, of course, for those who don't know the language.'

I gather from the way he says this that he doesn't include himself in this lot of ignoramuses.

'Well I don't mind these foreign films when there's a bit of tit or summat to see,' I say, watching his face out of the corner of my eye. His nose curls as though he's just noticed a bad smell and he blushes ever so slightly. 'But I can't stand having to read what they're saying at the bottom of the screen. Give me the good old English language any day.'

'Everyone to his taste,' Rawly says, and turns and says something to the bod on his other side.

I'm a bit sorry now that I've gone out of my way to make him think I'm just another cloth-head. But then, I think, what do I care what a nig-nog like Rawly thinks about me anyway?

The waitress puts a plate of sponge pudding and custard in front of me and I'm just going to start in on it when I hear chairs squeaking and see that Ingrid and her pals are leaving. She passes so close to me her sleeve brushes my shoulder but she doesn't flicker an eyelid to show she knows I'm there. So much for that. I don't know what I'm flogging myself to death for. But it's getting worse. Only just before the holidays I put eight-foot-two over a row of dimensions that totted up to nine-foot-seven and Bob Lacey, my section leader, pointed it out to me in a friendly way and told me to watch what I was doing. It's a good job Bob did spot it or there would have been a lot of angle-iron cut and wasted in the shop. I'm getting so I expect to drop clangers now and I nearly always check my drawings myself before I pass them on to Bob. But one of these days I'll slip up and we'll all miss it and the next thing I know I'll be called down into the Works to look at a pile of scrap iron worth maybe hundreds of pounds. Then I'll have really had it.

I'm nearly sure that Hassop's got his eye on me as well. He seems to be always nosing round, creeping up like he does, in these school-issue glasses he wears, and breathing his bad breath all over you. He's a littlish bloke with ginger hair. He hasn't all that much left on his head now but there's always a fair amount sprouting out of his nose. He always wears the same kind of bluish grey suits that look neither new nor old, and he just seems to wear one till it gets too shiny and then comes in another just like it. You wish sometimes Hassop would get his hair off and really bawl you out, but he never does. If he gets really mad he goes white, but he hardly ever lets go except on the younger lads. He daren't, that's his trouble, and everybody despises him for it. But nobody goes too far because right behind Hassop there's Mr Althorpe and he's a different kettle of fish altogether. Tell anybody to go to blazes, Althorpe would, and make no bones about it. So everybody respects him, even if they don't like him like they like somebody like Miller, for instance.

So it seems to me that sooner or later, the way I'm going on, I'll wind up on Althorpe's carpet, and I can't see any way out of it because I just can't get my mind off Ingrid. It's this not knowing. If only I knew one way or the other just how I stand . . .

III

First you take an old knife (I used the broken one the Old Lady scrapes potatoes with) and get rid of all the mud, doing a bit of prising if it's caked up solid under the instep. Then when you've given them a good going over with a stiffish brush they're ready for the polish. (You really should take the laces out but I can't always be bothered going to that trouble, even though tonight I'm doing a special job.) I like to clean shoes, especially when I've got something on my mind, because giving your hands something to do kind of helps you think and sometimes it even takes your mind off things. I like to poke into the waxy polish and spread it all over the shoes and go at them like mad with the brush and watch the shine break through and deepen; then finish off with a velvet till the toecaps are like black glass. Tonight I'm cleaning the shoes because I'm going out; but I've got something on my mind as well; and every now and again I have to stop and tell myself it's true and it's really happened to me.

It was the same day I borrowed the bus fare from Ingrid. I got the feeling stronger than ever in the afternoon that old Hassop had it in for me and when he sidles up at ten to five and tells me a drawing I've had on the board since a week before Christmas is wanted first thing in the morning, I'm more sure than ever. It means I'll have to work over, and bang goes my chance of seeing Ingrid on the way home. Well, I have it to do whether it's really wanted or Hassop's keeping me back out of spite, so I settle down to it and hope it won't take me long. There's plenty of work in the office and one or two sections stay behind most nights of the week. But tonight being the first day back after the holidays nobody's in the mood and at half past five everybody packs up to go. The board lights click off as they all slope out in ones and twos. The tracers come through, wafting face powder all over the place and chattering fifty to the dozen like birds do. Then by twenty to six there's only me left

52

besides Hassop and Miller, who always leave after everybody else. At five to six I unpin the sheet and take it up to Hassop's office. Another five minutes goes by while he reckons to look it over and drops hints right left and centre about my work. Then I'm free to go.

Half the lights are out in the corridors and I can hear the cleaners' buckets clanking somewhere. I go down the stairs and I'm pushing on the big door when I hear these high heels come tapping along the corridor behind me. I must go psychic for a minute because I know straight off who it is and my heart gives a little flutter. I turn round and she flashes a smile as though she's glad to see me.

'I'm going your way,' she says.

I hold the door open for her and get a gorgeous whiff of her scent as she goes by. We say good night to the commissionaire and walk off down the lane. It seems she's feeling a bit peevish.

'Some people . . .' she says. 'They don't think of starting their letters till everybody else is going home.'

'You've got one an' all, have you?' I say.

'Have I got one!'

'An' who's yours?'

'Leslie Felton . . . You'd think some people hadn't got homes to go to. Not that you can blame him, I suppose, with a wife like he's got.'

'What's wrong with his wife?'

'Oh, she's a real shrew, by all accounts. Don't tell me you didn't know? I thought everybody did.'

It seems there's a lot I don't know and she starts to bring me up to date. I don't have to make the conversation tonight; she just rolls it out. She's as full of scandal as the Sunday papers and by the time we get to the bus stop I know more about the people who work at Whittaker's than I've learned all the time I've been there.

I get both fares into town and she says, 'That makes us quits,' and smiles.

She picks up where she left off and starts chattering

again; but I'm not really listening now. My mind's working like mad on how I can make the most of this chance. I try to think of a way to get started and all the time the bus is tearing down the road into town. When I see the Grammar School sail by I kind of panic because we'll be in the station any minute now.

'Look, there's something I –' And she starts talking again at the same time. We both stop. 'Go on,' I say.

'I was just going to ask you if you'd seen that new musical *Rise and Shine* at the Palace,' she says. 'I was wondering what it was like.'

I haven't a clue what it's like, to be honest, but I say. 'I think it's good,' and I'm thinking, Now, now, now: What are you waiting for? 'I was thinking of going to see it myself one night this week, as a matter of fact,' I say. This is another fib, but I don't care. I have to clear my throat. 'P'raps . . . er mebbe you'd like to come with me . . . see it together . . .'

She says, 'Oh!' just as if it's the last thing she'd have thought of and I begin to think how I can pass it off if she turns me down. 'Well, when?'

I can hardly sit still in the seat. I want to jump up and shout, I'm that excited. 'I'd thought of going tomorrow, but any night 'ud suit me really.'

'Tomorrow's New Year's Eve,' she says, 'and I'm going to a party. Can you make it Wednesday?'

'All right.' Wednesday, Thursday, Friday, Saturday, or Sunday. I can make it any night or all of them. I just want it to be soon.

'Wednesday, then,' she says, and I nod. 'Wednesday.'

Before the bus pulls into the station we've fixed up what time we'll meet and where and everything. And to think, only this morning I wouldn't have given a bent penny for my chances. But that's how things work out sometimes.

Wednesday . . . I just don't know how I'll live till then.

But course I do, and now here I am waiting on the corner at twenty-five to eight. She's late, but only five minutes, and I was here ten minutes early to make sure I didn't miss her so that makes it seem more. The weather's gone all soft all of a sudden. It's rained pretty hard today and though it's stopped now you can still feel it in the wind. The roads and pavements are shining in the lights and the car tyres sizzle as they go by. A black Super Snipe slides up to the kerb and I step back smartish as it throws water up out of the gutter. I look after this car and watch it stop and let a bloke out. Then I watch it pull away and pick up speed with exhaust smoke curling in the tail lights. Now if I had a car . . . Dames go for bods with cars. It's only natural. And having a car would give you confidence, a sort of air, like. I imagine myself behind the wheel of a snappy little two-seater convertible – no need for anything big and swanky – rolling up to the kerb where Ingrid's waiting and enjoying the look on her face as I open the door and tell her to jump in. 'Where d'you fancy going tonight? What about nipping over to Leeds or Bradford to a show?' *That's* the way to take a bint out on a first date. And after the show, parked in some quiet spot and me with my arm round her listening to her say she's been mad about me all the time . . . I can't even drive a car. I suppose I could learn soon enough, though. And I could probably afford to buy one if I saved up for about fifteen years and packed in smoking.

I'm all wrapped up in this and I don't see this other car whipping up for a stop till it goes by with a whoosh and shoots water all over my shoes and trouser legs. Bang goes the shine I spent so much time on till the Old Lady was getting suspicious. I think the creases in my pants will be all right, though, because my suit's Terylene, my new clerical grey that I got for Chris's wedding. And she won't notice my shoes in the dark. I'm pretty present-able otherwise, I think. I saved my shave till after tea and finished off with the after-shave lotion I paid six bob for on the way home from work so's I'd smell nice. And I've taken special care over brushing my teeth, making sure there was no tea-time sausage and chips stuck in the cracks. I reckon I couldn't do more for Diana Dors.

Quarter to. She isn't coming. That's the trouble with dames: you never know where you have them. Some blokes reckon that's all part of the game but I'm the type that likes things settled. I like to know where I stand. Like Chris and David do, for instance. They've certainly got something I'd like to find, but that's my secret and I don't tell anybody.

Ten to. You feel a bit daft standing on a corner with everybody passing by and knowing you're waiting for a bird who's late. They must know because nobody ever arranges to meet somebody at ten to and so she must either be late or not coming. I reckon a quarter of an hour's enough to give any bint but I'll give her till eight seeing as this is the first time. Then I'll just have to write it all off. Oh, but it's sickening the way you get all built up and then knocked down again.

'Hello.'

I jump and turn round and catch the fresh clean smell of her. Her eyes are sparkling in the lights and there's rain in her hair. Her lips are parted showing her teeth and she's breathing a bit fast a though she's been hurrying.

'I'm sorry I'm so late. I couldn't get away sooner . . . I ran all the way . . . I felt sure you'd have given me up and gone.'

'No.' It's all I can think of to say I'm so busy looking at her. Gosh, but she's a smashing piece, and she's run all the way to meet me. She just said so.

'I knew you'd come,' I say at last, when I've had my fill of looking at her for the minute. And when I say it it's just as though I really did know all the time. 'You're not the sort of girl to stand a bloke up.'

'Why should I do that?' she says. 'I could have said no in the first place if I didn't want to come, couldn't I?'

I give a nod, eating her up with my eyes again. I can't believe it. I really can't. There must be a catch in it somewhere for this to happen to me.

'Well?' she says, and I realize I'm embarrassing her a bit staring like I am. So I say, 'Righto,' and we walk along the road to the picture house where the lights are blazing and the commissionaire's leaning against the pay-box talking to the cashier because there's nothing else for him to do. I reckon he'll be for the push any time now, the way things are.

'It's very quiet,' Ingrid says. 'I thought we might have to queue.'

'Three or four years ago, mebbe,' I say; 'but not nowadays. Cinema owners are on their beam ends. Why pay to see a bad picture when you can see one on television for nothing?' I've read this somewhere but she laughs and I let her think I've made it up. I'm wondering where she wants to sit and I don't like to ask her for fear it's the best seats and she won't like to say. I get two tickets for the back circle, the next to the best. Now she won't think I'm showing off and I shan't have started something I can't keep up if this turns into a regular thing. When the bint with a torch sees the two of us she flashes us up into the back where the courting couples are snogging away among the empty seats. I'm surprised when Ingrid goes up past a lot of empty rows and leads the way on to the very back row. We push past a couple sprawled out holding on to one another and they take no notice of us. We sit down in a double seat with no arm rest between us, which I think is a bit of all right. Ingrid decides in a minute she'd like her coat off and I help her with it. I have to put my arm round her to do this and I wonder if I dare keep it there. But I think it'll be rushing things a bit and that would be a pity after we're off to such a promising start.

There's a snap like elastic breaking from the couple on the row and the bint giggles and wrestles with the bloke.

'I feel like the psychiatrist who went to the Folies Bergère and spent all his time watching the audience.'

'What?' Ingrid says, and I don't know if she hasn't heard me or not got the joke.

'Skip it.' I feel for my cigs. 'Smoke?'

'Here.' She fumbles in her handbag. 'Let's eat this

first.' She brings out a bar of chocolate and breaks it into pieces and puts them on her knee. We munch away and watch the picture. Fruit and nut, it is, and I'm very partial to it next to coffee cream.

We've come in near the end of the feature and I can't make much sense of it. The stories of most musical pictures are pretty silly, anyway. You nearly always have a hard-up company hoping their luck will change and somebody will put up the cash so's they can do this terrific show on Broadway. There's always a nice young producer chap who's in love with the sweet young bint and doesn't know it because the second fem lead, who's a regular bitch even if she has got bags of talent, has her hooks in him. And you always come to the place in the picture where somebody looks round this barn or whatever dump it is they're holing up in and says, 'But say, why can't we put the show on right here?' And from then on it's all plain sailing because there's sure to be a stinking rich backer in the audience on the night and while he's busy signing the cheque the nice young producer is backstage realizing all of a sudden how much he loves the sweet young bint and singing her a song to tell her so. Every so often you get one that's a cut above all this, but this one we're watching now isn't one of them. Not that I care, mind. I could watch Rin-tin-tin tonight because what I'm interested in isn't up on the screen, it's right here beside me. She's so near I'm dizzy with it, and I'm sneaking little looks at her all the time and wondering if she's really all eyes and ears for the picture like she seems, and how soon I can put my arm round her.

Now there's a few schools of thought about how you should carry on on a first date. Some say you shouldn't put a finger out of place, and patience pays. At the other end of the line there's the caveman school. I reckon their methods only apply when you're out with a certain kind of bint who knows why you've asked her and comes expecting it. Then there's the middle-of-the-road boys who reckon you should at least show you know the difference between boys and girls and that you're interested in it. It depends what you're after, I always think. There's no doubt what the bloke on the row's after, for instance; and from the way the bint's holding him down it looks like he'll get it. But that's not the way I feel about Ingrid. I only want her to like me and let me be good to her. I want to be kind and gentle to her so bad it gushes up in me like a fountain whenever I think about her. And now, with her here, so close, in the dark . . .

Well the way it happens is that the lights go up in the interval and the ice-cream comes round. I ask her if she wants some and she says no, so I don't bother myself either. I put my elbow up on the back of the seat while I'm talking to her and when the lights go down again all I have to do is drop my hand and it's where I want it to be. She's very cooperative, because as soon as she feels it on her shoulder she comes over and tucks herself away under my armpit and her hair's in my face and I've got this lovely smell of a high-class chemist's shop all round me. The next thing we know we're kissing for the very first time and it's marvellous.

There's quite a cold wind blowing when we come out of the pictures. We walk along the main road for a bit then turn off up the hill to where Ingrid lives. Neither of us says much. I want to say something that will fix what's happened in the pictures; only out here in the cold it's as though we've left it behind in the warmth and the dark and we might never find it again.

'I'm glad we came out together,' I say.

'You're not disappointed, then?' she says, and I feel like gaping at her. Disappointed!

'P'haps you'd like to try it again?' I say. 'What about the week-end?'

'If you like.'

And what if I don't like? Does it matter to her either way? What's a kiss on the back row of the pictures after all? It doesn't mean we've signed an agreement or something.

'No need to if you don't want,' I say, and I'm horrified at the way I'm inviting her to turn me down.

59

'I'd like to,' she says.

'Well, that's okay, then. We stop at the end of their avenue. It's certainly a cold wind. I shove my hands down into my pockets and hunch my shoulders up. It's going, all that in the pictures. I can feel it slipping away. For all I know it might have gone for good . . . If I could kiss her, though, maybe I'd catch a little bit of it to carry till next time. But here in the open we're like strangers again. I couldn't do it easy and natural the way it was in the pictures. It'd be like making a pass out here.

'Come on,' I say, 'I'll walk you to the gate.'

'You've no need to, y'know.'

'I want to.'

'Oh, all right, then.'

We walk up this curving avenue, not touching, a foot apart, till she stops at a gate.

'Is this it?'

'This is it.'

I look up at this little modern semi standing up above the road with the garden tumbling down to the fence. Two thousand five-hundred at today's prices, I reckon. Neat, though, and worth painting because it would look smart when you'd finished. Not like our house, dirty stone front, two storeys and an attic besides, and great big rooms. Not that it isn't cosy, because the Old Lady's good at making it that; but it needs a collier's coal supply to keep it warm and you could never call it smart. I don't know anything about Ingird really and I wonder about her family and her father and mother and what her father's job is. I think I'm maybe a little bit timid of Ingrid's dad though I don't know why I should be because I've never seen him and I've done nothing to be ashamed of.

'Any more at home like you?'

'No, only little me,' and she laughs. Her lips are purple in the lights and her complexion's a kind of dirty white colour. We can't stand here all night, I think, and I wonder about kissing her again. I wonder if she expects me to. It just isn't the same out here, though.

She clicks the latch on the gate. 'Well, I'd better be getting in. Thanks for asking me out. I've enjoyed it.'

'I'm glad. See you tomorrow then.'

Now – now's the time while she's still close and her face is turned up to me. She's waiting, wondering why I don't do it.

'Yes, see you tomorrow.'

Too late now; she's through the gate and shutting it behind her. I watch her climb the four steps then walk up the steep path to the corner of the house. She turns and lifts her hand up and I wave back.

'Ey!'

'What?'

'Happy New Year!'

She laughs. 'Thanks. The same to you.'

I walk off, wondering what we'll be doing in a year's time, if we'll still be seeing one another. Maybe I did right not to kiss her. Perhaps it'll have given her a better opinion of me. Roll on Saturday night. After a bit I break into a trot because I've a lot too much to think about for walking.

3

I

Saturday morning and I'm down snug as a bug under the
bedclothes and it seems like I'm dreaming somebody's
calling my name. I come out of sleep with a jerk and hear
the Old Lady at the bottom of the stairs, bawling fit to
wake the street.

'Victor! *Victor!* How many more times?'

I open my eyes. 'Righto, I'm up.' I look at the wallpaper
two feet from my nose. The Old Lady's choice it is: roses
as big as cabbages with trellising on a grey ground.
There's flowers on the window as well – frost flowers –
and when I put my hand out I can feel how cold it is in the
room. Just for a few seconds, as I'm lying there, it's any
Saturday morning, with me going to help Mr Van Huyten
in his shop. And then I remember what makes today
special and the happy feeling opens up inside me like a
big yellow flower, all bright and sunny and warm.

I reach out for my watch and see it's two minutes past
eight and I'm going to have to look slippy, or else. I chuck
the clothes back and swing my legs out and bring them
back sharpish when my feet miss the mat and touch the
lino, which feels cold enough to fetch the skin off. I hang
down over the side of the bed and grobble for my socks. I
put them on and then my slippers. I get out of bed and
then I have to take the slippers off again so's I can get my
pyjama pants off. My britches feel as if they could stand
up on their own; no losing the creases this weather. I'm
nipping across to the bathroom when the Old Lady

comes to the bottom of the stairs again and opens her mouth for another rallentando. It cuts off as though somebody's throttled her when she sees me.

' 'Bout time, an' all,' she says, and goes back down the passage to the kitchen.

I'm out in a couple of ticks and half-way down the stairs before I remember I won't have another chance for a shave before I meet Ingrid. I nip back and lather up and cut myself five times and bleed like a stuck pig. I meet young Jim on the landing and he eyes the bits of toilet paper stuck all over my jib. 'You'll have to get your knife and fork sharpened,' he says. 'Get lost,' I tell him as I patter downstairs. I'm in a bad enough mood as it is now thinking about meeting Ingrid with blobs of dried blood all over my face.

It nearly makes my guts heave to smell the bacon and eggs in the kitchen. The Old Lady slaps the plate in front of me as I sit down.

'If it's a bit frizzled,' she says, 'you've only yourself to blame. I called you six times. I don't know what you're getting like. It's like trying to raise the dead shifting you out o' bed. You even answer me in your sleep now.'

I get on with my chow and let her have a chunter. It does her good to bind a bit. She's been up since about five getting the Old Man off. The Old Feller's been telling her for thirty years that he can manage on his own, but she won't have it. She says he'll forget his snap or something if she doesn't see to him, and apart from the odd times when she's been badly she's kept up the routine.

She watches me clean the plate up with a piece of bread.

'Shovellin' your food into you like that,' she says. 'It can't do you a bit o' good. An' don't you want a cup o' tea?'

I tell her I do, and a slice of bread and marmalade, and she sets about the loaf. She always grabs a loaf like it's a chicken whose neck she's wringing.

'You'd better look sharp,' she says. 'You don't want to be late. You don't want to give a bad impression, especially after that five pound Mr Van Huyten gave you at Christmas.'

'One minute you're on about me bolting me food and the next you're telling me to look sharp or I'll be late.'

'You should allow yourself time to do all you have to do, then you could eat your meals in a proper manner and still get where you have to go on time. You want to take a leaf out of your cousin Walter's book. He has a system in a morning: so many minutes for this and so many for that. You never see him bolting his food or having to run for a bus.'

I pull a face. Cousin Walter's a tall thin cove with a big nose who works in a bank. I don't like him; partly, I suppose, because everybody in the family seems to think he's the last word. The first time cousin Walter's taken bad for a crap in the morning his system will go for a burton, I think to myself.

'I shan't be late', I tell the Old Lady, 'as long as you don't addle me with your nagging.'

'I'll addle your earhole, young man, if you talk to me about nagging. You're not too big for a good slap, y'know, even if you are at the shavin' stage . . . Just look at your face. Fancy having to go out like that in a morning to wait on people in a shop.'

'I'll clean it up when I get there,' I tell her. Actually I'm a bit bothered about it myself. There's nothing niggles me more than cutting myself shaving because you've to go extra careful for days after for fear you open the places up again. But still, it's done now and it can't be helped. As for the Old Lady and her giving me a slap – well, she'd do it an' all and no bones about it. She's got no sense of humour, you know, and everybody knows it, bar her.

Another two minutes and I've had a cup of tea and two slices of bread and marmalade and I'm out of the house and haring down the hill to the bus stop. The sun's getting out fairly warm now but the frost has left some icy patches and I nearly come a cropper once. What I'm after is that bus waiting on the corner at the bottom. The conductor's standing on the platform looking my way and I think at first he's waiting for me. But he rings the bell while I'm twenty yards away and I have to put on an extra spurt to catch the rail and heave myself aboard.

He's a miserable-looking bod with bad teeth that he's poking into with a sharpened matchstick.

'You'll kill yourself one o' these days doin' that,' he says as I'm hanging on there drawing every breath as if it's my last. 'I could stop the bus and make you get off.'

'You saw me comin,' didn't you? Did you think I was practising for the mile, or summat?'

'Plenty more buses. We've got a schedule to keep to, y'know.'

There's a nice little four-letter word on the tip of my tongue but I swallow it and give him my fare. 'Three-penny.'

'Where you goin' to?'

'Market Street.'

'Fourpence.'

'It's only threepence from up the *hill*.'

'That's the service bus,' the conductor says. 'It's four-pence on this route because we go round by the Town Hall.'

I hand over another penny. 'Anyway, you're four-pence better off than if I hadn't caught it,' I tell him.

He shakes his head and smacks his tongue behind his bad teeth. 'Not me, mate. Makes no difference to me.'

I take the ticket and go upstairs thinking that he's the most miserable bastard I'm likely to meet today and I've got him over early, anyway.

Saturdays I go to work in Mr Van Huyten's gramophone record and music shop in Market Street. There's only Mr Van Huyten in during the week, and Henry Thomas who does the repairs in the back; and on Saturdays I serve behind the counter and help with the week-end rush. Mr Van Huyten's father was a Dutchman but I reckon Mr Van himself is as English as I am and the only things Dutch about him are his name and the way he talks sometimes if he gets excited, and that's double

Dutch. People don't always know it's a Dutch name. They get the Van bit mixed up with Von, and that's German. That's why they chucked bricks through Mr Van Huyten's father's windows in the Great War. People weren't as educated then as they are now and they didn't know that Mr Van Huyten and his father didn't like the Gerries any more than anybody else in Cressley till Mr Van joined up and came home in his Tommy's uniform. The Old Man joined the same mob – the Koylis – and him and Mr Van became pals, though Mr Van was a grown man and my dad was only a bit of a lad, younger than I am now. Something happened to Mr Van Huyten's father's antique business after the war and he shot himself one night and left Mr Van on his own. Mr Van had a lot of bad luck because he got married soon after this and then his wife died of cancer after only a few years. So he was on his own again and he never got married a second time. He made a living for a long time playing the piano in theatre bands and for the silent pictures before he got the shop.

Mr Van Huyten's not exactly what you'd call a close friend of the family but the Old Lady and Old Feller always think about him and send him a card at Christmas and he was one of the first names on the list of invitations to Chris's wedding. How I got this job was from the Old Man seeing the ad for a part-time assistant in the *Argus* one Saturday and mentioning it. I saw a chance for a bit of extra lolly and I fancied the job itself so the Old Man went and fixed it up without more ado. That was twelve months since and I've never regretted it. I like serving all the people who crowd into the shop on Saturdays and seeing all the different faces makes a change from looking at all the same old ones like Hassop and Miller and Rawlinson and Conroy up at Whittaker's day after day. I sometimes think this is the kind of job I'm cut out for, only there's no money in it as a full-time thing, though the thirty bob Mr Van pays me for Saturday is a grand bonus on top of my regular wage.

It's going up to nine by the time I get to the shop and

Mr Van's already opened. The Morris is standing outside and Henry's waiting for me to help him load it. Pale blue, the van is, with Mr Van Huyten's name on it in black letters. It's still new-looking because it's only six months old. The one before he'd had since pre-war and it could have been anybody's driving about. Mr Van's got his head down over his books in the little frosted-glass cubicle at the end of the long counter. Henry and I lug out two new TV sets, three that have been in for repair, and a new radiogram.

'Some good sales this week, eh, Henry?' I say, when we've finished and we're having a breather by the van. 'Over two hundred quid's worth of goods there.'

Henry's a little weedy bloke with a fat wife and five snotty-nosed kids. He wears glasses and his hair won't stick down though it always looks as though he's plastered everything he can think of on it, from liquid paraffin to lard. He gets a dokka from behind his ear and sticks it in his jib and lights up. He shakes his head and I know he's having one of his sorrowful mornings. Not that he ever has what you could call a cheerful morning.

'I wish I thought it could last, Vic,' he says, and shakes his head again.

'Last!' I say. 'Watcher talkin' about, Henry? Business is booming. You just can't meet the demand.'

But this is Henry all over – always looking on the black side – and even inventing one if he has to. I think maybe I'd be like him if I had a fat wife and five snotty-nosed kids. I have Ingrid in the back of my mind all the time and when I think of her and look at Henry I feel sorry for him.

'How long will it go on booming, Vic?' he says, puffing at his cig, 'there's got to be a saturation point somewhere, hasn't there?'

'Just look at records,' I say. 'You'd have thought TV would ha' killed all that; but it hasn't – just the opposite. They see a bloke on TV and run out to buy his latest record. And there's new ones coming out every month.'

'But you don't buy a new television set every month, do you?'

'So what? There's maintenance, isn't there? And what about cars? Yes, what about them? Look at the rate they turn *them* out. Where do they all go to? I don't know. You'd think everybody in the country would have two apiece by this time; but I haven't got one and you haven't.'

'Ah,' says Henry, 'but that's a different kettle o' fish. That's a different thing altogether . . .'

I catch the gleam in his eye and see the way his hand goes up and I know all the signs. He'll be quoting statistics in a minute and once Henry starts quoting statistics you're done for. I don't know where he gets them all from and I sometimes think he must make them up in his sleep without knowing it.

'I've given this a lot of thought,' he says. 'It's a sort of hobby of mine, as you know; and I've come to one or two conclusions . . .'

'You'd better save 'em till dinner-time, old cock, or you'll have Mr Van on our tails for wasting time.'

Now Henry being conscientious, he sees the sense in this and shuts up straight away. But he sighs, and I reckon he's doing this all the time when people are stopping him having his say. He stamps his tab-end out and buttons his smock up and opens the cab door.

'All right,' he says. 'But we're all living in a fool's paradise, that's all. A fool's paradise, Vic. Full employment and business booming? It just isn't feasible, lad. Don't say I didn't warn you when the crash comes.'

'We'll go on the dole together, Henry,' I say, and grin.

He looks back at me. 'Dole?' he says. 'You ask your dad about the dole, lad.'

And with this parting shot, as they say, he shuts the door and starts the engine. A proper Job's comforter, the Old Lady would call him. I wait till he's gone off up the street and then go into the shop.

'You'd better sell out and put your money in green-grocery, Mr Van Huyten,' I say as I pass the desk, and Mr Van lifts his big shaggy head up behind the glass and gives me a serious look.

'Oh, and why is that, Vic?'

'Henry says we're living in a fool's paradise.'

'Oh, *Henry* says. Our backyard economist.' Mr Van laughs, opening his mouth and showing his teeth, all sticking out of the gums any-old-how like gravestones in a mouldy old churchyard where they don't bury people any more. 'What Henry doesn't know about the workings of a wireless set doesn't matter; but he's a little undependable on the financial aspects of business, I fear.' And Mr Van Huyten chuckles away as though Henry's the comic find of the year.

I give him a minute to get over it then I ask him what I have to do.

'Now let me see,' he says, pushing his specs up on to his forehead. 'Let me consider . . .'

Mr Van Huyten's a bloke with something about him. He says things I never hear from anybody else in real life. And he dresses the part of a distinguished old gent, in a black jacket and striped trousers and a Come-to-Jesus collar. You have to look close to see the bits of breakfast on his waistcoat and pants, and the cig ash. Mr Van smokes a lot, only he doesn't really smoke at all, if you see what I mean. He lights fags all day long and then lets them hang out of his mouth till the ash drops on to his books when he brushes it away kind of absent-minded like. Yes, he looks a real gent, and a touch I really go for is this white handkerchief that hangs half out of his top pocket. It's real casual, artistic like, as if he's saying, 'Oh, yes, I know this is the way to dress, but I can't be bothered with it really, you know.'

So he considers, and then he says, 'I think you might check over that new consignment of records, if you don't mind. I've no doubt some of them will be asked for before the day's out and we should know where to put our hands on them.'

'Right you are.'

'If you don't mind,' though. He's the boss, isn't he, so who am I to mind? But that's Mr Van all over, considerate, treats you like a person, and makes it a real pleasure to do things for him.

So I begin to go through these records stacked in boxes behind the counter. There's all the latest pop stuff here for the fans: Frankie Vaughan, Tommy Steele, and Elvis. And they'll be swarming all over the place this afternoon, buying loads of stuff and taking it home to play with the repeat on till both them and the neighbours are sick to death of it. Then they'll come back next week for some more. Every week-end they're here, buying records by big names who've been going years and blokes you won't be able to remember eighteen months from now. I don't take a lot of notice of Henry's moaning but I sometimes wonder myself if it can last. In the meantime Mr Van Huyten must be doing very nicely thank you. He's a Beethoven man himself, you know. I once heard him tell a customer he was very fond of the 'later quartets', whatever they might be. But he doesn't mind keeping the business running on the profits from the other stuff. Me, I like all kinds of things, stuff with a tune you can whistle. Let's face it, there's a hell of a lot of crap passes over the counter.

When I've checked the consignment over I pass the invoices over to Mr Van for spiking. I pick out the records that are on order and sort the rest out ready for filing in their boxes. The box system's my idea; before this Mr Van had his stock filed according to catalogue numbers.

'Look, Mr Van Huyten,' I said to him one Saturday morning; 'I've been thinking about the way you've got your stock filed.' And he stops what he's doing to listen to me.

'Now when somebody comes in for a record we look the number up in the catalogue and if we have it we make a single sale. Right?'

He nods, very patient like. 'Right.'

'And if we haven't got it we offer to order it. But they don't always want to wait and so they might go somewhere else.'

'That's right,' Mr Van says. 'We can't stock everything.'

'No, we can't. But supposing we put the records in boxes and label 'em according to the artist – or the composers for the classical stuff. Then when a bloke comes in for a Perry Como, say, we get Perry Como's box down and look for it there; and we let the customer look as well. That way he actually sees the records we've got instead of just names in a catalogue, which we might not have anyway. Ten to one he'll spot something he's forgotten or didn't know about. That way we could sell mebbe three or four records for every one we sell now.'

He's looking at me over his glasses. 'You mean to let them browse, as they do in bookshops?'

'That's it. You'd never make a bookshop pay if you only let the customer see the one book he wants. Many a time they don't know what they want, and this way we could have people coming in just to look through a box of the sort of records they fancy. Course, we'd have to keep an eye on them, see they don't do any damage . . . You see what I mean, Mr Van Huyten?'

He nods. 'I see what you mean, Victor. I'll think about it and let you know.' He goes back to his books but I know he will think about it like he says and then let me know what he thinks.

He brings it up again the next Saturday. 'I like that idea of yours, Vic,' he says. 'How could we introduce it, do you think?'

I'm itching to get started straight away. 'It shouldn't be hard,' I say. 'All we need's plenty of boxes, and I've got a kid's stencilling outfit at home I can do the labels with.'

'It's the reorganization I'm thinking about, Victor. It will take time and you're only here Saturdays, our busiest time.'

I tell him I'm willing to come in after work a couple of nights and he looks doubtful. 'If you're sure you don't mind sacrificing your spare time,' he says.

'It'll be a pleasure. I like doing jobs like that.'

'And I'll pay you the same rate as Saturday, then.'

'Well, I wasn't thinking about the money, Mr Van

71

Huyten,' I tell him, and I wasn't. I don't want him to think I'm on the make. It's the idea that counts.

'Well you just think about it now, my boy,' he says. 'You give me your time and I pay for it. That's business.'

Anyway, I did the labels at home and went into the shop every night one week and got the sorting done. I've got a pretty good memory for anything I'm interested in and by the time I'd finished I thought I nearly knew the stock off by heart and could say practically without checking whether we had a record in or not. The first two nights Mr Van stayed with me but on the others he left me to lock up and take the key up to his house when I'd finished. It made me feel good to have him trust me like that. I mean, I could have walked out with nearly anything and he wouldn't have known. Anyway, it started me thinking about something else – staggering the dinner hour on Saturdays so's we didn't have to shut the shop at the busiest time. We started doing this after a bit.

Anyway, now I've finished sorting the new records and I take a look round the shop. One time the customers used to listen to records on any old gram that was handy, but now there's a couple of soundproof listening booths at one end of the shop. Even these aren't enough some Saturdays, though, and I'm thinking about something I've seen in Leeds: a kind of arrangement of turntables and earphones so's you can listen in private right out in the shop. I wonder if Mr Van Huyten would be interested in this idea and I think I'll mention it to him some day soon.

II

'Hello,' she says. 'I've brought my friend along. I hope you don't mind.'

'Oh, no . . . no,' I say, like a clot. But what else can I say, for Pete's sake? My heart's dropped down into my boots with a thud because I know straight off my number's up. This is one way of doing it, giving you the shove. They don't refuse the date but they bring a girl friend along to keep you at arm's length; and if you don't ask them again, well, that's okay, because that was the idea in the first place.

I look at them standing arm-in-arm under the lamp: Ingrid all neat and clean and fresh-smelling as usual, and this plain Jane with a muddy complexion, a big nose, and a mouth like a crack in a pie. I often wonder what it is makes bints pair off like this, one lovely and one horrible. You see it all the time and it must have turned more lads against one another than nearly anything else because if you're hunting in pairs somebody's got to have the horror. As it is, it looks as if I've got both of them and neither. And if the fact that she's here isn't enough the look this girl friend's giving me says a mouthful.

Tonight's Sunday and we were out together for the second time last night. It wasn't like the first time, though. We went to a plushy cinema in the middle of town and all we could do was hold hands. Well that wasn't bad but once we were outside again we seemed to lose all the headway we'd made, just like we did on Wednesday night. So it was my idea to go for a walk tonight and see how we'd make out outside all evening.

And now this. This is a brush-off if ever I've seen one.

'This is Dorothy,' Ingrid says. 'And this is Vic.'

She was a nice girl as nice girls go and as nice girls go she went. This Dorothy says nothing but carries on giving me the look till I feel like asking her what she's got on her mind. There we are, standing under the lamp; three of us, one too many, and that one is me, Joe Soap.

'Do you know a girl called Mary Fitzpatrick?' this Dorothy asks me all at once.

This is plain bints all over, the way they shoot questions at you that seem to have all sorts of thing hidden in them. It makes me think she knows something nasty about me and I start to try and think what it can be. Plain bints know they can't blind you with their looks so they have to get at you some other way.

'Yes, I know her.'

73

'You don't know me, though, do you?' she says, and the way she says it makes it sound like 'But you'll wish you did in a minute!'

'I've never seen you before that I know of,' I tell her.

'But I know you,' she says, 'and I know Mary Fitzpatrick.'

'Give her my love next time you see her,' I say. What the hell's she getting at? I wonder.

'You used to give it to her yourself at one time, didn't you?'

'Me and Mary Fitzpatrick? I don't know what you're talking about.'

Me and Mary Fitzpatrick used to live in the same street and I can remember dancing with her one time and another time walking her home because she was on her own and I was going the same way anyway. That's all, and it's a fact; because though I think she quite liked me she wasn't my type and anyway she was a Catholic and I'm C. of E. when I'm anything and it's no use letting religion in to balls things up. From the way this Dorothy's talking though you'd think I put Mary Fitzpatrick in the family way.

'I hardly knew her,' I say and I wonder if Ingrid will believe this. But what does it matter now whether she believes it or not? She's looking from one to the other of us like she's taking it all in and I feel like slapping this Dorothy across the face because I know just what type she is now and it's a type I don't like a bit.

'Well,' Ingrid says, 'which way shall we go?'

'Any way you like,' I say. The walk doesn't seem like a good idea any more. It just makes me look too skinny to take her to the pictures again.

'Shall we go this way, then; up towards the park?'

'If you like.'

At least that's going away from the centre of town and cuts down the risk of anybody I know seeing me with the two of them.

So we walk up the hill and they're still linking on the pavement, holding on to one another as if they expect somebody to jump on them from round the corner. There isn't enough room on the pavement for three abreast so I have to walk in the gutter. This seems to cut me off from Ingrid more than ever and I get a real strong feeling that I'm not wanted round these parts. I wonder how long I can stick it before I make an excuse and blow. It's a grand night, though. As we come up over the hill where there's houses on one side only we can see over the edge of the cliff to all the lights in the valley and up the opposite side where the road goes over the top to Calderford. It's just the kind of night I was wishing for, hard and dry, just the night for walking and talking and getting to know somebody better. As it is, it's all gone wrong and I'm getting nowhere. I haven't said a word in over five minutes. This Dorothy cramps my style no end, and there's not much point in making an effort anyway now all the signs are out. I'm not the brightest geezer in the world but I can read the writing on the wall as well as the next man.

Dorothy's on the far side of Ingrid and she's saying something I can't hear. It sounds like some private joke from the way she's keeping her voice down and when she stops they both giggle. I feel they're making cracks about me, and even if they're not it's rotten manners to carry on like that.

Then Dorothy lifts her voice and says, 'Look that's where Ralph Wilson lives now.' There's some pretty posh houses up on this side of the park and she's pointing to this big place standing back behind some trees. I catch a glimpse of a car, maybe an Armstrong Siddeley, standing in the drive.

'I didn't know they'd moved,' Ingrid says.

'Oh, yes, they've been up here a bit now,' Dorothy says. 'Proper stuck-up, he is, as well, since they went to live in a big house. He hardly speaks when he sees you.'

It sounds to me as though this Ralph Wilson's a man after my own heart as far as Dorothy's concerned.

'I don't see why he should get stuck-up all of a sudden,' Ingrid says. 'That house they lived in before was big

75

enough and his family was always well-off. Anyway, he's always friendly enough with me when I see him.'

'Well, I think he should be friendly with you, if anybody,' Dorothy says, and she's got that tone of voice out again, like she knows a lot more than she's saying. But Ingrid takes her up on it.

'What d'you mean?'

'I mean after that time at the tennis club when you and him were locked in the changing-rooms and nobody could get in.'

'You know very well it was Harry Norris who did that. He had the key all the time.'

'Oh, I know; but I'm talking about what went on inside. You didn't seem so bothered about getting out so quick, either of you.'

'Just what everybody wanted, wasn't it, for us to make a fuss?'

'Everybody except Ralph Wilson. I think he put Harry Norris up to it in the first place.'

'Well he didn't get anything out of it if he did.'

'That's not what he said after. I heard some of the things he told the lads.'

'I don't know why you have to bring all this up,' Ingrid says. 'I'm sure Vic isn't interested in old gossip like that.'

'Oh, I don't know,' Dorothy says.

'You're everybody's best friend, aren't you?' I say.

'What d'you mean by that?' Dorothy says.

'You know what I mean. First off you try to make out something about me, and now it's Ingrid.'

I've had enough of this and I've a feeling I'll say something any minute that'll gum the works up good and proper. But I'm past caring. If this Dorothy's spoilt our date she's not going to get off scot free.

'Who d'you think you are, anyway?' she says to me. 'I know things about you that you wouldn't like spreading about.'

We've stopped walking now and I look her straight in her horrible clock. 'You can't scare me with that kind o' talk,' I tell her. 'You don't know anything about me that

76

nobody else knows. And if you're thinkin' o' making something up you'd better think again.'

'Why, what will you do?' she sneers, ever so clever.

Well I've got my rag out now and no mistake. I think of all the time I've been wanting Ingrid and the way I hoped we'd be tonight. And now she's here spoiling everything with her mucky talk. So I let her have it, and to hell with everything.

'I'll take your pants down and slap your bloody arse,' I tell her. 'A pity nobody ever did it before.'

'You lay a finger on me and I'll have the police on you.'

'After you've wiped the grin off your face.'

'How d'you mean?'

'I mean any bloke who laid a finger on you 'ud deserve a medal. He'd have to have a sack over his head before he'd take you into a tennis pavilion.'

I think for a second she's going to fly at me biting and scratching and I step one pace back and half lift my hands to keep her off. Then all at once she turns her back and bursts out crying like a kid.

'You shouldn't have said that,' Ingrid says.

'Oh, what the hell,' I say. 'Why should she have it all her own way?'

Dorothy begins to walk away up the road, still blubbing, and Ingrid looks after her. 'Look, she's going.'

'Well, what are you going to do?'

'I can't leave her now.'

'After what she tried to make out about you?'

'You don't know her. That's just her way. She didn't mean anything.'

'That's what they all say, all these old gossips who go about making trouble. They never mean anything.'

'You don't know her.'

'I don't want to know her. I've seen enough of her.'

She stands on the edge of the pavement like she can't make up her mind what to do, and I wonder why she keeps up the pretence.

'Well I can't leave her.'

'What did you bring her for? You had a date with me, didn't you?'

'She just came to our house for tea and I didn't want to send her away on her own. She's my best friend.'

'I'd never have known if you hadn't told me.'

A likely story, I'm thinking. Why doesn't she say straight out what she thinks? Why keep on pretending like this? Dorothy's a good twenty yards away by now. She's got her head down so it looks like the waterworks are still in operation.

'I shall have to go to her,' Ingrid says. 'You've hurt her, y'know. She's very sensitive, really.'

'Why doesn't she think other people might be?'

'It's just her way . . . I must go now . . .'

'Okay.'

'I'll see you at work on Monday.'

'I'm usually there.'

She walks backwards a few paces. 'Good night then.'

'Good night.'

She swings round and sets off after Dorothy who's gone out of sight round a corner. I watch till she turns the corner herself then I walk back down the hill. I'm so miserable I just don't give a damn for anything.

4

I

There's only one good thing about Monday morning and that is Hassop's away. I'm up talking to Miller in his office when the inter-com starts buzzing and Mr Althorpe's light goes on. Miller lifts the receiver up and presses the switch and listens for a minute. Then he says, 'No, he hasn't come in yet, Mr Althorpe . . . Well, he did seem a bit under the weather on Friday . . . Yes, righto, I'll come in now.' He puts the receiver down and shoves a note-pad in his smock pocket and makes for the door. Most of us in the D.O. wear smocks because it's surprising the amount of muck there is about, what with pencil dust and grit from the Works. We had a bloke started once who wore a white one and set everybody off making cracks about ice-cream men because the standard colours are khaki and a sort of mucky grey. He didn't stop long, this bod, because he didn't fit in somehow.

'I'll see you later, Vic,' Miller says as he's going out.

'What's up with Hassop?'

'*Mister* Hassop,' Miller says, and goes out without answering.

I go back down the office and Jimmy looks up from his board next to mine. 'Where's old Dogknob this morning?'

'Mister Dogknob to you,' I say.

'Mister Horace Edward Hassop Dogknob, Esquire,' Jimmy says. 'Some say 'good old Hassop'; others know the blighter.'

I give myself the pleasure of sharpening a brand-new

pencil. 'Looks as if he's badly. With a bit o' luck it might turn into pneumonia and we shan't see him for six months.'

'A week'll do for me,' Jimmy says. 'I'm grateful for small mercies.'

Conroy comes past with a roll of prints under his arm. He's got his big head down in his shoulders and he looks as brussen as he always does.

'What's up with Hassop?'

'Looks like flu.'

He gives a grunt and moves off. I'm not sorry. Conroy's one of the bods at Whittaker's I can do without very nicely, thank you.

I file the pencil point to a chisel shape and give the board a flick over with a duster. Everybody seems to be working even if Hassop is away. But Miller and the section leaders can keep order, and anyway, keeping your nose down is the best way of making the time pass. As soon as I try to settle down though, I start thinking about Ingrid and last night. I try to get my mind on my drawing, and do a few lines; but it's no use – I just keep thinking about her. I look over at Jimmy and think I'd like to tell him and get some advice. But then I think I've made a twerp of myself and there's no point in telling anybody else about that.

Miller comes back in a bit and calls me up to his office.

'How d'you feel about a trip into town?'

'I don't mind,' I tell him. 'It's not a bad morning out.'

'Mr Hassop isn't on the phone and Mr Althorpe wants a message taking to him and some papers bringing back. Do you know where he lives?'

'Somewhere up Bradford Road, doesn't he?'

'That's right. Here, I'll jot the address down on a bit of paper.'

He hands me the paper and an envelope with Hassop's name on it that he's brought out of Althorpe's office.

'Righto, then, don't be too long. And no stopping off for morning coffee on the way.'

'I'm missing my tea break, remember,' I say, and Miller

80

says, 'Gerrout of it,' with a grin. He feels in his pocket. 'Here's a bob for your bus fare. You can keep the change.'

'I suppose it'll turn out to be sevenpence each way,' I say as I go out.

I go and take my smock off and throw it over my buffet.

'Taking the rest of the morning off, Brown?' Jimmy says in his managing director's voice.

'I'm off up to see Hassop,' I tell him. 'Makes a change, a trip out in the middle of the morning. Any messages?'

'Tell him we'll buy him a grand wreath,' Jimmy says.

Outside it's bright and fine and there's big white clouds scudding across the sky just like in spring, only it's none too warm and you have to keep moving or you soon feel the cold. I amble down to the corner to wait for a bus. I feel in my pocket to make sure I've still got the envelope for Hassop. I hope Mrs Hassop, or whoever answers the door, won't ask me up to see him because I know I shan't know what to say to him. I get my cigs out and when I open the packet I see there's three gone already this morning. I'm smoking like a mill chimney these days. I'll be up to twenty a day if I don't watch it, and I can't afford that. Sometimes when I'm broke and I read about it causing lung cancer I think I'll give up, but I can never be bothered to make the effort; and anyway, I like it. I put the packet away and decide I'll wait till I drop off for a cup of coffee on the way back.

When I'm on the bus I start to think about Ingrid again. What I mean is, I'm always thinking about Ingrid but a lot of the time I have to think about other things as well, only now I can give all my attention to it. Oh, but she's a swell piece! The more I see her and think about her the more I think she's a real bobby dazzler. I reckon I can't grumble really and I'm lucky to have taken her out three times. Well, twice, because you can't count last night. That was a proper washout. Thinking about it now I wonder if I wasn't a bit, well, cruel like with Dorothy. Not that she hadn't it coming, mind. She must have been going about for some time saying just what she liked and getting away with it; but she tangled with the wrong bloke when she picked on me. I told her. Awful, though, the way she folded up soon as I really went for her. You could tell it hurt. Poor ugly bint. It cooked my goose with Ingrid, though, I bet, even if the oven wasn't warming up already. Women are funny like that; they're as catty as can be about one another, but let a man start and they don't half close ranks in double-quick time.

The bus runs down through the shopping centre. There's a lad with dusters tied round his feet dressing Granger's big window and a fat woman with great big arms down on her knees scrubbing the foyer of the Plaza picture house. A bint with the neatest pair of gams I've seen in a fortnight stops for a minute to look at the stills in the boxes outside. Ah, well, there's plenty more fish in the sea . . . I try to think this but it doesn't help much. I change to a Bradford bus in the station and sit downstairs near the door because I'm not sure how far I have to go. The conductor comes in laughing at something a tart conductor has just said to him and rings the bell. I give him my fare and tell him I want to get off at Providence Avenue.

'Watch out for the Maternity Hospital,' he says. 'You get off there.'

It's only when he says this that I see the two bints on the bus with me both have buns in the oven, and three more get on up the hill. The conductor winks at me when he's taken their fares. 'We give more free rides than any other route,' he says, and I grin.

'Had any embarrassing moments?'

He laughs. 'Aye, I have that, lad; but not on a bus!'

When I see the Maternity Hospital standing back behind these huge lawns I get off with the five pregnant bints and watch them waddle across the road with their shoulders back. I wonder for a minute what it must be like to have a kid and then think I'm glad I'll never know. I wonder about the other thing as well, and if women enjoy it as much as men. I've an idea they don't, and anyway, it might not be all men crack it up to be. I don't know, but I wonder. I wonder about it quite a lot these days, and as I'm going up the road to Hassop's I think there might be a lot to be said for these knocking-shops blokes who've done military service abroad tell you about. You feel the need and you pay your money and get what you want. Just like drinking a glass of water when you're thirsty. Nobody spends all his time thinking about water, except the bloke in a desert where there isn't any. Some chaps spend a lot of time thinking about wine, though; but that's drinking for pleasure like going to bed with a bint you're in love with. When that happens with everything else you have together it must be just about the most wonderful thing in the world. But that's love and it comes some time. The other thing's biology, and you have that all along.

I think I've made a mistake till I check the number on a bit of paper Miller gave me. The house stands back from the road and there's a lot of black soil packed down hard that must have been a garden at one time. It's big and square, the house, and it looks a lot like a broken-down Working Men's Club. I reckon it must have been standing right there the best part of a hundred years because the stone's all grey-black and the flags round it are all sunk and sticking up in the corners any-old-how. There's a bit of a porch with some coloured glass windows in it, red and yellow and green, round the door, and I go along the path and knock, still thinking somebody's slipped up and given me the wrong address. There's a kind of rising sun in frosted glass in the top half of the door and I give it a push and go into the porch when nobody answers my knock. Inside there's the house door and a mat that's worn nearly to strings on the step. There's a pile of sacks and a rusty old paraffin stove and a crate of empty stout bottles as well. Everything smells damp and you get the idea it's all rotting away here and nobody cares a hang. It's a real rum do. I don't like it much.

But there's the number on the door all right, like the one on the paper, so this must be it. I get hold of a little bell-handle that's in a kind of socket on the wall and pull on the chain. I put my head up to the door and listen for the bell but there's no sound. I reckon that hasn't worked since the Charge of the Light Brigade, so I give a sharp rat-a-tat-tat on the letter-box knocker.

Well I seem to have been standing there half the morning, and if it was just my say-so I'd have been off long since, when I hear somebody sliding a bolt on the inside. The door opens maybe six inches and this woman's face appears in the gap. Her voice gives me a start; it's as deep as a man's.

'Yerss?'

'I've called with a message for Mr Hassop,' I say, watching this phizzog in the doorway. It's long and baggy and sort of yellowish brown in colour and the eyes are stuck half-way out of it like brown marbles.

'For Mr Hassop?' the face says.

'I'm from the Works – Whittaker's. Mr Hassop does live here, doesn't he?'

'What is the message?'

When she talks she shows the biggest bottom teeth I've ever seen, square at the top and tapering down to the gums.

'It's written down.' I show her the envelope. 'Mr Althorpe sent it. He thought Mr Hassop must have flu when he didn't come this morning. We knew he had a cold on Friday. I hope it's nothing serious, only there's so much flu about you can't be too careful . . .'

There I go, yattering on and hardly knowing what I'm saying. But it makes me feel queer standing there in front of this face with these two marbles watching me. All at once a scrawny hand comes round the door and flicks the envelope away from me.

'Wait.'

The face vanishes.

I stand there thinking this is the queerest do I've ever come across. I wait a good five minutes and then the door opens a bit wider as though a little puff of wind's blown it. I push it open more and step inside.

I'm in a big hall with a bare tiled floor. There's lots of nearly black unvarnished doors leading off, all shut. The stairs go up at the far end and there's a tall window with a half-round top and some more of the coloured glass in it. There's a smell of gas that's not burning properly coming from somewhere and in a bit it seems to settle on my stomach and I don't feel too cracky. But I hang on and there's not a sound for maybe ten minutes and I'm beginning to think I must be at the wrong address after all and this woman is a loony who's buzzed off with the envelope and isn't coming back. I begin to work out what I can say back at the office and then all of a sudden a door opens upstairs somewhere and I hear these two voices going at it hammer and tongs bawling one another out. I can't tell what they're saying but in a minute they stop and this woman comes to the top of the stairs. I get a good view of her now and it makes me wish I'd stopped outside. If this is Hassop's missis it's time he put her back where he dug her up from. She comes down the stairs with her head back like a horrible imitation of a countess arriving at a ball or something. Her hair's a dusty black and it's piled up all any-old-how on top of her head. She's got some kind of dressing-gown on made of a thin stuff, grey and dirty yellow, with like a feather collar to it. The marbles are on me as she gets to the bottom of the the stairs and comes across the hall. When she gets nearer I find there's a queer smell about her and I wonder if she's had a bath since the Great War.

She gives me the big envelope she's carrying and says in this basso profundo voice, 'There was no need for you to come in.'

I say sorry and ask how Hassop is.

'It's all in the envelope,' she says.

'Oh, well, righto, then. I'll go straight back and give it to Mr Althorpe. Hope he'll soon be up and about again . . .'

She says nothing and these marbles are fixed on me and I wonder what we're both doing standing there while I babble on. It seems she's not going to show me out, so I say, 'Well, I'll be getting off, then,' and walk to the door. She stands stock-still, just the marbles swivelling as I get to the door.

It's only when I swing the door wide open and a great ray of sunshine shoots in that she moves. Then she suddenly half-runs towards me with her hands up as though she's after clawng my eyes out.

'Close the door,' she says. 'Close the door.'

Well, I'm all for this, but with me and her on opposite sides, so I say good morning and nip smartly out. The door slams as if she's thrown all her weight behind it and the knocker jumps and gives a rap. I hear the bolt shoot home again and I get out of the porch and walk smartish up the path and don't look back till I'm out on the pavement. I'm thinking then that if that's what Hassop has to put up with it's no wonder he isn't the life and soul of the party.

II

I drop off in town for a coffee at the Bluebird Snack Bar, and I light that cig up I promised myself earlier. It's something unusual for me to be downtown on a working morning and I'm a bit surprised, like I always am, to see so many people about. I don't mean just women shopping and that, but blokes wandering about as they like while me and my kind are tied up earning a living. Quite a few of them are coloured bods, Indians and Pakistanis mostly. They all look alike to me, with long faces and high cheek bones, thin wrists and big teeth. They have right thick black glossy hair that shines as if they use half a bottle of cream on it at a time. I've never seen a well-dressed one yet and I don't suppose most of them are well-off. I reckon even the ones who aren't working though are better off on National Assistance here than they would be working at home; and I suppose there'll be some of them who don't bother about getting a job so long as the Government's willing to keep them. That's what a lot of people have against them, but I always think you can't just lump people together like that. I reckon there'll be right 'uns and wrong 'uns among them like there is with anybody else. They don't seem to cause much bother, and mind their own business. All the same, though, I wouldn't like to be a bird walking home late at night by myself up Colville Road. There's so many of them living up there the locals call it the Road to Mandalay. God! I'm glad I'm English. I'm glad a dozen times a week when I read in the papers all that's going on in the world.

It's quiet in the snack bar and I enjoy my coffee and sit there thinking how nice it would be if Ingrid was to walk in and we could have a quiet little chat and I'd maybe get to know where I stand. Not that I don't know already. I reckon it's all up. But I still can't take it somehow that it's all over after just two dates – three if you count last night. We were getting along fine as far as I could see. There wasn't the slightest sign of anything going wrong till that Dorothy turned up. I wonder if I got Ingrid wrong about that. Perhaps Dorothy did just turn up and Ingrid couldn't get rid of her, like she said. If she did I made a real mess of things by going for her like I did. Oh, I don't know. Bints are the very devil to understand.

I'm feeling a bit peckish so I go to get my cup filled again and buy a sausage roll to stave off the pangs till dinner-time.

There's only one way to find out and that's to ask her for another date. If she says yes, all well and good. If she says no it can't be any worse than now when I'm wondering and imagining the worst and hoping for something better. So I decide: I'll ask her, and if I can't screw myself up to doing it to her face I'll write her a little note and get young Laisterdyke to give it to her.

I'm sitting there drinking my second cup of coffee and thinking about Ingrid and hearing somebody bashing pots about in the back place when who should walk in but Les Jackson with his left hand all done up in a big boxing glove of bandages. He spots me as he turns round and he lifts his eyebrows and brings his cup over to the table, holding his bad hand up against his chest. The bandages are all fresh and clean.

'Howdo, Vic.'

' 'Lo, Les. What the hell you been doin' to your hand?'

'That dame,' Les says. 'What thighs!' He sits down laughing. 'I had an argument with a drilling machine Friday morning.'

'Is it bad?'

'Slit all down the side of me hand an' taken the tip off one finger.'

'Christ!'

Les sips his tea and I take my cigs out and offer him one. 'Have a picture of Queen Victoria.' I take another myself and we light up. Les pulls on his like he hasn't had a smoke in a week.

'Just what I need,' he says. 'I've been up to the Infirmary. I've to go up every morning to have the dressings changed.'

'Give you some stick?'

'It's not so bad now. Gave me gyp Friday, though, when I just done it. I nearly passed out on 'em. They've one of the tough Irish sisters in Casualty up there. I told her they ought to give you a whiff o' summat afore they start messing about. "What, a big husky chap like yourself?" she says. "You're soft, man." '

'Aye, an' I'm soft an' all when it comes to owt like that,' I tell him. I'm looking at the bandages and imagining the mess underneath and I can't help turning cold and shivering.

'What you doing out this time o' morning, anyway?' Les says. 'Are you laiking?'

'No, I've just been taking a message to my boss's house. He's off badly.'

'Having ten minutes at the firm's expense now, eh?'

'That's the idea.'

'Got it cushy, you office boys.'

'Come off it. It's your own fault if you're wearing overalls instead of a collar an' tie. A grammar school lad drilling lumps o' metal.'

'Aw, I like to make things. I allus did. I couldn't abide sitting at a desk all day. Too much like school . . . I say, guess who I ran into just now – Old Roster.'

'Gerraway!'

'I did that!'

'Old Roster . . . I haven't seen him in years. Did he speak to you?'

'Oh aye. I said good morning like and he stopped and took a good look at me. You know the way he does it – first over his glasses then through 'em. Then he says. 'Jackson, isn't it? Yes – Jackson. Good heavens, boy, what have you done to your hand?' We must have stood for a good ten minutes talkin' about this an' that. Fancy him remembering me name, though.'

'Oh, he's not a bad lad, Roster. Plenty worse than him.'

'I'll say.'

'He didn't remind you about the time we sewed the armholes of his gown up, did he?'

We have a laugh as we think about that, then Les shoves his cup to one side and leans over the table and lowers his voice a bit. 'Didja hear the one about the chap with a wooden leg who went on his honeymoon?' he says.

I haven't heard it.

I get back to the office about half-eleven and take the envelope in to Miller.

'Did you see Mr Hassop?' he asks me.

'No, just his wife.'

'It must have been his sister; Mr Hassop isn't married. Did she say how he was?'

'She said it was all in the envelope.'

Miller looks at me as if he thinks I'm trying to be funny. 'How d'you mean, in the envelope?'

'That's what she said. I asked how he was and she said it was all in the envelope.'

Miller turns the envelope over in his hands. It's got Mr Althorpe's name on it so he can't open it.

'Have you seen her, this sister?' I ask him, because

89

now I'm back in the office I'm wondering if I can have imagined it all.

'No, I don't know much about Mr Hassop's private life. He's very reserved about it.'

'I don't wonder. Honest, Jack, she's the queerest bird I've ever run across.' And I start to tell him all about it and he rests his behind on his desk and shoves his specs up on his nose with his forefinger now and again, the way he does, as he listens to me.

'Hmmm,' he says when I've finished. 'Well, you'd better not say anything about it in the office. We don't want Mr Hassop's personal affairs bandying about the place.'

I say no, course not, and Miller picks the envelope up to take it in to Mr Althorpe. He looks back as he's going out. 'You say this dressing-gown thing had a feather collar on it?' he says.

'Looked like feathers to me.'

He says 'Hmmm' again, and beetles off out.

I go down the office to my board.

'And how's the draughtsman's friend, this morning?' Jimmy says.

'It's all in the envelope,' I say, and start laughing. It's got all the makings of a good catchphrase for Jimmy and me once I've told him the tale.

'What's so funny?' he says.

'Tell you later.' I reckon it'll be okay to tell him outside. It'll have to be; I can't keep a thing like that to myself. I go over and lean on his board. 'Didja hear the one about the bloke with the wooden leg 'at got married and went on his honeymoon?'

He hasn't heard it either.

III

Now I've decided to ask Ingrid out again I can't think of anything else for wondering how I'm going to go about it and what she'll say. I see her at dinner-time in the canteen only I can't keep my mind right on her because Ken

Rawlinson's yattering away about a symphony concert he's been to in Leeds Town Hall on Sunday night.

'. . . and it's tragic to think he never actually heard the biggest part of his own music.'

'What?' I say. 'Who's that?'

'Beethoven.'

'How's that? Did he snuff it young, or summat?'

'He was afflicted with deafness.'

'Well how could he compose music if he was deaf?' The stuff this bighead Rawly comes out with. He'll be talking about blind painters next.

'It was all in his mind,' Rawly says. 'All he had to do was write it down.'

'Without hearing it?'

'Of course. All this business you see in films where the composer sits picking out a melody at the piano is a Hollywood myth. Or at least, it's grossly exaggerated. A musician of the first rank has only to see the music to hear it in his mind. And a composer has no need actually to hear the music to put it down on paper.'

This is interesting. It even makes me forget Ingrid for a minute. Course, I don't believe all Rawly says, because he's a big show-off, but I can always check on this with Mr Van Huyten. He's sure to know.

'A first-class musician', Rawly says, 'can read an orchestral score as easily as the average person can read a book.'

'And he's only himself to blame if anybody plays a wrong note, eh?'

'Exactly. In fact some musicians so despair of hearing the perfect performance of a favourite work that they give up *listening* to music and read scores instead.'

'Like playing with yourself because you can't find the perfect woman,' says Conroy on the other side of Rawly, and Rawly goes as red as fire and carries on with his dinner without another word.

I have to smile at this because although I don't like Conroy any more than I like Rawly I think it's a very smart remark and I'm ready to see Rawly taken down a peg any time. It's shut him up, anyway, and now I can concentrate on Ingrid again. I like her. I like everything about her. I like the way her hair's cut short and waves over her ears. I like the little dimples at the corners of her mouth and the mouth itself, all soft and full and made for kisses. I remember me kissing it and wonder if I ever will again. She knows I'm watching her and just once, for a second, her eyes slide round to mine. Then away again. You might think we've never spoken two words to one another. All that in the warm and the dark in the pictures; you might think it had never happened.

I'm still dreaming about her at half past three when she comes through the office with her notebook and pencil to take some letters for Miller. I let my eyes slide up over the top edge of the board and follow her all the way. Such a trim little behind she has in that skirt, and them darkish nylons show her legs off a treat.

'Isn't it sweet, Jeff?' somebody says near by, and I jump. Conroy and his pal Lewis are leaning on Conroy's board watching me. They're both laughing in that sarcastic way Conroy has and Lewis copies.

'Doesn't it do your heart good to see it?' Conroy says.

'What's up wi' you two?' I say, as if I didn't know.

'Don't come it, young Browny,' Conroy says. 'We know you're doing a bit for our Miss Rothwell, the Siren of the Typing Pool.'

'Why don't you mind your own bloody business?' I say, and look down at my board as if I'm going to carry on working.

'I don't suppose you've got into the front room yet, young Browny.' Conroy says. 'A bit of knee-trembling up the back passage just now, eh?'

'Up the front passage an' all, I'll bet,' Lewis sniggers.

I'm going red and I can feel myself getting mad in a hard lump in my chest. I say nothing, because it'll only make them worse. But one of these days I'll give that Lewis one right in the guts. Conroy's too heavy for me, but Lewis is just my barrow and one day he'll open his big gob too far when there's nobody around to keep the peace . . .

They haven't done yet, either.

'You want to be careful there, young Browny,' Conroy says. 'She's a hot bit o' stuff, our Miss Rothwell. A bit out of your class, I'd say. You want to leave her to the men.'

I keep my head down, reckoning to be drawing. But they won't lay off. My heart's hammering now and I can't hold the pencil still, so I grip it and press it down hard on to the paper so it won't show.

'Know what they call her?' Conroy says. 'What her nickname is? They call her the Praying Mantis. You know what a Praying Mantis is, don't you?'

I say nothing, holding myself in tight, waiting for them to lay off.

'Well it's an insect, something like a big grasshopper, and the female eats the male while they're actually on the job together. Just gobbles him up bit by bit.'

'And you can guess which bit she leaves till last,' Lewis says, nearly killing himself with laughing.

'That's a bloody rotten thing to say, Conroy,' I say, bringing my head up. 'Why don't you mind your own business, you lousy swine!'

'What's that?' Conroy says, and gets off his elbows. 'Say that again, you young sod, an' I'll –'

I'm saved in the nick of time when Miller opens his office door and shouts for Conroy. He goes off and Lewis comes over to me and sticks his face over the edge of the board. He's nicely shaved and his hair's slicked back with a dead straight parting. They always say Lewis has a haircut every ten days. Very particular about his appearance he is. Clean as you like on the outside and as mucky as a sewer in.

'You want to be careful with your language, young Browny,' he says, 'or you'll be getting a thick ear for your cheek.'

This is about as much as I'm taking and I grap for Lewis's tie and nearly throttle him pulling him over the edge of the board. 'You say much more, Lewis, an' I'll wrap a bunch o' fives round your bloody neck.' He waves his arms about and goes red in the face as I hold him. 'You're a poor bloody fish without Conroy to back you up, an' don't forget it.'

I give him a push as I let go and he stands there gasping and pulling at his tie as he wonders whether to make anything of it. Then Miller and Conroy come down the office to Conroy's board and he can slink away without losing any more face.

IV

I don't get a chance to talk to Ingrid going home Monday and I hope I might do better next morning. Instead, though, I get tied up with Jimmy in the middle of a whole drove of people while Ingrid walks on in front with some more women.

When I get into the office I scribble a quick note asking if I can see her tonight. I roll a couple of drawings up and mosey down to the print room. The machine's humming away in there and the lamps are trundling to and fro along the rails with the light from them swooping about the walls and ceiling. Phoebe Johnson's on her own, doing a few little dance steps in front of the machine as though it's a juke box in a coffee bar. Phoebe's at this sort of thing all day long: humming calypso songs to herself and twitching her elbows and shoulders about. She's only sixteen but she's a real voluptuous-looking bit with curvy hips and two at the front any film star would be proud of. There's rumour about among the lads that she's a sure thing, but that's just wishful thinking because I happen to know a couple of blokes who've dated her and there's nothing doing. Phoebe believes in Romance and that's got nothing to do with what nearly every bloke she goes out with is interested in; though I reckon she knows she'll have to put up with it when she gets married, whoever the bod happens to be.

I lean on the trimming table and watch her for a bit. 'Where's young Colin?'

She shrugs without stopping this little dance she's doing. 'Dunno.'

Tell the truth I'm just a little bit scared of Phoebe because she says just what she thinks when she thinks it. She does her job well enough to keep out of trouble but one of these days she'll speak her mind to the wrong bloke and then she'll be out. Not that she'll care because it's obvious she wouldn't care a hoot if she got the sack tomorrow. That's the kind of lass she is.

'Has he turned in this morning?'

'I haven't seen him.' She makes a few more steps then a spin that brings her round to face me. 'I don't like your tie.'

'What's up with me tie?'

'It's not modern, up-to-date,' she says. 'It's an old man's tie.' She reaches out and flicks it out of my jumper, calm as you please, so's she can see it all. She shakes her head and dances away with her hands up and her fingers clicking.

I tuck the tie away again. 'What sort o' tie do you think I should wear, then?'

'Well, a slim jim, or summat else modern. You've seen 'em in the shops.'

'Aye, an' they can stop in the shops for me. I wouldn't be seen dead in 'em.'

'If you want to walk about looking like your grand-father,' she says.

'I don't want to walk about lookin' a freak . . . An' why don't you stop jigging about a bit? You'll have St Vitus' dance, if you haven't got it already.'

Phoebe knocks off dancing and pulls herself up straight, sticking this lovely chest of hers out, and says in her duchess's voice, 'If you're going to be insulting, Mr Brown, you may leave the room.'

I get off the table, grinning at her, and toss her the roll of drawings. 'Here, run us one off each o' them, will you?'

'When?'

'Oh, any time as long as it's in the next ten minutes.'

A bit later I see Phoebe go out of the print room and I pop down to catch young Laisterdyke on his own.

'Here, Colin; you know that good-looking dark-haired

lass in the typists'; Ingrid Rothwell her name is?'
Laisterdyke nods. He knows them all. He's one of these
cheeky undersized kids that women seem to take to, like
they want to mother them or something. I take the note
out of my pocket. 'Will you give her this?'

He grins. 'I'll think about it.' He takes the note and
puts it in his pocket.

'You know what I mean. On the quiet like.'

'I know.'

I'm a bit uneasy about it as I leave him. Somebody else
knows about it now, and if she turns me down I'll look
more of a twerp than ever.

There's nothing doing in the way of a reply till after
lunch. Once, in the canteen, I catch Ingrid's eye and she
seems to smile for a second before she looks away. Then
about two o'clock Phoebe walks by and throws a letter
on to my board and says in a loud voice, 'A lass in the
typists' asked me to give you that.' I put my head down
and lock my fingers over my forehead. For a minute or
two I daren't look up because I'm sure everybody heard.
I wait till my cheeks stop burning then sneak a look
round and see everybody apparently minding their own
business. I pop the letter into my pocket and nip along to
the river caves where I can read it in private. I'm so
excited I'm all fingers and thumbs opening the envelope.

It's a very short letter. 'Dear Vic,' it says. 'I'm sorry
but I can't come tonight because we have a cousin of
mine staying with us for a few days, Ingrid.'

And that's that. How many times do you have to be
told? I hear somebody come in and run one of the taps so
I pull the chain before I open the cubicle door and walk
back to the office. It's like a big heavy weight inside me.
I'm like that all week, miserable as sin, going through the
motions but hardly seeing what I'm doing, even though I
know it'll all very likely catch up with me later and get
me into trouble. But I can't help it. And I know I'm a fool
but when it gets to Friday I know I'll have to ask her just
one more time. This time the chance comes like a charm.
What happens is I'm by myself in the print room when

she comes in to ask about some prints for Miller's letters.

'I don't know,' I say, rummaging about on the table. 'You'll have to ask young Colin. I don't think he's done 'em yet.'

She says all right, she'll finish the letters and come back, and she starts to go out.

'I say!'

She stops and turns round and doesn't look at me. I think she knows what's coming and she's embarrassed because she's going to say no.

'Are you er ... doing anything special tomorrow night? Have you anything fixed up?'

She says no, she doesn't think so, still keeping her eyes down.

I'm fidgeting my behind on the edge of the table trying to look casual and snapping my penknife open and shut. I wish she'd look at me so I might guess what she's thinking.

'Well, look, I was thinking ... wondering, would you like to go out with me? We could go to the flicks first, then on to a dance, if you like.'

It seems like there's about ten years between me finishing and her speaking. Then she says. 'All right,' and that's all. But it's enough. Phoebe comes in jigging her hips as if she's got all the office behind her in a conga chain and when I look round again Ingrid's gone. But she said yes! Yes, yes, yes. I seem to float off the table and I grab hold of Phoebe and do a few steps with her.

'What d'you know!' she says. 'It's come to life!'

5

I

Saturday night sees me standing with my hands shoved deep into my overcoat pockets looking in at the suits on the dummies in Montague Burton's window. I'm wondering how I'm going to pass the evening on now when a hand drops on my shoulder and Willy's voice says, 'Now then, tosh.'

I look round. 'Howdo, Willy.'

'What you doin'?' Willy says.

'I was just wonderin' where to go. Where you off to?'

'I was just plannin' on havin' an odd 'un an' then catching this new Western at the Ritz.'

'By yourself?'

'Aye. Fancy it?'

'Okay.' It doesn't matter much one way or the other what I do now the evening's spoiled. But I reckon I'll be better off with Willy than moping on my own. Not that I'll be much company, the way I'm feeling.

We walk past all the shops lit up on Cooperative Street. One of Granger's windows blazes at us across the junction and a copper on the beat stops a minute to look at a few hundred quid's worth of fur coats.

'Who's in this picture?' I say as Willy nudges me to cross over the street.

'Burt Lancaster and Kirk Douglas,' Willy says. 'In colour an' all. Should be good. I like a good Western.'

Willy likes nearly any kind of picture. He goes three and four times every week and you can hardly mention a flick he hasn't seen. Beer and the pictures are Willy's hobbies. If you can't find him in a pub you know he's at the pictures. We're crossing the road towards the lights and this jangly piano coming from the Weaver's Arms.

'Let's find a quiet 'un,' I say when Willy makes to go in.

'It's good ale here,' Willy says.

'Mebbe it is; but I don't like pub pianos.'

Willy shrugs. 'Okay, I'm easy. I think there's another round the corner.'

We set off again.

'Didn't she turn up, then?' Willy says after a few steps.

'Who?'

'This tart you were waiting for.'

'Who said I was waiting for a tart? I was just looking in Burton's window and wonderin' where to go.'

'I wa' talking to a mate o' mine on the corner for five minutes afore I came across,' Willy says. 'I saw you walkin' up an' down an' looking at your watch.'

'All right, I was waiting for a bint, then.'

'And she didn't turn up?' Willy says. 'Well, it's not the first time it's happened.'

'It's the bloody last time it'll happen with me!' I say, letting some of it come out, though it's not mad I feel at all really.

'Famous last words,' Willy says, then stops. 'They've shifted it.'

'What?'

'That pub . . . I'll swear it was here a fortnight sin' . . . Fancy me losing a pub in the middle of me own home town. I must be getting soft in the head.' He stands looking round a minute, then gets his bearings. 'I know.' He starts off again. 'C'mon.' I follow him.

'Oh, why did she do it?' I'm thinking as I catch up with Willy and get into step again. Why, why, why? Why couldn't she say no straight out instead of having me waiting twenty-five minutes with nothing at the end of it? All day I've been thinking about it. Knowing I was going to see her was like having a jewel in my pocket and every now and then I'd take it out and turn it over and gloat over it. Minutes like that I could remember just exactly what she looked like when I asked her in the print room. Shut my eyes and I could see how the light fell on her hair, and her face, and the way she wouldn't look at me (and I know why she couldn't now, the deceitful bitch . . . No, I don't mean that really, either. I'm not mad, just miserable, and I'd run to her tomorrow if she wagged her finger at me). She had a pale pink blouse on with a high neck that came up on her throat, her plump little throat that I wanted to stroke, like I'm always wanting to stroke her, soft and gentle and quiet. And now . . . why? Why should she do this to me? Where did I go wrong? That's what I want to know.

We go into this pub – I believe it's called the Cherry Tree – and get a couple of pints of bitter and take them to a table.

'Have you been out with her afore?' Willy says. 'Or is this the first and last time?'

'I've been out with her twice,' I tell him. 'Three times really, only I don't count the last time.'

'How's that?'

I see straight away I've said too much and I run my fingers up and down in the moisture on the outside of the glass before I say anything else. 'She brought a mate of hers with her.'

A big grin breaks on Willy's face. He drinks from his glass and he's still grinning when he puts it down.

'Would you believe it?' I say, putting on a show for him. 'Brought her mate!'

'You should ha' called round for me,' Willy says. 'I'd ha' taken care of her for you.'

I shake my head as I remember Dorothy. 'You wouldn't ha' liked this one, Willy. Feet little fiddle cases, mouth like a crack in a pie. You'd need a strong stomach or too much ale to make a pass at her . . . Imagine what I felt like, though, walking up an' finding two of 'em.'

'Didn't she say why she'd brought her?'

'Oh, she spun me a cock an' bull tale about this pal

turning up for her tea and she couldn't get rid of her without offending her. Course, I didn't fall for that one.'

'Doesn't look like it,' Willy says.

'How d'ye mean?'

'Well, you must've asked her again or you wouldn't ha' been stood up tonight.'

'I wanted to test her like. You know, sort of find out where I stood.'

'Well now you know,' Willy says.

'Aye, I do.' I lift my glass and have a drink. The ale's cold and refreshing, just the way I like it. I haven't enjoyed, a drink as much for a long time. Still, I'm half wishing I hadn't met Willy because the way the conversation's gone I feel a proper Sammy.

'Mebbe you were a bit hasty for her,' Willy says, watching me. 'Scared her off.'

'I never laid a finger on her.'

'Well you were too slow, then.'

'Well . . . we did a spot of neckin', y'know. But I wouldn't ha' dreamed o' trying anything else. Not with this one. She's not like that.'

'Not like what?' Willy says.

'Well . . . she's different.'

'How's she different?' Willy says. 'She's got two at the front and one in the middle, hasn't she, like all the rest?'

I don't like this kind of talk where Ingrid's concerned and I feel my face tighten. 'She's a decent bird, Willy, that's what I mean.'

'Decent enough to leave you standin' on a corner, you mean?' Willy says.

'Mebbe she got held up or summat.'

'Mebbe she dropped dead after tea or summat,' Willy says.

'Oh, belt up, Willy,' I say, and have another drink. Willy's glass is already empty.

'Okay,' Willy says; 'we won't fall out about a bird. Specially one 'at doesn't turn up. Let's have another pint.'

'No, let's beat it.' I've bought the ones we've just drunk

so I can say this without it looking as though I'm trying to skip my round. 'We might miss the start of the big picture.'

This Western's all about Wyatt Earp, the famous Marshal, and Doc Holliday and their fight with the Clanton gang at the O.K. Corral. I enjoy it, especially the last bit where they're all going at it hammer and tongs blowing the daylights out of one another. They look as though they really mean it. Real peevish, they get. Anyway, it takes me out of myself for a bit and there's times while I'm watching it when I might never have known any bint called Ingrid Rothwell. But once we're outside again in the cold it all comes back.

'We've time for a quick 'un afore they close,' Willy says. We're standing on the causeway in front of the pictures, making the people coming out down the steps walk round us. 'Naw, I don't really feel like it, Willy. I think I'll beetle off home.'

'I was thinking o' going on to the Gala Rooms after,' Willy says. 'Why don't you come on? Forget about this bint an' we'll pick some fresh talent up.'

I run my shoe along the edge of the step. 'Naw, I think I'll go an' get to bed.'

Willy looks at me. 'Gi'n you a turn, hasn't she? You must ha' been getting serious.'

'Naw, it's not that, Willy, honest. I've had a hard day at the shop, that's all. Been on me feet since nine o'clock this morning. I don't feel like ploughing round a dance-floor now.' I could have done it with Ingrid, though, on feet as light as air.

'Well, just as you like, tosh,' Willy says. 'I'll be seein' ye, then.'

'Aye, be seein' ye, Willy. Adios!'

'Boners' noses,' Willy says.

The bus I catch doesn't go up the hill and when I get off at the corner I catch the smell of fish and chips and I cross the road and go into the shop and buy a fish and four pennorth of chips. I sprinkle them with salt and vinegar and eat them out of the paper as I'm going up the hill. I really like fish and chips and there's no better way of eating them than in the open air, straight out of the pan, all piping hot. These are so hot they nearly burn my mouth and I break the batter, all goldy brown, round the fish and let it cool in the fresh air. I have to hold them away from me because I've been a bit too liberal with the vinegar and soon it starts seeping through the paper on to my fingers. They last me till I reach the gate and then I wipe my hands on the paper and screw it up into a ball and drop-kick it ten yards up the road.

It's half past ten and the Old Lady and the Old Feller are sitting with the table-lamp on watching television when I go in.

'D'you want some supper?' the Old Lady asks me.

'I've had some fish and chips.'

'You'll want a drink o' something, I suppose?'

'It's okay, don't bother; I'll make some cocoa.'

I go into the kitchen and make the cocoa and bring it back into the living-room and sit on the sofa at the back and light a fag. I'm thinking about Ingrid as I watch the picture that's on TV. I've a feeling I saw it just after the war when I was a nipper. The Old Man stretches his legs out and sucks at his pipe and the Old Lady knits away in the dim light. A picture of perfect contentment, you might say.

'Where've you been?' the Old Lady says in a minute and I know she's got one of her newsy moods on.

'Pictures.'

'By yourself?'

'With Willy Lomas.'

'Willy Lomas? I don't think I know him, do I?'

'He's a mate of mine. I used to go to school with him.'

'Grammar School?'

'No, Elementary.'

She grunts and I think, there, if I'd been out with Ingrid she'd either have got to know all about it or I'd have had to lie. And even if everything was all right with Ingrid I wouldn't want the Old Lady to know about it yet.

103

She hears wedding bells a sight too soon for my liking. She sets the pace and puts you out of your own stride.

The Old Man leans over and knocks his pipe out on the grate. 'I don't know why you pay good money to go to t'pictures when you can see 'em at home for nowt.'

'All these are old stuff.'

'What be that? They're pictures just same, aren't they?'

'You can't show colour and Cinemascope on TV.'

'Cinemascope?'

'Wide screen . . . bigger.'

He sucks at his empty pipe. 'I don't see as havin' a bigger screen makes pictures any better,' he says.

I don't bother to argue about it. The picture's finished and there's a toothpaste ad on and I get up and throw my cig-end in the fire.

'Going up?' the Old Lady says.

'Aye, I'm ready for it. Had a busy day today.'

'You haven't forgotten we're all going to our Christine's for tea tomorrow?'

'No, I haven't forgotten.'

I say good night and go upstairs. There's light in Jim's room and the door's ajar. I go into our bathroom that's like a big cold cave, all pipes and tanks and bare painted walls, and wash my face and brush my teeth as quick as I can. As I'm coming out I hear Jim give me a call and I go and stand in his doorway.

'What's up?'

He picks this pale blue envelope out of his book and flicks it down to the foot of the bed. 'Letter for you.'

I pick it up an look at it. I look at my name in this handwriting and all at once I begin to get excited.

'Where d'ye get this?'

'I found it behind the front door as I came to bed. Somebody must have pushed it in while we were watching television. There's no stamp on it.'

There's no address on it, either; just my name. I hold myself back from tearing it open there and then.

'Have me mam an' dad seen it?'

'No, I came straight upstairs.' Jim gives me a sly look. 'I wouldn't say it was a man's handwriting, would you?'

I'm grinning at him, grinning all over my face, even though I don't know what's in the letter yet. 'Thanks, lad. I'll remember you in my will for this.'

'Don't mention it,' Jim says.

'Don't you mention it, either.'

'Mum's the word.'

'That's the ticket.'

I go across the landing and shut my door behind me before I rip the envelope open and take out this one sheet of matching notepaper. 'Dear Vic,' it says, 'My cousin decided to catch a later train and I went with her to Leeds to see her off. The train was late and it was after half past seven when I got back into Cressley. I went to where we'd arranged to meet but of course you'd gone. I wondered what on earth you could be thinking of me so I thought I'd better write this letter and explain or you wouldn't be on speaking terms by Monday. I'll be at the same place tomorrow night (Sunday) if you can manage it. If you don't come by 7.15 I'll know you can't get. Hoping you can, Love, Ingrid.'

That last word jumps out and hits me in the eye. Love! *Love!* I throw the letter up in the air and do a standing jump on to the bed and bounce about like a clown on one of those trampoline things at the circus. She *hasn't* stood me up. She couldn't help it. And she sends her love. Her *love!* I jump down and feel in my back pocket and go back to Jim's room. 'You know that speedometer for your bike 'at you're saving up for?' I throw a couple of half-crowns on to the bed. 'There's five bob towards it.'

I'm back across the landing again before I think that one half-crown would have been enough. Then I think, Oh, what the hell! What's money anyway? Good old Jim. Good old me. Good old everybody, and lovely, lovely Ingrid. Oh, what a lovely tart she is: what a luscious, lovable bint!

II

Sunday afternoon, then, we all troop across town – the Old Feller, the Old Lady, Jim, and me – to Chris's new place up a little avenue off Dewsbury Road. It's high up, like our house, and they've got a view as good as ours only with it being an upstairs flat they can see it from the living-room and ours only shows from the bedrooms. Chris and David have only got back from their honeymoon yesterday and there's kisses and hugs all round when she opens the door for us. And then we're all invited to look at the furnishings in the flat that Chris hasn't let any of us see before because she wanted to keep it all as a surprise for when they were actually living in it. Well it looks real smart and I wouldn't mind a place like it myself. It's done out in contemporary style with light-coloured furniture with splayed legs that you catch with your feet if you're not careful and a kind of mauve fitted carpet and two different pattern papers on the walls. They haven't got a three-piece suite like ours at home but a couple of easy-chairs and a studio couch that makes up into a bed if they want to put anybody up for the night. The Old Lady looks round at it all, taking all in, and says, 'Yes, very nice, love, very nice,' in a tone of voice that says straight out it is very nice if you like that sort of thing but it isn't her cup of cocoa by any means.

David and the Old Man get together at the window and look out. 'That's what I call a real West Riding view,' the Old Feller says. 'A bit of everything.'

'Better than the view from my old digs,' David says. 'A coal-dealer's yard, half a dozen rows of terraced houses, and the biggest Nonconformist chapel I've ever seen.'

'Have you never been to Cleckheaton?' the Old Man says, his face never slipping. 'You want to get our Chris to take you sometime. A lovely spot. They've got biggest Methodist chapel there 'at I've ever seen. An' another nearly as big on t'other side o' t'road.'

'Ghastly places,' David says.

'Ho'd on, lad,' the Old Man says. 'They were built to the

glory of God, young feller. Just imagine the spirit 'at went into putting 'em up.'

'Oh, yes, agreed,' David says. 'It's pity that they're mostly white elephants today. It's the architecture I'm referring to. Why must almost all the big building in the West Riding be either Greek or Italian? Every other one you see looks like the Parthenon covered in soot.'

'Because we believe in having t'best there is,' the Old Feller says.

'But is there no typically Yorkshire architecture?'

'Aye, Collinson's mill,' the Old Man says, grinning. He points. 'That one wi' t'biggest chimney o' t'lot.'

David smiles. 'Well, I must admit that the West Riding isn't as bad as it's painted. I've been pleasantly surprised since living here.'

'It's not everybody's cup o' tea,' the Old Man admits. 'Some fowk like summat a bit ... well, *softer*, if you know what I mean ...'

They get on talking about various parts of the country because the Old Man fancies himself as having knocked about a bit, and every now and again he has to admit that other places might have something. I get up and wander over to the bookcase by the fireplace. There's a chinking of pots from the little kitchen and every now and then either Chris or the Old Lady will march through with something else to put on the folding-leaf table they've got opened out in the middle of the floor. David's chief subject is English Lit. and there's a lot of Shakespeare and dull classics stuff on the shelves. I'm just browsing there, passing time on till the tea's ready, and this fat book with a green back takes my eye. I pick it out and notice one thing on the spine, what I took to be a snake, is a bow like they used in ancient times. I look at the title, *Ulysses*, and the name of the author, James Joyce, and they don't mean a thing to me; but seeing as I've got the book out I open it and leaf a few pages over. The next minute I've dropped on a bit near the end that nearly makes my hair stand up. As far as I can make out it's a bint in bed or somewhere thinking about all the times she's had with blokes. It knocks me sideways, it really does. I mean, I've seen these things what sometimes get passed on from hand to hand on mucky bits of typing paper – you know, all about the vacuum cleaner salesman who goes to a house and finds a bint in on her own – but I've never seen anything like this actually *printed*. Well, I'm racing through it, catching up on my education fast (it's the sort of stuff you race through because it's her thoughts, see, just as they come – and nothing left out, believe you me – and there's no commas or full stops or anything and all the sentences run into one another just the way they do when you're thinking yourself, I suppose). Anyway, I'm standing there taking all this in – or at least, all the spicy bits – when David comes over and asks me if I've found anything interesting.

I'm a bit embarrassed, though I don't know why because it's his book, not mine, and I say with a little laugh, 'This is a bit hot, isn't it? I didn't know they let 'em print stuff like this.'

'It went through several courts before free publication was sanctioned,' David says.

'I'll bet . . .' and I'm thinking, well, fancy old David reading stuff like this, and leaving it around for Chris to see an' all. 'Is it supposed to be good or something?'

'It's a masterpiece,' David says. 'There's no other word for it. It's one of the most significant books in the language.'

I'm thinking I'd like to have a go at it when I'm on my own and I say, 'You'll have to lend it to me sometime.'

'I'm afraid you'd find it very dull,' David says. 'It's not an easy book to read. There's so much below the surface that it takes several readings before you begin to grasp it . . . Anyway, I shouldn't want your mother, for instance, to pick it up and open it where you did. She mightn't understand.'

'You bet your boots she wouldn't. What does Chris think to it?'

'She hasn't read it. She knows what it's about, and its

reputation, and she says she doesn't feel obliged to go any further.'

He takes another book out. 'What about this?' I look at the title. 'Oh, Raymond Chandler. Yes, I've read this one. I've read three or four of his: all they've got in the library.'

'You like to read?'

'Oh, yes; I'm reading all the time. Beats television into a cocked hat, reading does.'

'What kind of books do you read?'

'Oh, thrillers, war stories, that sort of thing. You know ... Why don't you write a book, David? A war book, I mean. You've had plenty of adventures, haven't you?'

'Too many...' He puts the Chandler back on the shelf. 'I did start one once, a book about my experiences in the prison camp ... But there have been so many it didn't seem much use.' He pulls another book out and hands it to me. 'Now if I could write a war story as good as that one it wouldn't matter how many there had been before.'

It's called *For Whom the Bell Tolls*. 'I've seen a picture of this,' I tell him as it comes to mind. 'It's a fairly old one but they re-issued it a while back. Gary Cooper and Ingrid Bergman were in it ... It was good.'

Ingrid ... Ingrid ... I'm hardly listening when David says to take the book with me and see how I like it.

A bit later I nip into the kitchen for a word with Chris while the Old Lady's out for a minute. 'I say, Chris, you won't mind if I beetle off about half-six, will you?'

She's slicing hard-boiled eggs for the salad. 'I shall be mortally offended,' she says. 'Invited for the first time to my new home and you can't get away soon enough. Is it something important?'

'Top priority. I wouldn't have gone out tonight only there was a bit of a mix-up and now I really have to.'

'What's her name?' Chris says.

'Oh, you don't know her.'

'I shall know her a bit better if you tell me what they call her. You do know, I suppose?'

'Course I do. They call her Ingrid Rothwell. You'll not

say anything to me mother about it, will you? You know how she is. I mean, well, I'll tell her myself sometime, if . . . you know.'

Chris smiles, one of them lovely little smiles she has that make you feel everything's all right with the world and everything. 'I know,' she says.

The Old Lady bustles in licking butter off her fingers and wiping them down this apron of Chris's that she would put on. 'C'mon,' she says to me; 'out of it. Can't do wi' men cluttering the place up, hindering the job . . . How're we doing?' she says to Chris. 'I think we're nearly ready aren't we?'

'If you wouldn't mind mashing the tea.'

'Right you are, love.'

A few minutes later we're all sitting round the table and Chris starts talking about some of the things they saw on their honeymoon and this gets the Old Man started on London. It's one of the things about the Old Feller that niggles you a bit the way he thinks he's an expert on London because he was there a bit in the Great War and he's been two or three times since to brass band contests or Rugby League Cup Finals. It doesn't put him off a bit that he's sitting next to David who was born in the place. In a bit he gets so much at sea that even Chris has to pull him up.

'But the place you're talking about isn't even in Leicester Square, Dad,' she says.

'It wa' t'last time I wa' there,' the Old Feller says. 'Are you tryin' to tell me I don't know London?'

'He'd tell Joe Davis how to play billiards,' I say and the Old Man says, 'You keep a still tongue in your head, young feller,' and lifts his first finger up to lay the law down. 'I'm tellin' you 'at when Ezra Dykes an' me were down for t'*Daily Herald* Brass Band Contest in 1949 . . . No, wait a minute . . . war it '51? . . .' He turns to the Old Lady. 'You remember that year. War it '49 or '51?'

'I don't know owt about it,' the Old Lady says, poker-faced, 'You'd better shut up an' get your tea.'

And David, who's sided with nobody, looks up at this and gives me a quiet wink.

At twenty-five past six I go into the bathroom and have a wash, then while the Old Lady's busy in the kitchen helping Chris with the washing-up I get my coat and nip out down the stairs.

She is waiting for me on the corner by Barclays Bank. She's got a blue coat on that fits to her figure, with a big fur collar and no hat. Her shoes have the highest heels I've ever seen her in. I see her before she sees me and it's like half of me's over there with her before I start to cross the road.

'Hello.'

'Hello. You got my letter, then?'

'Yes, I got it.'

I'm holding her hands with gloves on and looking at her while she babbles on all about why she was so late last night. Now I know it wasn't deliberate I'm not interested, but she will go on, giving me every little detail.

'What was his name?' I say, breaking into it.

'Who?'

'This porter you got to help you with the case.'

'How should I know?' she says, and then she sees I'm taking the mickey and she says, 'Yes, I do go on, don't I? And it doesn't really matter, does it?'

'Not a bit.'

'I don't know what you must have thought of me, though.'

'Forget it. It's okay now.'

'What did you do?' she says. 'Did it waste your evening? Did you wait long?'

I tell her I went to the pictures with a pal and ask her how she came to think of writing the note. Because this is the real good bit about it all. She meant to come all right, and that's something; but to think of writing the note when she was late, that meant she cared about it and couldn't just let things slide. She had to *do* something.

'It just came to me,' she says. 'I thought if I let you know straight away you'd realize I couldn't help it. If I'd waited till Monday it would have had all week-end to pile up in – you know what I mean? – and it would have taken a lot more putting right then. I was afraid you might think I'd done it on purpose you see.'

'But how did you know where I live?' There's another thing: she must have been interested before to have known that.

She gives a little smile, not looking at me. 'Oh, I knew,' she says. 'P'raps I know more about you than you think.'

I feel like singing and shouting right there in the street. Oh, she's a peach. She really is.

III

'Well, where shall we go, then? Pictures?'

'I'd rather just walk and talk,' she says, and this suits me fine. It's what I wanted last Sunday when that Dorothy came and put her big feet in it. By, but when I think how near she got to busting everything up . . . What I'd have missed – all this, being here with her now and knowing she's definitely interested in me, like I am in her. But maybe it's all for the better that we have had some trouble because it's made Ingrid come right out and let me know she's interested. We've kind of gone back a couple of strides and advanced a dozen. I reckon we really owe Dorothy a vote of thanks.

'Did you have any trouble meeting me tonight?'

'Well, I really shouldn't have come,' I tell her, and think that man-eating lions on the streets wouldn't have kept me away. 'We've all been to tea at my sister's new flat. She just got back from her honeymoon yesterday.'

'Oh, yes, Christine. You told me about the wedding.'

So I did, nearly a fortnight ago. And look how much has happened since then! I got to know Ingrid, then thought I'd lost her, and now I've found her all over again. And I still can hardly believe she's here with me now, and not at my invitation, but her own! I take hold of her hand and pull her arm up through mine and she turns her head and looks at me and smiles; and at the same time I get this gorgeous whiff of the scent she's wearing.

'I like your perfume. What is it?'

She giggles. 'Its called *Desire*.'

'Living dangerously, aren't you, wearing stuff like that?' I think of the sort of joke somebody like Jimmy Slade might make – a chastity belt given free with every bottle – and grin to myself.

'It's quite expensive, as a matter of fact,' she says. 'I only wear it on special occasions. It's not for everyday use.'

'I don't know whether to be flattered or not.'

'Why?'

'I don't know whether it means you trust me to behave or trust me not to.'

She giggles again. 'Now, now. Keep the party clean.'

We get to talking about our families because we don't really know much about each other, and I find out that Ingrid's dad's a site engineer for a big constructional firm out Manchester way and his work takes him all over the country and sometimes abroad. 'He's really hardly ever at home,' Ingrid says. 'Mother says it's like being married to a sailor.' (I notice the way she says 'mother' and not 'my mother' or 'me mam', and this puts her family a notch above mine straight away.) 'Then again she says it has its advantages. You never have a chance to get fed-up with a husband who's only at home occasionally. They're like a proper couple of love-birds when he does turn up. You'd think they'd been married a month instead of twenty years ... Of course, it'll be different when she hasn't got me for company. It'll be a bit lonely for her then.'

'Are you thinking of leaving home, then?'

'Well, I suppose I shall one day, when I get married, I mean.'

'How old are you, Ingrid?' I've guessed but I'm not sure.

'I was eighteen just before Christmas.' I'd have given her another year. 'You're only a kid,' I say to tease her a bit. 'You won't be leaving your mother for a while.'

'Well you've got to think about the future, haven't

113

you? Many a girl's married and started a family at eighteen. Anyway, how old are you, Father Time, if it isn't too personal a question?'

'Twenty.'

'I couldn't really tell. It was the grey beard that put me off.'

I laugh. 'Okay, okay.' And inside I'm singing and shouting again. It's all right, we're getting along grand.

'And what sort o'chap are you goinna marry? Somebody like your dad who's away all the time?'

'No fear. I want a husband who's with me all the time, and I'll risk getting fed-up with him.'

Just the way I want it: living and loving and laughing together, every day. It must be wonderful if you can hit it right. 'You'll have to wait an' see about that till he turns up. He might turn out to be a sailor or something and that'll be worse than ever.'

'How d'you know he hasn't turned up already?' she says, and I give her a quick look, wondering what to make of this.

'Well what are you doing out with me, then?'

'Making him jealous,' she says.

'I see. Is he a big bloke?'

'Oh, I wouldn't say that. He's quite well-built, though.'

'Handy with his fists?'

'I don't know. I should think he can take care of himself.'

'Hmm.' I pretend to raise my hat and turn back the way we've come. 'Well, good night.'

She laughs. 'Come on, I'll take care of you.'

We've walked up this residential avenue that branches off the main road that runs out to Greenford past Cressley Moor and now we can see the big gates of Ravensnook Park with all the fancy ironwork and shields, and a little side gate standing open, Ingrid suggests we walk through that way and we go in past the lodge which is in darkness and on to one of the wide tarmac avenues where there's empty flower-beds on each side and big trees.

114

'What *did* you think when I didn't turn up last night?' she says after a bit.

'I didn't know what to think, really.'

'I suppose it did occur to you that I might have got held up somewhere?'

'It did cross me mind.'

'You didn't really think I'd made the date and then deliberately not turned up, did you?'

'It has been known, y'know.'

'Well you don't know me very well if you think I could do a thing like that,' she says, and it seems to me there's a touch of frost in her voice now.

'Well I don't know you very well, do I? We've only been out together three times. Only twice with just the two of us. When you turned up with that Dorothy the other night I –'

'I *didn't* want her to come, you know. Only she often pops over on Sunday afternoons and stays to tea. I wasn't expecting her last week and when she came I didn't have a chance to explain to her till we were out of the house and then I couldn't get rid of her without offending her. She's like that, y'know. She got it into her head that she was coming to have a look at you and that was that. She said she'd only stop five minutes and then go.'

Well that clears that up. Now it's just like we're beginning again, only the funny thing is that Dorothy's got us off to a flying start this time. I'll bet she'd be mad if she knew!

'You know what happened after that,' Ingrid says.

I do. Not half. Is she ticking me off just a little bit? I wonder. Maybe she is, and she's probably right, because the mood I'm in now I can even think about Dorothy without wanting to puke.

'I didn't mean to open up on her like that, you know; only I couldn't stand all them insinuations of hers. Not after the two dates we'd had. And when all that happened and you didn't turn up last night, well, I just thought we'd had it. I thought you didn't want to see me any more and you didn't like telling me to me face.'

'And it wasn't that way at all!' she says. 'Doesn't it just show how misunderstandings can come about? It's a good job I did think of writing that note or I don't know what might have happened.'

'I can tell you what would have happened,' I say. 'I shouldn't have bothered you again.'

The bandstand, a big one shaped like a fancy cake, looms up out of the dark. I say, 'Let's sit down,' and steer Ingrid round a corner that's a mass of rhododendron blossom in early summer on to a sidepath where I know there's a seat.

'Would it have bothered you if I hadn't asked you out again?' I say and it seems like a kind of shyness comes over her because all she says is, 'What do you think?' I say nothing to this but I show her by lifting my arm and putting it round her shoulders. She moves a bit nearer to me on the seat and I think how funny it is what can make the difference between you jogging along from day to day and thinking that life's absolutely wonderful.

'What on earth's that you've got in your pocket?' she says.

I take my arm away and sit up straight again. 'A book.'

'It feels like a brick.'

I take the book out of my pocket and hold it in my hands. 'It's *For Whom the Bell Tolls*. Have you read it?'

Good heavens, no, she says, she can't read books. She gets three magazines a week and can hardly get through them for watching telly. 'Telly.' I don't like that word somehow. It always reminds me of fat ignorant pigs of people swilling stout and cackling like hens at the sort of jokes they put on them coloured seaside postcards; all about fat bellies and chamber pots and that sort of thing. You know. So I just go on holding the book and say nothing. There's something just in the *feel* of a book, I always think; something solid that's here to stay. Not like television, switched on and off like a tap. I think it's a pity she doesn't read because it means we shan't ever be able to talk about the books we've both read and recommend them to one another.

'They made a picture of it,' I tell her, for something to say. 'Gary Cooper and Ingrid Bergman.'

'My namesake.'

'Eh?'

'Ingrid Bergman. That's who I'm called after. Mother was mad on her at one time. Her and Leslie Howard. If I'd been a boy I'd probably have been called Leslie.'

'I thought it was a queer name for an English girl,' I say. 'I was going to ask you about it.'

'I don't think it's queer. I like it.'

'I don't mean queer that way. I mean unusual.'

'Would you rather I was called Mary or Barbara, or something like that?'

'Dorothy,' I say. 'That's a name I've always liked.'

She digs me in the side. 'Go on with you!'

I laugh and put the book away in the other pocket. 'I like you just the way you are,' I tell her.

There's a little silence before she says, 'Do you, Vic? Honest?'

I'd like to tell her I love her, I'm mad about her, but I can't do it in cold blood like, so I make do for the time being by saying, 'I wouldn't have run after you like I have otherwise, would I?'

'No, I suppose not.'

I slide my arm round her again and she comes over till her hair's on my face. I turn my face and brush my mouth across her cheek and a second later I'm covering her face with little short kisses, planting them all over, on her forehead, her cheeks, her eyes, her nose, and then on her mouth. I kiss her the same way on the mouth, as though one long kiss isn't good enough and I've got to go on kissing and breaking away and kissing again; and all the time I'm whispering her name to her over and over again.

And then, in a bit, we ease up and break away for a breather.

'Phew!' she says with a little laugh.

'It's rotten being a girl sometimes,' she says after a bit. 'Suppose you'd never asked me again after last Sunday.

117

It might have been ages before I could make you see I still wanted to go out with you.'

'That Dorothy. She nearly gummed up the works.'

'She wouldn't have minded, y'know. She's a bit of a cat, really, even if she is a friend of mine. She's jealous, y'know, because I'm going out with you. That's her trouble: she's jealous.'

'Why doesn't she find a chap for herself?' I say, easy because I've got Ingrid and anybody can have Dorothy that fancies her.

'She reckons she doesn't like men. She pretends she's above that sort of thing.'

'Don't any of 'em ever ask her out?'

'I don't think so.'

'Hard lines.'

'Well, she's not attractive, is she? I mean, let's be honest, you didn't find her attractive, did you?'

'I find you attractive,' I say thinking it's time we were making contact again. We kiss again, a real long slow one this time that melts me to the soles of my boots till I think I might pass out from the way I feel about her. When we break off this time we keep our faces together and I run my fingers ever so gently across her forehead and down her cheek and then we kiss again, and all at once she begins to do exciting things with her tongue and I'm holding her and holding her because I can't hold her close enough. And my mind's working away now because as I see it the way she's kissing me now she's as good as giving me the green light to go a bit further and I wonder if I'm right because I'll blow my brains out and no mistake if I balls it all up by offending her after all this. We kiss again and again she starts these wonderful tricks with her tongue and I think well that's it all right and no mistake and she will think me a Sammy if I don't do something now. I slip my hand into her coat and she twists a bit on the seat to make it easier for me. In a minute I'm inside her blouse but then I'm scuppered by all the harness and whatnot she's got on underneath. She says something and pulls away a bit and puts her own hand up to her shoulder. Then she comes back and whispers 'All right,' and my hand's in there again and I'm feeling the soft firm weight and the tip coming up hard under my thumb, and my guts are melting with tenderness for her. 'God,' I'm saying to her. 'God, I'm crazy about you, Ingrid,' and her fingers are up in my hair at the back and she's curling and twisting them and saying, 'Vic, oh, Vic,' over and over again, and all I can think of is this is what I was born for, this is what I've been waiting for as long as I can remember. And that's not all, because later, when my hand moves somewhere else, it's as though she's feeling just the same way as me, as though it's what she's been waiting for, because she quivers at my touch and sighs and then rests back in my arm and makes little noises in her throat as I love her like I never thought was possible except in imagination.

It's not till after that she seems to wonder and then she says in a little whisper as she leans against my shoulder, 'Vic . . . You don't think I'm common, do you?'

'Why?'

'Because of . . . of just now?'

'You haven't to think that,' I tell her. 'Don't think it.' And then I'm covering her face with them little kisses again, covering every square inch because I want her to see I'm thanking her as well as loving her and that after tonight I love her more than ever.

It's late when I get in and the Old Lady's waiting up for me, standing with her back to the fire and winding the alarm clock for morning. The Old Man's gone to bed apparently.

'You're a fine one,' the Old Lady says as I'm blinking in the light.

'How's that?'

'Getting invited out to yer tea and then slippin' off like that. I don't know what David thought, I'm sure.'

'Did he say owt?'

'He's too well-mannered for that. You could take a lesson or two from him on how to behave yourself.'

'I told Chris, y'know. She said it was okay.'

'Oh, our Christine 'ull stick up for you: she allus did. An' anyway, what else could she say? She couldn't keep you there if you said you were going out.'

I sit down in the easy chair and unlace my shoes. I know my face is a bit hot and red but my mouth's set because I'm not going to let anything spoil tonight.

'You should be ashamed of yourself,' the Old Lady says.

'Look,' I say, 'I was invited to tea at me own sister's, not Buckingham Palace. To tea. It didn't mean I'd to stay till supper-time.'

The Old Lady picks her cup off the fireplace and drinks the last of the tea in it. 'When you're invited to tea,' she says, nagging on, 'you don't just slope off the minute you leave the table.'

'You're exaggerating, as usual. Anyway, I explained it to Chris and she said it was all right.'

'Explained what? I don't even know where you've been that was so important.'

I get up and turn my back to her as I hunt for my slippers behind the chair. 'I had a date.'

'With a lass?'

'Yes.'

'But you knew a fortnight ago you'd be goin' to our Christine's today.'

'I was supposed to meet her last night but there was a bit of a mix-up and we had to put if off till tonight.'

'I thought you said you were out with a mate of yours last night?'

'I was. I told you, there was a mix-up.'

'It's all mixed up to me,' she says. 'Hole-in-the-corner work.'

I'm getting wild because she's doing it. She's turning it all wrong. I can nearly hear her if she knew what happened in the park tonight, the way she'd turn it into something shabby and dirty, when it wasn't like that at all. I put my slippers on and keep my face down, but I know she's still watching me.

120

'Do I know this lass?'

'No.'

She says nothing else for a minute, then she says in a funny tight little voice, 'Well, I reckon you'll tell me what you want me to know about her in your own good time.'

'What's for supper?'

'There's a long-bun in the bread-bowl and you can make yourself a cup o' cocoa. I'm going to bed.'

'Have we plenty of milk?'

'We're not without.'

'I'll have a glass of milk, then.'

'Leave enough for your father an' me for breakfast, that's all.' She moves towards the door, carrying the alarm clock that's ticking away like billy-ho in the quiet. 'Don't be too long as you come up, and don't leave any lights on.'

I go into the kitchen and find the long-bun and slice it in two and spread it thick with best butter. I'm wondering why the Old Lady didn't press a bit further about Ingrid; and then I come to the conclusion that she was pleased enough at the bottom of her to hear I've been out with a lass.

I take the long-bun and the milk and go and sit down in front of the fire. The trouble is that underneath it all *I* think it's shabby and dirty as well, because it's something nobody talks about, something you put up with because it's necessary to make the world go on, and people who enjoy it are in the same class as drunkards and gamblers. And I can't help thinking this even though I know it isn't like that at all; not with Chris and David, surely, and not with Ingrid and me.

6

I

Next morning Hassop's back, I think sooner than we expected and I'm dead sure sooner than we hoped.

'I thought we might have another quiet week,' Jimmy says as the boss goes into his office and shuts the door behind him. 'Didn't his sister give you any idea?'

'It must have been in the envelope.' I say with a grin. What do I care if Hassop *is* back? I'm happy, that's the thing. Old Hassop isn't so bad. He does his job in his own way and if he does turn nasty once in a while, well, that's a boss's privilege. He's got his trouble . . . That sister . . . If I had to live with a weird old bird like that maybe I'd be a bit bloody-minded at times. But, like I say, I'm happy. I haven't actually spoken to Ingrid this morning but just to see her legs twinkling away in front in the mist was enough to bring last night back with a rush and make me think what a lucky, lucky dog I am. I feel like liking people. I can even see good points in the brussen bastard Conroy. Well, till dinner-time I can, anyway . . .

What happens then is that there's half a dozen of us hanging about round the plan files near the door, having a natter before the bell goes. Somebody's just saying Conroy's name when the door bursts open and in marches Conroy himself. He stops. 'Who's talking about me?' he says. 'Who mentioned my name?'

Well it wasn't me, as it happens, but this sharp answer's on the tip of my tongue without me hardly thinking and it's too good to hold back.

'I did,' I say. 'I was just saying I'd bought a pig and I didn't know what to call it.'

Somebody behind me cracks out laughing and there's grins on all the faces I can see except Conroy's. He just stares for a second, going all stiff with rage. 'Wha ... you cheeky young bleeder ...' And he comes for me with his arms punching out to either side, pushing lads away to clear a path to me. I stand my ground. I didn't want to pick a quarrel, not today when I'm feeling so good, but I reckon it had to come sooner or later. My heart's thumping because I reckon I'm in for a hiding; but I'm not going to let everybody see me back down.

I know the only way to save myself is to get in close, so I dodge the first punch that Conroy swings at my head and duck and throw myself forward under his fists and grab hold of him round the middle. I see the lino coming up to meet as I go down, taking Conroy with me. We roll about on the floor, bashing against plan files. I catch my ear on one of the drawer handles and nearly shout with the pain, and all the time I'm getting these short jabs on the side of the head as Conroy punches away and pushes and pulls at the same time, struggling to get free so's he can really let me have it. Well, I'm soon nearly weeping, the punishment I'm taking and I'm scared I might show it any time. I pull away and twist my head to try to get it out of the way and I see Conroy's fat leg right in front of my face with the trousers pulled tight across it. I don't stop to think whether it's fair fighting or not; I just dip my face and bite as hard as I can.

That does it, all right. Conroy lets out a yell and rears up and breaks away. He shuffles off on his knees holding on to his crotch with both hands. 'Oh, me cods,' he says. 'Oh, Christ, me cods.'

Well, everybody's laughing fit to bust, bar me. I'm watching Conroy and wondering if I've done any damage, because that wasn't where I intended to bite him at all, only he must have moved.

The door opens and in comes Hassop. He stops when he sees Conroy, still on his knees, holding his cods and moaning to himself. I'm just getting up and everybody else is doubled up laughing. Well, they all knock off laughing pronto when they see Hassop and he looks down at Conroy who's kneeling right under him now, like he's begging from him.

'What's going on here?' he says, and Conroy looks up then looks away again without saying anything. 'Have you been fighting, Brown?' he says to me.

'Just acting the fool a bit, Mr Hassop,' I say. I'm brushing my suit down with the flat of my hand and watching him, his face gone white, standing there as though he's trying to think up the best way to bawl us out. But he doesn't. He just twitches for a minute, then says, 'Well, this is neither the time nor the place. Get to your work, all of you, and let's have no more of it.'

He walks away to his own office and Conroy picks himself up and goes to his board where he pulls himself up on to his buffet and sits with his head in his hands. I watch him for a minute then go round to him. 'Are you okay, Conroy?' I say, and Conroy says, 'Bugger off,' without looking up. So I go back to my board and get on with my work. But I can't help looking over at him now and again because I'm a bit worried, wondering if I've really hurt him. My right ear tingles all afternoon.

Well if we were thinking it was done with we were wrong, because next morning Hassop stops by Conroy's board and says, 'Mr. Althorpe wants to see you in his office, Conroy. You, too, Brown.'

Conroy lifts his big head up and stares Hassop out before getting off his buffet and making for the door, with me following him. 'You know what this is, don't you?' he says when we're out in the corridor. 'Our pal Hassop's been telling tales again. He hasn't the bloody guts to bawl us out himself so he gets Althorpe to do his dirty work.'

'What are we going to say?' I ask him, wondering if we can concoct a decent tale before we go in.

'Don't worry, mate,' Conroy says. 'If I know Althorpe we shan't get a word in edgeways.'

We stop outside this big heavy varnished door with 'Chief Engineer' painted on it in gold letters. 'Step through here,' Conroy says, 'and you're in the presence of two thousand a year . . . Here goes.' He raps with his knuckles and sticks his ear against the door. A typist trots by and gives us the once-over. I wink at her though I never felt less like winking at anybody. I hear a voice shout in the office and Conroy turns the knob and we go in.

Mr Althorpe is a big chap with smooth silvery hair that shines in the light coming through the big window behind his desk. He finishes the letter he's dictating and then tells the typist to scram and she picks her notebook and pencil up and pads out across the carpet through a connecting door. Mr Althorpe takes a cig out of the packet of twenty Players lying on the blotter and lights up. It's only eleven o'clock but the desk ashtray's nearly full of dog-ends and matchsticks already. He waves us nearer and takes his heavy glasses off and puts them on the desk and gives us a real keen look which he holds till I feel the last of my confidence vanish.

'Now then, you two,' he says. 'I hear you've been indulging in a bit of horse-play in the office. Rolling about on the floor and clouting one another.'

I wonder if he expects us to say something, but I wait for Conroy and he keeps mum and so I look out of the window behind Mr Althorpe and watch a bright yellow fork-lift truck, unloaded, the forks sticking out like a circus clown's big feet, come down the yard.

'Well I'm not having it, see?' Mr Althorpe says all at once, and he brings his hand flat down on the top of his desk, making me jump a foot off the carpet. 'If you've got differences and want to settle 'em that way, do it outside. I'm not standing for it in the office. You come here to work and get the job done. That's what you're paid for and if you don't like the arrangement you can take your hook somewhere else. I won't have the office turned into a monkey house. If I'd carried on like that when I was a lad I'd have been out in the street without any warning.

But we valued our jobs in those days; they were harder to come by.'

I'm looking at Mr Althorpe's tie now which is a neatly knotted blue with little white spots. I wonder if I'll ever sit behind a big desk with two thousand a year and tell a couple of bods off for scrapping in the office. I think after that this was one of the times when I knew I didn't really care one way or the other for the job.

'You're old enough to know better,' Althorpe's saying to Conroy. 'You shouldn't have to be told these things; and it's up to you older chaps to set a good example for lads like Brown here. I've no complaints about your work, Conroy. You've got a good engineering brain and we've always had high hopes of your ability. It's time you grew up.'

He swivels his eyes to me and pins me like a butterfly on a board. 'I'm not so sure about you, Brown,' he says. 'Mr Hassop hasn't been altogether satisfied with your work lately. You seemed a promising lad when you first came to us, but you haven't shown much sign of it recently. What's up, are you busy thinking about some lass when you should be watching what you're putting on your drawings!'

I blush and open my mouth, thinking he wants an answer. Then I shut it again when he carries straight on talking.

'Just get your ideas straight and look to your work if you want to stay with us.' He picks his glasses up again and puts them on. 'I don't know what you were scrapping about and I don't want to know. But don't let me hear any more of it.'

He looks down at his papers and I know he's finished. I'm just thinking it hasn't been too bad and let's get out of here when old Conroy, who hasn't said a dicky bird so far, says something that makes my spine go cold, and Mr Althorpe takes his glasses off again.

'What was that?' he says.

'I said I don't know what all the fuss is about,' Conroy says. 'A bit of alecking about in the office. I don't see why it couldn't have been dealt with in the office for what it was worth.'

Now this is as good as saying Hassop's a tale-telling bastard and I watch Mr Althorpe's face go pink and his eyes stare as he throws his specs down and stands up to lean forward on his hands.

'Are you telling me how to deal with my staff, Conroy?' he says. And then he begins again and says all he's already said and more besides only this time he decorates it with words that make me look away and wish a hole would open up in the floor, I'm so embarrassed. It sounds to me nearly as bad as if the Old Feller had come out with a mouthful. Maybe he thinks it's the only kind of language we understand but I reckon a man in Mr Althorpe's position shouldn't use language like that and I know I'll never have the same respect for him again. Once I sneak a sideways look at Conroy and see him standing there, his mouth set, and not knuckling under at all to what Althorpe's saying.

'Now clear out,' Althorpe says; 'both of you.' And he drops back into his chair and reaches out for his glasses again.

Conroy's doing some swearing himself when we get out into the corridor. He's nearly climbing the walls, he's so mad. As for me, I'm trembling all over and my heart's bumping away. 'Christ' I say, 'I could have dropped through the floor when he started effing and blinding it.'

'He knows all the words, doesn't he?' Conroy says. 'One thing about him, he has the guts to use 'em and speak his mind.'

'You know, I reckon this is all my fault for cracking at you the way I did.'

'Hassop's fault, more like. I'd like to smash his yellow teeth in, the snivelling little sneak.'

I'm looking at Conroy and I'm nearly liking him, and I'd never have thought that. I know I'll always remember how he stood up to Althorpe, anyway.

'I'm sorry I bit you, Conroy,' I tell him; 'only, you were giving me a real leathering.'

'Oh, forget it,' he growls. 'I thought for a minute you'd blighted me efficiency. Anyway, I reckon we're even now. I got your back up before that with what I said about that bird . . . You won't be seeing much more of me around this place, I can tell you. I've had my bellyful of this shower. Be damned if I'll stick here and be talked to like a labourer off the shop floor.'

He hits the office door with the flat of his hand and barges in. The door swings back on the spring and I have to put my arm up quick to stop it hitting me in the face. Conroy walks straight up the aisle till he gets to Whymper, a little middle-aged draughtsman, and a wage-slave if ever there was one.

'Where's that *Manchester Guardian* of yours?' he says in a voice everybody can hear.

'You can look at it at lunch-time, by all means,' Whymper says, giving a startled look up at Conroy standing over him glowering.

'Bugger that,' Conroy says. 'I want it now.'

Whymper shrugs. 'If you insist.' He opens a drawer on his left and looks away and carries on with his work.

Half the ofice is watching when Conroy takes the paper back to his own board and spreads it out and starts turning the pages just as if he's in the reading room at the public library. When he gets to the situations vacant pages he stands there reading and running his finger down the columns.

In a minute or two Hassop cottons on that something's up and he comes out and soft-foots it down the office to Conroy, who takes not one bit of notice of him at all. 'Do you have to read the paper during office hours, Conroy?' he says, sarcy as can be; and Conroy goes on reading as though he doesn't know he's there. 'I'm talking to you, Conroy,' Hassop says, getting his rag out a bit.

Conroy turns his head and looks at Hassop. 'I'm looking for a job,' he says. 'And if I don't find anything in here I'll look in the *Yorkshire Post* an' all.' He starts warming up. 'I've had enough of this bloody lot, Hassop, and I'm getting out. I'm not one of your frightened little time-servers cowering over his board every time he hears the boss's voice. I'm a lad 'at knows a thing or two and I'm taking me talents elsewhere. I shan't have to look long, either; there's plenty of firms crying out for blokes who can think jobs out on their own. And they're paying more brass than this bloody sweat-shop an' all!'

Well, this is telling him, and no mistake, and everybody's straining so's they don't miss a word and waiting to see what'll happen. That Conroy, I'm thinking, he's a buggeroo if ever there was one. There's no stopping him when he gets his dander up. Old Hassop's face is as white as lard and his mouth is twitching away like it always does when he's worked up. 'You'll be applying for a new job sooner than you think, Conroy, if you carry on like this.'

'You sack me if you want to,' Conroy says. 'You'll be doing me a favour.'

A vein comes out on Hassop's forehead and just for a couple of seconds we're all waiting to hear him tell Conroy to get his cards. But we ought to know he hasn't the guts to do a thing like that in front of the whole office. He stands there, and he stands there a minute too long. Then he says in a strangled voice, 'You've had your warning, Conroy. You'd better watch out.' And he turns and walks away to his own office.

Conroy watches him till the door shuts behind him, then he goes back to his reading, licking his finger-end to make turning the pages easier.

II

One night when I get home the Old Man's upstairs practising. He's quite a lad with the trombone, the Old Feller, and I mean that. He's had offers from some tip-top bands in his time, only he didn't take the ones from South Yorkshire because the pits down there are too deep and hot for him, and with the others it would have meant him leaving the pit altogether and taking an unskilled job in a factory, and the money wasn't good enough. So he's always with Cressley Town, which is no Fairey Aviation, but a pretty good second section band, for all that. I don't play anything myself, but I'm rather partial to a brass band, especially on the march, and one of the biggest kicks I know is to see the Old Feller out there in front, throwing the slide out, and hear the trombones rasping away under the rest of the band.

He comes downstairs while I'm having my tea and picks a postcard off the fireplace. 'You haven't forgotten this, have you, Vic?' It's notification of a blood donors' session round at Shiregrove Road Council School. The Old Man has one as well, and we usually go together.

'I had,' I say, 'but it's okay; I've nothing else on.'

'All this givin' your blood in the middle of winter,' the Old Lady says. 'I'm sure it weakens your resistance to colds and disease.'

'Gerraway,' I say.

'I should imagine it's quite beneficial in some ways,' young Jim says. 'Bloodletting was considered a cure for almost everything at one time.'

I pull a face at Mister Know-all and the Old Lady says, 'Well they don't do it now, do they? They've learned better.'

The Old Man's polishing his boots by the fire. 'I don't see as how it can do any harm,' he says. 'An' what drop they take out o' you does some poor soul a power o' good.'

'Ah well,' the Old Lady says, 'I reckon it's up to everybody to do their bit. That's what makes the world go round. But I do think you should take some malt and cod-liver oil in winter, Victor. Help to make up for it a bit.'

I pull another face. I haven't taken malt and cod-liver oil in years.

'Jim's used all his up. I'll get a new jar from the chemist's tomorrow.'

'Get some capsules; I'm too old to take it out of the jar.'

I hold my cup out. 'Is there a drop more?'

The Old Lady picks the teapot up out of the hearth and pours me another cup. 'You're never too old to take what's good for you; and that includes your mother's advice.'

'Lecture coming up.'

'A thick ear coming up, young man, if you start cheeking me. Advice is cheap for them as'll take it.'

I jump up from the table and throw my arms out and go into my Al Jolson take-off. 'Mammy, how I love yer, how I need yer, my dear old mammy . . .'

She can't help smiling, though she does her best.

'Gerraway with yer, you great clown.'

The school's all lit up and we walk across the playground to the door we usually go in and check the notice which says 'Blood Donors this way', with an arrow. There's a bloke and a middle-aged woman waiting with their cards outside the door on the left and two or three more people sitting outside the room where they actually take the blood. Me and the Old Man tag on to the line. I'm easy about giving blood now; it's a doddle; but I can never get used to the hospital smell they bring with them when they come and set up for the job. The Old Feller goes in and I follow in half a minute and sit down in front of this bod who takes my card. He shows me another card which I have to sign to say I've never had yellow jaundice, malaria, cancer, kidney disease, and a lot of other nasty complaints. They don't want your blood if you've had any of these and you have to sign the card every time you go, in case you've had a dose of something since the last time you were here, I suppose. Then this bloke gives me a post card and asks me to write my name and address on it. I'll get this through the post in a couple of weeks telling me what my blood's been used for. He hands me all my record cards and whatnot and I move on to the bint in the blue inform who takes hold of my hand and jabs a needle in my thumb and squeezes a drop of blood out which she catches in a little glass tube and drops into some chemical or other. She blows into this chemical through another little tube and watches it change colour. From this she can check my blood group against the record card. I go out, holding a bit of cotton wool over my thumb and hang my jacket on a hook and join the others waiting for their turn.

They have all the trolleys set out in the assembly hall and a nurse leads me to one of these and I get up and lie on my back. The nurse there shoves a length of like brush-handle into my hand and I'm supposed to grip and relax on this while she winds a rubber bandage round my arm above the elbow and pumps it up to make the vein stand out. Now we're all ready and in a minute a woman doctor comes over and gives me a nice smile like she always does and asks me if I'm keeping well. I say I am and she slips the needle in and makes the connexion without me feeling a thing except the light touch of her fingers. I watch her face while she's doing it. It's a clean, fresh face, without make-up, and I always think how nice she is and wonder why she isn't married because I'm sure she'd be real good for some bloke.

'Is that comfortable?'

'Fine, thanks.'

She smiles again and goes off to see to somebody else. I feel like shutting my eyes but I think I might drop off to sleep if I do so I keep them open and look at the ceiling and now and then take a butcher's at this nurse who's sitting by the trolley knitting a jumper while my blood runs into the bottle on the floor. The old place is ready for decorating. As I remember, it was always ready for decorating. It's ten years since I sat my County Minor in this very room and passed to go to Grammar School. Ten years! They say time passes quicker the older you get, but even I can look back ten years and more and remember what I was doing at the time. And ten years on . . . what will I be doing then, when I'm thirty? Probably married, maybe with some kids. But who to? Who would the bint be? Now a couple of weeks ago I might have thought Ingrid, maybe, but now . . . It's the funniest thing about Ingrid. I'm out with her twice and three times a week now and you might think I've got all I was always hankering after in that direction. Maybe I have, but somehow, I don't know, there isn't the magic there was at the beginning, though it's still exciting enough at certain times. Anyway, when I think of getting married I don't think of her, that's all . . .

About twenty minutes later, when we've had a lie-down and a cup of tea, the Old Man and I are walking out through the gate, all done and dusted.

'Comin' straight down home?' the Old Man says, and I say, 'I suppose so; I've nowt else on tonight.'

We walk down the hill till we come to the Bunch of Grapes, which is one of these nice quiet pubs with notices up inside telling you singing isn't allowed. The Old Man fair surprises me when he stops and says, 'Could you do with a drink?' I'm surprised, you see, because although he must know I have a drink now and again like any other young chap, he's never really acknowledged it by inviting me into a pub with him.

'I don't mind an odd 'un, Dad.'

'Get a bit o' strength back, eh?' he says, and I see him grin in the light coming from the window.

'That's the ticket.'

The landlord knows him and says, 'Evenin' Arthur,' when we go in. 'How you keepin'?'

'Evenin', Jack. Fair to middlin', y'know. Mustn't grumble. How's yourself?'

The landlord says he can't grumble either and asks us what we're having. The Old Man looks at me and I think it might be policy not to seem too used to all this, so I say, 'Whatever you're having, Dad,' and the Old Feller gets two halves of mild (I prefer bitter really) and twenty Players and we go and sit down at a table near the fire. The only other customers are two blokes talking about football on the other side of the fireplaces.

The Old Man lifts his glass. 'All the best.'

'Cheers.'

He drinks and put his glass down and sits on his buffet

with his hands resting on his knees. 'What you grinnin' at?' he says in a minute.

'Oh, nowt much.'

But I'm grinning because I can't help it; because I'm thinking this is a kind of milestone in my life, like my first long pants and being able to smoke in the house. It's like the Old Man's kind of acknowledging I'm grown up and not a kid any more.

'Nice quiet place, this,' the Old Man says. 'Never any rowdy customers. Ever been in afore?'

I say no, I haven't.

'You do take a drink now an' again, though, don't you?'

'Yes, I like a glass occasionally.'

He nods. 'I see no harm in a young feller takin' a drink in moderation. so long as you don't have eight or nine pints an' start wantin' to gob everybody.'

'That's silly.'

'Aye, it is, but there's plenty on 'em do it.'

'It's a nice drink, this.'

'Aye, he keeps a good drink, Jack does.'

We sit without saying anything for a while, then the Old Man says, 'How you gettin' on at your work?'

'Oh, okay.'

'Still liking it, are you?'

'Yes, I like it all right.' I know this isn't exactly the truth, somehow, but I let it go because it would be too hard to explain to the Old Feller when I can hardly reckon it up for myself.

'Seems to me there's good prospects in your line. T'evenin' paper's allus full o' vacancies for draughtsmen.'

'Oh, there's plenty o' jobs about.'

'What d'ye think about Whittaker's? D'ye reckon you'll be settlin' there when you get on to full rate?'

'Well I'm not thinkin' o' moving yet. I'll have to see when I'm twenty-one. They pay union rates and the work's as interesting as any other branch of engineering, I reckon. Course, I could probably get the same line o' work somewhere else. I don't know that there's much chance of promotion at Whittaker's. Too many keen young chaps in the office.'

'If you made a move in t'same line it'd mean you going away, happen?'

'Yeh, I'd have to do that. Manchester, maybe, or Birmingham.'

'Aye.' The Old Man nods and appears to weigh this up for a minute. Then he says, 'Well, there comes a time in most chaps' lives when they've to strike out on their own if they're goin' to make headway. And the time to do it is while you're still single, without ties.'

'I suppose so.' Me and the Old Man haven't talked like this for a long time. Come to think of it, we don't talk much at all except to say where's the boot polish and pass the salt.

'I'm not tryin' to push you off or anythin', mind,' he says. 'I just want you to know 'at I see the position and if you do decide it'll be best to make a move it'll be up to you. I don't want you to think there's anybody here holding you back.'

'No, I see that.'

'Course, your mother'll not like it. You're still nobbut a bairn to her.'

'If I'd been in another job she'd maybe have had to like it or lump it a couple of years ago.'

'You mean your National Service?'

'Aye.'

'D'ye think you'll ever have it to do now?'

'I don't think so. There's a lot of us up at Whittaker's got deferment. I don't think they'll ever bother us now. They'll be packing it up altogether soon by the looks of things.'

'Well, that's all right, then.'

'I wish I had gone up sometimes, y'know.'

'You'd just ha lost two years' experience an' wasted your time.'

'I think it might have given me a fresh slant on things. You know, broadened me outlook. I talk to these lads who've had service abroad and I think I've never seen anything stopping at home.'

'Well, it gets a lad away from his mother's apron string,' the Old Man says. 'Teaches him to stand on his own feet. But for broadening your outlook, I don't know. I reckon it depends on the man. I knew fellers in 1916 'at were just as gormless when they came out as they were when they went in. It didn't learn 'em owt. Except 'at politicians makes wars an' us ordinary chaps has to fight 'em.'

He empties his glass and I reach for it as he sets it down. 'Have another?'

He looks up at the electric wall-clock and says, 'Aye, all right.'

'I wa' thinkin' o' poppin' over to see Huddersfield Town a Saturday,' he says when I come back with the new drinks. 'Fancy an afternoon out?'

'I shall be at the shop, Dad,' I remind him.

'Oh, aye, o' course. I wa' forgettin'. Ah well, it can't be helped. Seems a long time sin' we had a day out together like that.'

It does. I can't remember the last time. I lift my glass. 'Well, we're having a night out now.'

The Old Man twinkles. 'Aye, you're right, lad, we are. We shan't have to be too long, though, as your mother 'ull be wondering where we've got to.'

I'm watching a little feller who's buying a pint at the back counter and looking across at the Old Man. In a minute he comes over with his glass and puts his hand on the Old Feller's shoulder.

'How go, Arthur? How ye keepin', lad?'

The Old Man looks up. 'Well, I'll be blessed if it isn't Herbert! Wha, I haven't seen thee in ages, lad. Sit thissen down, lad, sit thissen down.'

The little feller pulls a buffet up and sits down. He's quite well-dressed in a grey tweed overcoat and a green trilby, but there's no mistaking what he is, even without the blue marks on his face and hands.

'You don't know my lad, do you, Herbert?' the Old

136

Man says. 'My eldest lad, that is. T'other's still at school, but Victor here's a draughtsman up at Whittaker's, y'know.' There's a touch of pride in the Old Man's voice and I'm surprised because it's never occurred to me he might be proud of me. Of Chris, yes, and young Jim, but not me.

'Is he, by gow?' the little feller says. 'A draughtsman, eh? That's better na t'pit, eh?'

'You're dead right,' I say.

'I allus said 'at mine wouldn't be forced into t'pit like I wa',' the Old Feller says.

'This is a golden age for young fowk, Arthur,' the little chap says. 'Not like our young days. Then there wa' nowt else but pit or t'mills. An' us fathers were on'y too ready to send us down to addle 'em some brass. I have a lad o' me own in t'Coal Board offices, y'know. He's allus grumblin' about size of his wage packet compared wi' mine. I tell him he doesn't know he's born. It's worth three quid a week to go to work at nine o'clocks an' be able to see daylight through t'winders. My job 'ud kill him in a week. Less.'

He lifts his glass and sinks half his pint. I watch the level fall and know he's a chap who likes his booze. As if he's read my thoughts, he says, 'I don't know what I'd do wi'out me pint, Arthur. I sometimes think it's t'only thing 'at keeps me goin'.' He brings a packet of Woodbines out and hands them round. 'They ought to give us a free ration of it, like they do coal,' he says, and laughs.

'Where are you working now then, Herbert?' the Old Man asks him when we've all three lit up.

'I've been at Roundwood for t'past three year, fillin' on t'days.'

'Roundwood, Wakefield?' the Old Man says. 'That's a tidy way to travel, isn't it?'

'Oh, I have a car,' the little feller says. 'Gi'n over bussing it years sin'. I can be at work in twenty minutes thru stepping out of the house.'

'Doing it in style, eh, Herbert?'

'Why not?' Herbert says. 'We've never had it as good

as this last ten year, Arthur, an' I'm makin' t'best on it while it lasts.'

'How d'ye mean, while it lasts? You don't think there'll be a slump, do you?'

'It won't allus be like this,' the little chap says. 'I've seen too much o' t'shabby times and to think 'at this'll last for ever.'

'Oh, I don't know, Herbert. I don't see why it shouldn't.'

'Funny thing happen, Arthur. You'd think 'at fowk 'ud allus want coal. An' so they will for a long time yet. But we've both seen times when fowk had empty grates and coal were standin' in mountains in t'pit yards, doin' nowt. It's a question of economics, Arthur; an' chaps like thee an' me know nowt about that. All we know is coal-gettin', when they'll let us do it . . .'

I listen to them natter on. From coal-gettin and economics they get on to politics. They're both Labour, of course, so they've nothing much to argue about there. Then they get on to sport and Huddersfield Town where they can have a difference of opinion on one or two points; but all very matey like. While this is going on the little feller gets himself another pint and has our glasses filled up. Then the Old Feller buys him a pint and we have our glasses filled again. I'm thinking it's a good job it's mild we're drinking because by the time the clock shows twenty to ten we've had five glasses apiece and the little feller's well on with his fourth pint.

'Just look what time it is,' the Old Man says. 'Wes'll have to be off.'

'It's taken you some time tonight,' the Old Lady says when we go in. The house is lovely and warm and full of the smell of ironing.

'Aye,' the Old Man says, and Old Lady takes a quick look at both of us. 'I see,' she says. 'That's where you've been spending your time.'

'Aye, we just felt like an odd 'un,' the Old Feller says, taking his jacket off. The beer's put a twinkle in his eye

138

and the OLd Lady can't bear to think she's being laughed at any time.

'You want taking Victor into such places,' she says. 'Learning him bad habits.'

'I reckon it's about time he learned to take a drink in moderation,' the Old Man says. He sits down in his chair and crosses his legs to take his boots off.

'They learn soon enough on their own, these days. An' you want to remember you've another son an' all. You want to set an example for him.'

Jim's sitting reading and taking not a bit of notice of all this.

'I reckon my example's good enough for any son o' mine,' the Old Man says, and winks at me while the Old Lady's got her back turned. I wink back. I'm feeling a bit drunk and I'm keeping my mouth shut and moving very carefully so's the Old Lady won't notice.

It looks for a minute as if she's going to say some more on the subject; then she seems to decide to let it drop and goes on ironing, hanging the clothes on the bars of the clothes-horse as she finishes them.

7

I

'Was that right?' she says into my ear. 'Did I do it properly?'

'Yes,' I say, 'that was right.'

I'm down flat on my back on my raincoat by her side and looking at the branches of the trees between us and the sky. It's a high sky tonight, big and pale, with dark shadows of clouds chasing across it, and you can't see the moon. For a few seconds there's nothing; I'm empty, not thinking, kind of not living nearly. Then there's a twinge of shame; that's the first thing that comes. I find out after it's always the first thing that comes, but I'm a bit more hardened to it then than I am now. And now I'm thinking straight: I've nothing else on my mind. I'm thinking straighter and clearer than I ever have since I first looked twice at her and wondered what my chances were. I'm thinking straight and clear and it's terrible, because I don't love her, and that's the awful truth. I don't even *like* her much now. Not because of what we've done, though that's the way I know that after the first few dates, when I wanted nothing from her except to be with her and have her like me, that was what was stopping me from seeing I didn't love her after all. And I never did have a chance to get to know if I liked her – like you like some people just for what they are and nothing else to it – because the first time I really noticed her I loved her and I hadn't spoken two words to her in my life. Now I wonder how I've stood it as long as I have: her gossip and silly scandal and her small talk about television and quiz shows and every little detail about how some lucky housewife from Wolverhampton or Tooting won a refrigerator or three thousands pairs of nylons and a holiday in America by answering questions you'd have got your arse tanned if you didn't know the answers to in Standard Four. But now I do know how I've stood it and that just isn't here any more and there's nothing else – just nothing. And when I think that only a matter of weeks ago I'd have gone to the ends of the earth for her nearly I just don't understand it. I don't understand it at all.

'You're quiet,' she says.

'Am I?'

'Haven't you got anything to say?'

She turns her face and I feel her breath warm on my cheek. 'Vic.'

'Hmm?'

'I thought at first, you know, just then, that you wanted to . . . you know, do everything.'

I did want to, I remember; and there's nothing I want to do less right now.

'I might have,' I say, 'but I wasn't daft enought to try it.'

'D'you think it's anything like that?' she says in a minute, and I think, Oh, Christ! does she have to talk about it? It's over, why can't she leave it alone?

'I suppose it must be' I don't know.'

'I wondered,' she says, and I think that maybe that's her way of trying to find out if I've ever gone the whole hog with anybody.

All of a sudden I feel like hurting her and I say, 'You talk as if I'm the first chap you've ever been out with.'

'You don't think I've ever gone as far as that with anybody else, do you?' she says. 'Is that the kind of girl you think I am?'

'How should I know?' I say. I don't really want to hurt her, but I've kind of got to work something off on her. I'm sorry when I see her look away and say, 'I didn't mean that. I know you haven't. I know you're not that kind of girl.'

'I sometimes think I must be,' she says.

'Come off it.' Now she's wondering if she's been too easy and I'll like her less for it. Well I do like her less but not for that. And I can't be bothered with her feelings – I'm too busy with my own. All of a sudden I feel about five years older, and to tell the truth, a bit muckier about the edges. And I think, So that's what it's like after with somebody you don't love; because as far as the feeling's concerned there's no difference between what we've done and going all the way.

'Anyway,' she says all at once, 'I don't think it's wrong or anything to be ashamed of. Not when you're fond of the person.'

But what about when you're not? What then? And you don't always know till after because it kind of blinds you. I know now, and the thing is, what am I going to do about it? How can I break it off now when it's only a few weeks since I told her I was mad about her, and meant it? How can I tell her I've been taken in because sex and a dream have got all mixed up inside me? How can I tell her I've been all wrong and we'd best call it off? How can I tell her all that after tonight, when she's shown me she's fond of me, that she loves me, because I'm pretty sure she does. She'll never understand. She'll think I've been working up to this all the time and now I've had what I wanted I'm not interested any more. And it isn't like that at all. But then again, maybe it doesn't mean all that much to her – as much as it might to another bint, I mean. Oh, I'm not thinking she's nothing but a young bag. I reckon she wouldn't carry on like that with just any Tom, Dick, or Harry; she'd have to be fond of whoever it was before she did. But maybe she gets fond pretty easily, and there's no getting away from it, she's a pretty hot bit of stuff. She gave me the green light okay the way she kissed me that night on the seat down there, or I'd never have gone as far as I did then. And you can look at it another way – I'm not the last word in

142

ladykillers. There's plenty better-looking bods than me about and I'd be a bit big-headed to think I was the only bloke who ever got her worked up . . .

It starts to rain. Not much, but it must have been spitting for a few minutes before I notice it. It's as good an excuse as any for breaking it up.

'C'mon, we'd better make for the shelter.'

She starts to fuss about with her clothes, tidying herself before she gets up. When she's on her feet she brushes herself down with her hand, then picks her handbag up. I give my raincoat a shake and put it on as we cut across the grass to the shelter. When we get there she starts to mend her make-up as best she can in the dark and I watch her, thinking how irritated it makes me and how much I'd have liked to see her doing it not long ago. I don't get it; it's beyond me. How can you think you've found so much and then suddenly wake up and see you've found nothing at all? And if I can't understand it what hope have I of making her see it?

She finishes what she's doing and clicks her compact shut and drops it into her bag. We sit a bit apart on the seat and watch the rain. In a minute she starts to tell me a bit of scandal about one of the bosses at Whittaker's. I don't much like this bloke she's talking about and I'm interested in what she's saying; only somehow it rubs me up the wrong way. I want to contradict her. I feel if she said black was black I'd say it was white just to be awkward.

I say something and she says, 'I always thought you didn't like him. You've said so to me.'

'I don't; but I don't see 'at that's any reason to believe everything anybody says about him.'

She knows I've snubbed her. I've never used that tone of voice to her before and I know she feels it. She doesn't say anything, though, but dips into her handbag and fishes out a packet of fags and offers me one. She always has cigs when we're out on a date and she usually won't smoke mine. 'You spend enough on me,' she'll say, 'without me smoking at your expense as well.' I've always

143

thought this was nice of her, and I still do for that matter. Oh, she's a decent kid, the sort any bloke would be glad to take out. It's no good me trying to make out she's common and easy, because she's not. She's just easy with me. And I don't want her any more . . . It's the awful truth. I smoke my cig and look out at the rain, waiting for it to stop so's we can beat it.

'Blasted weather,' I say once, and she looks at me.

'You're not in a very good mood tonight, are you?'

'I hadn't noticed.'

'I had,' she says. 'Is it something I've said or done?'

'No, course not.'

I suppose this is the time I ought to tell her how I feel; but I just can't start to do it. How can I after half an hour ago? She'll never understand. She's bound to think I planned it all from the start.

'There is something wrong, though, isn't there?' she says.

'Oh, I'm a bit fed-up all round. I'm not very happy at work just now. I don't know what it is. I allus used to be content enough.'

'P'haps you ought to look for another job,' she says.

'Mebbe that's it. Mebbe I should move right away, to Birmingham or Manchester . . . have a real change.'

'Would you like to do that? Move right away from Cressley?'

I give a shrug. 'I dunno. Mebbe I'd be just as bad off. I sometimes think it's the job itself I'm fed-up with. Althorpe had us on the mat the other week, y'know. Me an' Conroy . . .' And I tell her about the fight, leaving out what really started it and that I bit Conroy.

'Don't you get on with Conroy, then?'

'Oh, he's a clever devil, allus throwin' his weight about. I couldn't help making that crack when he gave me the opening. Still, I like him better now than I did. He didn't flinch when old Althorpe opened up, an' it was a fair treat to see the way he stood up to Hassop afterwards. I wonder he didn't sack him on the spot. You could nearly see Conroy daring him to.'

'I always think he's a funny sort of man,' Ingrid says. 'I shouldn't want to be on my own with him.'

'Who, Conroy?'

'No, Mr Hassop.'

Why, what's up with him?' This is a new slant on Hassop for me.

It's the way he looks at you. Old X-ray eyes, the typists call him.'

'Who, old Hassop? Does he ever try it on, then?'

'Oh, no, he's always very correct and distant. Never says a wrong word, in fact. But he's got a way of looking right through your clothes that gives me the creeps.'

'Well, I never knew he was that way inclined. I never told you about the time I went to his house with a message when he had flu, did I?' I know that telling Ingrid is as good as telling all the female staff but somehow I don't care whether it gets round and Miller knows I've talked or not. It's something to talk about now till the rain stops and we can go.

'. . . and then she come down the stairs in this kind of dressing-gown thing with this great envelope in her hand an' I'm standing there spouting all sorts of rubbish about hoping Hassop 'ull be up an' about again soon, an' all she says is, 'It's in the envelope.'

'She said what?'

'It's in the envelope. When I asked her how Hassop was that's all she said, and shoved it into me hands.'

'Good heavens!'

'But the funniest thing was when I was going out . . . I opened the door and the minute she saw the sunshine she gives a yell an' comes for me shouting 'Shut the door! Shut the door!' Anybody 'ud've thought she was scared o' shrivellin' up and turning to dust or something like vampires are supposed to do.'

'Ugh!' Ingrid shivers. 'You're giving me the creeps. What did you do then?'

'I hopped it out, pronto. I'd just got me foot off the step when the door banged shut behind me. Five seconds slower and I'd ha' been catapulted out through the porch windows.'

Ingrid says, 'Well, I say . . .' and giggles. She folds her arms across her bust as though she's hugging the story to her ready to tell her mates. It'll be all over the firm by dinner-time tomorrow, but I don't care. I look out across the park.

'It's not doing much now. We'd better be off.'

We have to have another titivating session before she's ready to go and I walk about on the concrete getting more and more irritated. I want to be away from her, on my own, this minute, so's I can think about what's happened and what I'm going to do about it. But I know I'll have to take her home; and I'm glad it's dark because, funny thing, I don't want anybody to see me with her now. It'd be just too bad if somebody we both know saw us now and jumped to conclusions – all the wrong ones.

She finishes at last we set off towards the gates.

'Have you got your dinner suit pressed?' she says.

I'm still feeling a bit contrary so I say, 'Dinner suit?' though I know very well what she means.

'For the Staff Party.'

'Oh, that! I'm wearing me tails; didn't I tell you?'

And this is another thing. I was looking forward to the Staff Party because this year I'd have a girl of my own to take. I was so happy. Why can't you stop in love with a bird once you've fallen for her. Why has everything to be so complicated? Better now if I'd never picked her out from the crowd that first time. That first date, though. I didn't know where to put myself, I was that chuff with everything, And now . . . I'll never be able to explain it to her. I know I won't.

'What's the matter?' she says.

'Why?'

'You're sighing. You sound as if you've got the whole world on yours shoulders.'

I feel as if I have; and what a blooming queer world it is!

'You're not sorry now, are you?' she says. 'About tonight, I mean.'

'Course not.'

Why should I be? If I'm feeling a bit disgusted at myself

146

it's not because of that altogether. It's because it's shown me there's nothing between us. It's not only bints who have something to lose; I've lost something tonight, and to a lass I don't much like, let alone love. I suppose I've gained something as well: a bit of experience, if you look at it that way. I suppose you could put it down to experience.

I'm brooding about it all the way across the park and through the streets to her house. I'll just have to let it die a natural death, I'm thinking, let it cool off gradually. I reckon she's a right to something better than this, but I know I'll never be able to tell her and explain to her face.

'When shall I see you again?' she says at their gate.

'Tomorrow.'

'I mean outside work, silly.'

'Well, not this week-end, I'm afraid. An old pal of mine's coming over this week-end. I haven't seen him for years. Anyway, I'll always see you at work. We can fix something up any time.'

I reckon she can't help but notice I'm not interested, even if she does know I'm lying about this mate. I bet she doesn't know how interested I really am, though. How can she?

'All right,' she says, and I'm glad she doesn't make anything of it.

She waits. We don't say anything. She doesn't lift her face and she doesn't even look at me but I know she's waiting to be kissed. And why not, after tonight? I only hesitate a second, then I put my hand under her chin and lift her face up. I kiss her on the mouth, but not for all the gold in the Bank of England can I put my feeling in it. She must know now, I think on the way home, even if she didn't before.

II

I manage to steer clear of it for a few days by keeping away from Ingrid herself, but then she sends me a note by young Laisterdyke. I read it in the river caves and wonder what I'm going to reply. The easiest way is to just ignore it, act as if I've never got it. But that's not fair, I think. I can't just brush her off like that . . . I think about it for a bit, then I come up with a reply that doesn't say anything straight out but has a lot between the lines. 'Dear Ingid, I can't see you tonight because I've somewhere else to go. I've started Tech again now and I'm sitting for the National this time and I'll have to work on other nights beside class nights if I want to get through. So I shan't be able to get out much and I don't think it's fair to tie you down when I don't know when I'll have a free night, Vic.'

When I read it through I'm a bit ashamed of it but I can't bring myself to be more blunt. So I give the note to young Colin and slip him a tanner at the same time. 'Here, give her this – and keep your mouth shut.'

'A pleasure,' he says, pocketing the tanner. 'Special deliveries a bob.'

'A bob on your earhole if you don't watch out.'

There's a reply next morning. 'Dear Vic, I was surprised to read your letter. I don't see how you going to night school makes any difference to us. I know you won't have much free time but that doesn't matter if you really want to see me. I thought something was wrong the other night, and now I'm sure. If it's something I've done I wish you'd tell me what it is. Ingrid.'

I'm feeling pretty low when I read this. She's wondering what's up and feeling miserable herself and I'm sorry about it. It's disappointing all round. But you can't help the way you feel, can you? Anyway, that just about winds it up. She'll be too proud to write another note if I don't answer this one; and I don't intend to do that.

Part Two

1

I

Next week it's the Staff Party.

Every year about this time Whittaker's take over the Town Hall and invite the Staff to this do. If you're married you can take your other half with you, and if you're single a boy friend or a bird. There's whist and dancing and a stand-up supper and a bar, and it's all free for nothing except the booze, and you pay for that out of your own pocket.

Mr Matthew makes a little speech and tells the Staff how well they've done this last year and how much better he's sure they'll do next. Nearly always the same speech, it is; and then if there's any old coves saying good-bye to it all the gold watches are dished out and there's a lot of shaking hands and clapping. I mean, you're forced to give a clap when some old keff what started in 1907 totters across the floor for his present, because you get kind of awe-struck when you think he was working thirty years before you were born, and you start to wonder if some lad born thirty years from now will stand here thinking the same thing when you hobble up for your watch or whatever it is they'll be presenting in fifty years' time. Somehow I can't see it for me. To begin with, I can't imagine myself at that age with all my troubles behind me and nothing left but pottering in the garden till the end.

Anyway, that's what happens at these do's, and there's nearly always a presentation to somebody

151

because Whittaker's is the kind of firm blokes stay with for life.

There's enough booze put away at one of these do's to float all the battleships in Portsmouth Harbour and the bosses and the men get real friendly together. You know what I mean: lots of joking and back-slapping and introducing wives and thinking that old so-an-so isn't such a bad bastard after all. Course, they're all back on two sides of the fence again next morning but it's nice while it lasts, I suppose.

The women look forward to it more than anybody. All you can get out of them the minute Christmas is over is the Party. They parade their new frocks and their husbands or boy friends, not missing what the others have got, and saving it all up for after. I sometimes wonder which they like best, the Party itself or the tittle-tattle in the cloakroom after. Birds are queer. You can get two blokes who don't think much to one another and on a night like this they'll be like old pals. But get two women like that and a party only seems to make it worse.

Anyway, it's a real good do, a grand night out.

Well, things being different I'd have taken Ingrid but now I get there on my own about eight. I have a couple of glasses of bottled beer that blows you up and a dance or two and a natter with any of the lads I run into. Going up to ten I'm standing on the edge of the floor when Conroy pushes past me. I can see he has a bit of load on and I watch him go down to the bandstand and have a word with the leader between sets. This bod, name of Oscar Winthrop, a tailor's dummy type with patent-leather hair and a pencil-thin moustache, looks a bit doubtful at Conroy and gives a little smile. I see Conroy throwing his head about and pulling a face as if to say, 'Come on, don't be a nig-nog,' and in a minute Winthrop seems to give way and Conroy climbs up on to the stand and shakes hands with all the blokes in the front row of the band. They're grinning at Conroy and one another, but Conroy's face never slips. Tom Evans, the construction shop foreman, who's always M.C. at these do's because he's a real keen dancer and looks good in tail, moseys over to see what's up. He has a word with Winthrop and Conroy, who takes next to no notice of him, then walks away again as though he's washing his hands of the affair whatever it is.

Jimmy Slade comes up behind me. 'What's Conroy up to?'

'Dunno; just wonderin' meself.'

The leader puts his stick up and the band blow a chord.

'Ladies and gentlemen,' this bod says, 'we have had a request from one of your own Staff members to sing a number with the band. Never let it be said that Oscar Winthrop failed to encourage new talent. I give you, ladies and gentlemen, the singing sensation of Dawson Whittaker and Sons – Al Conroy!'

There's a bit of a laugh at this and one or two people clap. Conroy steps up to the mike, his face all red and serious, and bows all round. The leader gives the down-beat and Conroy buckles at the knees, throws his arms out and bawls into the mike:

Babe-e!
Who were you with last night?
A-huggin' an' a-kissin' in the bright moonlight.
O-hoh,
I won't have nobody flirtin' with my baby,
I tell you this, oh baby, an' I don't mean maybe.
If you wanna keep me lovin',
A-huggin' an' a-snuggin'
Then save your lovin' kisses just for me.

When he's finished his chorus and the band's having a turn Conroy starts to prance about the stage, twisting and shaking himself as though he's got half a dozen scorpions up his vest. By this time the audience is going mad and the Drawing Office lads are sending up cheers over the noise of the band.

A voice right behind me says. 'Isn't that one of your staff, Hassop?' I sneak a quick look round and see it's Matthew Whittaker, the big boss himself.

Hassop sort of clears his throat and I bet he's wishing he could disown Conroy. 'Hmmm, er um, er yes, it is.'

'Good worker, is he?'

'Quite a clever young man,' Hassop says. 'A little too head-strong and irresponsible for his own good, though, I'm afraid.'

I'm all ears waiting to see what Mr Matthew will say to this, but Mrs Whittaker, a dark woman, quite nice-looking to say she's past her first youth, says with a laugh, 'He doesn't sound as if he'd starve if he ever gave up draughtsmanship.'

They all laugh, and when I hear a noise like water trying to get out of a stopped-up drain I realize Hassop's joining in.

They move off as Conroy finishes his number with a chorus of scat singing that's a proper marvel the way he gets his tongue round it; and at the end he stops his capering about so sudden he nearly throws himself off the stage into the potted ferns. He gets a terrific hand. I'm clapping like mad and so is everybody else I can see, including the band. Oscar Winthrop slaps him on the back as he comes down the steps.

Conroy makes his way across the floor and people are laughing and saying things to him all the way. He comes up to me.

'Seen Jeff Lewis?'

'Not lately.'

'He owes me a quid.'

'Mr Matthew and old Hassop have just been talking about you,' I tell him.

'Nothing complimentary, I hope,' he says, getting on his toes and looking all round for Lewis.

'Hassop said you were a clever young man.'

'You're a lying swine, young Browny.'

'Honest. He said you were headstrong an' all, and too irresponsible for your own good.'

'That's more like it,' Conroy says. 'I can believe he said that.'

I tell him what Mrs Whittaker said as well but he's got his mind on something else. Lewis, I think.

'I'm more interested in my quid,' he says. 'Come and help me find Lewis and I'll buy you a pint out of it.'

'Okay.'

We split up and work through the crowd and into the passage that leads to the bar. I haven't gone far when I come on Lewis from behind. He's standing in a group of four or five, chewing the fat and looking real keen, I have to admit. He's one of the few blokes apart from the bosses who's wearing a dinner jacket. Everybody else is wearing the suit they keep for weddings, funerals, and boozing on a Sunday dinner-time.

'Conroy's looking for you,' I say, clapping him on the shoulder.

'Oh, what for?'

'Because you owe me a quid,' says Conroy, coming up from the other side. 'You bet me a level quid I daren't do a number with the band.'

Lewis gets his wallet out and opens it. 'Ten bob, wasn't it?'

'A quid, you chiseller,' Conroy says, and reaches over and plucks a pound note out of Lewis's wallet. He half turns away, then turns round again. 'Put another quid up an' I'll do another number,' he offers.

But Lewis won't throw his money away so easy, and Conroy says to me, 'C'mon, then, young Browny; let's see about that pint.'

On the way into the bar we meet Ken Rawlinson and his girl friend coming out. She's a thin blonde piece with a way of looking straight through you as though you're not there.

'How do, Rawly,' Conroy says, and I see Rawly flinch. 'How d'ye like my number?'

The blonde bit focuses her eyes on Conroy as though she's just noticed him crawling out from under a stone.

'It's not whether I liked it or not that matters,' Rawly says, real distant like; 'but what the management thinks.'

155

'Pity I forgot me fiddle,' Conroys says. 'I'd've given you a violin concerto. A bit of Debewssy, eh?'

'Debussy didn't write a violin concerto,' the blonde piece says, and takes Rawly by the arm and pulls him off into the crowd.

Conroy's laughing like a drain as we go into the bar. 'Bag a table,' he says, 'while I go get the wallop.'

I find a place by the wall under the mirrors and in a minute or two Conroy comes over with his big hands round four glasses of beer.

'Who're all the these for?' I say as he lowers them on to the table.

'For us,' he says. 'Two apiece. They don't sell pints. Too refined. Like Rawly.' He laughs. 'Old Rawly.'

'Seems to me he got one up on you there, though, Conroy,' I say. 'About the violin concerto, I mean.'

Conroy's taking a long pull at his glass. He shakes his head as he puts it down. 'He didn't say it: *she* did. Shouldn't be surprised if Rawly doesn't know Debussy from the Chancellor of the Exchequer.'

I notice now that Conroy pronounces the name like the blonde bit did and I begin to see that he was laying it on thick for Rawly's benefit. And I'm beginning to wonder if there isn't more to Conroy than meets the eye.

'On the other hand, maybe he does,' Conroy says, taking another swing at his beer. 'He knows most of the names and he drags 'em out at every opportunity. He's the sort of bloke who goes once a year to a symphony concert and talks about it at the top of his voice on the bus next morning. I can't stand him, young Browny. Him and his lousy Beethoven and bloody Dostoyevsky. He knows the da-da-da-daa bit from Beethoven and I'll bet not another note. And he wouldn't recognize a line of Dostoyevsky if you bawled it in his ear. He's a lousy fake, young Browny, and if there's owt I can't stand it's a fake.'

Conroy's not letting talking stop him from drinking and he's already emptied his first glass and started on the second.

'He buys *The Times* and the *Guardian* and the posh Sunday papers and reads all the critics and thinks that's it. He likes to blind you with a lot of names and facts. He can very likely tell you that Tolstoy had duck-egg and chips for his tea on 13 March 1888, but you ask him what they called Anna Karenina's fancy man and he'll look at you gone out.'

'Who's Anna Kar . . . what's her name?'

'Karenina. She's a woman in a book of that name.'

'How do you know?'

'Because I've read the bloody thing,' Conroy says; 'that's how I know . . . What's up – surprised? Thought *Reveille* was my steady diet, did you? Well don't get me wrong, young Browny. I might be a loud-mouthed bastard at times but there's two sorts of them. I'm one and Rawly's another. And I don't like his sort. If you like Dostoyevsky and lousy Beethoven – all right. I reckon you're getting summat you won't get of *Peg's Paper* and last week's Top Ten. But there's no call to go about letting everybody know what a fine cultured bod you are and thinking everybody else are peasants.'

He finishes his second glass and pushes it away. I'm only halfway down my first one and he looks at the full one.

'Want that?'

'No, go on, you have it.' I push it towards him.

'I'll get you another for it in a minute, only I can't be bothered getting up just now.'

He takes a pull and smacks his lips.

'And what's more,' he says, 'I don't like this pansy approach to it all. Let's grow long hair and manicure our fingernails, or else fill 'em with coal dust to show we can't be bothered with a little thing like keeping clean. It must make some of these blokes turn in their graves the types who lick their shirt-tails.'

Well, I'm fascinated at the way he's talking. I watch his hand on the glass as he lifts it again. Short and square-fingered, it is, with a fuzz of dark hairs on the back. Conroy doesn't look too intelligent, you know. He's got a square sort of face with a low forehead and deep-set eyes. But I know he's got a good engineering brain and he can turn out a line drawing that's a model for anybody in the office. He's also rowdy and coarse and foul-mouthed. And now here's a new slant on him altogether. Here's a Conroy who knows a lot about books and music – good music and good books – real heavyweight stuff that you think only horrible types like Rawly and old stagers like Mr Van Huyten are interested in. You sort of never associate that sort of thing with a liking for beer and dirty stories. Least, I never have till now. The long and the sort of it is, Conroy's a Highbrow.

'By shots, Conroy,' I say, 'I've never heard you talk like this afor.'

'No,' he says, 'you haven't. Because when you see me I'm sober; and now I'm pissed. Or near enough to make no difference. Some blokes want to fight, others to shag every bird in sight, and others just flake out. Me, I just talk . . . more and more . . . just talk . . .'

He empties his glass and looks into it kind of sorrowfully like. Then he drops a real bombshell.

'Did I ever tell you about my missis, young Browny?'

I'm gawping and he's not too drunk to notice.

'Shouldn't have said that,' he says. 'Tales out of school.'

'I didn't even know you were married.'

'I'm not married now,' he says. 'And as far as anybody else is concerned, I never have been. You let the cat out of the bag, young Browny, and I'll knock your block off.'

'Oh, I shan't tell,' I say. 'No need to worry about me telling.'

'No, you're not a bad lad, young Browny . . .' He looks round at the bar as if he's wondering whether to go for some more beer. All at once he pushes his chair back and gets up. 'Have to go shake hands with an old friend,' he says, and he goes off into the crowd.

A bit later I'm standing in the ballroom doorway when I see Ingrid by herself not far away. She's wearing a yellow frock with big blue flowers on the skirt and gold-coloured dancing shoes. I think she looks real keen and it's a pity I've fallen out of love with her. I watch her for a minute or two and then something makes me go over to her and ask her to dance. She glances at me just once when she accepts and not again during the ten minutes we're on the floor. We don't say much either.

It's a slow waltz and they've turned the lights down a bit. I find I like having her so near and I know the other signs, the way my heart's fluttering and I'm breathing as if I'm on top of a mountain. It's just the way I feel when I look at some of these nudes in magazines. I have my right hand in the middle of her back, on the fastening of her brassière, and I move it further over so she has to come closer. Still she doesn't look straight at me or say anything in particular. It's just as though I'm just any one of the bods.

I don't know what to make of myself now. Here I've been telling myself I don't love her any more, and now I'm wanting her again. But not in the old way. Once I'd have given anything just to be here with her like this, but now I want her like I want the bints in the magazines. It's not really *her* I want at all, if you see what I mean.

Maybe it's this and maybe because I think I ought to be nice to her that makes me wonder if I should offer to take her home after the Party. After all, it was more or less fixed that I'd bring her, and now she's on her own. But when the set finishes I decide not to say anything right now. If I see her at the end of the Party and she's still on her own, then I might offer to see her home. I'm not sure. I don't know really how I feel. Looking at her now I'm nearly sorry I broke it off like I did.

II

First the bar packs up and then the clock in the tower strikes midnight. The Party begins to fade away, all the life going out of it as people begin to collect their coats before the rush starts. As I come out of the cloakroom they're singing 'Auld Lang Syne', and then the 'Queen' strikes up.

Jimmy comes over to me. 'How're you getting home?'

'Shanks' pony. It's the chauffeur's night off.'

'Miller's got his car outside. He's giving me and Pauline a lift. He said to see if there was anybody else. Come on, you may as well.'

I've sort of been half-looking round for Ingrid, but I'm not all that bothered so I follow Jimmy across the foyer to where this red-headed bint from the typists', Pauline Lawrence, who Jimmy seems to have got very friendly with tonight, is standing with Miller and his wife.

'Ah, Vic,' Miller says. 'You joining us? Good ... You've met my wife, have you? Vic Brown, one of our bright young men.'

I say howdedo to Mrs Miller, who's a plainish sort of woman, a bit on the dumpy side, and we all go out to the car park. Miller's car's a biggish pre-war Lanchester in a sort of metallic fawn colour that I believe he picked up for a song. He's the sort of bloke who's always running down post-war jobs because he says they're tinny and have nothing in them. I pile in the back with Jimmy and this Pauline. He seems to be doing very nicely for himself there because he puts his arm round her straight away and she settles down against him as though she's been doing it for months. Miller gives the windscreen a wipe over with a cloth and gets in next to his missis.

'All okay back there?' he says, starting the engine.

'We're okay' I tell him, 'except I'm the odd man out. I hope you're not making me responsible for these two lovebirds.'

'Wrap up,' Jimmy says, 'and look the other way.'

Pauline giggles and Mrs Miller looks over her shoulder and laughs. She seems like a good sort. But then, so is Miller. He's looking back towards the Town Hall entrance. 'Just a tick,' he says, and hops out, leaving the engine running, and disappears. He's back in a couple of minutes with somebody else. He opens the back door. 'Here, this will even things up a bit.'

A lass bends her head to get in and I move up to give her room, wondering who it is. Then my heart gives a knock, because it's Ingrid.

'Now we don't know who's sitting on whose knee,' Jimmy says. He turns a bit sideways to make room for four of us and Pauline snuggles up to him. Making a real play for him, she is. I wonder how long this has been brewing up and think Jimmy's a deep 'un for not mentioning it. Then I realize I'm just as deep because I've never said anything to him about Ingrid.

'What does it matter?' Miller says. 'All pals together.'

We move off out of the car park and down the hill into the shopping centre. Miller's not a very good driver really. He's kind of all tensed up all the time and he goes in fits and starts as if he can't make up his mind where he's going. There's still a few shop windows lit up in town but hardly a soul about. At first Miller tries a bit of general conversation but he soon gives this up and talks to his wife. It's quiet in the back seat. Jimmy and Pauline are necking away like mad. I don't know if it's the same kiss they started when the car began to move or another one. All I know is I haven't seen anybody come up for air yet. I shuffle about a bit and ask Ingrid if she's comfy.

'I'm all right,' she says.

We're close together, real close, because we can't help it. I'm getting the same feeling now I had while we were dancing. Only now we're more private like and with Miller and his wife with their backs to us and Jimmy and Pauline occupied with their own affairs we're practically on our own. It's dark, and my leg's touching hers, and her face is less than a foot from mine.

'Get a load of those two,' I whisper to her.

'Mmmm,' she says, 'Very friendly, aren't they?'

I move, as though I'm shifting about to get more comfortable, and put my arm on the back of the seat. I touch her shoulder and pull her towards me. For a second maybe it looks as though she's not having any; then she comes, bringing her head near so I can put my mouth on her neck under her left ear. In a minute I lift my free hand and turn her face and kiss her. She lets me, but there's nothing much coming back. I'm between her and Jimmy and Pauline and they can't see a thing if they're looking, which they aren't, so I slip my hand into her coat and squeeze her gently through her frock. A minute or two of this and she begins to wake up and act interested. By this time I'm thinking about that last date in the park, and wondering how soon we can have another one.

'When can I see you?' I say into her ear.

'I thought you didn't want to.'

'I do . . . When can I? Tomorrow?'

'Not tomorrow.'

'When then? The day after?'

She's quiet for a minute. 'All right.'

'Does anybody know where we are?' Miller says. 'You'd better watch out in the back there. I'm just keeping going. If I overshoot and reach home you'll either have to walk back or kip down in the garden shed.'

Jimmy tears himself away from Pauline long enough to look out of this window. 'You turn left at the next crossroads,' he says; 'then it's about two hundred yards down on the left before the church.'

'Who lives there?'

'You can drop both of us. I'll see Pauline home from there.'

'Sure you can trust him, Pauline?' Miller says.

'Trust me to what?' Jimmy says with a dirty laugh.

'Now then, keep the party clean,' Miller says. 'Once you step out of this car with a wolf like young Slade the responsibility is yours, young lady.'

'I'll risk it,' Pauline says.

'So be it,' Miller says, and swings the car round the bend.

He pulls into the kerb down the road where Jimmy said and smothers a yawn as he lift his hands off the wheel. 'It makes you think, driving a car at night when everybody's gone to bed.'

'Makes you think what?' I ask him.

'Makes you think you should have been there yourself hours ago.'

'Oh, come now, Jack,' Mrs Miller says; 'you know you've enjoyed it. I think we all have, haven't we?' she says, turning round to us.

We all agree with her and Pauline says, 'I think we should have a party every month.'

'God forbid,' Miller says. 'There'll be enough thick heads in the morning as it is.'

'What did you think to old Conroy's turn?' I say.

'Quite a diversion,' Miller says. 'I must say I didn't think he had it in him.'

'He's had more than a drop to drink,' Ingrid says. 'You could see that.'

'He did it for a bet,' I tell them. 'Lewis bet him a quid.'

Miller turns round in his seat. 'Did he really, Vic?'

'I saw him collect his winnings. Lewis tried to make out it was only ten bob, but Conroy took the quid. He bought me a drink out of it.' For some reason I feel kind of proud to be able to say I had a drink with Conroy after his number.

'You and Conroy drinking together?' Jimmy says. 'Whatever next!'

'Oh, he's not so bad when you get to know him. I had a real long natter with him in the bar. I'll bet you didn't know he –' I stop, because I'm just about to spill the beans about Conroy being married and I promised not to tell. 'He knows a lot about books and music,' I say, covering up. 'More than Rawly does; only he doesn't make a song and dance about it.'

'I can't stand either of them,' Ingrid says. 'Ken Rawlinson's a terrific snob and Conroy's just like a big animal walking about.'

The talk's getting a bit catty now so Miller breaks it up. 'C'mon, kids, out you get. Let the old man get home to his beauty sleep.'

'Why, Mr Miller,' Pauline says, 'you're not old!'

'Flatterer,' Miller says. He reaches right over behind his missis and opens the door for Jimmy and Pauline. They get out and shout good night back into the car.

'Well, there's a couple who've certainly had a good

time,' Miller says, and Mrs Miller asks if they've been courting long.

'I didn't even know they were friendly,' Miller says.

'I don't think they've spoken more than two words to one another before tonight,' Ingrid says.

'Like that, is it?' Miller says. 'You can't deny the Party brings the Staff together.'

He drives on for a bit.

'What about you two?'

'If you turn down at the next traffic lights you can drop me right at the door,' I tell him.

'And you, Ingrid?'

'I'll show you when we've dropped Vic.'

'I'm sure I never meant you to come so far out of your way, Jack,' I tell Miller.

'Think nothing of it,' he says. 'There'll be a small deduction from salary on Friday.'

As he turns into our street I pull Ingrid over to me again and kiss her. 'Friday night, then?'

'All right.'

The car stops and I get out. I bend down to say good night.

'Thanks for the lift, Jack. Very good of you. Goo'night, Ingrid. Goo'night, Mrs Miller.'

I watch them go, the exhaust smoke pink in the tail lights, and then I feel for my key and go up the path. There's a big ball of fluttering excitement in me at the thought of seeing Ingrid on Friday night. I remember how I felt after last time, but somehow it seems different now, and I can't think about that. All I can think about is seeing her again, and after can take care of itself.

III

One day about a fortnight after the Party Conroy doesn't turn in and nobody knows why he's away. The next day he comes as usual and about half-ten he goes into Hassop's office and spends a good half-hour in there chewing the fat about something. Young Colin Laisterdyke takes Hassop his morning cuppa and comes out and tells us he's heard him say to Conroy that he doesn't suppose he can make him change his mind if he's made it up; and it doesn't take a genius to reckon up from this that Conroy's handing his notice in.

There's nothing official and Conroy doesn't say a dicky bird, but on Friday of the week after this Jeff Lewis goes round the office with a box and a sheet of paper collecting money for Conroy's leaving present. It's a good collection to say Conroy's not everybody's best friend, and even old Hassop coughs up half a quid. We all say it wouldn't have been more than two bob, like all the rest of us put in, though, if Lewis hadn't been crafty enough to have this sheet of foolscap with all the names signed on it and how much they've given.

A week after this Conroy leaves. He spends nearly all afternoon walking round the Works saying so long to all the blokes he knows down there, and then about five we have a little ceremony up by Hassop's office and Conroy's presented with a matching fountain pen and propelling pencil set. Hassop makes a little speech about how much Conroy's going to be missed and everybody's embarrassed and wishing he'd belt up because we know he doesn't mean a word of it. There's Conroy's name in gold letters on the pen and pencil and it seems to touch him when he gets them. He swallows a time or two and then manages to say, 'Thanks very much, lads. Bloody good of you.'

And that's all. Five minutes later he's got all his books and drawing tackle in a little attaché case and he's ready for off.

He comes and holds his hand out to me.

'So long, then, young Browny.'

'So long, Conroy. All the best.'

'Watch out for the women, lad; and go easy on the beer.'

'I'll see to it.'

'That's the ticket. And *Nil illegitimum*.'

'What's that?'

'*Nil illegitimum*,' Conroy says. 'Don't let the bastards grind you down.'

I'm laughing. 'I'll watch it.'

And then he's away, and the queerest thing is this lump in my throat like a bird's egg seeing him go out of the door. I've only just got to know Conroy, the other Conroy under the brag and bluster, and I think we might have been good mates. I sit on my buffet and look at his empty board. I look at Lewis and Rawly and Whymper and the rest. It's not going to be the same without old Conroy. Somehow it hasn't been the same lately anyway. I fiddle about with my scale. I can't concentrate any more today. I'm a bit fed-up all round and I wonder if a change of job mightn't do *me* good.

IV

In the meantime there's this business of Ingrid. I've seen her three or four times since the Party and every time I leave her I think that's the last time and I don't care if I never set eyes on her again. Then one day I'll look at her and get this feeling and we're off again. There's no love in it as far as I'm concerned and I can think that I don't much like her even when I'm all het up to get her out again. And I feel rotten about it. I feel lousiest when I've just left her. I think then I should tell just how it is and I don't think it's fair I should take her out like this. But I never do, because just then I don't want to go deep into things and start explaining. And it's easy when I'm wanting her to tell myself that she wants me and she'd rather have me this way than not at all. It's a mess.

2

I

I arrive at the shop one Saturday morning and find Henry standing outside with the door still shut and no sight of Mr Van Huyten.

'I don't think he was feeling too good yesterday,' Henry says when I ask him what's up. 'He was out in the rain earlier in the week and he thought he'd caught a chill.'

'Who'll be looking after him?'

'He'll have to look after himself,' Henry says. 'He has a woman coming in to do for him two or three times a week, but he lives on his own.'

Poor old geezer! I know how it is when you have flu and you want coddling. 'Why, he could flake out,' I tell Henry, 'and nobody 'ud be any the wiser.'

Henry strikes a match and lights a dokka. 'That's what it's like when you're old and on your own in the world.'

Well, I don't know what to say to this. I can't remember it happening before. You know Mr Van Huyten's old but you kind of never think of him falling ill or dying or anything.

'Well what are we goinna do? We can't stand here all morning. There'll be customers arriving afore long.'

Henry gives a nod. 'And I've a couple of sets to deliver . . .' He studies a minute, then he says, 'I'd better go up and see what's doing.'

'Want me to come?'

'No need. I shan't be long. I really ought to get them sets delivered, if nothing else.' He goes over to the van, which he's had at home overnight.

'Does it mean the shop'll have to stay shut all day?'

'It did the last time he was badly,' Henry says. 'There was nobody else to look after it.'

'Well there is now,' I tell him. 'Look, Henry; tell him I can manage. He can't shut Saturday; it's his best day. Look at the trade he'll lose. It might mean thirty or forty quid on records alone.' I grab Henry's arm as he's climbing into the van. 'Tell him we can manage, Henry. You can demonstrate the sets while I look after the counter. You can always leave the repairs a day.'

Henry chucks his dog-end away as he gets into the cab. 'I'll see what he says.'

He's away half an hour and I'm on eggs all the time, walking up and down in front of the shop and thinking he won't be telling Mr Van Huyten right and I should have gone and talked to him myself. It nigh breaks my heart to think of the shop being shut and all that trade being turned away.

Once a middled-aged bloke comes up to the door and tries the handle. 'Aren't they open today?'

'In about half an hour,' I tell him. 'Mr Van Huyten's poorly but we'll be open in about half an hour if you can come back then.'

He studies a minute. 'It's my daughter,' he says. 'It's her birthday next week and she's mad keen for one o' these long-playing radiograms. I thought I'd surprise her like ... I didn't know whether to come here or try Norton's. Their winder's full of 'em ... televisions an' all ...'

'We can fix you up,' I tell him. 'We've got a good selection in our inside showroom – H.M.V., K.B., Bush ...' I feel like grabbing his arm and chaining him to the door till Henry gets back.

The bloke nods. 'Aye, well ... I'll just walk up the road and call back later.'

I can see him slipping away to Norton's and being

roped in by that horrible flash type who waits on there. Just then Henry draws up in the van. I say to the bloke, 'If you'll wait just another minute . . .' and jump at Henry as he opens the cab door and gets out.

'What does he say?'

'He says okay, we've to open up an' do the best we can. He wasn't too keen on it at first.'

I'm grinning all over my face. 'We've got a customer already. Gimme the key.'

I open the door and ease this cove in before he gets any more ideas about going somewhere else. Me and Henry show this bloke the lot, both in the shop and the back room, and when I give Henry the nudge he starts blinding him with gen about input and output and baffles and speakers and I don't know what else. Neither does this bloke but you can see Henry impresses him and he's thinking he's come to a shop where they know what they're at anyway.

After about twenty minutes of this the chap settles on an H.M.V. console job with V.H.F. radio, and I start to give him the patter about hire purchase and what not; and this is where I nearly slip up because I've weighed this cove up wrong. He just stands there for a minute or two listening and then he brings this dirty great roll of notes out of his pocket and says, 'I'll pay cash.'

Just like that. My hands are trembling so much I can hardly count the money.

'When can you deliver?' he says when I've made his receipt out.

'Any time,' I tell him.

'Righto.' He writes something on a bit of paper and gives it to me. 'You deliver to this address next Wednesday morning. Not before, mind. I want it there on the day.'

I take a quick butcher's at the name on the paper. 'We'll attend to it, Mr Wainright, don't worry.' I come round the counter and walk to the door with him. 'Thank you very much, sir. Good morning.'

As soon as the door's shut I dash into the back place to

Henry. He's got his overall on now and tinkering inside a TV set.

'Seventy-four guineas, Henry. Seventy-four bloody lovely guineas. Just wait till we tell Mr Van Huyten about this. If we only sell a couple of packets of needles all the rest of the day it's been worth opening for.'

Henry's poking a screwdriver into the innards of this set. He nods. 'Not bad,' he says. 'A pity it can't last.'

I give up and go back into the shop.

Course we sell more than a couple of packets of needles. Before long the rush starts and the fans are crowding me at the counter and I'm whipping record boxes down right and left and ringing up the old sales in the till. By the time we shut up and I start off to Mr Van Huyten's with the key, I'm dog-tired. But happy.

II

Mr Van Huyten's playing Brahms on the gramophone when I get there. He shushes me as he lets me in and I sit down and wait while the music's finished. I think Brahms is Mr Van Huyten's favourite composer. He told me once that Brahms might not be the greatest composer who ever lived but nobody ever wrote music that sounded more like great music should sound. It all sounds much of a muchness to me. No beat, no melody, and it goes on and on from now to Kingdom come.

Well after I've been sitting there about three hours this piece finishes and Mr Van reaches out and knocks the gram off. I've hardly said a word up to now and he waits for all the news. I ask him how he is first and he says he's not really poorly on himself but he's got a chill and he thought it wisest to stay at home today. I tell him about the radiogram we flogged and show him the details of the day's trade where I've written it all down on a bit of paper.

He says very good, very good, a few times, nodding his head, and I can tell he's pleased.

170

'You see it was worth opening for, Mr Van Huyten,' I say. 'I was on eggs thinking you'd tell Henry not to bother.'

He looks at me from where he's sitting in this big old wing-chair by the fire. 'It was important to you that the shop should open today, then, Victor?'

'Well, look at all the trade we'd've turned away. And you don't know how many new customers might never have come again if they'd once got to Norton's.'

'Quite so,' Mr Van says. 'You've done very well. And this is the first time you've attended to the shop on your own for the day. Of course, I knew you were capable or I shouldn't have given Henry permission to open . . .'

I lean back in the chair. I really am dead beat and Mr Van Huyten notices it.

'You wouldn't be sorry when it was time to close, eh?' he says, and I grin at him. 'Can't say I was. I haven't had a minute all day.'

He doesn't say anything to this and he appears to be thinking about something as he stares into the fire. So we sit there in this big room with the high ceiling and the old furniture and this old-fashioned gramophone with the massive horn sticking out into the room. It's all shabby and it would give me the creeps to live here. I wonder why Mr Van hangs on to this old gramphone from the year dot, for instance, when he's got all the latest electric long-playing ones in his shop. Must be sentimental reasons. He rests his elbows on the arms of his chair and puts his finger-ends together. He's wearing a big wool dressing-gown and a scarf round his neck. He doesn't look well. You get the feeling you can see through his skin and his face seems thinner than usual.

'How do you like your work, Victor?' he asks me all of a sudden, and I give a shrug. I hate to admit it but I have to be honest with Mr Van Huyten. 'Oh, so so.'

He looks at me over his specs. 'Only so so?'

'I liked it well enough for the first two or three years,' I tell him, 'but now, just lately . . . I've been a bit unsettled, as you might say.'

'You don't think it's just a change of scene you need? There comes a time in every man's life when he feels the need of a change.'

'I don't think its that, Mr Van Huyten. I'm just tired of the work. I want something different altogether. I feel I want to meet different people . . .'

'You like it in the shop on Saturdays?'

'I enjoy it. It's grand.'

'Have you ever considered doing something like that full time?'

I'm a bit embarrassed at this. 'Well, to tell you the truth, Mr Van Huyten, I don't think the money's there. In my job a thousand a year's not too much to hope for. More than that, even, if you get to be a chief draughtsman in charge of an office. And all the time you hear of shop asistants going to work in factories to get more money.'

He nods. 'I agree. The money isn't very good for the ordinary shop assistant. One must have er . . . an interest in the business for it to be worthwhile.'

He sits back in his chair and his face goes into the shadows thrown down by the standard lamp behind him. They make the lines on his face look deeper than I've ever seen them before.

'I'm an old man, Victor,' he says. 'Older than you probably think. I have a sound business which looks as though it will continue to prosper.' He smiles a bit. 'Despite Henry's gloomy prophecies . . . There's even room for expansion, but I'm past the age for striking out that way . . . I'm an old man,' he says again, 'and I have no living relatives. I was never fortunate enough to have children.' He lifts his hand. 'I may have a few cousins or half-cousins in Holland, but I don't know them and they don't know me.' He stops for a minute. 'I don't want to say too much, Victor, because you're still a very young man, not yet of age . . . But I will say in all honesty that I'm very fond of you and have every faith in your character and ability.'

This gets me. I'm touched, and when I remember the

172

dates with Ingrid I'm a bit ashamed as well.

'You've become rapidly familiar with the business even though you spend only one day a week with us . . .'

I'm wondering what he's driving at. Is he trying to tell me he wants to leave me the shop? I begin to feel excited, and a bit scared at the same time. He sits up in his chair and blows his nose with a loud noise. I catch the smell of the eucalyptus stuff he has on his hanky.

'The immediate problem, Victor, is that I'm going to be compelled to take on a full-time assistant in the shop. I want someone whom I can like and trust, someone to whom eventually, when I decide to retire and take things more easily, in a few years' time, I can hand over the day-to-day running of the business.'

Now I see he's taking thought for the time when he won't be around any more, and I don't know what to say to him. Here it is – here's how loneliness gets you in the end. You think if you find your dream, the person you're looking for, it'll be the end of loneliness for ever. And then, at the end, it creeps up on you again and finds you sitting in an old wing-chair in a gloomy old house, on your own, with everybody gone, and nothing to do but wait for the end. And maybe this is the worst loneliness of all, because you've got no hope of anything else.

Mr Van Huyten coughs and says, real delicate like, 'What are your present wages, Victor, if I might ask?'

I tell him I'm on seven-ten a week at present. 'If they come through with union rate when I'm twenty-one it'll be nearer ten pound.'

'You think they will give you the union rate?'

'I think it's practically certain. We've a pretty strong union membership at Whittaker's and all the older chaps get the rate.'

'And in future years? Does it rise any more?'

'Till you're twenty-five. It's about fourteen-ten then.'

Mr Van lifts his eyebrows. 'Fourteen-ten. And after that, what happens?'

'Well as far as the union's concerned, that's it. If the firm thinks you're worth a bit more they might give it to you. Like I said, there are jobs going that carry a thousand a year.'

'Hmmm.' Mr Van Huyten nods. 'I've never known just how well or how badly draughtsmen were paid. I've always thought they should be paid a reasonable wage considering the skill and training involved . . .' He clears his throat and feels for his hanky, bringing the smell of eucalyptus again.

'Well,' he says, 'no doubt you've followed the trend of what I've been saying. As I said, it's too early to make promises and raise hopes. What I require immediately, or as soon as it can be arranged, is someone whom I can like and trust to come and assist me.'

'What you're saying, Mr Van Huyten, is that you'd like me to come and work full-time in the shop.'

He nods again. 'Correct,' and he puts his hand up as I'm going to say something else. 'Apparently you've never seriously considered it before and the last thing I want to do is divert you from your chosen course. That's why I asked you how you liked your job. Now assuming the money was, shall we say comparable, and there were prospects of a future when – not next year, mind, but sometime – when you wouldn't be just a shop assistant in a dead-end job, what would you say then?'

'I don't know, Mr Van Huyten.' I think about it for a minute. 'I rather fancy the idea. I've always liked working in the shop, as you know . . .' I realize he's not expecting an answer off the cuff, and I say, 'Thanks very much for your offer, Mr Van Huyten, and I'd like to think it over, please.'

'Well done,' he says. 'A very reasonable answer. The last thing I wanted was for you to jump to a decision without considering every side of the matter.'

'I'll have to talk it over at home, you see.'

'Of course, of course. Naturally. I was going to suggest that I might discuss it with your father.'

'I'll tell him and maybe he'll call in one day on his way home from work.'

I don't stop long after this. Mr Van Huyten thanks me

again for looking after the shop for the day and gives me a ten-bob bonus over what he usually pays me. I don't want to take this but he won't let me go without it.

I put it to my mother and dad at supper-time the same night.

'Mr Van Huyten's offered me a full-time job at the shop,' I say, and watch the Old Lady's face.

'What did you say to that?' she says.

'I told him I'd think it over an' see what you an' me dad thought about it.'

'I think you're all right as you are,' the Old Lady says. 'What prospects is there in a shop?'

'Hold on a minute,' the Old Man says. 'Just ho'd your hosses. It's not like a job in just any shop. Mr Van Huyten thinks a lot about our Victor. He nearly looks on him like his own lad . . . Just what did he say, Victor? He didn't come out with it just like that, did he?'

'Oh, no; he went all round the houses, talking about how old he was and he has no relatives and he didn't want to divert me from my chosen course. You know how Mr Van Huyten talks.'

The Old Man nods. He's pretty sharp in a lot of ways, the Old Man, and he's on to this situation a sight quicker than the Old Lady is.

'Aye,' he says, 'he's a real gentleman all right.'

'But there's no money in being a shop assistant, Arthur,' the Old Lady says. 'Victor's nearly twenty-one an' he'll be due for a substantial rise then.'

'Oh, we talked about all that. He said the money would be all right.'

'D'ye fancy it, though, Victor?' the Old Man says. 'You know you allus wanted to be a draughtsman. You remember how chuff you were when you got that letter to say you could start at Whittaker's?'

'I was only sixteen then. I'm not sure I want that kind o' work now. It's not what Mr Van Huyten said makes me say that: it's been coming on for some time . . .' I feel myself beginning to grin. 'I wouldn't mind, y'know. I rather fancy the idea.'

175

'I think happen I'd better have a word with him,' the Old Feller says.

'Oh, aye, he said he thought you two ought to talk it over. I told him you might call in on your way home from work one day.'

'I shan't that!' the Old Man says. 'I shan't call an' see Mr Van Huyten in t'clothes I go to an' from t'pit in. I'll go up an' have a talk with him one night when I'm washed an' changed.'

III

A week later it's all settled. I'm to go and work for Mr Van Huyten at eight pounds a week. When I'm twenty-one he'll make it nine and he says I can depend on him to see I'm all right after that.

The first person I tell at Whittaker's is Jimmy Slade. I tell him straight after the Easter holidays.

'How d'you go about handing your notice in?'

'I think the correct way is to write to the Managing Director and say something like, "Will you please take this as notice of my intention to terminate my employment with the Company on such and such a date," '

'And how much notice do you have to give?'

'I think you're only bound to give a week but a fortnight's fairer. And I should have a word with old Hassop first and tell him what you're doing: then it doesn't make him look a Charlie.'

'I'm not looking forward to that.'

'They reckon he even tried to get Conroy to stay on,' Jimmy says; 'and I always thought he hated his guts.'

'He was pretty hot stuff, old Conroy. Hassop knew he was losing a good man. I don't reckon I'm in his class as a draughtsman.'

The dinner-time bell rings as we're talking and we follow everybody out of the office.

'Funny thing about Conroy,' I say, 'I was just beginning to like him when he left.'

'Oh, Albert wasn't such a bad sort of chap,' Jimmy says. 'Once you made allowances for his ways you could get on with him okay. I always did prefer him to Lewis.'

'Me an' all, any day.'

'Ah, well,' Jimmy says. 'If you've made your mind up you've made it up. I'll miss you, old cock.'

'Oh, come off it,' I say. 'I'm not emigrating to Timbuktu. We can have nights out together.'

'Aye, right enough.'

We've got along the corridor nearly to the door when all of a sudden we hear a bint cry out and there's a commotion at the bottom of the stairs. When we get nearer we see a crowd of birds and one or two bods gathered round somebody lying on the floor.

Somebody says. 'No, don't move her; run for the Nurse,' and one of the blokes goes dashing through the door.

We can't see a thing from where we are and we can't get past to get out. When one of the bints turns away I ask her, 'What's up? Who is it?'

'It's Ingrid Rothwell,' she says, all in a flutter and a flap. 'She's fallen down the stairs. Right from top to bottom. She couldn't save herself. She just gave a shout and went straight down.'

'Is there anything we can do?'

'I don't think so. They've gone for the Nurse. She's passed out and we daren't move her.'

My heart's going like a tom-tom and I don't know where I am for a minute. Jimmy gets hold of my arm and steers me away. 'C'mon; we're only blocking the way. Let's go to the canteen.'

We go back the long way round and hear about it later on. Ingrid's come round by the time the Nurse gets there and she gets a couple of bods to carry her into the waiting-room while she rings up for an ambulance. Next day we hear they've X-rayed Ingrid at the infirmary and she's broken her left arm. I get all this from Jimmy, who's got it from Pauline Lawrence, who got it from the Nurse. I'm glad it's not serious but now the shock's passed I don't feel much else. Anyway, I have to do something so I splash eight-and-six on a pound box of chocolates and send them with a little note by Pauline who's going to visit Ingrid one night. I just say in the note I'm sorry it's happened and I hope she'll soon be better again. I don't mention about leaving Whittaker's. She can't write back because it's her left arm and she's left-handed so she just tells Pauline to say thanks for the chocs, which she does.

When I think about it I'm glad she can't write because it means she can't pin me down. What with her laid up and me leaving Whittaker's I reckon this is the time to break off properly, for good. Then I might feel better all round and not so much of a louse. It'll be all right if I don't see her. I just shan't think about her then.

That afternoon I tell Mr Hassop that I'm handing my notice in at the week-end. I don't meet with much opposition. Maybe he's not bothered either way, whether I go or stay. We have quite a long natter, though, and he tells me all the disadvantages of being a shop assistant and the opportunities open for draughtsmen. I tell him I've thought about all that and this isn't just another shop assistant's job because I've kind of got an interest in the business, and we leave it at that.

On the Friday morning I take my letter in to Miss Padgett, Mr Matthew's secretary, and a fortnight later I'm away, just like Conroy, with my tackle in a case and a very nice pigskin notecase with my initials on it and a quid inside from the Staff.

Right at the last when they're giving me the wallet and Hassop's giving out with the bull like he did for Conroy, I'm swallowing hard and looking round at all their faces and having a last-minute touch of panic for fear I'm doing the wrong thing. Because now I can only remember the good times early on, when it all seemed exciting, before I got restless; and I think what a good bunch of lads they are, as grand a bunch all round as you'd meet in a day's march, and I know I'll miss them.

And that's it. The next Monday morning I go to work full-time for Mr Van Huyten in his shop.

3

I

I settle down pretty quickly at the shop because I like the
job as much as I thought I should. Mr Van Huyten tells
me all about invoicing and the books and soon he's
leaving me to deal with all this on quiet days during the
week. I get as I know the record catalogues inside
out – even the classical stuff as well, and I begin to like
hearing some of this as well as the jazz and pops, though
I can't really take to Mr Van Huyten's Brahms and the
'later quartets' by Beethoven, the one Rawly was talking
about having gone deaf that time. Chamber music's not
in my line: I like plenty of tunes and lots of bash and
clatter in the orchestra and before long I find that old
Tchaikovsky's right up my alley. I get to know more
about all this because Mr Van Huyten starts taking me
over to Leeds and Bradford in his car when there's some
crack orchestra playing. A lot of it's fit to put you to
sleep but every now and then you get a real kick out of
something they play, and sometimes you get a feeling
you don't like a certain piece now but you might if you
heard it a few more times. Mr Van Huyten talks about
music all the way there and back and I like hearing him
tell the tale about the great composers and how some of
them struggled to get a name and nobody cared for their
music when it first came out. He's real genned up, Mr
Van Huyten is, and he makes it interesting: all about
Mussorgsky going off his nut and Tchaikovsky writing to
that old bint all those years without seeing her and

179

trying to do himself in by drinking poisoned water. Some '
real boyos there were among them. Mr Van Huyten tells
me to have patience with music and it'll all open out like
a big flower some day.

'Why do they make it so hard to listen to?' I ask him
one night when we're coming back from a Hallé concert
in St George's Hall in Bradford.

'But they don't set out to do that, Victor,' he says.
'That's just the point. These popular tunes that you have
in the . . . what do you call it – the Hit Parade? They're
so simple they go in one ear and out the other. How long
do they last? A few weeks, or a month or two at the most.
But this is music which endures for hundreds of years. It
will be listened to as long as men live. Can you expect
music of that stature to have the immediate appeal of a
popular song? Someone once said that great art doesn't
reveal all its secrets at one glance. Be patient, let it work
on you, let it flow over you. One day you'll hear the most
glorious music where you now hear only a din. You'll
hear it all, Victor, I hope. The thunder and majesty of
Beethoven, the grace and tragic beauty of Mozart, the
glorious singing of Brahms, the noble sadness of Elgar.
It's like a wonderful voyage of discovery, Victor, with
magic over every horizon. Here is all the music in the
world just waiting for you to find it. How I wish I could go
back fifty years and discover it all afresh!'

When I've been at the shop awhile Mr Van Huyten lets
me have a two-speed record player and some records
cheap. I can see he's out to turn me into a real music-
lover; but I don't mind. It's like he says, a new discovery
over every horizon, and it seems like each week I'm finding something new to like.

Sometimes I go out on jobs with Henry, mainly to help
with the carrying and such, but I'm learning all the time,
and in the quiet spells I go back into the workroom and
watch him do the repairs and it's surprising how much
technical stuff you can pick up that way. At nights and
week-ends, besides playing records and the times I go
out with Mr Van Huyten, I might have a night at the

pictures with Willy or Jimmy, and the odd pint. Sometimes I go to a dance. I still think about this girl I'm going to run into one day, but I'm happy enough now and there's no great hurry.

I hardly think about Ingrid at all. Out of sight, out of mind certainly works where she's concerned. One time she sends me a picture postcard from Skegness where she's convalescing at her aunty's. There's an address on it but I think at first I won't bother writing back because it's all over. Then I think there's no harm in being civil so I get a picture of Cressley Town Hall and send her that. I write on it: 'I don't think I'll come here again for my holidays because it's a mucky place and it rains all the time. Hope you're properly better soon.' When I'm putting it in the letterbox I wonder if I'm not encouraging her and it might be better to tear it up and forget it; but I let it go.

II

The days draw out, the weather gets warmer, and it's what we call summer, with a bitter laugh when we've said it.

One day towards the back end of June I'm leaning on the counter in the shop, feeling a bit cheesed. Mr Van Huyten's doing his accounts in his little glass cubby-hole and Henry's busy in the back. Things are a bit slack this morning and by ten o'clock we've had a woman in for a record catalogue, another woman with an electric iron for repair, and a bod who's wandered round looking at TV sets and radiograms and wouldn't let me tell him anything about them. 'I'm just looking,' he says. I know his type. He'll go home and tell his family that the assistants at Van Huyten's are too pushing. And if you take no notice of people when they come in they go away and say we don't give them service and attention.

Anyway, I leave him be, and in a minute or two in comes a sprightly-looking bint with a hedgerow hairdo

181

who asks for a record of Tommy Steele singing: 'I'm the Only Man on the Island'. I serve her and take her money and watch her go down the shop. She's wearing spike-heels that she's not too steady on and a tight skirt that cuts her stride to about six inches. I wonder what happens if she ever forgets and tries to run for a bus. I notice skirts are getting shorter, which is something I don't mind at all, and I'm looking at this bint's legs as she prissys her way out and letting my thoughts wander a bit in the direction of subject normal when the door opens and another pair of legs comes in: a pair of neat slim legs in darkish nylons that I'd know anywhere. And all at once it's just as though somebody's given me a clout on the chest over the heart and I can't breathe properly.

She comes up to the counter and says, 'Hello, Vic.'

'Hello, Ingrid. Are you better?'

'Yes, thanks. I'm going back to work on Monday.'

'Taken a fair while, hasn't it?'

'There were complications. It didn't set right the first time and they had to break it again.'

'You'll have to take it easy a bit pounding the old typewriter.'

'I suppose I shall. I expect I've lost my speed and everything now.'

'How did it happen? I never did get the proper tale.'

'Oh, I was wearing a new pair of shoes with high heels.' She laughs. 'That's what vanity leads to.'

'Anyway, so long as you're all right now.'

She looks okay, pretty much as usual, in fact. She's a bit tanned, and maybe a wee bit thinner than before. But not much, and not in the places that matter. I know, because I can't help looking. She's wearing a fawn short-sleeved jumper and the points of her threepenny bits are pushing the weave apart so you can see the white of her bra through.

'It was nice of you to send the chocolates.'

'Oh, that was nothing.'

'I'm sorry I couldn't write a note to thank you but it was my left arm, you see.'

'That's okay, Pauline said thanks.'

She looks down the counter at Mr Van Huyten doing his accounts and taking no notice of us. She opens her bag and takes a bit of paper out.

'Have you any of these?'

I take the paper from her. My hand's not too steady what with seeing her again so sudden like. There's the titles of three popular records on the paper and down at the bottom she's written 'When can I see you again?' Just for a second I think this is another record and then I catch on and, of all things to happen, I start to blush.

I turn round to the shelf and get the boxes down and I can feel all the old excitement knotting up in me.

'We have the first two,' I tell her, getting the records out, 'and we can get the other one in a couple of days.'

'I'll leave that one,' she says, and I notice that she's coloured up a bit as well and she can't look me in the face. 'Can I listen to the others, please?'

She's probably heard them both a million times apiece already but I say, 'Sure,' and go round the counter and open the door of one of the listening booths.

'How d'you like your new job?' she says when we're in the booth.

'Oh, it's grand.'

'I was surprised to hear you'd left Whittaker's. A bit sudden, wasn't it?'

'Oh, I don't know. I'd been a bit restless for some time. When this chance turned up I took it.'

I'm putting the first record on the turntable and I'm thinking that more than anything I want to see her again. I have to see her however I might feel later. I say, 'Tonight, half past seven, the park gates nearest your place.'

She says okay and I let the needle down on the record. There's a brassy intro and then this bod starts to yawp, 'I can't getchew out of my mind, What ever I do, oh baby, I find, I keep thinking of ye-ew . . .' It's crap, but if she likes it it's her dough.

When she's gone I nip out back to the bog because my

183

guts seemed to have turned to water. It's no good though because it's all excitement, excitement at the thought of seeing her again and . . .

III

'Do you love me, Vic?' she says, and I put my face down in her neck where she can't see it. All I want now is to get away from her because I feel as lousy as I ever did about it all. And to think not an hour ago I didn't know where to put myself I was so mad for her. If only she hadn't come into the shop I think now. I was doing all right without her. I hardly ever thought of her. But no, she has to come in and let me see her again and set me off remembering what it's like to kiss her and hold her, remembering how firm she is and how soft her skin is in places you can't see. The private places. And maybe that's half the attraction – they're private to everybody bar me. In a way it's a gift the way she is about me and somebody like Willy would be sure to say I was a twerp if I passed up the chance . . .

But now she's got to talk about loving and I thought she'd got the position about that straightened out long since.

I know she's waiting for me to say something and I can't tell her a barefaced lie. And how can I say no, straight out, after the way we've just been? I wonder if she'd understand if I could explain it all – just how I feel. What I want is somebody to explain it to me! I wonder anyway if a girl could ever feel the way I do, and I reckon women are different that way and they have to have love.

Well, she's asked me and now she's waiting for an answer.

'I don't know,' I say.

She waits a second or two, then she says, 'D'you love anybody else?'

'No.' And that's a lie in a way, only not in the way

184

she'd call a lie because I don't suppose she means a bint I've never yet laid eyes on, that exists only in my mind.

We're lying on my raincoat under some trees up the top end of the park where nobody ever goes except courters. It's a fine night for a change; the sun's warm and there are leaf-shadows on the grass round us. I'm looking away down the slope and it's nearly as though Ingrid reads my mind when she says, 'D'you remember that night on the seat down there and what you said?'

'Yes . . . I remember.'

'Did you mean it then, Vic?'

'Well, I must have done or I wouldn't have said it. I was a bit carried away.'

'You meant it then,' she says. 'I know you did. You didn't want to see me then just for what you could get, did you?'

Put like that it's a bit straight from the shoulder and I feel myself colouring up. It's one thing feeling you're a bit of a louse at times and another being as good as told you are. And the thing is, I'm not *like* that really. I'm not. I don't want to be rotten to her or anybody else. I don't want to hurt her. But she wants me to go out with her, doesn't she? And as for all this – she started it, didn't she?.

'I'd never have gone as far as I did that night if you hadn't let me know you wanted me to.'

'Let you know?' she says. 'How did I let you know?'

'Kissing me that way . . . You know . . . with your tongue. I thought you were inviting me . . .'

'I didn't know it meant that. I just wanted to kiss you properly . . . You'll have been thinking all this time I'm easy, then?'

'No, I haven't. I didn't think so then and I don't now. I . . . oh, I can't explain, that's all: I just can't explain.'

I want to tell her I know she loves me and that's what makes the difference; but how can I come out with a thing like that without sounding conceited? And anyway, it would make me seemed to be taking advantage more than ever.

'You didn't believe all those things Dorothy said that time, did you, Vic? You don't think I've done all this with anybody else, do you?'

'No, course not.'

I don't really care I don't think for a minute I'm the first bloke who's had his hand up her skirt, but maybe that's all. And she'd have to think a lot about whoever it was to let him that far. She's that sort of girl.

She slides her arm up round my neck and pulls me down to her. 'You know I like you, don't you, Vic? I've liked you since before you asked me out.'

And that's one of the funniest things about it: the way the whole thing's switched since the beginning. Well, I have to kiss her when she says this but it's a dead loss as far as I'm concerned.

A couple saunter down the slope not far from us and I say, 'C'mon, we'll have the park-keeper after us.'

'Why should he bother us?'

'Anyway, it's getting late.'

She sits up and take her powder compact and lipstick and comb out of her handbag and starts titivating her-self up. I lie there and watch her, wishing she'd make it snappy so's we can go. I can't understand it. I just can't understand what goes on inside you to make you change like this. She checks that all her buttons and zips are fastened and I tidy myself up, itching for her to get a move on.

'How's everything at Whittaker's?' I ask her for some-thing to say as we walk down to the gate.

'Oh, pretty much as it always was.'

We reach the gate where she goes down the road to her house and I cut back down the edge of the park to ours. She looks at me and I know she's waiting for me to say something.

'Can you take phone calls?'

She nods. 'The best time's during the dinner hour. About twenty past one when we're back from the canteen.'

'Well I'm pretty busy just now. I don't know when it'll

be, but I'll give you a ring one day next week. Okay?'

'If you like.'

I can tell from the look on her face that she's thinking I don't mean it. Maybe it's just as well. Maybe if she was to turn round on me right now and tell me to take my hook for good it would be the best thing that could happen.

But she doesn't. She says okay, and we say good night and I watch her walk away down the avenue. I can tell she's feeling pretty miserable and I don't feel exactly on top of the world myself.

IV

And that's the way we go on right through the last of the summer and autumn and into winter again. Sometimes I'll see her twice a week and other times a fortnight might go by. Then she either rings me or I'll ring her and we're off again. She never talks about love again and it seems we've both come to accept things the way they are. She wants me as she's got me if the only other way is not having me at all; and as for me, there's times when I feel I never want to see her again and others when all I want is to take all her clothes off and roll her on a bed. Only we don't go that far. I don't know what she'd say if I offered and I'm not daft enough to take the risk if she was willing. Only I can't help thinking about it.

I have my twenty-first birthday in October and I start paying my board at home. I think the Old Lady's always fancied throwing a party for me, but I'm not in the mood, so her and the Old man buy me a gold wrist watch, a real beauty.

I see Ingrid a day or two after. She's sent me a card and I thank her for it, though I wish she hadn't done it because naturally the Old Lady was on to it like a shot.

It's a cold night and teeming down with rain and we don't fancy any of the pictures showing in town so I take her into the Bluebird for a cup of coffee. I don't usually

187

take her into places like that because we might see somebody I know and they're sure to get all the wrong ideas.

'I thought you weren't coming,' she says when we get sat down at a table at the back. She's wearing a green mack and it's wet on the shoulders. She takes her head-scarf off and her hair's dampish and pressed down to her head.

'I've been to the blood donation centre. I'd forgotten it was tonight or I'd have said half-an-hour later.'

'I didn't know you gave blood.'

'Every now and again.'

'How did you come to start doing that?'

'Oh, they had a bit of a drive on to find new donors and a chap came to the door one night. I reckoned if it was all that important to 'em I might as well give 'em a pint now and then.'

'Does it hurt? When they take it, I mean.'

'Naw, there's nothing to it. Me dad goes an' all. They got two new names when they came to our house.'

She sips her coffee, dainty like, with her little finger sticking out. She's got all sorts of little ways that put me on edge.

'I don't think I could face the sight of so much blood,' she says. 'Especially my own.'

'You don't see any blood. The bottle's on the floor all the time. You can see it if you lean over, but you don't have to.'

'But I thought . . . I've seen them on the pictures.'

'That's when they're being given blood. That's when the bottle's up above.'

'Oh, I see.'

'Then they send you a card to tell you how it's been used.'

'Have you ever had yours used in anything exciting?'

'Well I'm a common group – "O" – and I've only been four times.' I fish out the little blue card and show her the stickers on it, one for each visit. 'Usually it's just ordinary transfusions after operations. But it all helps.

188

You're got to think of all the poor devils who need it and remember you never know when you might be in the same boat. It'd be hard cheese if they hadn't any, wouldn't it?'

She shivers. 'I hope I never need any. I hate the thought of hospitals and operations. I had enough with my arm.'

'You never know,' I say.

She drinks some more coffee, and I look past her at the room. It's fairly full, it being a wet night, and there's all sort of people in, but mostly young 'uns passing the time on the flirting with one another, like that crowd in the middle with the lasses with hedgerow haircuts and jeans and the lads in jeans as well, some of them, and striped sweatshirts under their jackets. One of them has a leather jacket and a crewcut. He looks as though he's walked out of an American picture. It's all Yankeeland these days. If it goes big in America it takes here, like rock 'n' roll for instance. Me, I like to look English because I reckon it's the finest country in the world, bar none. Not that it's heaven for everybody, I suppose. There's an old keff sitting on his own down there by the wall and I wonder what he thinks to it. Even from the back you can see he hasn't had a shave for a week and he can't have sat in a barber's chair for months. There's a ragged hole in the top of his old trilby and he has a double-breasted navy blue overcoat that's dusty and without buttons and tied round the waist with a length of string. It gives you a kind of shock to see people like him about these days and you can only think it's their own fault. He might have boozed his way into that condition for all I know. He might be a no-good waster that's scrounged his way through life, too idle to do a day's work. You don't know.

But whichever way it is, there he is, old and on his own, and probably without two ha'pennies to rub together and you can't help feeling sorry and kind of sick inside to look at him.

'What are you looking at?' Ingrid says, watching me.

189

'Nothing, I'm just looking. My face is pointing that way.'

'Are you scared you'll see somebody you know?'

'Why should I be?'

'I sometimes think you're ashamed to be seen with me,' she says, looking down into her cup.

'Why should I be?' I say, feeling my face go hot.

She shrugs. 'I don't know. I just get the feeling sometimes.'

I'm drawing patterns with a matchstick in a drop of split coffee on the table-top and she turns her head and takes a look round the place herself.

'Well,' she says in a minute, 'how does it feel to be a man?'

I give a laugh. 'Ask me another.'

'Did you get any nice presents?'

I stretch my arm across the table to show her the watch. 'Me mother an' dad bought me this. Isn't it a gem, eh?'

She takes hold of my wrist and turns it so she can see the watch better. 'It's lovely . . . What else did you get?'

'Oh, Jim bought me a tie and Chris and David got me a book of crime stories and an L.P. record of Tchaikovsky's Pathetic Symphony.'

'My, my,' she says, lifting her eyebrows. 'Haven't we gone Highbrow lately!'

This niggles me no end. She's so satisfied that these yawping crooners are the last word.

'Well, what's wrong with it?' I say. 'It was written for people to like, wasn't it? What's wrong with me liking it?'

'Oh, nothing at all. Only there's lots of people who pretend to like that kind of thing just because they think it makes them Somebody.'

'You know me better than that.'

She shrugs. 'Oh, if you like it you're welcome to it. Personally I can't stand it. I like something with a tune.'

'But there's bags of tunes in Tchaikovsky,' I say. 'You can't get away from 'em . . .' I stop. Be damned if I'm going to defend myself for liking something that's worth something instead of the latest boy wonder from Clack-necuddenthistle who gets on television because he happens to have a check shirt and a guitar and a lot of bloody cheek.

We just sit there propping our chins on our hands and say nothing else for a bit.

'Would you like another cup o' coffee?' I asked her after a minute or two.

'May as well,' she says. 'We can't go anywhere in this rain.'

'It might have stopped now.'

'The grass'll be wet.'

I look at her. 'You're in a funny mood tonight. What you want to make a crack like that for?'

'Anyway,' she says, 'it's the wrong time.'

'Oh, that's what's wrong with you, is it?'

'That and other things.'

I look away from her and wish I hadn't come. I didn't know I was walking into this. I've never known her like this before. Quiet sometimes, brooding a bit, maybe; but she's never been sort of bitter like this. Well . . . I can't really blame her, I suppose . . .

'I'll get some more coffee'

I go over to the serving counter that runs down one side of the place with glass cases on top full of sandwiches and sticky cream buns and éclairs and whatnot and this big shiny steaming coffee machine in the middle. It kind of puts you off, the sight of all that grub when you're not hungry.

When I get back to the table I see a flat brown-paper package on the table by my place.

'What's this?'

'Open it and see.'

I strip off the brown paper and take this cig case out and hold it in my hands.

'Many happy returns,' she says.

I turn it over, looking at it. There's a little square with my initials engraved in it: V.A.B. She's even remembered

191

my middle name. All of a sudden I'm touched, right deep down. I want to take her hand and say, 'I love you, Ingrid. From now on it's all going to be different.' But I can't do it, because it wouldn't be true.

'Do you like it?'

'It's lovely . . . honest it is . . . Thanks ever so much, Ingrid. It's just what I need as well. . . I haven't got one . . .'

I look at the case and not at her when I say, 'I . . . I wish it could be different, Ingrid. I really do.'

'But it can't, can it?'

'I don't want to be rotten to you, y'know.'

'I don't think you do.'

I open the case. 'How many does it hold, fifteen?'

'Yes, fifteen.'

'And it's got one o' them metal things for holding the cigs. I like them better than the springs: they don't squash the cigs.'

'I was going to fill it for you,' she says, 'but I didn't have time to get to a tobacconists'.'

'Did you buy it today?'

'They were engraving it. I collected it tonight, after work.'

'Well it's lovely, Ingrid it really is.'

I snap it shut and look at the time by my new watch. 'What say we try and make the last show at the Ritz? It's that war picture. It might not be so bad.'

She nods, 'All right.'

We drink up and go out. As we pass the old keff I see that he's making his tea last as long as he can and just as I'm going by him something makes me put my hand in my pocket and fish half a crown out. 'Here you are; have another one on me.' I drop the half-dollar by his cup and he just looks up sort of bewildered like as I move on and follow Ingrid out.

'What was he saying to you?' she says as we go down the steps.

'Oh, nothing much.'

'Did he ask you for money?'

'No, he never said a word.'

'You gave him some, though, didn't you?'

'Well, what if I did?'

'How much did you give him?'

'Half a crown.'

'Half a crown! Whatever made you do that?'

'I just felt sorry for him, that's all. There's no law against it, is there? You make me feel as if I'd thrown half a crown down a drain.'

'You probably might just as well have. Very likely he'll make a bee-line for the nearest pub.'

'Well, that's his fault, isn't it, not mine? If he's daft enough to booze it, it's his lookout, not mine.'

We're walking along side by side and she takes my arm and gives it a squeeze. 'You're a funny lad,' she says.

'Don't I know it,' I say.

A while later we're together in the dark at the back of the picture house and I'm holding her and kissing her and for a while it's nearly like the first time I ever did it. Nearly – but not quite.

4

I

Comes another Christmas. The day we shut the shop for the holidays Mr Van Huyten has a little chat with me and tells me how pleased he is with the way things have worked out. It's nice to know you're giving satisfaction somewhere, anyway, I think. Mr Van Huyten gives me a Christmas bonus of five pounds and I go out and blue three-ten of it on a powder compact for Ingrid.

On Boxing Day Chris and David invite us over to celebrate their first wedding anniversary. It doesn't seem possible that it's a whole year since they got married, and still, when I think of all that's happened to me . . . The Old Man's full of corny jokes about the first seven years being the worst and they've only another six to go. They laugh this off like they do the way the Old Lady's always talking about the kids they'll be having, though there isn't a sign yet. I wonder if they're having trouble in this direction and then think they've only been married a year anyway and when they have kids and how many is their business and nobody else's. It's typical of the Old Lady, though. First she couldn't wait to get Chris married and now she's all agog to be a grandmother. I don't know what she'll pester about after that. Me, I suppose. She'll be dropping hints in my direction any time. Not that I'd mind if I could find the right girl and be sure she was the right one and not just a passing fancy like Ingrid. It seems to me being married must be something special if you can look as happy as Chris and David

194

do after a year of it. As it is, seeing the way they are only shows up the difference between the way I thought of Ingrid a year ago and the way I am with her now.

One morning in January there's a letter by my plate when I come down to breakfast. I recognize Ingrid's writing on the envelope and as I sit down and pick it up I feel the Old Lady watching me through that second pair of eyes she has in the back of her head.

'From your girl friend?' she says.

'What girl friend?'

'*What* girl friend?' There's the sizzle of the eggs as she breaks them into the frying pan. 'That lass you're knocking about with,' she says. I think for a minute she's seen me with Ingrid, then she says, 'That lass 'at sent you the card for your twenty-first and bought you the cigarette case.'

'Oh, *that*. That was months ago.'

'Don't you see her nowadays, then?'

I don't know how much she knows. You can never be sure with the Old Lady. 'Oh, on an' off. We're friendly like.'

'Well, then, what are you goin' all round the houses about it for?' she says. 'Are you ashamed of her or summat?'

She turns round and I keep my face down over my cornflakes. 'I just don't want you to get the wrong idea, that's all.'

She turns her face away again and splashes fat over the eggs.

'What sort o' wrong idea?'

'That it's serious or anything.'

She shakes her head. 'I don't know how it is wi' young fowk nowadays; they don't seem to know their own minds. Just want to play fast an' loose with one after the other. In my young days we either courted properly or left it alone.'

She brings the frying pan over from the cooker and lifts the eggs out on a knife – one on to Jim's plate and one on to mine. She shares the bacon out as well, then puts the pan back on the cooker and turns the gas off. She picks her cup up and has a drink of tea, watching the two of us tuck into the bacon and eggs.

'It's different now,' I tell her. 'Times change. You know what they say nowadays – Play the field before you get married and you won't want to after.'

'There's a lot o' fowk got married quicker than they thought they would through playin' t'field,' the Old Lady says.

I haven't liked this conversation from the start and I like it even less the way it's going now, so I shut up and say no more. The minutes tick away as we go on eating, and after a while the Old Lady says, 'Well . . . aren't you goin' to open your letter?'

'Read the letter, Vic, there's a good lad,' Jim says; 'then you can tell us all the news.'

'You'll get a good clout if you don't hold your tongue,' the Old Lady says; 'and there's a bit o' news for you!'

Jim's sitting with his back to her and he pushes his tongue down between his bottom teeth and his lip, tucks his chin down into his neck, and rolls his eyes.

'I can read it on the bus,' I say, trying not to grin and bring the Old Lady down on Jim. 'It isn't important.'

'It can't be,' the Old Lady says, real dry, 'or she wouldn't have bothered to write to you.'

Well, she does her best, but I'm not having any, and the letter's still sealed in its envelope when I leave the house and walk down the hill to the bus stop. I'm pretty mad with Ingrid for sending it and starting all that with the Old Lady and I wonder why she couldn't ring me up if she wanted to tell me something. I open the letter at the bus stop.

'Dear Vic,' she says, 'I've been off work today with an upset stomach and as I shan't be going back tomorrow (Thursday) I shan't be able to come out to meet you. My mother's going out, though, and you can come up to our house if you like. You know where I live. Just come to the back door and knock. Love, Ingrid.

'PS. Don't come before 7.30 because she's not going out till seven.'

Now I like this very much. I've never been in Ingrid's house but they're sure to have a couch or a comfortable chair, and it'll be a lot cosier than the park.

II

'I couldn't ring you up because Mother didn't go out all afternoon,' Ingrid says. 'So I scribbled the letter and pretended I wanted a little walk for some fresh air to give me a chance to post it.'

'You haven't told your mother about me, then?' I say.

'Well, no, I haven't. I mean, it's not as if we were . . . well, courting, is it?'

'No . . . no, it isn't.'

'Your parents don't know about me, do they?'

'Well they do and they don't. I mean they saw your birthday card and they know a girl bought me the cigarette case; but they don't know how often I see you or how it is between us.'

Ingrid blushes a bit. 'I should think not . . . That's the trouble isn't it? I mean, we couldn't tell anybody how it is, could we?'

'As far as anybody else is concerned – anybody who happens to see us out, I mean – we're just friends who go out with each other now and again.'

She says nothing to this, but looks into the fire, reaching out once, out of habit I suppose, to pull her skirt down over her knees. She's showing quite a lot of leg actually, because her skirt's on the short side and you sink right down into the velvet cushions in these chairs of theirs.

It's the dining-room we're in. I suppose they're like us and don't use the front room every day. This room's cosy, though, with this leather three-piece suite and a fitted carpet in rust. There's a console TV on one side of the fireplace and a little wireless on a table on the other. Ingrid's ma must be a Royalty fan because there's a big coloured photo of the Queen in her Coronation outfit on

197

the wall over the fireplace. There's a good fire and I'm feeling nice and comfortable and I've taken my jacket off and hung it on one of the dining-chairs.

I think Ingrid's a bit excited at having me here while her mother's back's turn because she's in a sort of light-hearted nervous mood and she laughs a lot. Or she was doing before we started talking about how it is with us and now she's gone a bit quiet, as if it's started her on studying, while she looks into the fire. I was just thinking before this that I'd have to get up and kiss her any time now. And the way we are, cosy and private for the first time, who knows what might happen then? I look at the shape of her under this pale pink blouse and I want to look at her properly. I want to find out if my hands have been telling the truth about how lovely she is.

I stand up to get a fag out of my jacket. As I get the cig case out of my inside pocket I pull some more stuff out with it: my comb and wallet, and a little book of pin-ups that took my fancy in a shop where I was buying fags a day or two since. Ingrid's just got up to straighten the curtains and there's no hiding this book from her because she sees it there on the floor with this bint on the front revealing all. The next minute she's bent down, got it, and jumped away as I try to grab it back.

'C'mon, gimme,'

She laughs. 'No. I'm going to look and see what a dirty-minded old thing you really are.'

She gets behind her chair and I know if I want the book I'll have to chase her and take it off her. I'm a bit red, but I'm not going to make a song and dance about it, so I sit down in my chair and light my fag. When she sees I'm not bothering she comes round and sits down and starts to turn the pages. She seems to get real interested, having a real good look at every picture, just like a lad might do, and once or twice she gives a little giggle, when she comes to one she thinks is a bit more saucy than the rest, I suppose. I go over and sit on the arm of her chair and look down over her shoulder. I get a funny kind of thrill looking at pictures like these with her and I can feel the blood in my throat and my hands aren't steady.

'I don't know how they can do it,' she says, 'standing in front of a photographer like that.'

'I don't suppose they think anything of it. It's a job. Exploiting their natural assets, you might say.'

'I'll bet there's some carrying on.'

'Now who's being dirty-minded?'

'Well if you were taking photographs of women like this all day wouldn't you feel like it? Now you can't pretend you wouldn't.'

'Well, I'm not used to it. And anyway, I don't know where you drop on jobs like that. There'd ha' been some sense in it if me dad had apprenticed me to one o' these blokes.'

She gives my leg a dig with her elbow. 'Go on with you!'

She turns the pages. '*She's* lovely, though. Isn't she *firm*?'

'No nicer than you,' I say, and I'm glad she can't see my face because my cheeks are on fire.

'Get away,' she says. 'You don't mean that.'

'I do, though. I think your figure's every bit as nice as hers.'

'Look at her bust, though. I'll bet she doesn't even need a bra.'

I have to swallow a couple of times before I can speak. 'Well, I think you've got . . . got lovely breasts. I've always thought so.'

'Shut up,' she says. 'You'll make me blush.' And I can see her coming up pink about the ears and neck.

'Course, I couldn't swear to it, like . . . I mean . . .'

'I know what you mean,' she says. 'You don't have to go into details.'

I bend over her and lift her face up to mine. I kiss her but she doesn't respond much. 'I wish we could,' I say.

'Could what?'

'Go into details.'

'You want a lot, don't you?'

I keep my face down, talking soft into her ear as she goes on turning the pages of the book, pretending to look to the end. Then I take the book off her and put it away. I go round the front of her chair and pull her to her feet by both hands and kiss her again. There's still not much coming back; and I thought she was in a frisky mood. I'm mad for her now, though, and I'm sure she can feel my heart pumping away against her. I've got one hand between us, holding her through the blouse.

'You know how I am about you, Ingrid,' I say, spreading my feet to balance us.

'That's the trouble,' she says. 'I don't know.'

'Nobody's ever got me this way before,' I tell her, and it's no lie.

'But you don't always feel like this, do you? And then you're not bothered about me.'

I'm a bit ashamed. What can I say to her?

'I don't know how I do feel half the time,' I tell her. 'I've never been through this kind of thing before. I know I must seem a louse at times, but I don't mean to be, and I'm not like that really. It's just that sometimes I feel rotten about it all and then I think it's not fair to either of us to carry on . . . I did try to break it off, y'know, when I found out it wasn't the same as I'd thought . . .'

'But I came running after you . . .'

I'm not liking this. We've managed pretty well without talk before, because I thought we both knew just how it was, and Ingrid seemed to have decided to make the best of it, even though it wasn't what she wanted. But at least talking does give me a chance to make some excuse for myself and show her I know how she must feel even if on the outside I just seem selfish and out for my own ends. The trouble is there's two sides to everybody and Ingrid brings out all the worst in me instead of the best.

It's hard to say, the mood I'm in just now, but I reckon I owe her the chance if she wants to take it. 'D'you want to pack it in?' I say. 'I reckon I can't blame you if you do.'

She seems to think about it for a few seconds, standing close up to me and looking at the floor by my feet. Then she says, 'No, I don't want to pack it in.' And when she lifts her face and kisses me there's everything in it that she was holding back before.

I start to unbutton her blouse up the front and she doesn't object to this because it's no more than we've done before. It's only when I start pulling it free of her skirt that she puts her hand over mine to stop me.

'What's wrong?'

'Somebody might come.'

'You're not expecting anybody, are you?'

'No, but you never know.'

'Lock the door.'

'I already have.'

'Well if anybody does come you can pretend you were in the bath or something,' I tell her, saying the first thing that comes into my head.

'Oh, Vic . . .'

'C'mon, Ingrid, c'mon.'

'It's nothing, you know, really.'

'Not to you. You're a girl. It's a lot to me. I think about nothing else sometimes. I lie in bed and imagine . . .'

'Well I can't do it while you're here. You'll have to go out.'

'Oh, c'mon. I'll do it for you.'

'No, I can't, Vic, honest. You'll have to go out.'

'Okay, then,' I say, thinking you can't expect everything at once. 'I'll go up to the bathroom.'

'Its round the corner at the top of the stairs. You'll give me time, won't you?'

I look at my watch. 'It's half past now. I won't come back till twenty to.'

She switches on the standard lamp by the television set and douses the main light. Then she goes to the fireplace and stands with one hand on it, looking down into the fire.

I go out and along the passage and up the stairs. The carpet's thick under my feet. The house isn't big but I'm impressed by the furnishings. It seems Mr Rothwell must have spent a load of dough making it comfortable for Ingrid and her ma while he's away on his travels. The bathroom has pink walls with black tiles to about chest height. Our bath at home stands on four cast-iron rest like animals' feet but this is one of the modern boxed-in efforts, in black to match the tiles.

I wonder how I'm going to pass the next ten minutes and then I catch sight of myself in the glass over the washbasin and decide my hair needs combing; so I spend a bit of time on that, easing the waves in with my fingers till it's just right. Then I wash my hand with the piece of blue scented soap and hold my hand under my mouth and try to smell my breath. It's not a very good method but I'm not bothered because I don't think I have any trouble that way. I put the lid down over the lavatory and sit down. My watch shows another five minutes to go. I sit down and think about Ingrid downstairs and wonder just what she's doing. All at once I remember the Old Lady saying something to me a long time ago after I'd been in some kind of scrape – I can't remember just what it was. But I remember she said, 'Never do anything you'd be ashamed of your mother knowing about,' and I'm thinking Oh, Christ, if she could only see me now, because if it depended on what she's told me – or the Old Feller for that matter – I'd still be thinking you got babies by saving Co-op Cheques and that there isn't any difference between men and women except women grow their hair longer and don't have to shave. And then I get to thinking what a funny business it all is, this sex and blokes going mad over women and doing all sorts of daft things because of them. And it's been the same since the world began and now here I am and it's my turn and it makes you wonder where it'll all end.

I deliberately wait two minutes over the ten I said before I go down. Then my legs are like jelly on the stairs.

III

A few days after, the first real snow of the winter arrives. It falls during the night and by the time people are up and getting on their way to work the snow ploughs have been busy clearing the roads. The snow lasts for nearly a fortnight and even after it's gone there are still grubby patches of it in the fields and the corners where nobody walks. And it stays cold. In fact it's colder than when the snow was here. Everything gets frozen up and the way the frost bites at you makes you wonder if it'll ever turn warm again. This is the worst time of the year for open-air courting and Ingrid and I mostly go to the pictures on our night out. But now and again we just have to go into the park, even if it's only into a shelter. Nights like this, when your hands are like blocks of ice, I think about their comfy dining-room and the fire and the couch. But we never get a chance like that again.

And now something's changed. One time I'd never have thought of going all the way with Ingrid, like a bloke short of money wouldn't think of robbing a bank. I'd be just asking for trouble. But since I've seen her and know just what she's like, how gorgeous she really is, there's always temptation like a little chap sitting on my shoulder and whispering in my ear, 'Go on, find out what you want to know. Twenty-one years and you've never done it with anybody. You've gone so far, why not go that little bit further? It's okay, thousands are doing it all the time, and she's willing.' Well, one night when the freeze is suddenly over and everything's mild again we go to our old spot under the trees. This little chap is extra persuasive and it seems like either him or a mate of his is talking to Ingrid as well, because it happens. I don't have to force her or even persuade her really; she seems as ready as I am; and it's not till after that we stop and think about it.

'It'll be all right, Vic, won't it?' she says in a whisper.

'What? Course it will.' How the hell should I know? I'm thinking. It had better be, that's all.

'But we won't risk it again, will we?'

'No; I'll get something.' When I'm in the mood again I'll see about getting something. I don't know just how. I can't see myself walking into a shop like buying a packet of fags. But I can ask Willy and he'll know. Just now I couldn't care less if we never do it again. Now that it's over I'm wondering what all the fuss is about and wishing we'd played safe and had our fun without any risk like we've always done.

But a couple of days later I'm all for it again and feeling quite a lad about it. I feel like a proper man of the world with a willing bint laid on like this. So I keep an eye open for Willy, but somehow now I want him specially he doesn't seem to be about. One night I set off to call for him and see if I can catch him that way. I've only ever been to Willy's house once and I didn't like it. It's a terrace house in a ropy street off Gilderdale Road where there's always a crowd of snotty-nosed kids hanging about with their britches' behinds hanging out. Willy's brothers are a crowd of roughs and always on the booze and his ma's a bit of a slut. My mother's broad-spoken and all that, but she'd have no room for Willy's old lady and her mucky ways.

A kid comes out of an entry bawling as I go up the street. He's maybe five or six and real grubby. It's the way he's blubbing, though, that gets me. I mean kids are always roaring about something but there's crying and crying and this kid sounds real heartbroken. I've never heard such misery in a kid's crying before and it fair turns me over.

Willy isn't in when I get to their house and I ask his mother if she knows where he is. 'Nay lad,' she says, standing on the step with her arms folded over this mucky apron, 'how should I know? He never tells me where he's goin'. Have yer tried t'pubs he usually goes to?'

'I haven't tried anywhere. I came straight here.'

'D'yer know which they are?'

'I know one or two places he likes a drink.'

'Aye, well try them. Or he could ha' gone to t'pictures.

Spends half his time in t'pictures, our Willy does. He'll ruin his eyesight afore he's finished. I've told him so time an' time agen.'

'I'll have a look around, then.'

'Aye, you do that, lad.' She eyes me up and down, looking at my clothes. I can tell she doesn't remember seeing me before. 'War it owt important yer wanted him for?'

'Oh no. I'm a mate of his. I haven't seen him for a bit so I thought I'd look him up.'

She nods. 'I see. Aye, well you go an' look in one'r two pubs. You'll happen run across him.'

I walk off down the street and she watches me from the step. I haven't gone far when she calls me back.

'It's just come to me,' she says. 'I believe he did say summat about havin' a game o'billiards. D'yer know where t'saloon is?'

I tell her yes, and I'll try there first. Then I go off, thinking she doesn't care a damn where Willy is as long as he isn't hanging about under her feet. I wonder what it must be like to have a mother like that and think I'll take mine every time, even if she does want to know a bit too much at times.

There's a flight of wooden stairs to the billiard saloon which is on the corner of Cooperative Street across from the market place. If you're up there on a market day you see out across all the tarpaulin roofs of the stalls to the glass roof of the covered market-house. I find Willy in his shirt-sleeves playing on one of the four tables under the big shaded light.

'Howdo, Willy.'

'Ah, Vic, me old cock sparrer. How ist?'

'Pretty fair.'

Willy finishes chalking his cue and bends down to take his shot. 'Come for a game?' he says.

'No, I was looking for you. I've been up to your house. Your mother said I might find you here.'

'Owt special on your mind?'

'No, I just thought I'd see what you were doing. I haven't seen you for a while.'

'Right enough,' Willy says.

There's four or five other blokes in the room and I don't know this lad Willy's playing with. They're playing snooker. Willy makes his shot and sends balls clickety-clicking all over the place.

'I'll just show Fred here the way home an' then we'll adjourn for a jar, eh?'

This lad called Fred gives a guffaw. 'Tha won't show me t'way home wi' shots like that, Willy,' he says.

'Ah,' Willy says, dead-pan, 'it's not how good you are but how much fun you get out of it. I get a lot more fun than tha does, because tha plays to win an' I don't give a bugger either way.'

I unfasten my raincoat and light a fag and sit down to wait for the game to finish. This lad trounces Willy and Willy grins and winks at me as he puts his cue up in the rack.

'Right, now for that jar. Are you comin', Fred?'

I'm glad when Fred says no, he's stopping for another game, because I want Willy on his own. We go downstairs and into the Crown next door. It's a quiet night and we nearly have the place to ourselves. We drink for a bit and talk about one thing and the other before I get to the point.

'Willy, when you get yourself fixed up with a bird – you know, on a sure thing – where d'you get your tackle from?'

'Oh, ho!' Willy says. 'That's it, is it?'

You have to lay it on thick for Willy so I say, 'I've got a bint lined up an' she's all ready for it; only I don't want to take any risks.'

'How about letting me in on it,' Willy says. 'Share an' share alike, y'know.'

'She's not a bag, Willy. She just likes me, that's all. I've been working on it a bit now.'

'What's her name? Do I know her?'

'No, she doesn't live round here . . . Anyway, that's all I need and I'm set up.'

'Lucky dog,' Willy says.

'Where d'you get fixed up? Have you any on you now?'

' 'Smatter o'fact I'm right out at the moment. But you

can buy 'em. Just walk into a shop an' ask for 'em.'

'Which shop?'

'Oh, any chemist's. Doesn't your barber flog 'em?'

'I don't know.'

'A lot of 'em do.'

'Anyway, my barber's a pal of the Old Feller's.'

'Well there's plenty o' places.'

'Suppose you go into a chemist's and a bird comes to serve you?'

'So what? She knows what they're for just like anybody else.'

'I couldn't ask a bird, Willy. I'd be embarrassed.' I take a pull at my pint. 'Look, Willy, if I give you the brass will you get some for me?'

'But what's to stop you gettin' 'em for yourself? You've got to do it sometime, haven't you?'

'I don't think I could do it, Willy. I'd be scared they might ask my age or something.'

'Well, you're old enough.'

'Aye, but it'd be embarrassing.'

'Aw, there's nowt to it.'

I'm getting a bit suspicious the way Willy's hedging and beginning to wonder how much of him is just talk.

'Who was the first bint you ever had it with, Willy?'

'Oh, a bint you don't know.'

'When was the last time?'

'The other week.'

'Aye, in your flipping imagination, Willy, I know.'

'Why don't you mind your own bloody business?' Willy says.

I'm grinning as I reach for Willy's empty glass. 'C'mon, let's have another.'

IV

Did you get anything . . . you know . . .?' she says.

'No. I went downtown on Saturday but I couldn't bring meself to go into a shop an' ask.'

'We'd better not . . . you know . . . go so far, then, had we?'

'No, we won't go so far.'

I push her back on to my coat and kiss her, holding her to me full length till I seem to be sinking into her, and I'm thinking what a mug I am with it here for the asking for the first time in my life and I'm letting a little thing like bashfulness stop me.

And after it's just like it always is, as though I'm finished with it and I'll never look twice at a bint again. Only times like this, when I'm seeing things more clear than I can any other time, I feel it's like being let out of prison must be, when you think you've got a clear field in front of you and all the good things to enjoy without having something else nagging at you like it is when I can't read a book or listen to music or enjoy a picture for thinking about her and touching her and her touching me. To get really free, though, I have to get right away from her because while I'm still with her I've got that feeling that I'm just about the rottenest devil alive, for treating her this way. I reckon people sometimes are just like animals, just like randy dogs having a go in the street and not giving a cuss for all the traffic belting up and down round them. Only dogs have some sense: when they finish they just walk away, and people have to talk. And I don't want to talk to Ingrid: I want to get up and walk away, free, and not have to stick around and listen to her yatter about something and nothing and say yes and no and I think this and I think the other when I don't think anything at all except I want to get away where I can enjoy being rid of her and wanting bints at all. Only, the thing is, I'm not rid of wanting bints except in that way. There is another way, and with a real bint, the sort I've always wanted, it would be this way and I'd want to stay with her and talk and laugh and maybe touch her, but tender like and soft. And when I think about that it comes on in a deep ache as I wonder if I'll ever find her.

I sit up and look round. I can see the grass sloping

away to the path, and the pale line of the path and the bandstand just to be made out in the trees, and I feel suddenly so awfully lonely that I'm scared and I say the first thing that comes into my head, which is: 'Turned a bit cold, hasn't it?'

She's still lying there on the coat and I wonder what's keeping her so quiet when she usually has so much to say.

'Like to walk a bit?' I've got to be on the move. I can't stay here any longer.

She says nothing but just lies with her face partly turned away from me.

'You okay?' I ask her after a bit of this and she mumbles something that I take to be 'yes'.

'Let's walk a bit. I'm turning cold.'

She says something I don't catch and I say, 'Beg pardon.'

'I think something's gone wrong, Vic,' she says.

I catch this all right, and no mistake. My heart sort of slips sideways and there's panic like big bats flying about inside me. 'How d'you mean "wrong"?' I know very well what she means but I'm hoping I'm mistaken, just the same.

She says in a quiet voice that I know means she's dead serious, 'Something that should have happened hasn't.'

'How d'you mean it hasn't happened?' My voice is a bit rough because I can't control it properly and it's either that or letting her see how scared I am.

'You know what I mean.'

'Well, how long?'

'Ten days.'

'Ten days . . . That's nothing, is it?'

'It is with me. I'm like clockwork usually.'

'Not this time, anyway.' I'm surprised the way my voice sounds now. Here I am all chewed up and panicky inside and the way it comes out you'd think I hadn't a care in the world. 'C'mon,' I say, 'let's walk.'

'It's never happened before, Vic,' she says, still not moving.

'Look, how can anything have gone wrong? How can it?'

'You know very well it can.'

'Look, people try for ages before it comes off. My sister's been trying for months and there's not a sign yet. I'm not even sure we did it properly . . . I don't have to go into all the details. You know.'

She sits up now but her head's hanging down and she's pulling her hanky about with her fingers. 'All I know is I'm ten days overdue and it's never happened before . . . I'm scared, Vic.'

So am I. Oh, brother, am I scared! I feel like getting up and running like mad across the park, putting as much distance between me and her as I can. As if that would do any good. But still, I've got to get away from her, on my own, so's I can think this thing out without having to put a show on for her benefit. Oh, Christ, what have I got myself into!

'You're scared about nothing. C'mon, let's walk.'

'I wish I'd your confidence.'

You wouldn't want it if you could see it, old girl, I think. 'All you've got to do is stop worrying. You're probably stopping it happening by worrying about it. It's a vicious circle . . . C'mon, let's go.' If I have to ask her once more I'll shout it.

She stands up and tidies her clothes. I pick my mac up and shake it and think about the number of times I've done the same thing just here. I don't know when I'm well-off, that's my trouble. There I was, happy as a lark, free as you like, and I have to go and get myself into a mess like this. And I didn't even enjoy it really. Well never again. If this turns out all right it's the finish. And I mean that. It's the end.

Down at the gate I say to her, 'Now stop worrying about it. By the time I see you again everything'll be okay.'

'I hope so,' she says in a dull voice. 'What will we do if it isn't, though?'

God, I can't think about that!

'I tell you it will be, so stop worrying.'

I've a feeling she'd like to hang about a bit longer because she doesn't want to go home with it on her mind. Maybe she's scared of giving the game away. Not like me. *I* should go in for amateur dramatics or something. I never knew I was such a good actor.

Well I get plenty of practice the next few days. I can't remember a worse four or five days in my life, while I'm walking about putting on the big act, pretending I haven't a care in the world, and all the time this thing's boiling inside me. I learn how people can hide a big load of worry if they have to, because nobody, not even the Old Lady, as much as guesses there's anything wrong. All the time I'm wanting like mad to ring Ingrid up and hear her say it's come right, but I daren't for fear of hearing the opposite. I think she'll ring me anyway when it does happen; and then again I think maybe she won't because I might have sounded too confident about it, and why should she ring me to tell me something I knew would happen all the time? *I might have to marry her.* I've got to face it; if this doesn't turn out right I might have to marry her. I break out in a cold sweat at the thought of it. I suppose there are places in the world where you could marry a bint who was having a kid and then call it off after. But not where I live. People do get divorced now and then, and split up, but when bods like me get married it's nine times out of ten for life. A life sentence, and make the best of it. And anyway, I don't like to think about marriage in terms of getting out of it. Marriage shouldn't be like that: it should be like it is with Chris and David; like it could be with me and that girl . . . the right girl . . . But with the wrong one . . . Never again, I tell myself. If this works out I'll see her just once more to explain how I feel and that'll be the end, *finis, kaput.* No matter how much I might want to do otherwise.

Well, at the end of this five days, or five years to me, the phone rings in the shop and Mr Van Huyten says, 'It's for you, Victor. A young lady, I believe.' My heart's hammering as I pick the receiver up and I look round to see if anybody's listening and take a deep breath before saying anything.

'Hello.'

'Hello, is that you, Vic? This is Ingrid.'

'Hello, Ingrid. How's tricks?'

'I've been waiting for you to ring me, Vic. I thought you must be away from work or something . . .'

'Oh, no, no . . . I've been a bit tied up with one thing an' another.' I slip my hand into my jacket and feel my heart doing the polka.

'Vic – it hasn't happened. It's over a fortnight now.'

'You're not pulling my leg, are you?' Like hell, she is!

'You know I wouldn't joke about a thing like that.'

'Well, there's still time, isn't there?'

'I suppose there's always a chance . . . Look, I've got to see you, Vic. We've got to talk about it. I can't talk over the telephone. Can I see you tonight?'

'Well, I'm not sure about tonight . . .' I haven't a damn thing on actually, but my first instinct is to put her off.

'Please, Vic, tonight. Don't put me off, please. I've got to see you.'

She sounds to me as if she'll go round the bend if she doesn't talk to somebody, and better me than anybody else. You never know with these birds. Some of them tell their pals every damn thing.

'Okay, tonight, then. Usual time and place.'

I put the receiver down and get hold of the counter with both hands. I know as sure as God made little apples that it's not going to happen and she's pregnant.

V

'Let's get it straight, then. You're a fortnight overdue . . .'

'Fifteen days,' she says.

'Okay, fifteen days. Is it such a long time? I don't know much about it, but don't women have this happen to them sometimes?'

'Some women do, but they come to expect it. I'm not

like that. I told you before, Vic, it's never happened with me. I can nearly tell the date by it usually.'

'Well, maybe you're run down and need a tonic or something. Maybe you should see the doctor.'

'I've a feeling I shall be seeing the doctor before long,' she says; 'only it won't be for a tonic.'

'Whatever you do, don't get panicky. There's always a chance. There's always hope.'

We're in the shelter in the park and it's a fine warmish night with a clear sky. But we're sitting about four feet apart and neither of us feels much like going out on the grass.

'There's something else,' Ingrid says. 'I couldn't tell you over the phone . . . My mother knows. I had to tell her.'

I feel as if somebody's planted a size ten boot right in my guts. It winds me. 'Oh, for crying out loud, Ingrid, why did you have to do a daft thing like that? Couldn't you have kept it dark a bit longer?' Oh, Jesus, now we are in trouble.

'I had to tell her, Vic. She knows as well as I do how regular I am. She started asking questions. You don't know my mother how she can worm things out of you. I just broke down and told her.'

As long as she doesn't break down now, I'm thinking. As long as she doesn't start bawling on top of everything else.

'How much did you tell her?'

'Well . . . enough . . .'

What does it matter what she told her? There's only one way to make a baby, after all. It's the oldest pastime known to man, don't they say? I think of how many blokes must have been in this pickle before me and imagine them all stretching right back to ancient times. Wherever they all are now they must be nudging one another and sniggering and saying, Look, there's another poor sod gone and got his wick wet.

'Oh, Christ . . . What did she say?'

'What d'you think she said? She was livid. I've never

213

seen her so angry . . . I daren't tell you all she did say.'

'About me?'

'Well, can you blame her?'

So if nothing worse comes of it I've got a woman walking about thinking of me as the dirty little tyke who nearly got her daughter into trouble. I'll be lucky if she doesn't spill the beans to the Old Lady. Any day might bring a letter telling all . . .

'She made me have a hot bath and drink some gin. I think she wishes she hadn't now, but she was in a real flap.'

'It didn't work, though?'

'No. I couldn't stand the bath hot enough and I was sick when I'd had one glass of gin.'

'It's . . . it's a kind of murder, in a way, that . . .'

'I suppose it is, in a way. But I'll bet plenty of women try it on, and you wouldn't have minded if it had worked, would you?'

'What's she going to do now?'

'She says she'll wait another week and then take me to the doctor's.'

'I suppose she'll want to see me then?'

'She said she'd write for me dad to come home. She says you'll have a man to face when you do come.'

'Oh, Christ, what a lousy mess.'

'I suppose we should have thought about it before.'

'But it's a bit of bloody hard luck when we get caught first time and there's people trying for ages to have kids.'

'You'll have to write a letter to somebody about it,' she says. It's the best joke I've ever heard her make but I'm not in a mood for laughing. I can't even raise a smile.

I get up and walk up and down on the concrete a bit. There's no way out, though. I've had it, sure as eggs are eggs. I take my cig case out. 'May as well have a smoke. We're not dead yet. Here . . .' She takes one and we light up.

'Vic,' she says, 'what are we going to do? What can we do?'

214

She's upset, real upset, I can tell. I'm not the only one to have gone through it this past few days. And before that – she was carrying it around with her for days before she told me. And it'll be worse for her in one way because she'll be the one who'll have the big belly to hump around for everybody to point at and talk about. Except, of course, that once that's over she'll have what she wants – me. And a bloody fine catch I am. Maybe that's what's worrying her now, maybe she's wondering if I will marry her if the worst happens. Maybe that's what's getting her down . . .

I know she's pregnant. I know for sure. I know for sure I'm not going to get out of this one. I'm caught and that's a fact. Capital F-a-c-t. This is where all the dreams end, Vic Brown. No need to go on looking for that girl. You've found her, the only one you'll get now. You're trapped and there's no way out. Oh, what a fool; what a bloody, bloody fool!

So that's it. It only wants saying, and I lean my head against the roof post and look out over the park and say it.

'Don't worry. We'll get married. That's what we'll do.'

She says nothing and in a few seconds I hear a little noise and I turn round and see she's crying.

'Don't worry, I said, we'll get married. You didn't think I'd let you down, did you? You didn't think I'd take my hook and leave you to face it all on your own, did you? I'm no bloody angel but I'm not that kind of louse.'

She's sobbing away like billy-ho now. The hanky's out and the waterworks are turned on good and proper.

'I've always wanted to marry you, Vic,' she says. 'I've often imagined how you might propose to me. And now it has to be this way. Forcing you into it. You'd never have asked me but for this, would you? I know you wouldn't. I know you don't love me like I love you.'

Well, she can't have it both ways, can she? Just like a woman to want it, though.

'I've asked you, haven't I? I've said we'll get married, haven't I?'

'You've no need to if you don't want to,' she says all at once. 'I shan't force you.'

This is a laugh. Even if she won't force me, what about everybody else? I can just imagine them all if I make so much as a sign that I don't want to go through with it. I can just see them all putting the screws on. It'd take a better man than me to stand out against all that.

'You know damn well you won't turn me down, though,' I tell her, and if it sounds conceited I can't help it. It's not much joy to me to know she loves me. If she didn't we should probably never have got into this mess.

Me saying that turns the waterworks on in a fresh gush. 'I won't,' she says. 'I won't. I've always wanted you. You know I have.'

I turn round again and look at the park.

'Well,' I say in a quiet voice, 'now you've got me.'

And as I'm standing there I wish to God, I wish more than I've ever wished for anything else, that I'd never laid eyes on her.

5

I

I watch the water go down the plug-hole. Anti-clockwise.
Due to the sun's pull, or something, they say. It goes down
clockwise in the southern hemisphere. I wonder what it
does on the equator. Goes straight down, I suppose. I
think it might be a good wheeze to take a holiday walking
down Africa, watching water go down the plug-holes
every place you stopped at. You'd know when you got to
the equator when it changed. Maybe you'd get a town
slap bang on the equator with a street where it went
down anticlockwise at one end and clockwise at the
other. And straight down in the middle. Doing all that
walking you wouldn't have time to get into trouble. Take
years to walk all that way . . .

'Victor, your tea's on the table.'

'Coming.'

It's Monday and the room's all warm and cosy with the
ironing. There's finny haddock for my tea and I usually
enjoy this, lying there all crispy gold on the plate with
great dollops of best butter melting over it till it's nearly
afloat. But today it's just like cardboard in my mouth and
I can hardly get it down. The Old Lady watches me struggling with something I usually scoff in no time and she
says:

'You're not getting your tea, Victor.'

'I don't feel up to it today.'

'You reckon to be fond of a bit o' finny, don't you?'

'I like it all right. I'm just not hungry, that's all.'

Half past six. I'm meeting Ingrid at a quarter past seven and she'll expect me to have something to tell her. Funny how many times I've sat down to a plateful of finny haddock for my tea and then leaned back pogged and with nothing more on my mind than which picture I fancy seeing best.

The Old Man's cleared a space on the other side of the table and he's got his pools coupons spread out. He likes to fill them in early so's he won't forget.

'Have you been filling yourself with all sorts o' peg-meg this afternoon?' the Old Lady says.

'I haven't had a thing.'

I'm going to Ingrid's house tonight and I've told her I'll tell the Old Lady and the Old Feller first . . . The ironing board creaks under the weight the Old Lady's putting on the iron. I'll be getting that in the earhole any minute now . . .

'I'm talkin' to you, Vic,' the Old Man says.

'Eh? What?'

'I said what do you think of Sheffield United's chances this week.'

'How the heck should I know?' I say, letting some of it out. 'They don't call me Old Moore.'

' 'Ere, 'ere,' the Old Man says. 'I asked you a civil question, young feller-me-lad.'

'Well I don't know everything about football. Why don't you use your own judgement, 'stead o' keep askin' me?'

The Old Man lifts his eyebrows over the frames of his glasses and looks at the Old Lady.

'What's wrong with you, Victor?' she says. 'Have you been having sòme trouble at shop, or summat?'

'I'm okay.'

I get up from the table and go and sit down with the evening paper. I intended softening them up a bit before springing it and now I've gone and done just the opposite. What I need is some kind of opening so's I can break it gently like. As if you can break a thing like that gently! I read the paper from back to front without taking in

218

hardly a word and then it's ten to seven. I can't put it off much longer. It's got to be any minute now. The Old Man's breathing heavy and muttering to himself as he puts his forecasts in with his ball-point pen. The ironing board goes on creaking as the Old Lady goes steadily on with her work.

Nobody says anything for a minute or two and then all of a sudden I hear this voice speak, just as though somebody's popped his head round the door to share a bit of news.

'I'm thinking of getting married.'

And by the way everything goes quiet I know it's me.

The Old Lady stands there with the iron up in the air and it even brings the Old Man out of his pools. The Old Lady drops the iron with a clatter on to the stand, but she's too flabbergasted to say anything for a minute.

'Who you thinkin' o' marryin'?' she says when she's got her wind back.

'A lass called Ingrid Rothwell. She lives up on Park Drive.'

'How is it we haven't heard owt of it afore?'

'I didn't know before. I've only just made me mind up.'

The Old Lady's sharp enough sometimes and she seems to get this situation weighed up in double-quick time. 'It's happen a case of you've *had* to make your mind up, is it?'

I shift in the chair. I can't look at her. She's watching me, and so's the Old Man, but he hasn't said anything yet.

'*Is* it a forced do, Victor?' the Old Lady says straight out then.

I open my mouth to say something but nothing comes out. Then I shrink back small as the Old Lady comes at me across the hearth-rug. She's got her hand up I'm sure for a minute she's going to clout me one. Then she drops it and lets me have it with her tongue.

'You girt fool,' she says. 'You girt silly fool. You with all your future afore you lettin' yerself get entangled with some cheap young piece 'at knows nowt but carryin' on an' gettin' down on her –'

'She's not like that. She's not like that at all. You stand

219

there callin' her all t'names under t'sun and you don't even know her.'

'I know this much about her – she's trapped you nicely. When I think of all the decent respectable lasses you could ha' married and you come home an' tell me you're weddin' some little slut 'at's got her claws into you this way . . .'

I'm on my feet shouting. I'm surprised at the amount of feeling I can put into sticking up for Ingrid. 'She's not like that, I tell you. You don't even know her.'

'Nah just a minute, you two,' the Old Feller says. He gets up and walks between us so's we have to fall back. 'It's allus been my experience 'at there's two folk to reckon wi' in cases like this.'

'Your experience?' the Old Lady says. 'What do you know about it?'

'Well I'm sixty-one-year old,' the Old Man says, 'and I courted thee an' married thee an' helped thee bring three bairns into t'world, so I think I can say I know a bit . . . Now fair's fair, an' I don't like to hear you carryin' on about this lass afore you've even seen her. I don't know who's most to blame, but it's bound to be a bit o' both. I reckon our Victor's on'y yuman like any young feller an' if this lass is a bit soft-hearted like, an' affectionate, summat like this can happen. It's not first time an' it won't be t'last. An' if our Victor's had his fun he's a right to pay for it just like anybody else.'

'How old is she?' the Old Lady asks, surly like, but quieter now the Old Feller's had a say.

'Nineteen.'

'Nobbut a bairn,' the Old Man says.

'There's many a lass at nineteen these days knows more than I do at my age,' the Old Ladys says, letting the rag show a bit again.

'Aye, happen there is, an' happen she's not one of 'em. If they'd both known a bit more they might not ha' got into this. We'll know more about that when we've seen her. When are you bringin' her home with you, Victor?'

'I reckon it can be any time now.'

'I'm not sure I want her in my house,' the Old Lady says.

'You can't turn your own daughter-in-law away, Lucy.'

'She's not me daughter-in-law yet.'

'Seems to me the quicker she is the better for everybody.'

'An' what are all t'neighbours an' everybody goin' to think?' the Old Lady says. 'Such a lovely wedding our Christine had . . .'

'We'll let neighbours attend to their own business and we'll see to ours.'

Well, I've never seen the Old Man like this before, taking charge with a firm hand. But I wish it was something else brought it on.

'Have you seen her parents yet?' the Old Lady says.

'I'm going tonight. I wanted to tell you first.'

'Very thoughtful of you,' the Old Lady says. 'Well just watch your manners. We don't want 'em thinkin' you come from any sort of family. And not a word to our Jim 'at it's not all above board. There's plenty of time for him to get to know about such things.'

I catch the Old Man's eye. He's got an expression on his face that I can't weigh up. I look away and go and get my coat.

II

'Did you tell 'em?' Ingrid asks me.

'Yes, I told 'em.'

'What did they say?'

'Pretty much what you'd expect. Me mother was wild. I thought she was going to clout me with the iron at one bit. The Old Man was reasonable enough, though.'

'I don't know how I'll ever face them.'

'Oh, you'll manage okay. You'll get on straight away with me dad but you might have to dig a bit deeper with me mother. She's all right when you get to know her,

221

though, and she'll see straight off 'at you're a decent lass.'

'Is that what you told them?'

'What?'

'That I'm a decent girl.'

'Well, you are, aren't you? You know I've always thought so.'

She's got her arm through mine in a possessive sort of way she's never shown before and now she gives it a squeeze. When I look at her I catch the sparkle of tears in her eyes.

'What's up now?'

She shakes her head. 'It's nothing. It's just when you're nice to me, that's all.'

God, what a louse I must have been to her sometimes!

It takes only a few minutes from the end of the road and we're going up the steps to their house. She's got her hand on the door-handle when she says, 'Remember to act as though you've never been in the house before.'

'You didn't tell them about that, then?'

'Gosh, no. They don't even know you've been here before.'

'Okay, I'll remember.'

Ingrid's dad's a shortish neatish sort of bloke, about forty-five, I'd say. His hair's black and smooth and parted down the middle. His eyes are nearly black as well but they don't look too unfriendly to me as we shake hands when Ingrid's introduced us to one another. He's got suède fur-lined slippers on, grey flannels with a good crease, a red long-sleeved cardigan over a grey shirt, and a heather mixture tie.

'Nippy out tonight, is it?' he says, standing with his back to the fire. 'I thought it might be. Turning colder again . . . Well, you'd better sit down, er . . . er, Victor. Take his coat, Ingrid; make yourself useful.'

She takes my raincoat over her arm and asks where her mother is.

'Upstairs, tidying up, I think. She won't be long.'

Ingrid goes out and doesn't come straight back. Mr

Rothwell waves me to a chair and we both sit down. He's in the chair Ingrid was sitting in that night. I look at the couch and remember her there as bare as the day she was born and wonder what her old man would say if he knew. I think now I might as well have made a job of it then while we were warm and private if I only had to go and do it later in the park, when it was cold and neither of us enjoyed it.

Mr Rothwell reaches out for a twenty-packet of Players from on top of the television set. 'Do you smoke?'

'Oh, yes . . . thanks.' I take one and we light up.

He's got his eye on me now and I wish Ingrid would hurry up and come back.

'I don't suppose you've been looking forward to this?'

'Can't say I have. I had to face it, though.'

'Right enough. I'm glad to know you're prepared to face your responsibilities all round. Ingrid's told us you've asked her to marry you.'

'Oh, yes . . . well, I mean, I did straight away when I . . . when she . . .'

'It came as a bit of a shock to you, did it?'

'I'll say it did.'

'You must have known, though, that it might happen . . . didn't you?'

My face feels as if it's on fire. 'Well, I . . . I suppose I knew it was possible. But it's not as if we'd . . . as if we'd –'

'Made a habit of it?'

'Yes, that's right. There was only the one time, y'see.'

He doesn't say anything to this but just watches me with his dark eyes. I can't tell what he's thinking, whether he believes me or not. I suppose what we did the other times is just as bad in principle like even if it isn't dangerous like going all the way is. I wonder if he knows about all that, if Ingrid's told him.

'Of course, you know, Ingrid's not of age yet. I believe you've reached your majority.'

'Oh, yes; six months ago.'

'And you've told your parents about all this?'

I nod. 'Yes, they know.'

'What was their reaction?'

223

'Pretty much what you'd expect. They were upset. Me father seemed to take it a lot calmer than me mother.'

'Yes, I expect so. Women are always a lot more emotional about these things. It's their nature, I suppose. You'll find it the same with Ingrid's mother. A man's too busy thinking what's to be done.'

I'm wondering where Ingrid and her ma have got to. Mrs Rothwell's certainly keeping me on edge waiting for her.

'I understand you were a draughtsman at Whittaker's before you went into the shop.'

'That's right.'

'I'm in engineering myself, y'know. As a matter of fact, I worked for Whittaker's for a few years as a young man. I was surprised to hear you'd given up a good trade like draughtsmanship to go into a shop. I shouldn't have thought the opportunities compared at all.'

'Well, of course, I thought about all that before I decided,' I say, and begin to try to tell him how it is with me and Mr Van Huyten. I don't make a very good job of it because it's something I haven't got really cut and dried myself and I think by the time I've finished I've given Mr Rothwell the impression that it's already in the will that I come in for everything when Mr Van Huyten cocks his clog. Maybe this isn't a bad thing, though, because he seems to take better to the idea now.

'And what's your salary now?' he asks me.

I tell him and he nods. 'That seems reasonable. You seem to have found yourself a very good opening. This Mr van Huyten must have a considerable personal liking for you.'

'We get on well,' I say, and I'm glad to say it because maybe this is the best testimonial I could have.

The door opens and Ingrid comes in with her mother. I remember it's polite to stand when a woman comes into the room and I get up. One look at Mrs Rothwell's enough. I don't like her.

She's a little woman, maybe a bit younger than Mr Rothwell, with blonde hair cut short and pressed tight to

224

her head in little waves. She's got a turquoise jersey frock on that shows her figure off – or at least, what's left of her figure, because it might have been good at one time but now it's mostly bust and behind. You can see she's well corseted in, though, and there's a couple of rolls of fat she can't get rid of up under her arms. I don't know straight away what it is makes me take a dislike to her on sight, and then I realize it's her eyes, pale blue with a sort of crafty stupid glint in them that tells me I'm going to have some trouble there sometime if nowhere else. It's awful to think I'm going to have to see a lot more of her and Mr Rothwell in future, whether I like it or not. I can feel it all closing in round me like a big net. Oh, what a chump I've been! And if only I could get out of it. Even now, at the back of my mind, I can hardly believe it's true, and there's no way out.

'Mother, this is Vic.'

I say good evening and kind of half-lift my hand. She nods, real short like, and says good evening back. I feel as if I ought to say something. 'Er . . . I'm sorry we have to meet in circumstances like these.' The truth is I'm talking because I'm as nervous as hell and I know straight away it's come out in the wrong tone of voice, just as if I think it's really all a bit of a lark.

'It's a bit late to think about that, isn't it?' she says straight out.

Ingrid looks at the floor and I feel this smile, that's absolutely out of place anyway, fade off my face.

They come round the sofa and sit down. Mrs Rothwell's frock's a bit on the short side and she shows a lot of leg while she's settling herself. I'm looking at it an' all. I couldn't care tuppence about Mrs Rothwell's legs actually but you know how it is when a woman's showing a lot. You can't keep your eyes off it. Nearly any woman – she doesn't have to be attractive. Anyway, just for a minute I'm looking at her legs, which aren't anything to write home about at all, and she's looking at me looking and I feel myself coming up in a huge blush. I can imagine her talking to Mr Rothwell when I've gone and saying something like, 'Did you see the way he couldn't keep his eyes off my legs? He's be trying to get into bed with *me* if we have him about the house!'

I hear a voice talking to me and see Ingrid's dad holding the packet of Players out again. 'Cigarette?'

'No, here, have one of mine.' I get my case out and offer it to him. Then I remember Mrs Rothwell. 'Sorry, do you smoke?'

She hesitates for a second before she takes a cig out of the case.

'That's a very nice-looking case you have there,' Mr Rothwell says. 'D'you mind if I have a look?'

I pass the case over and he takes a good butcher's at it, opening and shutting it and turning it over and back, feeling the weight of it.

'V.A.B.,' he says. 'What does the "A" stand for?'

'Arthur – after me father.'

'I see . . . Yes, it's a very nice case indeed. It must have been quite expensive.'

'I've no idea how much it cost. It was a present, y'see.'

'I bought it,' Ingrid says, 'for his twenty-first birthday.'

'You bought it?' her mother says, and holds her hand out and takes the case from Mr Rothwell. 'Rather an expensive present for you to buy, wasn't it?'

'Oh, it wasn't all that expensive,' Ingrid says, and she colours up a bit as though she expects her mother to ask how much.

But her ma passes the case back to me without pressing the point.

'How long have you known my daughter?' she says now, like a duchess asking a gardener for his references. I nearly expect her to say 'Brown', but she doesn't call me by any name all evening.

'Well we've known one another by sight for a long time, but we've been friendly about eighteen months.'

'Friendly!' she says, screwing her little mouth up. 'I suppose you realize that this business has upset Ingrid's father and I very much.'

'I suppose it must have. It's only natural.' I try to look

226

shame-faced and it's not so hard because I'm feeling that miserable.

'I expect your parents have had something to say about it as well?'

'Oh, yes, well, I mean . . .'

'And I suppose they're trying to pin all the blame on Ingrid, saying she enticed you into it.'

'Oh, no, I wouldn't say that.'

'Well I'll have you know that we think there's very little blame on Ingrid's side at all. I know the way I've brought my daughter up and I know what sort of a girl she is. She'd only do a thing like that under extreme persuasion.'

(Oh, not too much persuasion, Mrs Rothwell. Not too much when it came to the point.)

'I've brought her up to be a decent, honourable girl who could be at ease in the very best company . . .'

(So she thinks she's got class, does she? Why, she hasn't a quarter of the class our Chris has!)

'We have very good connexions and we've always had high hopes of the match she might make. We don't like having the pistol levelled at our heads in this way.'

She's talking as though I've deliberately put Ingrid in the family way so's I can marry her, when all the time it's *me* the pistol's pointing at. It'd be funny if it wasn't so bloody tragic. I look at Old Man Rothwell but he's watching his missis and letting her have her say.

'You realize that Ingrid is well under age and needs our permission before she can marry?'

'Now just a minute, Esther,' Mr Rothwell chips in. 'I don't know much about the law but I don't think you could get away with that in court. I think they'd give permission straight away if only for the sake of the child.'

As if I'd ever take them to court to make them let me marry Ingrid! Why, the best thing that could happen would be for them to stand up straight and say, 'We don't give our permission. Ingrid won't marry you.' They wouldn't see me for dust! The kid, though . . . I've never really stopped to think about it before. I wonder if it will be a boy or a girl. Whatever it is it'll be mine, mine and Ingrid's. And I'm not ready to be a father yet. I'm just not ready.

Just for a minute Ma Rothwell glares at Mr Rothwell as if to say, 'Whose side are you on?' and then she climbs down off her high horse a bit.

'I just want to make it clear that this sort of thing involves other people besides the two of them.'

'Yes, I think Victor appreciates that,' Mr Rothwell says. 'I think he's as sorry about it now as any young man could be.'

(Sorrier than that, old lad, if you did but know.)

'He's had his parents to face as well and I expect that wasn't too easy. I don't like the idea of young people starting married life this way any more than anybody else does, but the damage is done now and we shall just have to make the best of it. Victor's come straight out like a man and said he'll marry Ingrid, and I respect him for it. As for Ingrid, from what she's told me I think she'd like nothing better than to be Victor's wife, baby or no baby.'

This makes Ingrid blush a bit but she doesn't look up.

Well, considering all the circumstances and the fact that I wish I'd never had to meet him, I'm beginning to like Ingrid's old man, and I reckon he doesn't think I'm all that bad either. Her mother's got her little mouth all pursed up and reckon she's disappointed at not being let shout the odds a bit longer and a bit put out because her hubby's put all his cards on the table so soon. She says nothing, though, and I wonder what she's going to turn out like when Mr Rothwell isn't around to keep her in check. I'm not very hopeful.

'I think we ought to get down to practical matters,' Mr Rothwell says, like a bloke who wants to get his business wound up because he hasn't a lot of time to spare. 'Such as how soon the wedding can be and where they're going to live. I think the wedding should take place as quickly and as quietly as possible, with no fuss. I should say in three or four weeks' time. What d'you think, Victor?'

'I think that'll be all right.'

May as well be tomorrow if it's going to be at all. I can't say anything else but okay because it's got beyond me now. I'm not in charge any longer. I'm horrified, though, at how fast things are beginning to move. A month ago I was free to come and go as I liked, and a month from now, at this rate, I'll be a married man with a wife I don't particularly like, let alone love, and a chico on the way! Oh, what a mug, what a mug!

'Of course,' Ingrid's dad says, 'there's still a chance that it's a false alarm. A small chance. But in that event you'll be married anyway, so it doesn't really matter.'

That's the maddening thing about it all, the way everybody's looking at it upside down. They all think we've been courting in the ordinary way and got a bit impatient and jumped the gun. They've got no idea the way things have really been and I can't tell them. All I can say is it'd be real rich if I wind up married to Ingrid and it does turn out to be a false alarm after all!

'Registry office, of course,' Mr Rothwell says, and Mrs Rothwell's bottom lip starts to tremble and she feels for her hanky.

'When I think', she says, nearly repeating what the Old Lady said, 'of the nice wedding I've always imagined Ingrid having. All in white, at church, with the choir and all our relatives and friends there. When I think what a proud day it would have been . . . And now this . . . this hole-in-the-corner affair . . .'

Ingrid puts her hand into her ma's. 'It doesn't matter, Mother. I don't mind.'

'But I do,' Mrs Rothwell says. 'It's a mother's proudest day.'

'Well I'm afraid there's nothing we can do about that now,' Mr Rothwell says, 'so we'll just have to put it out of our minds. The next important matter is where they're going to live. Have you any ideas on that, Victor?'

'Well, I don't really know . . .' It's all happening so quick, without giving me a chance to think. All I could think about was would I get out of it, would it be all right. I've always imagined that when I met that girl we'd have

229

a house all lined up, or at least a flat to begin with. Somewhere private and cosy, just for the two of us. 'I haven't had time to think about it,' I say. 'I suppose we could live at our house for a while. We don't stand a chance of finding a house of our own straight away.'

'To rent, you mean?'

'Yes. I can't afford to buy one.'

I fancy Ingrid's mother curls her lip at this but it might be just imagination. I'm in the mood for fancying that sort of thing.

'What do your parents think to that idea?'

'Well I haven't actually mentioned it yet. I don't think they'd mind, though. We've plenty of room.'

'Well I have a suggestion,' he says. 'We talked it over before you came. I'm away most of the time and if Ingrid leaves too it'll mean that her mother will be on her own. Of course Ingrid can't stay to keep her mother company for ever, but for the present there's no reason why you shouldn't live here. The next few months will no doubt be a bit trying for Ingrid and it'll help her if she's near her mother. That will give you a breathing space to look for a house to rent, or save up enough to put a deposit on your own. What do you say?'

Here again, what can I say? They've got it all worked out. I look at Ma Rothwell, who's saying nothing. I fancy they've talked this over and left it open till they saw what sort of a bloke I was and whether they could bear me about the place. Well, it seems I've passed muster on that one, anyway. Still, I'd've preferred to be in a place I know, especially now I'm not sure about how Ingrid's ma will turn out. But I'm not calling the tune.

'All right . . . Thank you.'

Well, the conversation carries on in a general sort of way now and they begin to fish for information about the family. I tell them about the Old Man and the Old Lady, and about Chris and Jim, and David. I think Mrs Rothwell would be happier if the Old Man was a doctor or a solicitor, or a business man even, rather than a miner, but I've never been ashamed of the Old Man's job before and

I don't intend to start now. I think Chris and David help to make up for it a bit as far as Ma Rothwell's concerned, because she's a snob, no doubt about it.

A bit after nine, when I've had a cup of tea and a biscuit and promised to fix up for Mr Rothwell and the Old Man to meet each other and have a natter, I beat it. Ingrid comes with me to the corner.

'Well?' she says as we walk along.

'It wasn't so bad. And anyway, it's done with now.'

'Think about me,' she says. 'I've got it to face yet.'

'Oh, you'll be okay. They won't eat you. Just be yourself and don't put any airs and graces on and they'll take to you okay.'

Why shouldn't they take to her? I think. She's a nice enough kid and they haven't to live with her for the rest of their lives. Forty years, maybe longer. It's a *real* life sentence, and no time off for good behaviour . . .

'What will it be?'

'I suppose the sooner the better now. What about tomorrow night?'

'Oh, dear . . . Well, all right.'

A bit farther on I say, 'I like your dad.' I'm thinking it's a pity he'll be away most of the time because having him around would probably increase my chances of rubbing along with Ingrid's mother. Anyway, I shan't be the first bloke who didn't care for his mother-in-law; or his wife, for that matter. Not that that's any consolation at all. Not a bit.

III

'Well he seems a nice enough chap,' the Old Feller says when we get back home. It's Wednesday night now and we've been to meet Mr Rothwell in the lounge bar of the Craven Arms. 'Talks reasonable an' quiet an' doesn't go flyin' off the handle about summat 'at can't be altered.'

'You want goin' an' talking over your children's futures in a pub,' the Old Lady says.

'It isn't a pub,' the Old Man says, 'it's t'best hotel in Cressley. It wa' good enough for our Christine's weddin' reception, wadn't it?'

'That wa' different,' the Old Lady says. 'We had a private room: we didn't go into the bar.'

'When a couple o' fellers get together to talk things over they have a drink,' the Old Man says. 'I'll bet there's more important matters settled there than anywhere else in Cressley. 'Xcept maybe t'Con Club. An' anyway, I told you before, we had to meet on neutral ground like. If he'd come here he'd ha' felt at a disadvantage, an' I know I should if I'd gone to their house. Besides,' he says, giving me a sly wink, 'we didn't want any women about throwin' spanners in t'works.'

'Oh, aye,' the Old Lady says. 'Oh, aye, leave it to t'men an' it'll be all right. I know.' She nods her head a time or two. 'Well them 'at lives t'longest 'ull see t'most.'

She goes into the kitchen and comes back in a minute with a couple of mugs. 'Here's your cocoa, if you can stomach any more liquid tonight.'

The Old Man lifts his eyebrows at me but says nothing.

'Well I must say,' the Old Lady says, sitting down, ' 'at Ingrid seems a decent enough lass. I'll admit I was quite prepared to dislike her, but I changed me mind when I'd seen her. Time'll tell whether I'm right or wrong, but I don't think our Victor's getting a bad lass for a wife. He could ha' done worse.'

This is high praise from the Old Lady, and something to tell Ingrid when I see her again.

'What's her mother like, Vic?' the Old Feller asks me. 'D'you think you'll get on with her?'

I pull a little face and shake my head. 'She's a bit of a rum'un, Dad. I don't rightly know.'

The Old Feller looks at me and there's a kind of frosty smile in his eyes. 'Tha're goin' to have plenty o' time to find out, lad,' he says.

'Married?' Mr Van Huyten says. 'Well, bless my soul! Congratulations, Victor. This is rather sudden, isn't it? Or have I been out of touch?'

'We kind of decided all at once.'

'Ah, well, you impetuous young people,' he says with a twinkle. 'Of course you can take your first week's holiday when you like. You must have a honeymoon.' He makes a note in his diary. 'The second week in May. No, I don't see any objection to that.'

'I'm afraid we shan't be able to ask you to the wedding, Mr Van Huyten. It's going to be a very small affair, y'see. Just close family like.'

'Oh, that's all right, Victor. I understand perfectly.'

I wonder if he does. And if he does he says not a dicky bird about it either now or later. He's like that, of course, is Mr Van Huyten.

Henry's a great believer in marriage.

'Best thing you could do,' he says when I tell him. 'Marry early, get some kids and responsibility. It's the making of a man, responsibility. And remember, marriage is what you make it. Look at me, for instance.'

I'm looking at him and think if he's a for instance I don't want any.

'So a wife and six kids on my wage isn't everybody's cup of tea,' Henry says. 'But I'm happy with it, Vic, and that's the main thing.'

And so he is. A wife with as much glamour as an old doormat; house like a pigsty from morning till night with kids bawling and wiping jam and bread on the wallpaper and crapping all over the place. And old Henry's happy on it. And many a bloke with five thousand a year's getting ulcers and worrying himself into the cemetery. It just goes to show. But what it goes to show I don't rightly know, except maybe that people are different. And that's the big snag; you can account for nearly all the trouble in the world when you say that.

All my mates, Jimmy Slade and Willy Lomas and the rest, I'm avoiding like the plague. And all the time I'm waiting for a miracle to happen to make it all come right and put things back where they were again.

6

I

But this is no fairy-tale and no miracle happens. The cell door shuts behind me and the key turns in the lock at eleven o'clock in the morning on the first Saturday in May at the registry office in Huddersfield Road. David's my best man and Ingrid has a cousin of hers that I've never seen before as her bridesmaid. All I can think of when it's over and we're walking out into the sunshine again is how fast you sign yourself away. As we go through the gates into the street a bint goes by, wobbling a bit on stiletto heels. I sort of half-register the fact that she's got nice legs and then all at once it comes over me that I'll never be able to look at a bint with an open mind again. I'm a goner. The search is over for me. I'm a married man as of five minutes ago and soon I'll be a father. It all clots up inside me in a hard lump of misery and I just can't talk to anybody. Not that there's much merry wedding conversation going on anyway. They're all somehow feeling this wasn't the way they wanted it and what should have been a big important and happy time has sort of crept up on them and caught them napping.

We go back to Rothwells' and have a buffet meal and here the party begins to relax a bit. The Old Feller and Mr Rothwell get really chatty, but the two mothers are spending their time sizing one another up and kind of jockeying for position all the time as though they think the men are letting the side down the way they're talking about football and this, that, and the other, nearly like old mates.

At half past one Ingrid and I go upstairs for a wash. There's no changing to do because I'm travelling in my new dark blue suit and Ingrid's going in the grey costume she's worn at the wedding. When we come down we see her mother getting herself ready and Ingrid says, 'Mother, would you mind if just Jean and Christine and David came with us to the station?'

Ma Rothwell's jaw drops a mile at this. 'But whatever for?' she says. 'Don't you want your own mother to see you off on your honeymoon?'

'I'd rather it wasn't such a big party,' Ingrid says, and there's something about the stubborn way she says it that suits me fine. I don't want the band playing at the station, for one.

Well, Ma Rothwell looks as if she's going to cry and Mr Rothwell chips in and says, 'Yes, let her have her way, Esther. It'll perhaps be just as well.'

Well there's kisses and handshakes all round and I find Mrs Rothwell's pudgy cheek up against my face so I kiss that and taste face-powder. Mr Rothwell gets hold of my hand like he means it and looks me straight in the eye. 'I shan't be here when you get back, so I'll see you later. Just you look after her, now.'

'I will.'

We take Mr Rothwell's Oxford and David drives. We've timed it nicely and the train's in when we go through the barrier. When we're in the carriage and leaning out of the window for the last good-byes I meet Chris's look, it seems to me for the first time since I broke the news at home. Because if there's one person I've hated knowing about this, and felt ashamed in front of, it's her. Now I see she's smiling at me and I feel tons better just for that.

'Look after her, Vic,' she says. 'She'll need it. And you, Ingrid, be good to him. He's not a bad lad, your husband.'

'I know that,' Ingrid says, and all at once she's sobbing like a leaky tap, sniffing and blowing into her hanky.

David shakes my hand. 'All the best, Vic.'

And then they're waving to us as the train moves down the platform.

We sit down in opposite corners as the train pulls clear of the station and picks up speed. Ingrid blows her nose and puts her hanky away and gets her compact out and starts to cover the signs of her crying. She's looking very smart and attractive and the grey costume suits her. I suppose to look at us anybody would take us for a normal happy honeymoon couple, very much in love and all that. She puts the compact away and looks at me.

'Well, missis?' I say.

'Aye, mister?'

I smile at her. It's not much of a smile to tell the truth, but I'm surprised I can muster one at all.

II

Scarborough's sunny and a bit quiet because the season hasn't properly begun yet. We get a taxi at the station and it takes us up on to the Esplanade overlooking the Spa and South Bay where Mrs Rothwell's booked us in at a posher hotel than any I've ever stayed at before. There's even a bloke in a white jacket in the lobby waiting to take our luggage upstairs when we arrive; though it's no more than there should be for thirty bob a day apiece, low season rate. Just like Ma Rothwell to chuck my brass around, I think. But I don't mind too much because you can keep yourself to yourself in these better places, and anyway, you can't count the pennies on your honeymoon, can you?

When we're getting ready for bed that night we keep our backs turned to one another like a couple of bashful kids. But I catch sight of Ingrid in the dressing-table mirror as she slots the nightie down over her head and it seems to me her bust's filling up and she's showing a definite belly already. I never thought anybody could guess she was in the family way, but now I'm not so sure.

I'll be thinking about it all the week now and wondering if everybody knows, and us on our honeymoon.

'We get into bed and put the light out and I take hold of her intending to make the most of the fact that we've got a licence for it now, but she stops me short when she says, 'D'you think we should, Vic? Don't you think it might be dangerous?'

I'm flabbergasted. 'How d'you mean, dangerous?'

'For the baby.'

'But you're hardly three months gone yet, what the heck! It's ages yet before it gets dangerous. Didn't your mother say anything about it?'

'That's what I mean. She said I'd to be careful.'

'Hell! what's she trying to do, spoil our honeymoon?'

'She was only thinking about me, Vic.'

'And doing her best to turn you stone cold on our wedding night.' The bitch, I'm thinking, the damned interfering old bitch. And that's what I've got to live with . . .

'I'm sure she didn't mean any harm.'

'Oh, for Pete's sake, Ingrid, it's all in a book I bought.'

'A book?'

'Yeh, a book for people just getting married. It tells you how to go on.'

She giggles.

'What's funny?'

'Most people would say we knew "how to go on".'

'Well, I thought I might as well get genned up properly from the start. It says in there 'at you're okay till about six months. I looked it up specially. I've got it in the case. I'll get it out an' show it you if you want.'

'I'll take your word for it.' She snuggles up closer and I think this is a lot better.

'It's told me a lot more things as well . . .'

'Such as?'

'Such as how to get you where I want you. How to rouse you an' all that.'

She rubs her face against mine and I get hair in my mouth. 'You know you've always known how to do that.'

'Well, now I know even better.' I start giving her a bit

of the technique. 'What you got this passion-killer on for?'

'It's not a passion-killer; it's a passion-rouser. I bought it specially for you. It's sheer nylon. Don't you like it?'

'I like it when I'm looking. I'm not looking now.'

'Wait a minute, then.'

She pulls away from me and sits up in the bed.

'Put it under the pillow in case there's a fire.'

She giggles in the dark, and then she's back and there's nothing in the way any more.

'Better?'

'A lot better.'

I run my hand all the way down from her shoulder to her hips. 'Remember that night at your house? Gosh, but I'll never know how I held off that time, I wanted you that bad.'

'You can have me now,' she says, feeling for my mouth. 'Oh, Vic,' she says before she kisses me, 'I do love you.'

And I'd give anything in the world to be able to say it back.

We've only been there a couple of days when we have our first quarrel.

There's a couple stopping at this hotel. There's a lot more people like, but there's this couple who sit at the next table for meals and seem to want to be friendly. They're a youngish-looking middle-aged couple who have a green Ford Consul parked out in front of the place. They're not what you'd call well-off because you can tell that by his sports coat which has definitely seen better days, though she's quite a snappy dresser. All the same, they have this something about them that puts them a cut or two above Ingrid and me. A kind of air, it is, of knowing their way about and what things are best and what are common. *They're* not common, if you see what I mean. They talk nice as well. Not lah-di-da, but easy and natural, without any accent that shows where they come from. Anybody can place me straight away, and Ma Rothwell as well, no matter how she puts it on; but not these two.

Well it appears they live in Essex and this is the first time they've stayed on the Yorkshire coast and because Ingrid knows all round pretty well from having stayed here a lot as a kid she's soon talking away nineteen to the dozen, telling them all the places they should see. Which is all very well, but before long I begin to notice how her voice is changing; how she's putting it on like a telephone operator in a high-class knocking-shop. And it gets worse and worse and more and more obvious till I just can't stand it any more, I'm that mad and embarrassed, and I have to get up and go out.

I wait for her on the steps, looking out across the road at the bay and Castle rock sticking out into the sea with the little boats and pleasure steamers hugging under it like chickens under an old hen.

'What did you do that for?' she says when she comes out.

'What?' I say, sulky like.

'Barge out like that right in the middle of the conversation.'

'I can leave a room without asking their permission, can't I?' I start down the steps and she follows me.

'Well, what's wrong with them, for goodness' sake? I think they're very nice people.'

'Mebbe they are, but there's no need to throw yourself at 'em just because they condescend to exchange a few words about the weather.'

'And if they'd sat there all week and not spoken you'd have said they were stuck-up and snobbish. Well, it strikes me you're the snob – an upside-down snob.'

I'm getting pretty riled now, more so because I know I'm partly at fault. 'I've talked to better people than them in my time but they have to take me as I am, Yorkshire accent an' all. I don't put it on for anybody.'

'And who does?'

'You do. You sounded as if you were auditioning for the BBC and trying to kid 'em you'd come straight from

239

Eton, or wherever it is they send these posh bints.'

'I hadn't noticed,' she says, stiffening up.

'Well I did, an' I'll bet they did an' all. Why d'you want to throw yourself at people like that? Meet 'em half-way, be pleasant, okay. But there's no need to gush and preen yourself as if they were royalty or something. People don't think any better of you for trying to make out you're better than you are.'

She says nothing to this and a bit of me's sorry under the irritation. We walk on without saying anything for a bit, then I say, 'Okay, let's forget it.'

'I think we'd better,' she says, very quiet, and this is worse somehow than if she'd come out and bawled back at me.

We've got to the cliff lift now and there's one at the top standing with its door open.

'Where d'you want to go?'

'I'm not particular.'

'You want to go and look at the shops?'

'No, we'd better save that for later in the week when we know how much money we have left.'

'Well, I shan't have so much left if that bloke stands about in the hall so much more,' I say, trying to make a joke. 'I feel as if I ought to put a bob into his hand every time I pass him.'

'Shall we go down on the beach, then?' she says.

'Okay. We'll get the papers and a couple of deck chairs and take it easy like a real old married couple.'

'I suppose we ought to make the most of it,' she says. 'It's the last holiday we'll have on our own for a long, long time.'

It's these casual remarks about us spending the rest of our lives together that chill me to the marrow, reminding me that this is real and not a dream. We walk together into the lift and I look down at her in her summer frock and wonder if it shows.

III

Next week I move my gear over to Rothwell's ready for settling in. There's not much, just my clothes, a few books, and one or two gramophone records. I leave the gram at home for young Jim because Ingrid already has one. Ingrid's bed's a three-quarter size, which is fair enough when we're feeling matey, but not so good for sleeping comfortable; so we put this in the spare room and go into town and buy a new double one for us. This is our first bit of furniture and the only thing we need at present because the rest of the stuff in Ingrid's room – dressing-table, wardrobe, and drawers – is enough for both of us. On the face of it this should give us a chance to save up for when we can get our own place; but now Ingrid's packed her job in we only have my wage and by the time I've paid Ma Rothwell board and lodging for the two of us and I've had my National Health and income tax stopped at the shop we only have about fifty bob left over to pay for everything else – entertainment, clothes, and all the stuff we'll need for the kid when it arrives. At this rate I can see us being stuck with Ingrid's old lady for the next ten years and I don't like the thought of this one little bit; because from the day I go there to the day I walk out I don't feel at home in that house.

This is because Ma Rothwell and I don't get along very well, like I expected. We don't have words or anything like that (not at first, anyway) and there's nothing really you can pin down and tell anybody about because you have to be around all the time and see how things lead up to things and hear the tone of voice things are said in to get the idea.

I'm not so bothered that she's house-proud. I'm a pretty tidy sort of bloke myself and if she wants to empty ash-trays after me and shake the cushions about all the time and tell me she doesn't want me to smoke upstairs or go up there in my shoes, well it's her house and if she's proud of it she can have it that way. It does get on your nerves after a bit, though.

241

But not as much as the way she talks. She talks the most horrible bilge most of the time and freezes up as though you've insulted her if you dare to try to put her right. She has one or two favourite subjects. The Royal Family's one of them. She keeps a scrapbook of the Queen and Philip and the kids and she reads all these intimate stories about the way they live and takes them all for gospel. As if anybody really knows about them, and they wouldn't be allowed to write it if they did. Another favourite of hers is the way she puts shop-keepers in their places. To hear her talk you'd think everybody in Cressley was out to do her down. But she doesn't let them get away with it, Ma Rothwell doesn't. Oh, no, she puts them in their place all right. A proper putter-in-place, she is. She never seems to see that if she was the big lady she thinks she is they'd all be falling over themselves to be nice to her and so she ought to reckon they do even if they don't. Then there's politics. You don't need telling she's Conservative. What else could she be but real true blue and never a good word for the Labour Party and the trade unions. If she had her way trade unions would be abolished. And as for the miners, well, they're just holding the country up to ran-som, so she says, and making trouble at every turn. She's not forgotten the Old Man's a miner, but it doesn't stop her shooting her mouth off about something she knows absolutely nothing about. And I mustn't forget the col-oured people, the West Indians and Pakistanis and so on. She'd pack that lot off home, and sharp about it, because what with blackies on the buses and all you read about in the papers it's getting as a respectable Englishwoman daren't put her nose outside her own door. In fact, she can hardly open her mouth without showing everybody what a stupid, bigoted, ignorant old cow she is. And I've got to live with her.

As for Ingrid, I don't think she had a serious thought to call her own before she met me and I gave her something to think about, except what colour of coat she wanted for winter and whether she liked 'Criss Cross Quiz' better than 'Double Your Money', or 'Take Your Pick' better than both.

It's not having a life of my own any more that really gets me down, though. I don't seem to be able to do anything I want to do. I try playing my records once – but only once. Before the first side's finished both Ingrid and her ma are bored to death and I have to pack it in because they want television on. I always used to like television before I came to live at Rothwell's but now I hate the sight of it because it's on when I go in at tea-time and it doesn't go off till it's time to go to bed. I've got to watch it, though, because I can't read with the light out and I don't go out much without Ingrid because her ma doesn't think it's right.

I've been there about six weeks when we have our first little set-to. Mr Van tells me one day that the Philharmonia Orchestra's coming to Leeds and would I like to go over with him because it's a real crack outfit and you don't often get a chance of hearing them live.

'Well I don't know, Mr Van Huyten,' I say. 'I'd like to but I'm not my own boss now, y'know.' I try to laugh. 'Married man an' all that.'

'Bring your wife along, Victor,' he says. 'I'd be glad to have the company of you both.'

I tell him I'll see what she says and I ask her that night if she'd like to go, only I make the mistake of doing it while her mother's there. Like I expected, she pulls a face. 'I'd be bored to tears,' she says.

'Why don't you give it a try? There's always a first time.'

'Ingrid knows what she likes and she doesn't pretend to enjoy highbrow nonsense,' Ma Rothwell says, minding her own business as usual.

Well, I'm as wild as hell on a windy night at this and it's all I can do to stop myself telling her just what I think. 'It's a matter of opinion,' I say, holding it back. 'Makes a change from television quiz shows, though.'

She tightens her mouth up because she knows this is one for her.

'Anyway, I'd like to go if you won't.'

Now left to Ingrid this would be okay but the old cow has

to put her two cents' worth in again. 'You have to sacrifice things when you're married,' she says. 'Give and take.'

Now just what this has to do with me going to a symphony concert I don't know. It's the sort of thing that makes me want to climb the walls. It's stupid beyond belief.

'I don't see what that has to do with it. There's no harm in me goin' to a concert, is there?'

She shrugs. (She can shrug in a more maddening way than anybody I ever met.) 'If you want to carry on just as you did before you were married it's got nothing to do with me. Though I'm sure Ingrid will have something to say about it.' And she bows out now she's done the damage.

'I don't know what you're getting at,' I tell her, and I don't. You can't say anything when she talks like that because there's no sense to argue at.

'You don't mind if I go, do you?' I say to Ingrid.

'When is it?'

'A fortnight on Saturday.'

'I don't know. We might want to go somewhere else.'

For a second I hate her enough to slap her silly face. To think only three months ago I'd just to snap my fingers and she'd come running. Now I'm married to her and it's as if her mother puts her in a trance where she hasn't a mind of her own.

'Well, you'll have to forget about that,' I say, 'because I'm going.'

This puts me in the dog-house and with Ma Rothwell around I've no chance of sorting it out till we go up to bed.

'I didn't like the way you snapped at me tonight,' Ingrid says, pulling her jumper over her head and shaking her hair free again.

'I didn't like the way everybody was telling me what I could and couldn't do. I don't know what the hell's coming over you these days, Ingrid. You're just an echo of your old lady.'

244

'I'd rather you didn't call her that, if you don't mind.'

'Well you know who I'm talking about.'

'You should show a bit of respect for her, Vic. After all, we are living in her house.'

'Don't I know it?'

She finishes undressing and gets into bed. 'Are you going to this concert?'

'Yes, I am.'

'You're going to make an issue of it?'

'*Me?*' I stand there in my shirt and underpants, pointing my finger at my chest. '*I'm* making an issue of it? You let your mother drive me into a corner, don't do a thing to help me out, and then say *I'm* making an issue of it. Just because you'd rather stop at home yourself and watch some bloody silly television programme.'

'For goodness' sake keep your voice down. She can hear every word.'

'I don't care what she can hear,' I say, my voice getting louder still.

There's a tap on the door and Ma Rothwell says from outside, 'Are you all right, Ingrid?'

'Yes, Mother.'

I put the light out and get into bed. 'What the hell does she mean? Did she think I was hiding you or summat?'

She snuggles down under the clothes without bothering to answer me. Now she'll go to sleep and we've settled nothing. We'll wake up in the morning and it'll all start again. It's all boiling away inside me and there's no way of getting rid of it.

One day the phone rings in the shop and there's Jimmy on the other end of the line.

'Guess who walked into the office the other day,' he says. 'Old Conroy.'

'I thought he'd moved away altogether.'

'His family live in Bradford. He's not working at the moment because he's emigrating, off to Australia. He's fixing a get-together before he goes . . .'

We talk a bit (it's quiet in the shop) and Jimmy tells me they're all going out to the Lord Nelson, that's a pub on the way to Bradford, for a booze-up and would I like to go. It'll be a kitty do with everybody chucking ten bob in at the beginning of the evening and drinking till it's gone. I tell him I don't know how I'm fixed for that night, but I'll let him know.

I know now I shan't be going but I mention it to Ingrid just to let her know the sort of sacrifices I'll make for the sake of peace and quiet.

'I always thought you didn't like Conroy,' she says.

'I got to like him well enough before he left. And anyway, it's a chance to see some of the lads again.'

'It'll be a drinking do, won't it?'

'What else?'

'Have you told him you'll go?'

'No, I put him off. You know very well your mother 'ud go hairless if I as much as offered to go out on me own to a do like that.'

She looks at me sort of soft and gutless like. 'Oh, Vic, I don't want you to think you can't do anything on your own any more.'

'You want to tell your mother that sometime,' I say. 'If I set me mind on going, I'll go, and neither you nor your ma will stop me. But I'm all for a quiet life, and as I've got to live here I'll give it a miss.'

We're up in the bedroom as usual, the only place we can have a private talk – if we keep our voices down.

'I'll tell you straight, though,' I say. 'I didn't bargain for this bloody lot when I offered to marry you.'

'There's no need to swear,' she says.

'Swear?'

'Yes, swear. You do it so much these days you don't even notice it; and you never used to.'

'Circumstances were different. This is enough to make a parson swear.'

This is the way we always are now. The only chance we get to talk, except when we go out, which isn't often now that Ingrid's showing obvious (she's very self-conscious about it; and so am I, for that matter), is late at night and first thing in the morning. Well you know how you are first thing and at night it's as though we've time for nothing else but the grouses we've been saving up because we couldn't get rid of them earlier. So it seems like we do nothing but niggle and nag.

'You go if you want to,' she says.

'And get the big freeze treatment for it? No, thanks. I haven't forgotten the concert.'

'Well you went to that, didn't you?'

'And paid for it. Anybody'd have thought I'd spent the evening in a knocking-shop somewhere instead of a respectable symphony concert.'

'Well, it's up to you.'

'Aye, it's up to me. You never back me up, do you? You let your mother say just what she likes and you never think of siding with me, do you?'

'I don't see why I should fall out with my mother. I never used to and I won't start now.'

I chuck my keys and money with a clatter on to the dressing-table. 'Not even to save my face, eh?'

'She's my mother, Vic.'

'And I'm your husband; or have you forgotten now you've got the certificate to prove you have one? I know anybody 'ud take me for the lodger, but you can bet your boots I remember signing my name.'

'P'raps you're sorry you married me,' she says, and she should know better, she really should, with me in the mood I'm in.

'There's no bloody p'raps about it,' I tell her.

Well that sends her to bed in tears and leaves me walking up and down the bedroom itching to throw things about and break them from sheer frustration.

Oh, it's a great life, and we've only another thirty or forty years of it to come.

7

I

I get back from the shop about half past six one night at the back end of August, in the middle of a heat wave, and find the house all locked up. I haven't got a key and I can't get in till Ingrid and her ma come back from shopping or wherever they've decided to go without bothering to tell me.

I haven't been feeling so hot this afternoon. I've had a blinding headache since just after dinner and I'm dead-tired. I'm standing outside the back door with my hands in my pockets and wondering how long they'll be when Mrs Oliphant our next-door neighbour comes out to shake the tablecloth. She spots me as she turns round to go back into the house and stops and gives me what I fancy's a queer look.

'Looks as if I'm locked out,' I say, feeling a bit of a Charlie about it. 'I don't suppose you know where they've gone?'

Well now she looks at me proper odd and no mistake about it as she comes up to the fence with the tablecloth over her arm. Red and white check, it is.

'But they're up at the hospital,' she says. 'Didn't you –'

'Hospital? It isn't Ingrid's day for ante-natal. That's on Tuesday . . .' All at once it's as though somebody's kicked the bottom out of my belly and all my tripes are tumbling out. 'What's wrong?' I say. 'What you lookin' at me like that for?'

'But surely,' she says, still gawping at me. 'It's Ingrid. They've taken her to hospital. She's had an accident.'

The sun seems to be burning right through my skull and Mrs Oliphant's face goes all swimmy and out of focus in front of me. I take hold of the fence and feel myself sway a bit.

'As far as I can understand it, she fell downstairs and brought on a miscarriage. They rushed her into hospital early this afternoon. It couldn't have been much after two. You mean to say you didn't know?'

I shake my head, partly to say no and partly to try and clear it. My knees have taken their hook somewhere, leaving the rest of my legs to fend for themselves. I know if I don't sit down somewhere in a minute I might fall down.

'You'd better come in and sit down,' Mrs O. says, and opens the little connecting gate to let me through. 'It must have been a shock for you, but naturally I thought you'd know . . . Come along in and sit down for a minute. There's a cup of tea left. You'll feel better in a few minutes.'

Mr Oliphant looks up from his evening paper as we go in.

'Here's young Mr Brown, Henry,' Mrs O. says. 'I've just found him outside the house. He couldn't get in and he didn't know anything about Ingrid till I told him . . . You just sit down there and I'll pour the tea. You'll feel better after it.'

'He didn't know?' Mr Oliphant says. 'But I thought you said it happened just after dinner?'

Mrs O. must give him a signal from behind me because he lets it drop.

'I haven't been feeling well all afternoon,' I mutter, and he looks at me.

'And you'll be feeling worse now, eh?' he says. He gets up and comes over to me, a big chap, in his shirt-sleeves, and puts his big hand on the back of my neck and shoves my head down between my knees and holds it there for a minute. 'Now lean back and relax,' he says, letting go.

'There'll be a cup of tea for you in a minute and you'll feel better then.'

When Mrs Oliphant brings the cup and saucer I hold them tight for fear of dropping them and ask her if she's got a couple of aspirins to spare and she goes into the kitchen and comes back with the bottle. I swallow the aspirins and sip the tea. It's a bit weak and not very hot. The two young Oliphant kids come rampaging in from the garden and Mr O. turns them straight round and packs them off out again.

'I suppose Ingrid's mother would be too shaken up herself to let you know,' Mrs Oliphant says. 'You are on the telephone, I suppose?'

Yes, we're on the phone. And it's a good four hours since it happened. There's been plenty of time to let me know. I know it and so do Mr and Mrs Oliphant.

'Would you like to ring up from here?' Mr O. says. 'You can use our phone by all means.'

'Thanks,' I say. 'In a minute. I'll ring in a minute.'

Will she die? I'm wondering. What if she's dead already? What if I'm a widower just this minute and I don't know it? Free again . . .

I finish the tea and then Mr Oliphant shows me where the phone is on a little shelf in the hall. 'D'you know the number?' I shake my head and he flips through the directory. Then he lifts the receiver and says a number and waits. In a minute he says, 'Cressley Infirmary? Just a minute, please.' He holds the receiver out to me. 'Here you are.'

'Hello . . . I'm inquiring about a Mrs Brown. She was brought in this afternoon. She had an accident, a miscarriage, early this afternoon . . . What? This is Mr Brown. My name's Victor Brown, hers is Ingrid . . . Yes, all right.'

I look round but Mr Oliphant's gone. I stand there with the receiver to my ear and wait. There's a kid's pedal-car and a tricycle behind the front door and a rubber ball at the bottom of the stairs. I like the way the hall's decorated, with a light fawn paper on the walls and a

dark blue with like little stars on the ceiling. I believe Mr
O. does it all himself. I don't exactly know what he does
for a living but they seem comfortable. They're nice
people. Nice and steady and quiet and happy . . .

'Hello?'

'Yes?'

'I'm afraid we've no news at the moment, Mr Brown.
Mrs Brown is still in the labour ward.'

'When will you know?'

'You could ring in about an hour. Or you could come
up and wait. We'd tell you then as soon as there's anything to report.'

'All right, I'll come up. Thank you.'

Probably wondering why I'm not there already, I think
as I go back into the dining-room and tell Mr and Mrs
Oliphant.

'I'm sure she'll be all right,' Mrs O. says. 'I had a
miscarriage once and I didn't even go away. I've had
both my children since then, so you can see it didn't do
me any harm. And Ingrid wasn't very far gone, was
she?'

I wonder if she knows Ingrid was three months on the
way when we got married and I say, 'No, not far,' and
leave it at that.

'She'll be all right,' Mrs Oliphant says. 'You'll see.'

'Are you going up there now?' Mr O. says, and I nod.
'Yes, I thought I would.'

He gets up. 'I'll run you up in the car,' he says.

'That's very good of you.'

'It won't take five minutes,' he says. 'You don't want to
be hanging about waiting for buses at a time like this.'

'No. Thanks very much.'

'What about your tea?' Mrs Oliphant says. 'Have you
had anything to eat? You can't go running off on an
empty stomach. You might have to wait a while.'

'I don't want anything to eat, thanks.'

'I can make you some sandwiches in just a minute.'

'Thanks all the same, but I don't think I could face
anything.'

251

Mr Oliphant finishes fastening his tie and puts his jacket on. 'Come on, then,' he says. 'I'll run you up.'

The woman in the office isn't the one who was on the phone. Her voice was nice and clear but this one talks as if she's got a mouthful of toffee and she twists her words about it till you can hardly tell what she's saying.

I tell her who I am and what I'm here for and she asks me to sit down round in the hall. I go round the corner into this big high waiting-room with windows in the roof and long benches covered with blue leather and sit down. I seem to remember coming here when I was a kid. I look round at the brass plates with the names of all the local big-wigs who gave money to build this wing and at the double doors with 'Casualty Department' written over them. It must have been when I cut my head open on the railings and I probably sat here in front of these same doors, shivering from stem to stern, scared stiff at what they might be cooking up for me behind the port-hole windows. There's a light on in there now, but nobody else waiting. I suppose they're ready to deal with anything that crops up. Always at it, somebody needing help.

Is she going to die? I wonder again. Is this the way it's all going to work out, with her dying and taking the baby with her? And they say there's a pattern to life. A plan. What plan? For me to fall in love with her and then fall out of love with her but still want her enough to give her the baby, so that we have to get married when I don't love her and she can fall downstairs and kill herself and the kid and leave me free again? What sort of a plan's that, except maybe a plan to have me spending the rest of my life telling myself I killed her and if I'd held out that night in the park she'd be still alive?

I don't want her to die. I don't love her, but I don't want her to die.

The hospital smell's beginning to make me feel sick. I haven't got rid of the headache yet: the aspirins didn't do a bit of good. I don't like hospitals. I'm like thousands of others, I reckon – scared of the people who're here to help, scared of the pain that makes you better. I sit sideways on the seat and pull one knee up and rest my arm on the back so's I can put my forehead in my hand.

'Mr Brown?'

I jump, she's come up so quiet on rubber soles. I look at her, a little dark women with glasses and a white coat unbuttoned, showing a dark frock underneath.

'Yes.'

'I'm Doctor Parker. I've just left your wife.'

'How is she?'

'As well can be expected. She's had a very uncomfortable afternoon and lost a lot of blood, but we've given her a transfusion and she's going to be all right. I'm sorry about the baby, but I'm afraid we couldn't do anything to save it.'

'No.' I look at the floor.

'How long have you been married?'

'Three months.'

'I see . . . you . . .'

'She was having the baby before.'

'I see. Well, you'll have other children, all being well. This won't be the end of it for you.'

'Can I see her?' I say this without hardly thinking, as though it's something I think she's expecting me to say. But I'm not so sure I want to see her and it's a kind of relief when she says, 'I'd rather you didn't tonight.' I don't know how I'd feel to see Ingrid poorly. I might hate her and it show.

'Her mother's just left,' the doctor says. 'I'm afraid she wasn't very good for her. A rather emotional person. She's trying to get some sleep now. If you'd come earlier . . .'

'I didn't know.'

'But it happened quite early this afternoon.'

'I was at work. I didn't get to know till I came home.'

'You mean your wife's mother didn't let you know?'

253

'The neighbours told me. I'd be the last one *she'd* think of telling.'

She looks at me without saying anything and I stand up.

'You can ring up first thing in the morning and visit tomorrow night at seven.'

'If *she* doesn't come.'

'Oh, you'll have priority for visiting.'

She walks me out to the door. 'Will you tell her I've been, and I came up as soon as I knew?'

'Yes. Anything else you'd like me to tell her?'

I shake my head. 'I don't think so. You can tell her not to worry; about the kid, I mean. I couldn't get used to the idea of being a father anyway.'

There's a bus coming down the hill as I go out of the hospital drive and I run and jump on as it stops. I go upstairs. Somehow I can't care about the kid because it never really was a kid. It wasn't really anything except an egg growing in Ingrid; something that made us have to get married. It wasn't a person so I can't feel bad about losing it. It's rotten to think it would have been a person, though, sometime, and now it's finished like this, all mangled and dead from being bounced down the stairs. 'A very uncomfortable afternoon,' the doctor said. I shut my eyes and I can see her there on her back with her legs open and them pulling this bloody mess out of her.

The bus stinks of petrol and stale tobacco smoke and because it's practically empty it jolts and jumps about the road all down the hill, shaking my tripes about till I break out in a cold sweat of sickness. I run down the steps and jump off as it slows at the corner and make straight for a Gents across the road. I find a penny and go into one of the bogs and the bolt echoes about the place as it shoots home behind me. It all seems to hit me at once: being married, not loving Ingrid, Ma Rothwell, the niggling and nagging, now the miscarriage, and me not feeling well, and I lean over the lavatory and retch and retch fit to bring my boot soles up till finally I throw up. And then I'm saying out loud, 'Oh, bugger it, bugger, damn, and blast it all,' till there's nothing else to come up and nothing else to say and I'm just standing there trembling and empty and cold.

I must have made some noise because when I come out the attendant's standing their waiting for me.

'You don't want to take it if you can't hold it,' he says, the interfering little bastard, the bossy little shithouse cleaner like the world's full of.

I just walk past him and say, 'Go f – yourself,' as I go out. He shouts something after me but I take no notice.

I can't make my mind up whether to go to Rothwell's or go home. I've a good mind at first not to go to Rothwell's ever again after this lot but then I think what a rough time Ingrid's had and I can't add to her troubles. Let her get out of hospital first and then see what happens. I wander round town for a bit, knowing I ought to go up home and tell them what's happened and knowing I've only got a second-hand tale and they'll want to know more than I can tell them and then it'll bring it all out and I can't be bothered going over all that tonight. Anyway, in the end I go up there and reckon I'm in a hurry and I'll call tomorrow when I've been up to the hospital. Then I push off over to Rothwell's and walk in and find Ingrid's mother sitting with Mrs Oliphant, telling her all the tale – or her side of it. They've got the teapot going and Ma Rothwell's face is shocking to look at, all puffed up and ugly from crying.

Ma Rothwell won't look at me, but Mrs Oliphant says, 'Here's Victor now. How did you find her, Victor?'

'I haven't seen her,' I say, shooting a look at Ma Rothwell that's plain for Mrs O. to see. 'I was too late. She was going to sleep.'

All at once Ma Rothwell starts to cry out loud and it's horrible to hear her and watch the way her face kind of goes to pieces. 'I wish Ingrid had never laid eyes on him,' she says in a strangled sort of voice through this crying, and Mrs Oliphant says, 'Come now, Esther, you know it can't be Vic's fault. This sort of thing can happen to anybody.'

I'm standing at the back of the room and I feel myself going white and beginning to tremble with rage. It's only Mrs O. looking up and giving me a signal with her eyes that stops me from going for Ingrid's mother there and then. I go out and up to the bedroom and walk about there, still trembling and swearing out loud, calling Ma Rothwell every filthy name I can think of.

II

Late that night I hear a car pull up outside and when I get up in the morning Mr Rothwell's home. It seems she'd time to let him know even if she couldn't ring me. As it is I think it's only him coming stops me from having it out with her and packing up and leaving. He seems to calm her down and make her see sense. I don't know how much poison she drops in his mind about me but it doesn't seem to make any difference; he's the same with me as he always is when he comes home, quiet and friendly and decent. You kind of get the feeling with him that he respects you as a person like and not for the first time I think it's a pity he's not at home all the time.

Anyway, he takes a week of his holidays and stops till Ingrid comes home. They tell her they really should have kept her ten days or a fortnight but they let her come out providing she takes things very easy for a bit. Then Mr Rothwell's away back to his job and we're like we always were, only worse. It's like we're living in a dream, waiting for things to get back to normal, whatever that might be. Ma Rothwell hardly ever speaks to me and I don't say a dicky bird more to her than I have to.

It's Ingrid who gets my back up more now. Weeks after she's home her mother's still telling her how poorly she is and she mustn't do anything strenuous, and take it easy all the time. And Ingrid laps it all up and sits about all day as though she's in the last stages of a decline. To me she's just a pain in the neck, neither use nor ornament, sitting about like an invalid on Scarborough Spa all day and keeping me at a distance in bed. It goes on so long I tell her she ought to put a notice up: 'Fragile, don't touch.'

'How long's this going on?' I ask her one night when she's given me the cold shoulder again. 'You'll have to snap out of it sometime, y'know.'

'What d'you mean "snap out of it"?'

'What I say. You can't act up on the strength of your miscarriage for ever.'

'So you think I'm just putting on an act, do you?'

'Mebbe you don't know it. I think you an' your mother between you have got you into a frame of mind where you really think you're still poorly; and I'm getting a bit tired of it.'

'Always thinking of yourself,' she says. 'Never any consideration for me.'

'I married you when you were in trouble, didn't I? It's three months since the accident now and it's time I could make a pass at you without feeling like a dirty old man.'

She's drawn herself up all stiff and rigid now, just like her mother. If she knew how much like her mother she looks and how much I hate Ma Rothwell I don't think she'd risk getting on her high horse so much.

'If that's all you can think of,' she says, 'you'll just have to show a bit of will-power, that's all.'

It might be her mother talking, the way she says it. I look at her and I can hardly see the hot little bit I used to snog with in the park. I don't know what's happened to her. I think they must have taken away her sex glands with the kid.

'Till when?' I say. 'Till your mother gives the word? You know what your mother 'ud like to do, don't you, or are you too dense to see it? She'd like to make me do something that'd give her an excuse to push you into getting a divorce. Well, she's going the right way about it, I can tell you. I could have packed it in the day you had your accident for two pins. It took some doing, coming back here after the way your mother treated me.'

'Why did you come back, then?'

'Because we're married, and you'd got a plateful of trouble without me adding to it by walking out.'

'Very noble and kind,' she says, real sarcastic, as though she doesn't believe a word I've said.

'Well you think of a better reason, then.'

'I don't have to thank you for doing what any normal husband would do, do I?'

I could hit her, honest; I'm coming a bit nearer to it every day, and I've never struck a bint in my life.

'No, you don't. But it looks like I've to go down on my knees to get you to do what any normal wife would do. Well, I'll tell you straight now; I'm getting fed-up with this lot. I was all for making the best of it, but if we're married we're married. I'm not going to be just the lodger with special permission to share your bed providing I keep my hands to myself.'

And so on, etcetera, etcetera. And it gets us nowhere except maybe a bit nearer scratching each other's eyes out and dropping all pretence of making a go of it.

It's not hard to see that all these little dos are leading the way to a big dust-up. And it's not long in coming now.

I think it starts over a new winter coat for Ingrid. It's a small thing that's really a big thing and there's more to it than meets the eye. Anyway, Ingrid's got a wardrobe full of clothes, and I mean that. I think she must have spent all her money on them before we were married. Well, she needs a new winter coat like I need a new mother-in-law and besides that we've more or less agreed between us to do without things we don't really need so's we can save every penny towards the time when we can have a place of our own. And now here's Ma Rothwell talking Ingrid into spending twelve or fifteen quid of my money on something she can do without and never miss it. I tell her as much and we get lined up, Ma Rothwell on one side, me on the other, and Ingrid in the middle. As it happens I'm wanting to go out to the pictures that night and ask Ingrid if she fancies it, thinking that us going out will break the argument up before it gets going. Straight

away her mother tells that there's some television programme on she said she wanted to see.

So there we are: it's either pictures or television. On
the face of it, that is. But I know that here and now we'e
going to settle something. It's Ma Rothwell or me, that's
how I see it, and now's the time for Ingrid to show her
mother she's got a husband and he comes first.

She ums and ahs for a bit while I get wilder and wilder, and then before she can say which she's going to do
I settle it for her when I grab my coat and slam out in a
black rage.

I'm still trembling on the bus. I feel the only way to
relieve my feelings is by violence. I want to break windows, smash furniture up, and bash my fist into somebody's face. My idea of delight would be to get my hands
round Ma Rothwell's neck and squeeze and squeeze till
her stupid eyes drop out of her stupid head. I don't know
what's happening to me. I never used to be like this. I'm
beginning to get an idea of how blokes can be driven to
murder.

III

I'm actually going up the steps to the pictures and feeling in my back pocket for the money when it strikes me I
don't really want to go in at all now, and I stop. A bloke
blunders into me from behind and I give him a 'sorry'
over my shoulder as I turn round and go back to the
pavement. I stand there and think how I'm going to
spend the evening. I think about all my old mates and
wonder what they're doing. I had a lot of mates and we
had some good times together. Now I've nearly lost track
of them. I haven't seen most of them in months. Being
married's put me out of circulation and I haven't felt like
meeting them anyway after the Charlie I made of myself.
It's starting to drizzle and this only makes me feel lower.
I walk up the road a bit and take shelter under an archway that leads between the shop fronts into a little

cobbled back street. I stand there for a minute or two with a smart bint in a blue raincoat waiting for her boy friend. He comes along nearly straight away and collects her, a big fair lad in a short raincoat, and they walk off arm-in-arm to the pictures. I look round and see this pub-sign swinging up the street and I go under the archway and up to the door.

There's a bottle-blonde behind the bar in a frock made out of a sort of ice-blue chainmail that sparkles and glitters in the light reflected like splinters in the mirror that covers the top half of the wall behind the wine and spirit bottles and upturned glasses. Her skin's a nice soft creamy pinkish colour and she has a black beauty spot on her left cheek. I don't know what colour she'd be at half past seven in the morning with no heat in the bedroom and the curtains stiff with frost but I like it well enough now. The colour spreads from her neck on to her chest, which is nicely covered and promises well for lower down. I sit there with half a pint like this; real tough bints, hard as nails, know all the answers; ready to put blokes like me in their place in two ticks, but as sexy and willing as you could wish for with the right kind of chap. She comes and reaches down for something under the bar right in front of where I'm sitting and I see further into the top of her frock than's good for me in my frame of mind. Now, I think, if I'd had plenty of cash I could have picked up with a bint like this and I'd have been landed. Sex without complications, and love could wait till the right girl came along. Instead of that it all gets mixed up and complicated and before you know where you are you're miles and miles up the creek with not a paddle in sight. And then I get the old dragging feeling inside me, because I'm married, hooked, and even if I turn my head this very minute and see the right girl standing behind me with Welcome Vic, written all over her face there's not a damn thing I can do about it. I'm a marked man.

Well while I'm thinking this, which isn't more than a few seconds, the blonde's tinkering about under the bar

260

and I've got my peepers trained into the neck of her frock, but without really seeing what's there, which shows what sort of a state I'm in. Then she straightens up and this chainmail flashes and sparkles and brings me back. I know she's seen me looking and I'm caught a bit short; but I can't say I wasn't looking really and I didn't see anything beyond the first glimpse. So I try to look her in the eye like a proper man of the world and for a couple of seconds she looks back, real cold and hard, like she's a duke's wife and I'm some little runt of a footman who's tried it on. Then she moves off along the counter and I see her wedding ring as she lifts her hand to work the beer pump.

'It's no good giving Maude the eye,' says somebody at my side. 'She's spoken for.'

I look round as Percy Walshaw pulls himself up on to the next buffet.

'Doesn't look as though that'd stop her, Percy.'

'Ah,' he says, 'you can't always go on appearances. She's as respectable as the vicar's wife.'

'Which vicar's that?' I say, and Percy laughs as the blonde bint comes along behind the counter and says good evening to him. He says good evening back and calls her by her first name.

'The usual?' she says, and Percy nods. 'Please.'

She takes a tankard off a hook and draws half a pint of bitter. I watch Percy take a good pull at it.

'How come the tankard?'

'I'm a regular, old cock. They look after the regulars.'

Still the same old Percy, I think to myself. He's a bloke about my age who I was at Grammar School with for a while, till he left among a lot of rumour that he'd been kicked out for having a bash at one of the lasses during the lunch-hour (I never did know how much truth there was in it) and went to a boarding school in the Midlands somewhere. Good pals we were for a bit, me and Percy, and though we don't see so much of one another now-adays we've always kept friendly. What I always like about Percy was that he didn't throw his money in your face, though he liked to make the best of it. I had to find out he lived in a house with seven bedrooms and they had a maid and a housekeeper, and I liked him all the more for not bragging about it or thinking it made him any different from the other lads. I liked him even at his barmiest, and he could be pretty barmy at times, believe you me. I reckon it came from having too much money too young and an old man who didn't lick the tar out of him often enough. You don't have to look twice now to see there's plenty of lolly hanging on to him. He looks the part in this checked cap and fur-collared short overcoat that must have set him back nigh on thirty quid. And if I know him he won't have walked here either, nor come on the bus.

'Well, how's life, me old sweat?' he says. 'I haven't seen you around lately.'

The honest answer to this is 'bloody awful', but I give him the stock reply: 'Oh, just steady, y'know.'

'Still pushing a pencil?'

'No, I'm in a shop now. What about you?'

Percy empties his tankard and signals the blonde. He's fishing a fistful of silver out of his pocket. 'Same again?' I say thanks.

'I'm in the business, old lad,' he says when he's ordered the drinks. 'Finally capitulated. They're trying to make a salesman out of me. I think they'll do it too. I like beetling about the countryside flannelling people into placing orders. Just up my alley. Plenty of strange pubs. Bags of expenses.' He touches the bit of fair down on his top lip. 'That's why I'm growing the tash. People don't like to think they're dealing with a lad.'

The blonde puts the new drinks in front of us and Percy pays.

'Cheers.'

'All the best.'

Percy gets his cig case out and we light up. 'What's on the board tonight?' he says. 'Just passing an hour on?'

'Something like that.'

'You don't look too chirpy to me, Vic. Have you got the miseries or something?'

I admit I'm feeling a bit cheesed. 'You know how you get sometimes.'

'Hmm,' he says, as though he's never felt cheesed in his life but has to be polite. 'Started courting yet?'

Well, there's no getting out of it now.

'I'm a bit past that, Percy, lad.'

'Past it?'

'Aye, I'm married.'

Percy stares at me. 'You never are! Well you old dark horse, you. When did all this take place?'

'About six months since.'

'And you're sitting in pubs moping already?' He shakes his head. 'It's amazing what marriage will do to a good man.'

'Oh, wrap it up, Percy.'

'Takes away your sense of humour too.'

'I can laugh like bloody hell when I feel like it,' I tell him, 'only I don't feel like it tonight.'

'Proper browned off, eh?'

'To the back teeth.'

'Well, well . . .' He takes a swig from his tankard and reckons to wipe froth off his tash. 'I consider it me bounded duty to hoist an old school chum out of the doldrums,' he says. 'I'm at a bit of a loose end myself tonight. A date I had fell through at the last minute. What say we embark on a small crawl, eh?'

It sounds like a good idea. Not long ago I was wondering where my mates might be and now here's Percy – just the one to take me out of myself, if anybody can. I take my wallet out and check. I see I have a quid note in there.

'Righto, Percy, you're on.'

'Right,' Percy says. He swigs the last of his beer and waits for me to finish mine. 'Step this way,' he says, slapping me on the shoulder. 'The carriage awaits.'

Outside on the cobbles there's a two-seater sports job of a make I can't identify in the dark. 'Nice car,' I say as we get into these low bucket seats.

'Like it?' Percy says with pride in his voice. 'Triumph

T.R.3. I talked the Old Man into buying it when I went out on the road. He wanted me to have a Humber or an Austin. More dignified, he said; but I won him over.'

Like you've been winning him over all your life, you old so and so, I think. But it certainly is a nice car . . .

He starts her up and she coughs and growls as though they've got a tiger down in the pub cellar. I feel a thrill in my guts at all this power, and I'm a bit jealous that it's Percy and not me behind the wheel.

'Ever been to the Monks' Rest?' he says, and I say no.

'New place out on the way to Bradford . . . La Posh . . . Right, that's the first stop.' He revs up fit to bust the windows. 'Hold your hat on.'

It seems to me we sample the beer in half the pubs in the West Riding in the next three hours: two here, an odd on somewhere else, and always Percy with his hand on my arm, saying, 'C'mon, let's move on.' Until I lost count of the bars we've leaned against, the people, we've talked to, the brews of ale we've tasted, and the Gents we've got rid of it in. In one place in Leeds Percy nearly fixes us up with a couple of hard-faced gin-drinking bints who like his line in dirty tales and his easy way with his brass; and he only breaks it off when he remembers his car's only a two-seater and anyway I'm married and not my own man any more.

'P'haps I should ha' got the Humber after all,' he says as we go out and get into the car on the way to another port of call.

Closing-time finds us in a floodlit roadhouse full of yellow wood and shiny chrome fittings somewhere Harrogate way. We walk out down the steps and weave our way between the cars in the park. Neither of us is too steady now and as Percy settles himself in his seat and slams the door he suddenly bursts out laughing. Not loud, but that quiet, helpless kind of laughing like when you don't know what you're laughing about but you just can't help it.

'How're you feeling, Vic?' he says.

'Pissed, Percy lad,' I say. 'Pissed as a flamin' newt.'

And then all at once I'm at it as well and we're both lolling back in our seats gurgling like drains, going on and on till it hurts across the middle under the ribs.

Eventually we get over it and Percy says, 'Well, I reckon we shall have to be heading for home. Where are we?'

'Somewhere near Harrogate, I think.'

'Never heard of it,' Percy says and I begin to feel a bit uneasy as he starts the car and lets it roll down on to the road.

'Are you okay, Percy?' I ask him. I'm thinking that this is all very well but we're in a powerful car and Percy's a bit on the mad side at the best of times.

'Never felt better,' he says. He's leaning forward with the neb of his cap touching the windscreen. 'Which way?'

'I don't know.'

'Which way did we come in?'

'From the left, I think.'

'Okay, we'll go to the right. It's as good a way as any.'

He swings the car out into the road, changes up and puts his foot down hard. I feel as though a big hand pushes me back into the set as we zoom away up the road. It's when I begin to feel scared that the effects of the booze start to lift. I've never been scared in a car before but I am now. I stick it for a bit, clenching my teeth and stiffening my legs against the bulkhead, but then I have to say something.

'Take it easy, Percy.'

'What?' Percy says.

'I said take it easy. It isn't daylight, y'know.'

Percy laughs and twitches the car under the tail of a big long-distance lorry. For a second I'm ready to swear we went right underneath between the wheels. We roar up a narrow country lane with stone walls on both sides.

'Any idea where we are?' Percy says.

'Have I hell,' I say, startled. 'Dont' you know?'

'I haven't known for the last ten minutes,' he shouts, full of good cheer. 'Took a wrong turning somewhere back yonder.'

'Well, we'll be in Scotland afore we know where we are, going at this speed. I might have been feeling a bit low earlier on but I'm not ready to snuff it yet.'

I think of Ingrid waiting up for me and me not turning up. The police going and breaking it to her. I wonder if she'd cry. Then there's my mother and dad and Chris . . .

'Snuff it?' Percy says. 'What're you talking about? You're not scared, are you?'

'Yes, I am. It's dark, man, for Christ's sake, and you don't know the road.'

'We've got good lights,' is all he says, and on we go belting into the dark.

Well the headlights are powerful enough, admitted; but the dark's funny and shadows can look like real things and real things like nothing at all . . .

I catch a split-second glimpse of a sign. 'For Christ's sake, Percy, watch the bend. It's a right angle –' And then I can't talk, only shut my mouth and my eyes tight and brace myself for the smash as a tall drystone wall rushes at us up the beam of the headlights. I feel the sideways drag as Percy pulls the car round and hear the screech of stone on metal on my side of the car. Then we stop.

I stay like I am for a few seconds, with my head down. My heart's going like a donkey engine and my hands are trembling like leaves in the wind. We've no business to be unhurt and I can hardly believe we are.

Percy's jumped out as soon as we've stopped and run round to my side. He comes back now and gets in. 'A foot,' he says. 'Just another ruddy foot and we'd have made it.'

I say nothing. He starts the car up and puts it into reverse and pulls back clear of the wall. Then he gets out again. He taps on my window and I wind it down.

'Made a lousy mess of this wing,' he says.

I'm not bothered about Percy's wing, just my own skin.

'Could be worse, though. At least the wheels still go round.' He comes back round the other side and gets in again. 'We'd better beat it before we have parker trouble.'

I stop his hand as it reaches for the starter.

'Look, hold on a bit. I'm not ready for any more of that just yet.' I give a false kind of laugh. 'What time does the next bus go from here?'

Percy gives a short polite laugh and falls to drumming his fingers on the steering wheel.

'A foot, though,' he says in a minute. 'Another foot and we'd have cleared it. What lousy luck!'

'I call it bloody good luck,' I tell him. 'A foot the other way and they'd have been scraping me off the wall in the morning.'

Percy turns his head and looks at me. 'You really are in a state, aren't you?'

'I thought that was it, Percy. I don't want to come as near as that again for a long, long time.'

Percy feels in the door pocket on his side. 'Hang on a tick. I've got the very thing . . . Have I? Yes, here it is.' He's holding a metal flask and he unscrews the top before handing it to me. 'Have a pull at that.'

'What is it?'

'Brandy.'

'I think I've had enough to –'

'Go o-on. Do you good.'

I lift the flask and as I'm taking a swig Percy tilts it up so the stuff pours down my throat. I splutter and cough.

'How's that?'

'I'm on fire.'

'It'll change into a warm glow in a minute. You won't have a care in the world.'

He wipes the neck of the flask with his hand and takes a swig himself and says, 'A-agh!' Then he screws the cap back on and puts it away. He reaches for the starter. 'Ready now?'

'In a minute.' I open the door.

'What's up now?'

'I want a leak.'

'Okay. I'll back up and have a look at the sign.'

'Right,' he says when I'm back in the car. 'I know where we are now. We'll be home in quicksticks.'

'Take all the time you like, Percy lad,' I tell him. 'Take all night if you like.'

He laughs.

He's still laughing when he drops me off outside Rothwells' and shouts good night before rocketing away down the road like a bat out of hell.

IV

I'm not too steady on my feet. The brandy's stirred all the other booze up again and I'm as drunk as I was earlier. Only not in the same way: not laughing drunk now, but mean and nasty drunk, spoiling for trouble if there's any coming. There's a light behind the front-room curtains so somebody's waiting up for me. There has to be somebody waiting because I haven't got a key. I've never had a key to this house. Anyway, I think, Ma Rothwell should be safely out of the way in bed by this time and if Ingrid's got anything to say about me coming home sozzled at going up to midnight, well, let her say it and see what happens. Just see what happens tonight.

But it's the old bitch herself who turns her head when I stand in the doorway, blinking in the light.

'Ingrid in bed?' I say, a bit taken aback like.

'She's been in bed over an hour. I should have been too if I hadn't had to wait up for you. Don't you know what time it is?'

I know, but I look at the little imitation marble clock on the mantelpiece. 'Ten to twelve.'

'Yes, ten to twelve, and people being kept from their beds waiting on your convenience till you decide you'll come home.'

I can tell from the way she lets her eyelids droop and her little podgy chin's tucked in that she's got it in for me. Well, all right, I think, if that's the way she wants it. I've practised giving her a piece of my mind so often I could do it in my sleep and I've always dreamed of having a real set-to with her one day. If she wants it now she can have it.

I feel a kind of relief, as though a big weight's lifting off me as I start the ball rolling. 'Home?' I say. 'You don't really mean that, do you? You don't really mean this is my home? I haven't even got a key. If I had a key you wouldn't have had to wait up for me. But I'm no more than a lodger here and you don't let me forget it.'

I watch the way her head turns. She's so dignified it's painful to watch her. I'm wondering how far I'll have to go before she drops the act and shows what a common piece she is at bottom.

'When you have a home of your own you'll be able to do as you like,' she says, 'I expect people who live in my house to accept my standards. Even if they haven't been brought up that way,' she says, standing up and gathering her knitting and smoothing her skirt down over her fat behind with one hand.

'I can see me getting a house. I can't rent one and I can't afford to buy one. We might get out of here round about 1968 the way I see it.'

'You know,' she says, 'you obviously don't feel the smallest shred of gratitude that I allowed you to come here to live.'

'You've got it wrong,' I tell her. 'We came here as a favour to you because you didn't want to lose your lovey-dovey daughter. Well, you've no need to worry; I don't like it any more than you do and you'll be rid of me the first chance that comes.'

'Which as you say doesn't seem likely for a long time.'

I'm taking my raincoat off now and having a bit of trouble with the buttons. I know she's watching me more carefully than she pretends to be.

'As soon as Ingrid feels like going back to work we'll be able to save more. Then we can buy a place.'

'I don't know that Ingrid wants to go back to work. She thinks like me – that a husband should be able to support a wife, or he's a poor fish.'

This isn't the way I've understood it. It seems to me half my trouble is not knowing whether to believe what Ingrid says or what her mother says she says. I'm getting mad.

'Well, she'll have to get rid of her fancy ideas. If she wants a house of her own she'll have to help to pay for it. I'm no mill-owner's son. Maybe that's what you had in mind for her, eh? Somebody loaded with brass to keep her in luxury all the rest of her life.'

'You're certainly not what I had in mind.'

'Well I married her. And bloody glad she was to have me, make no mistake.'

'Is there any need for language like that?'

Somehow I feel I'm not winning and this makes me all the madder. Here I am telling her all I've ever wanted to tell her and somehow she's not reacting. She's just taking it in her stride and making me feel small.

'Like what?' I say.

'You just swore.'

'I feel like swearing. I've felt like it ever since teatime.'

'Well don't bring it in here. Save it for your friends. I imagine they're the type to appreciate it.'

'My friends,' I say, and I hear my voice rise to a kind of falsetto. 'You think your friends are the last word. A bunch of bloody jumped-up social climbers. I might tell you I've just been out with a bloke who's got more money behind him than you an' all your friends put together ever dreamed of.'

I'm feeling a wee bit queasy in the guts now. I think it's a mixture of petrol fumes, a pork pie I've had, and the brandy on top of all the other booze, that's done it. I make for a chair, nearly falling over a stupid rug on the way.

'It seems he's been spending some of it tonight on drink.'

'I've had a drink. I'm not denying it.'

'A drink. More like a dozen.'

'All right, I've had a dozen. And I enjoyed 'em. Is there any law against it?'

'There's an elementary sense of decency that stops a man coming home to his wife in such a condition.'

'So I've no sense of decency now, eh? I'd enough to

marry your Ingrid when she was in trouble. Oh, I know I got her into trouble, but it takes two to do that, y'know. And don't think she wasn't getting what she wanted when I married her. She'd have married me any time, baby or no baby.'

'She'd have been in a position to listen to advice if she hadn't been seduced.'

'That's a good 'un. D'you think I had to tie her down to do it? Don't worry, if it hadn't been me it'd have been somebody else.'

I don't think this is strictly true but I'm past splitting hairs. I'm out to get Ma Rothwell foaming and I'm coming pretty near it now.

She trembles with rage. 'How dare you make such disgusting accusations against my daughter's character! You come in here, you little upstart, drunk, as though you own the house, and sully a good girl's name with your filthy talk . . .'

Well now I've really got her going and she looks as though she's good for a while yet, only I cut her short as I feel this queasy feeling suddenly spread out and up and before I know it I've leaned forward and thrown up on the nice cream carpet right in front of her. It's the easiest thing I ever remember: no heaving and retching and sweating – I just kind of hiccup and there it is on the carpet between my feet, all my tea and the pork pie I've had in the pub since, everything in a sloppy pinkish blob about the size of a tea-plate, mostly soft and creamy but with whole bits of stuff that have never tried to get digested stuck among it.

We both sort of look at it in surprise for a second or two and then, maybe it's the beer and I don't give a damn anyway, I don't know, but I start to giggle.

Ma Rothwell's mouth is open as though she's going to let me have it any second now, but it's as though she can't get the words out. Her whole body goes stiff and her eyes bulge and her hands are clenched up in front of her and it's just as though her voice has packed in and she's fighting and straining like mad to bring it back again. She's paralytic with rage. Her face has got past red and it's purple now. And there we are, the two of us, looking at one another across this puddle of sick, me waiting for what's going to happen and her looking as though she'll fall down and kick her heels and foam at the mouth any second now.

And I'm just thinking what a repulsive old sow she really is and how much I hate her when her voice-box starts operations again.

'You filthy pig,' she says. 'You filthy disgusting pig.'

It should hurt like hell for her to call me that and it probably would have any other time, but all I can see now is the funny side of it. I feel another giggle coming up and choke it back and splutter over it. But it's no good and I have to let it rip. And then I'm rolling back in the chair and laughing. I shout with laughing. It's as though I've never laughed before and I've only just found out how nice it is, and how lovely it is to let it come till you're helpless with it and it begins to hurt right across your guts.

I hear Ingrid's ma give a little scream and then the door slams, fair shaking the walls, and an ornament bounces down off the piano.

And now it doesn't seem as funny any more so in a minute I manage to give up and I light a fag and stretch my legs out, careful not to get my feet in the mess. I begin to smell it before long. Rotten it is, enough to make you want to throw up again, except there's nothing left to come. So I begin to think about cleaning it up, because it's one thing to throw up on Ma Rothwell's carpet and another to expect her to clean it up. I think about it. Newspaper's no good because it might go soft and split and then I'd get it on my hands. And if I use the dishcloth I'll only have to wash that out after. So I decide the coal shovel's the best thing and I get up and go into the kitchen and open the coal-place door and get the shovel out.

I have to use a bit of newspaper in the end to scrape the stuff off the shovel into the fire, but I get it up off the carpet okay. There's a bit of a coaly patch on the carpet from the shovel when I've finished but I reckon that can't be helped and Ma Rothwell will soon shift that with a bit of panshine or something. The little china jug she knocked down is in bits on the floor. It said 'Best wishes from Llandudno' round the outside before it was smashed and I've heard Mrs R. say she thought a lot about it because she got it on her honeymoon. I get a piece of writing-paper out of the bureau and write I DIDN'T DO THIS – YOU DID and put it with the bits of jug on top of the piano. Then I sit down and light another fag.

In a bit it dawns on me I'm feeling randy and I reckon it's the beer and the fact that what with one thing and another I've been on starvation rations for the last three or four months. I wonder if Ingrid's asleep and if she'll come the don't-touch-me stuff if I go up and slip into bed and turn her over.

I get up and throw my cig into the fire. I fetch the fireguard and put it up and switch off the lights in the kitchen and the sitting-room, taking a last look at the patch on the carpet before I do. I know Ma Rothwell isn't going to like that, but I can't help it. I can't even be bothered to think about tomorrow. I reckon after tonight we can't carry on as per, but I can't be bothered thinking about it. All I want is to get into Ingrid's warm bed and make love to her like I've only just found out about it.

I go upstairs and start getting undressed by the landing light and I never think to look at the bed till I'm down to my underwear. Then I see that the clothes are pulled about and the pillow dented, but there's no Ingrid. I remember now sort of half-hearing voices while I was downstairs but I didn't pay any attention. I go out on the landing and knock on Ma Rothwell's door.

'Ingrid.'

There's no answer.

I knock a bit louder. 'Ingrid.'

Ma Rothwell's voice says, 'Go away.'

'I want Ingrid.'

273

'I won't let my daughter sleep with a drunken sot like you,' the old bitch says.

'You won't *what*?' This does it. I bang on the door with the side of my fist. 'I want my wife. Send her out, d'y'ear. Send her out.'

There's the sound of low voices, then Ingrid says something from the other side of the door.

'Go to bed, Vic.'

'You come on in here, where you belong.'

'I'm staying in here tonight.'

'I'll come in an' fetch you if you don't come out.'

'You can't get in; the door's locked.'

'Locked?' I try the handle. 'Dammit, what the hell are you playing at? D'y'ear? I said what the hell are you playing at?'

I thump on the door. I'm really going now.

'You'll wake the neighbours, Vic.'

'Bugger the neighbours. Let them see to their own troubles. Come on now, come out.'

'For the last time,' Ma Rothwell says. 'She's not leaving this room tonight.'

'All right, then, you old cow,' I shout, 'you've done it. She's made her choice an' now I know where I stand.'

I storm back into our bedroom and slam the door. I'd pack up and get out now, except I've no place to go. I finish getting undressed and I can hardly fasten my pyjama buttons I'm that wild.

I get into bed and lie there swearing in the dark, and then in a bit I cool down and begin to think about it all. This is what it all comes to, is it? I think. Bawling and swearing at midnight like people in a slum. This is where the dreams end ... I never wanted much in the first place, just a girl I could love, who loved me, one I could be pals with besides loving her and all that. Not much to want. Oh, I know I've brought it all on myself. I shouldn't have carried on with Ingrid once I knew how things were. But still, thousands must do it and get away with it and we have to go and slip up the first time. And now what happens tomorrow? Do I clear out and leave her? I can't stay now, that's for sure. I *won't* stay, and that's for certain. I've had what's commonly known as a bellyful.

I fall asleep thinking I won't and I have the most weird dream I ever remember. I'm walking along an ordinary street and I go into what looks like an ordinary pub. In fact it's the pub I met Percy in tonight. Only inside it's like a big hall, so big you can't see the walls, and there's a kind of swirly mist all round. As I'm standing there wondering what's going to happen I hear a horrible scream that dies away in a moan. I'm scared stiff, and all of a sudden the blonde from the pub comes out of the mist, walking a foot off the floor. She's stark naked and she's reaching out for me with hands that have finger-nails six inches long and painted blood-red. It's the way she's looking at me that starts me running. There's pure murder on her face, it's all twitching and twisting, and I see that it isn't paint on her nails at all, but blood, dripping and dripping. I'm running and running and making no progress because my shoes weigh about fifty pounds apiece, and all the time I can feel this raving bint gaining on me. And just as them great sharp nails are clawing out for me, I wake up.

I'm hanging head down over the foot of the bed and the eider-down and sheets are all over the floor. I'm in a cold sweat and my heart's thumping away like billy-ho. It's half past four. I tidy up and climb back into bed with a cig. I don't remember putting the cig out before I fall asleep again.

When I wake up the next time it's half past six and I know what I'm going to do. I get dressed with fifty little elves tapping away with hammers inside my head, but cut out washing and shaving for fear of waking the two of them in the next room. I pack as much of my stuff as I can into one case and open the window and drop it into the garden. Down in the kitchen I find half a bottle of milk and I swig this. I collect my raincoat from where I dropped it in the front room last night, put it on, and go and open the back door. As I step out and pull the door shut behind me I hear the Yale lock snap and I think, Now, it's done. No turning back now even if I wanted to. I collect the case from the front garden, trying to remember what I was thinking about to drop it out like that instead of bringing it down the stairs with me, and walk off down the steps to the gate and down the road.

8

I

As I come into the drive between the stone gateposts with the big stone balls on top I'm wondering what I'm going to say to her, and somehow, now, going to see Chris to tell her I've made a muck of it all and chucked the sponge in is the worst feeling of all. They might not even be up, I think, and I'll feel pretty silly then. I look at my watch and it's just after a quarter past seven.

I ring the bell over their card and in a couple of minutes the door opens and there's David in his pyjamas with a green Tootal dressing-gown with white spots over them.

'Hello, David.'

He looks gone out for a second as he sees me and the case standing there at the crack of dawn. Then he rises to it and says, 'Good morning, Vic. Come to spend your holidays?'

'If you'll have me.'

He stands to one side and lets me in and shuts the door behind me. He shivers. 'Ugh, a bit raw this morning.'

'Is Chris up yet?'

'Yes, she's getting breakfast ready.'

I know he's wondering what it's all about and probably making a good guess, but he's too polite to start noseying and he just follows me up the stairs, saying something else about the weather till we get to the door, then he goes in first and calls out, 'Here's Vic, Chris.'

Chris comes into the kitchen doorway with a coffee pot in her hands. She's got a pale blue dressing-gown or housecoat thing on, with a tight bodice and a high neck and a skirt that touches the floor. She says hello, Vic, not turning a hair, though I can tell her mind's beginning to tick over as well. She says something about the milk boiling over and disappears back into the kitchen.

'Sit down, Vic,' David says. 'Take your coat off. You've plenty of time before you're due at the shop, haven't you?'

'Bags.'

I take my coat off and David takes it out and hangs it in their little lobby while I sit down. They've got the electric fire on because I suppose they don't bother to light a coal fire till evening with them both being out all day.

David comes back and hangs about a minute, reckoning not to look at me; then he says he'll go and help Chris with the tray, and beetles off out to the kitchen, leaving me on my own.

'Will you have a cup of coffee, Vic?' Chris calls out.

'Please.'

She sticks her head round the door. 'Have you had any breakfast?'

'Well, no, I haven't, act'ally.'

'Boiled egg and toast go down all right?'

'Grand.'

Her head vanishes and I look round the room. All of a sudden I'm near to crying. I think about Chris and David and Ingrid and me, and I've all on not to let go. I'm all right again by the time David comes through with the tray, though, and in a minute we're sitting down at the table and I'm wolfing the egg and toast. It crosses my mind that if this was a picture they'd have me poking about in my grub and looking miserable till somebody asked me what was wrong. As it is, nobody says a dicky bird yet and I shift the egg and toast in no time, I'm that famished. I haven't had a bite since that pork pie last night and you can't count that because it ended up on Ma Rothwell's carpet.

Well Chris holds off and chats with David about this and that till I've finished eating and got my third cup of

278

coffee in front of me. Then she hands me a cig and as I'm having the first drag of the day she comes at me straight on.

'Well, Vic?'

'What?'

'What's the trouble? You didn't just drop in on your way to the shop, did you?'

'No.'

David pushes his chair back and gets up. 'I'll go and shave.'

'You can stop and listen if you want to,' I tell him. 'You'll hear all about it later, anyway.'

'No, really,' he says, and gives me his little grin. 'You two have a chat. I should be getting ready anyway.'

I start rolling the ash off the end of my cig on to the plate, wondering where to begin. Chris pushes an ash-tray across to me, watches me for a minute, then makes the opening for me.

'Is it you and Ingrid?'

I nod, without looking at her. 'I've left her.'

'What d'you mean? You mean you just walked out on her this morning?'

I nod again. 'My case is in the hall.' She's looking straight at me but I still can't look back.

'What brought this on?'

'That bloody woman,' I say. 'She brought it on. I just couldn't stand any more. It wouldn't have been so bad if Ingrid had been on my side, but she's right under her mother's thumb.'

Chris just sits and looks at me. I sneak a quick look at her and see the wheels turning behind her eyes.

'I had a bit of a row with Ingrid last night and went out and met an old mate of mine. I was fed-up so I got plas-tered. When I got back Mrs Rothwell was waiting up for me and I told her a few things I'd been saving up.'

'She didn't tell you to go, did she?'

'No, but she took Ingrid in with her and locked her door. We had a real old set-to then. It all came out. It's been piling up for some time and I'd had a drink or two

279

and was past caring ... I used some pretty bad language ... I couldn't have stayed after that, I don't suppose. Anyway, I'd made my mind up. I'd finished. I came away this morning before they got up.'

I'm watching Chris's hands and thinking how slim and neat they are when she gets up and walks away from the table.

'How long have things been like this?'

'Oh, it's been brewing up for ages.'

'Was it the miscarriage?'

'Not altogether. That just made it worse. I didn't get on with her before that. She took a dislike to me the minute she laid eyes on me. Not good enough for her daughter. Not her idea of a match. You've seen her; you know what sort she is. You know she never rang me up when Ingrid fell down the stairs. I didn't get to know till I got home and the neighbours told me. That's a fine thing, isn't it? Then she blamed me. As if I could help it. As if I pushed her downstairs. Things just got worse and worse after that. Well I told her. I told her I might not be good enough for her daughter but I was good enough to marry her when she was in trouble.'

'You got her into trouble, Vic,' Chris reminds me gently.

'I know. And I wish to God I hadn't. How I wish I hadn't!' I put my head in my hands. 'Oh, Chris, if only I could have met somebody like you: somebody who'd have made me better than I am, not worse.'

'But you did marry Ingrid, didn't you? You did choose to marry her.'

'Aye. You've had your fun and now you can pay for it. Is that choosing? You know there's only one thing to do round here when you put a girl in the family way and that's marry her. It doesn't matter whether you love her or not as long as you make her respectable.'

'*Is* that why you married her, Vic? I've wondered.'

'Well now you know.'

'But there must have been something, Vic.'

'You're a woman. I don't know if you'd understand.

You only know you and David and you want to thank your lucky stars for that. It doesn't happen to everybody. I thought it was like that with me an' Ingrid right at the beginning, but it didn't last long.'

'But you still went on seeing her.'

'Yes, I did . . . For other reasons.'

'Wasn't that . . . well, selfish?'

'I did pack it up once. I thought it was over. But she came after me. I knew I was being a rotten dog but she still wanted me so I thought I might as well have what was going. One night I went a bit too far and now I'm paying for it. It's worked out bloody expensive, Chris, I can tell you . . .'

I sit there with my head in my hands and Chris says nothing for a bit. When she does say something it makes me jerk my head up and look at her.

'Well, after all, Vic, you've made your own bed, haven't you?'

I'm stunned, as though somebody's hit me over the head.

'You say that? That's what everybody else'll say. Can't you say nothing else?'

'Well haven't you?' she says. 'It's the truth, after all.'

'I expected something different from you.'

'I'll have to be honest with you, Vic. I think you've only yourself to blame. If you hadn't played about with this girl you wouldn't be here like this now. Right's right and wrong's no man's right.'

I can't get over it. I hardly know her. This isn't the Chris I used to run to, the one you could depend on to show you the way out, the thing to do. Coming here was the first thing I thought of, and now I'm getting what I could have got free at home.

'You sound like my mother.'

'And why not? She knows and she'd say the same thing to you. You're married and you just can't dismiss the fact.'

I feel all the bitterness come up sour in my throat. 'I'm married all right. You all made sure I'd get married. You

281

all stood round pushing. There wasn't one of you said no don't do it if you don't want to.'

'It wasn't a case of wanting to or not wanting to. You pushed yourself when you did what you did with Ingrid. At least you had the backbone to face your responsibilities.'

'For life. Black's black and white's white. Haven't any of you ever heard of a bloody colour called grey?'

'You're swearing a lot, Vic. You never used to.'

Everybody's tell me that: that I'm swearing a lot. I wonder why it is . . .

'I don't know what to say, Chris,' I say in a minute. 'I could always talk to you. We seemed closer together. You could always understand better than they could.'

'Perhaps I understand now better than they would, but I can't simply wave my magic wand and make it all come right. You came here this morning with some vague idea that you could tell me all about it and it would all turn out to be like it was before you were married. That's it, isn't it? Trust Chris to get me out of it. Well, I'm sorry, Vic, but it can't be done. It's a bit too big for that.'

I turn round in my chair and look out of the window. They've got a nice view on a clear day but now it's just mucky and grey and damp and all you can see is the mills down by the river with the big chimneys sticking up into the mist.

'What are you going to do?' Chris says after a while.

'I don't know . . . I know one thing, though; I'm not going back to live with that old cow Ma Rothwell.'

'She probably wouldn't have you back now, anyway.'

'No . . .' I haven't told Chris about me throwing up on the carpet. It's one detail I'd rather she didn't know. 'Well that makes it easier.'

David comes in from the bedroom, stuffing cigs and matches and papers into his pockets. He buys nice suits, David, but he ruins them with the amount of stuff he packs into the pockets.

'Vic's left Ingrid,' Chris tell him.

'I'd gathered as much,' he says. 'I'm sorry, Vic. That it's come to that, I mean. Anything we can do?'

'It looks as though there is,' Chris says. 'We shall have to put him up here for tonight at least, I think.'

'Don't put yourself out for me.'

She turns on me. 'It's no use being silly-clever about it, Vic,' she says. 'Where else can you go? You won't want to go home just yet, I suppose?'

All of a sudden I feel my face begin to slip. I can't hold it, keep it together. It crumples up. 'I haven't got a home,' I say. 'I haven't got a bloody home.' And then my face is down in my arms and I'm crying without trying to stop it, crying away with it all coming out; all of six months bottled up and now coming away.

II

I sleep on the studio couch in the sitting-room that night and for a good few nights after. I don't know what I'm going to do. I've no plans. Any idea I might have of going back home and picking up where I left off is soon scotched because next day Chris tells me she's seen the Old Lady.

'Has she been here?'

'No, I called on the way back from school.'

'You told her, I suppose?'

'That's what I went for. She has to know, Vic, and it's better coming from one of us than from somebody in the street.'

'I suppose so. What did she say?'

'She was upset.' I see Chris hesitate. 'She says she doesn't want to see you till you've patched it up with Ingrid again.'

I feel my mouth tighten. 'If that's the way she wants it . . . She'll have to wait a long time, that's all.'

'I told her I didn't think she was being fair; that you should be able to come to her when you're in trouble. But she said you should have gone straight to her if you felt like that. I think she's hurt that you didn't go there first.'

'I wanted advice, not a row with all the old proverbs thrown in.'

'As it happens you didn't get much more here, did you?'

I shrug.

David comes in with a loaded briefcase. Exercise books, I suppose. He says, 'Hi,' to me and kisses Chris. I look away for a minute. I can't bear to watch them. It's the worst of being here, seeing how happy they are.

'I've just been talking to Fowler downstairs,' David says, dropping the briefcase in a chair. 'He's got a job in Canada.'

'Have they decided to go?' Chris says.

'Oh, yes. It's just a question of time now, apparently. Making all the arrangements and all that.'

I can see Chris has something on her mind.

'How long did he say it would be?'

'About six weeks or a couple of months, I think. They've only just decided.'

'What are they going to do about the lease of the flat?'

'Give it up, I suppose.'

Chris looks at me and David says. 'Oh, I see what you're –' 'Vic,' Chris says. 'Do you think you and Ingrid would have been all right if you'd been on your own?'

'I dunno. We'd have been better. At least we could have brought things out and talked about them and said what we had to say.'

'Suppose you could get the Fowler's flat, do you think Ingrid would come?'

'I don't know.' I can feel myself being pushed into another corner and I shy away from it. 'It's too soon, Chris. I don't know what I want to do.'

'Could you afford it?' she says. 'It's four pounds a week.'

'Not on my wage.'

'Suppose Ingrid got another job?'

'I suppose we could then. Only her mother doesn't want her to go out to work again. She thinks a husband should be able to keep a wife.'

'Let's leave her mother out of it. She's had too much to say already.'

'I don't know . . .'

'David,' Chris says, 'pop down and see Mr Fowler. Tell him you know somebody who might want the flat. Ask him how long he'll hold it before he advertises or asks anybody else. He might have somebody in mind, of course.'

David goes out again and I say, 'Look, Chris, I don't know. I'm all mixed up. I don't know what I want to do.'

'If he'll hold the flat it'll give you a breathing space while you decide.'

'Suppose the landlord's got somebody else on his list?'

'It doesn't work quite like that. These flats are leased year by year. It's up to the outgoing tenant who he surrenders his lease to, though the landlord can always refuse to renew it if he disapproves. The Fowlers only renewed their lease a couple of months ago.'

'But that means I'll have to find a lump sum and I just haven't got it.'

'Don't worry about that. We'll raise the money somehow and you can pay back week by week. Anyway, all that can be settled later. The point is, do you want it? Will you give it a try?'

'I don't know. I just don't know, Chris.'

She comes down on her knees in front of me and takes my hands in hers. 'Look, Vic, I know you're unhappy, and I want to help you. We both do.'

I turn my head away. 'I've had enough, Chris. It's just a big cheat. A lousy cheat.'

'I know what you wanted, Vic,' she says. 'It's what most people want, though they're not all conscious of it. They want the other half of themselves, the other person who will make them whole. I'm happy to say I've found that with David. There was no doubt in my mind at the beginning and there's been none since.

'People talk glibly of being in love. Magazines and films are full of it. But there's a difference between that and loving. You can be in love with someone you hardly know – all romance and rapture and starry eyes. Oh, it's all true, Vic. It can happen just the way they say it does. But you don't *love* a person till you know him or her inside out, until you've lived with them and shared experience: sadness, joy, *living* – you've got to share living before you can find love. Being *in* love doesn't last, but you can find love to take its place.

'Do you know what I mean, Vic?'

'Yes, I know.'

'With some people that shared experience drives them apart, but with others it welds them still more strongly together. Through losing your baby you and Ingrid have shared tragedy early. Don't let it drive you apart, Vic. Be strong. Let it give you something, not take away.'

'We never had it in the beginning,' I say.

'Well try to find it now, Vic,' Chris says. 'Think of Ingrid. She loves you, or she did, I know. Losing the baby was much more of an ordeal to her than it could be to you. She needs somebody, Vic – not her mother – but somebody strong, to look after her and comfort her and make her see that life can be good again. You could do that, Vic. You could do that for Ingrid.' She squeezes my hands. 'Be strong, Vic. Don't give up. Make your marriage work.

'I'm not offering you the easy way out, am I?' she says in a minute.

I haven't time to think up an answer to this before David comes back and Chris gets up off her knees.

'What did he say?'

'He's got nobody else in mind. He'll hold it for a week.'

I run my hand through my hair. 'Only a week. It's not long enough, Chris.'

She looks at me. 'I think it is, Vic. Quite long enough.'

'How are you fixed for money?' David asks me.

'I've about thirty quid. Not a lot, is it?'

'Well if that's all that's on your mind, don't worry. We can let you have a bit and you can pay us back when you can.'

I look up and there's Chris looking from me to David with that lovely little smile on her face that seems to say, 'There's my man. I didn't have to ask him – he knew.'

'It . . . it's really very good of you, David.'

'Glad to be able to help. Families should stick together, I always think.'

III

A couple of days later Mr Rothwell comes home. I suppose Ingrid's mother's sent for him. He'll be thinking he's had nothing but urgent messages to come home since he heard about me. Anyway, how I know about it this time is because he rings me up at the shop.

'Vic? This is Ingrid's father. I want to talk to you.'

I'm sure I don't want to talk to him. I imagine the way Ma Rothwell must have ranted on about me coming in drunk and spewing on the carpet and I think he'll probably want to take a poke at me when he does see me.

'Well, what about?'

'Don't be so bloody ingenuous,' he says. 'What do you think it's about?'

'Well, when, then? I'm working now.'

'Where do you have your lunch?'

'At a little café round the corner.'

'D'you know the Dolphin, that pub in Bread Street?'

I say I do.

'Meet me there at half past twelve . . . Hello? Are you still there? I thought we'd been cut off. You will be there, won't you?'

I say okay, I'll be there, and he rings off.

I've got butterflies in my stomach all the rest of the morning, wondering what he's going to say, but when I get there at dinner-time he seems quite reasonable, like he always is. We order and he doesn't start till the soup's served.

'It's quite a mess, taken all round, isn't it?' he says.

'I suppose it is.'

'I've a good mind to send you a cleaning bill for the carpet.'

I feel myself going red. 'I'm sorry about that. It was an accident. I was pretty sozzled but I didn't mean to do that.'

'It seems the beer loosened your tongue a bit, too,' he says.

I say nothing.

'Perhaps you had some cause to fly off the handle; I don't know. I've only heard one side of it.' He lifts his spoon and sucks in some tomato soup. 'Like to tell me your story?'

I shuffle about a bit on the chair. 'I don't see how I can, really.'

'You mean without offending me? Well try.'

'Well it's just that I don't think Ingrid's mother liked me from the start and she's never given us a chance. We've never seemed to be married at all, really. I never felt I could say what I thought without getting her back up. I don't know if you know it, but she influences Ingrid quite a lot.'

He nods. 'I know. Perhaps that's partly due to me being away so much.'

'Well it got so Ingrid listened to her mother first all the time. I felt like a lodger, only worse, because a lodger can come and go as he likes and she was always rubbing it in that I had obligations and responsibilities, but I never had a chance to take responsibility because I was just nobody about the place . . . Then when the accident happened and she never let me know I was so wild I nearly walked out there and then.'

'What do you mean, she never let you know?'

I tell him about coming home to find the house locked, and how Mrs Oliphant told me what had happened. I get a definite impression he didn't know about this, but he doesn't let on.

'She even tried to blame me for that,' I tell him. I'm not enjoying this. It's not easy to run down a bloke's wife to his face, even if he has invited you to do it. 'You might ha' thought I'd stood at the top of the stairs and pushed her . . .'

I'm hoping he'll say something about this and give away how much he knows, but he doesn't.

'Anyway,' he says, 'you decided to stay.'

'Yes . . . And then things just got worse. Ingrid didn't seem to have any life in her any more. She just moped about the place like she was going off into a decline and nothing I said could snap her out of it. She said I'd no consideration.'

'It was a big shock to her, you know.'

'I know it must have been, but she can't act as if it happened last week for the rest of her life. I just got the feeling her mother was encouraging her not to get better.'

'So you'd say, then, by and large, that Ingrid's mother was at the bottom of all the trouble?' he says, watching me.

'Well . . . yes, I would.' It *is* embarrassing, you know, calling a bloke's wife to his face, especially if he happens to be a decent sort of cove. And there's another thing – I have to lay all the blame on Ma Rothwell because I can't tell him what the real trouble is: that I never loved Ingrid in the first place and all this on top of that was a bit too much for anybody to take.

The waitress comes over and serves the main course. I look at it, mashed potatoes, cabbage, and mutton. I don't feel much like it.

'Like a glass of beer?' Mr Rothwell says.

'No, thanks. I shall feel sleepy all afternoon if I have any.'

He orders a pale ale for himself. 'Not much of a drinker, are you?'

'No, I'm not. I get drunk pretty easily, really.'

'Oh, don't feel ashamed about it,' he says. 'It's a point in your favour, actually.' He picks his knife and fork up. It doesn't seem as if this is putting *him* off his grub anyway. 'What are your plans now, then?' he says. 'Are you living at home again?'

'No, I'm at my sister's.'

'Not very well in with your father and mother, is that it?'

'Something like that.'

'You seem to be quite an outcast.'

'I'm getting used to it. I've felt like one long enough.'

'You know,' he says, waving his knife about, 'I get the impression that you feel badly done to and have for some time. Almost as though marriage itself was something that had been imposed on you.'

I begin to feel uncomfortable because he's getting too warm for my liking.

'Do you wish you'd never got married?' he says.

'Yes, I do.'

'Why did you get married?' he says, his eye on me. 'Because you loved Ingrid or because of the baby?'

I don't answer this one.

'All right, then; do you want to stay married to Ingrid?'

'I don't want to be married to both Ingrid and her mother.'

I couldn't be sure but I think he nearly smiles at this.

'You're in a pretty poor position too, aren't you?' he says. 'Nowhere to go, nothing to offer a wife.'

'That's right.'

'A pretty poor wicket, in fact.'

'Oh, it's not all that bad from where I'm sitting,' I tell him, getting a bit riled. 'I've walked out and now I can stay out if I want to. There's no baby to think about now, and nobody's going to push me into anything.'

'Who's pushing?' he says without rising.

'All right, p'raps you're not. But don't make it seem like I'm hanging around waiting for Ingrid to say she'll have me back. I did the walking out, remember.'

'That's right, you did. And anyway, you don't know that Ingrid wants you any more, do you?'

'She hadn't shown much sign of it for a bit.'

'Well then,' he says, 'perhaps it'll be better all round if we call it a day. Forget it ever happened. Six months isn't long. Ingrid could claim an allowance from you but I don't think she needs that. She'll want to apply for a divorce, of course. You wouldn't object to that, would you?'

'What grounds has she?'

'Desertion, I suppose. If we were in America we could probably add mental cruelty as well.'

'That's a good 'un, that is.'

'Yes, isn't it? Divorces always have their funny side.'

'I shall die laughing.'

'Well that's what it comes to, isn't it, Vic? You won't want to be tied to a wife you're not living with, and I'm sure Ingrid will want to be free. She's young and attractive. She'll want to marry again. So will you, sometime, I suppose.'

'I've had a bellyful of being married.'

'So now you're going to chuck it and get out.'

'I haven't said that.'

'I thought you had.'

'I only said I could if I wanted to. I said I wasn't waiting around for any favours and I wasn't going to be pushed into doing anything I didn't want to do. And you can tell Ingrid that from me, and her mother an' all.' I've got to the stage now where I don't mind being rude.

'I'm not carrying any messages, Vic. If you want to say anything to Ingrid you'll have to tell her yourself.'

'A fat chance I'd have with her mother on guard. She doesn't like me, y'know.'

'I know she doesn't. But I like you, Vic. I still think you're a decent lad and I don't shy from the thought of you being my son-in-law.'

'Thanks very much.' I try to make it sound sarcastic but underneath I'm pleased. It's getting to be quite a treat to know somebody likes me.

Mr Rothwell looks down at the menu as the waitress comes over again.

'What will you have?' he says. 'College pudding or apple tart?'

'I'll give it a miss and just have coffee.'

He orders two coffees and the waitress shuffles off again. She's an elderly bint with thick stockings and her little white hat-thing on crooked. It's not a very classy joint, all dark paint and grubby wallpaper, but it's pretty full, mostly of men, and I suppose it's got a name among a certain type of feller, travellers and such, as a place where you can get a plain meal and a drink with it. We're sitting in a corner with a hat-rack between us and the next table, which is why we can talk without anybody hearing.

'Suppose I said I'd the offer of a flat?' I say to him. 'What then?'

'I'd say it makes the situation much more promising,' he says. 'If you asked Ingrid to live with you there and she refused then of course you'd be the injured party. Legally.'

'And I could apply for a divorce?'

'I should think so.'

'D'you think she would come? She'd have to go out to work again to help pay the rent.'

'Why don't you ask her?'

'How the hell can I?' I say, getting riled again. 'Her mother 'ud go hairless at the thought.'

'I don't want a bald wife,' he says, 'but we'll have to risk it, won't we?'

'You mean . . .?'

'I mean that what Ingrid's mother thinks in this case is secondary to what Ingrid herself thinks. If you want to see her, then –' He stops. 'Do you want to see her?'

I wait a minute, then I say, 'I think maybe I should.'

'All right, then. Where?'

'Not at your house.'

This time he does smile, a real smile and no mistake about it. 'Now Ingrid's mother *would* go hairless if I suggested that,' he says.

9

I

It seems like ten miles we walk that night, talking and mulling over things together without having to keep our voices down because her mother's in the next room. We have plenty to talk about and plenty to think about – the next forty years, in fact. It's not something you make your mind up about all in a minute. The last time it was settled in a couple of jiffs in the park, but not this time. This time I've thought about it – I'm still thinking – and we're talking. We've never talked so much before – we were never very strong on talking – and maybe we'll never talk as much again. Perhaps if we had talked a bit more and messed about a bit less things would be different now. But they're not, and that's that. That's the way it is and we've got to make the best of it.

After what seems like hours of walking all over the town we come to the park and sit down in our old shelter.

'You know you're gunna have to stand up to her, don't you?' I say.

She nods. 'Yes.'

'You'll have to let her see you've made your mind up and you can't be talked out of it.'

'It won't be easy,' she says. 'She's dead set against you now.'

'Well, your dad's with us anyway.'

'He's a brick is me dad. I don't know what would have happened without him.'

'Aye, he's a right nice chap, your dad. I right like him.'

'Is it a big flat, Vic?' she says. 'Will it take a lot of furnishing?'

I can hear the excitement in her voice and I know that now there's some definite aim she'll find what she needs to stand up to her ma. I tell her for the umpteenth time that I haven't been in the place so I don't know.

'When d'you think we can look round?'

'Any time, I suppose. They'll be expecting us to look at it before we decide anything.'

'You want to take it, don't you, Vic?' she says.

'Beggars can't be choosers, can they?' I say. 'It's steep but we'll manage, I suppose.'

'I mean . . . what I mean is, you want to take it because it'll mean we can be together?'

I think for a minute how to answer her. 'I reckon we haven't had a fair try,' I say then. 'We're married and we ought to see how it works out with just the two of us. P'raps we'll be chucking pots at one another inside a couple o' months, but at least we shan't be able to blame anybody else if we are.'

'I don't think we will.' She moves closer and puts her head on my shoulder. I slide my arm round her just like in the old days. 'We've had a rotten six months, haven't we?' she says.

'I'll say.'

'If anybody had told me last year at this time all that was going to happen I'd never have believed them.'

'Yeh.' I'm thinking I'm going to kiss her in a minute. You couldn't believe how different she is when her mother's not around.

'Vic,' she says in a minute; 'all that time, you know, when I didn't want you to make love to me. Well it wasn't that I didn't want you to really; only it never seemed right somehow, while we were living at home.'

'I think I know what you mean.' I remember how I never got used to going up to bed at night in a natural kind of way, and how the bedsprings creaked and how I didn't like leaving anything in the drawers for fear Ma Rothwell went into them during the day. Though what the heck there was to be ashamed about I don't know; but she just made you feel that way.

So now I do kiss her because it's the one thing I've been bothered about. If that wasn't right it just couldn't have worked out at all.

'It'll be different when we're on our own,' she says. 'We'll be all right then.'

'Yeh, we can do what we like then . . .' I smile. It's funny how things come into your mind. 'I've never seen you in the bath except once on our honeymoon.'

'Do you want to see me in the bath?'

'Yes. There's something nice about you when you're all shiny and slippy with soap.'

She laughs. 'You're a funny thing.'

'Yeh, funny. But not queer.'

'No, not queer.'

'This is funny as well,' she says; 'us sitting here talking. It's about the first time we've sat here and just talked.'

'Except the night you knew you were having a baby.'

'Yes, then. That's when you said you'd marry me.'

Well I don't want to go into the pros and cons of that all over again so I tighten my arm round her and say, 'We can do something else, if you like?'

'Such as?'

I slip my hand into her coat. 'What d'you think?'

'It's a bit cold, though, isn't it?'

'We never used to bother about that before.'

It seems a bit funny an old married couple like us having to . . . to do it in the park. Suppose somebody comes?'

'Nobody ever did before, did they? An' anyway, like you say, we're married.'

'I haven't got my lines with me.'

'You've got your ring on.'

'You're the last person they'd think I was married to.'

Right at the last minute she says, 'Have you got something, Vic.'

I have to laugh. 'As it happens, I have.'

And then she's got both arms round me and she's holding me tighter than tight and saying over and over again, 'Oh, I do love you, Vic, I do love you, I love you . . .'

So that's all right, then.

II

Walking back to Chris's I turn it all over in my mind. She still loves me. After all that's happened – the way I mucked her about, the accident and losing the baby, the way her mother's tried to turn her against me, and the way I've behaved – after all that she still loves me and she's ready to try and make a go of it. Whether I love her or not's another thing altogether, but that's not what matters now. What matters is I know I'm doing the right thing. I'm tired of feeling like a louse and now I'm going to do the best I can. And who knows, one day it might happen like Chris said: we might find a kind of loving to carry us through. I hope so because it's for a long, long time.

Because now I reckon I've got a lot of things weighed up. All this has taught me, about life and everything, I mean. And the way I see it is this – the secret of it all is there is no secret, and no God and no heaven and no hell. And if you say well what is life about I'll say it's about life, and that's all. And it's enough, because there's plenty of good things in life as well as bad. And I reckon there's no such thing as sin and punishment, either. There's what you do and what comes of it. There's right things and there's wrong things and if you do wrong things, wrong things happen to you – and that's the punishment. But there's no easy way out because if you do only right things you don't always come off best because there's chance. After everything else there's chance and you can do the best you can and you can't allow for that. If you say, well why does one bloke have all bad luck and another one have all good luck when he might be a wrong 'un, well I'll say isn't that chance? And anyway, he might not be as lucky as you think because you can't see inside him and a bloke can have six cars and holidays in the south of France every year and it's still what's inside him what counts.

What it boils down to is you've got to do your best and hope for the same. Do what you think's right and you'll be doing like millions of poor sods all over the world are doing. And when it hits you, if it does, chance, call it what you like, you'll wonder like all the rest of them because you've always done your best and you don't deserve a rotten deal. But that's your story.

And now I'm going to do my best and see how it works out.

So endeth the lesson.

It's a chilly night and I shiver a bit as I walk. It'll be Christmas again in a fortnight.

THE END

The Watchers on the Shore
Stan Barstow

The second in a trilogy of novels featuring Vic Brown

Continuing the story of Vic Brown, we find that, having
been unwillingly thrust into the cold and murky waters of
matrimony in *A Kind of Loving*, and after three years of
trying to live with Ingrid, he is still struggling to keep
afloat. Their marriage has become a kind of living – until a
lifebuoy affair bobs on to his horizon, enlarging his world
and enabling him to break out from the bonds of
matrimony. It is Donna Perryman, a stunningly attractive
actress, and the devastating effect she has on his life, that
is the subject of *The Watchers on the Shore*, the brilliant
sequel to *A Kind of Loving*, now regarded as a classic of
post-war literature.

'A major novelist'
PUNCH

0 552 99189 9

BLACK SWAN

The Right True End
Stan Barstow

The third in a trilogy of novels featuring Vic Brown

A Kind of Loving and *The Watchers on the Shore*
immortalised Vic Brown, the working-class boy from the
North. *The Right True End* is the final book in this masterly
trilogy.

As a divorced man, Vic has made it on his own terms in
London. A prize job, a flash car, as much sex as he can
handle – these are the symbols of his success. But it is still
not enough.

Ten years ago, with Donna, he knew he had something real,
the way things should be between a man and a woman.
Something so bloody marvellous that when she comes back
into his life, he is scared to death he'll mess up his chances
the second time around . . .

'A major novelist'
PUNCH

0 552 99187 2

BLACK SWAN

A Raging Calm
Stan Barstow

Set in a thriving, recognisable urban city, *A Raging Calm* is a story of conflicting passions, of loyalty and betrayal, and of the agony of an illicit love affair.

'Stan Barstow is one of the very best of our regional novelists and *A Raging Calm* is a fine example of his work. It is humane and it is perceptive. It never fakes feeling in the interests of drama, yet it remains dramatically alive. Deeply felt and skilfully told, the novel will certainly enhance Mr Barstow's already high reputation'
EVENING STANDARD

'A major novelist'
PUNCH

0 552 99193 7

BLACK SWAN

The Desperadoes
Stan Barstow

Short stories by the author of *A Kind of Loving*

Although set in and about the West Riding town which formed the locale of the author's first novel, *A Kind of Loving*, there is, however, nothing provincial in the themes of these brilliant stories, even though Stan Barstow shows in them his continuing preoccupation with people rooted in a recognisable society. The moods vary from grave to happy, from sad to wryly humorous. The stories reveal that Stan Barstow, while keenly aware of the tragedy of life, is also fully responsive to the humorous aspect of the human predicament.

'The stories have that very rare compassion and pity that distinguishes the really good writer from the merely able. Some of them are right up in the same class as D.H. Lawrence'
THE GUARDIAN

'Extraordinarily good'
SUNDAY TELEGRAPH

'A major novelist'
PUNCH

0 552 99185 6

BLACK SWAN

Joby
Stan Barstow

To Joby Weston that summer, the world was surely a
strange and brutal place. It was the summer when he
should have been swollen with happiness at the knowledge
that he was going to Cressley grammar school in
September but which was clouded by his mother going into
hospital.

It was the summer when he tasted the bitterness of
injustice. And it was Joby's last summer of innocence in
which slowly and painfully, he learned the hard facts of
life and discovered the world of adults was also full of
tragedy.

'The observation is unfaltering and unsentimental. Joby
and his friends are real people and the achievement of the
novel is to catch you up in his life and make you want to
shake his parents into caring as well.'
EVENING STANDARD

'He communicates his nostalgia and his innocence in this
short, sad and sympathetic book. He does without strain
what so many writers strain to do: he takes us back.'
SUNDAY TELEGRAPH

'The story is told with beautiful delicacy and compassion
. . . A little gem of a book.'
YORKSHIRE POST

'In Joby, Barstow has pared everything down to essentials,
the essentials of reality.'
THE SCOTSMAN

0 552 99176 7

BLACK SWAN

The Doctor's Wife
Brian Moore

'One of the outstanding works of fiction of the year'
PETER TINNISWOOD, THE TIMES

Sheila Redden is on her way from war-torn Belfast to the
south of France where her husband Kevin will join her in a
few days to relive their honeymoon of fifteen years ago. But
Sheila had not reckoned on meeting Tom Lowry and finding
her life transformed. *The Doctor's Wife* is a brilliant
portrait of a woman who is suddenly confronted by the
devastating power of passionate, erotic love.

'Nightmare images of tanks cruising down empty night
streets, feverish erotic couplings with a stranger in foreign
hotels; a married woman with one son from a provincial
backwater breaking out on a trip abroad; a concerned
sibling observing a rebellious young sister; the palpable
absence of God in the central characters' lives and the
notion that art and sex might replace Him . . . the principal
ingredients of Brian Moore's fine new novel . . . a
splendidly bracing experience'
NEW STATESMAN

'The erotic force of the love scenes is considerable'
THE GUARDIAN

'The most alluringly complex adulteress to come along in
print for some time'
TIME MAGAZINE

'It is uncanny; no male writer, I swear (and precious few
females), knows so much about women'
JANICE ELLIOTT, SUNDAY TELEGRAPH

0 552 99109 0

BLACK SWAN

Borstal Boy
Brendan Behan

Borstal Boy is the classic story of prison and Borstal life, as near the bone today as it was on first publication. A brilliantly written, acidic, provocative account of life inside, it manages to capture the cruelty and pathos, brutality and innocence of bleak lives. Behan has never been so sharp, or so sure of his raw materials, and he has opened an important window onto a closed, corrosive and often frightening society.

Borstal Boy is the major work of a most original and unexpected literary talent.

'If the English hoard words like misers, the Irish spend them like sailors; and Brendan Behan, Dublin's obstreperous poet-playwright, is one of the biggest spenders in this line since the young Sean O'Casey. Behan sends language out on a swaggering spree, ribald, flushed and spoiling for a fight'
KENNETH TYNAN

0 552 99054 X

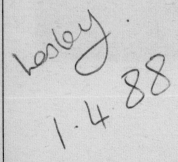

BLACK SWAN